## "WHAT ARE ~~WAITING FOR?~~
### HE ASKED.

She brought his wrist to her lips and gently, slowly touched her tongue to it. The taste exploded in her mouth. Whatever she'd expected, it wasn't this shivering of connection through her, pulling her deeper into Xia's mind, into the center of his magic. When she lifted her head, she had trouble getting her bearings. She sat on her haunches, trying to make the room stop spinning. Xia steadied her.

"I hate witches," he said. His hand, big and warm and more than capable of killing, followed the upward indentation of her spine. He brought her head to his and kissed her, hard, and Alexandrine returned his kiss with unrestrained passion. With one quick motion, he grabbed the top of her shirt and pulled at the buttons until they came free . . .

"Dark and sexy, MY FORBIDDEN DESIRE is a must-read for anyone who loves their romance honed to a dangerous edge. Carolyn Jewel's heroes are walking towers of sin—hot enough to make you shiver, so wicked you'll be screaming for more."

—Meljean Brook author of *Demon Bound*

Also by Carolyn Jewel

*My Wicked Enemy*

# ACKNOWLEDGMENTS

Calling out to the usual crew: Megan Frampton for reading my stuff before it's fully cooked. Thank you very much for that. My son comes in for his share of appreciation, too. You're a good kid, Nathaniel. Just remember, being taller than your mom means you are now the chief lightbulb changer. Consider this the official passing on of the stepladder. I love you. To my sister Marguerite for being everyone's Rite (she knows what that means) and to my parents for everything. Thanks are due to my wise editor, Michele Bidelspach. A saint, I tell you, with great insights. And to my wonderful agent, Kristin Nelson, for all her support and assistance. A very big thank-you indeed.

# GLOSSARY

**blood-twin:** A bonded pair of fiends who share a permanent magical connection. They may be biologically related and same sex. Antisocial and prone to psychosis.

**copa:** A plant derivative of a yellow-ochre color when processed. Has a mild psychotropic effect on the kin who use it for relaxation. On mages, the drug increases magical abilities and is highly addictive.

**cracking** (a talisman): A mage or witch may crack open a talisman in order to absorb the life force within and magically prolong his or her life. Requires a sacrificial murder.

**demon:** Any of a number of shape-shifting magical beings whose chief characteristic is, as far as the magekind are concerned, the ability to possess and control a human.

**fiend:** A subspecies of demon. Before relations with the magekind exploded into war, they frequently bonded with the magekind.

**kin:** What fiends collectively call each other. Socially divided into various factions seeking power over other Warlord-led factions. The kin connect with other kin via psychic links, often collectively. They typically possess multiple physical forms, at least one of which is recognizably human.

**mage:** A male who possesses magic. A sorcerer. See also *magekind*.

**mageheld:** A fiend or other demon who is under the complete control of a magekind.

**magekind:** Humans who possess magic. The magekind arose to protect vanilla humans from the depredations of demons, a very real threat.

**sever:** The act of removing a mageheld from the control of a mage or witch, through the use of magic.

**talisman:** A usually small object into which a mage has enclosed the life force of a fiend, typically against the fiend's will. A talisman confers additional magical power to the mage who has it. Sometimes requires an additional sacrifice. See also *cracking* (a talisman).

**vanilla:** A human with no magic or, pejoratively, one of the magekind with little power.

**warlord:** A fiend who leads some number of other fiends who have sworn fealty. Usually a natural leader possessing far more magic than others of the kin.

**witch:** A human female who possesses magic. A sorceress. See also *magekind*.

# MY FORBIDDEN
# DESIRE

# CHAPTER 1

An icy sensation prickled across the back of Alexandrine Marit's neck and raised gooseflesh on her arms. The significance of that ripple of cold should have penetrated, but she was distracted and not thinking clearly. Instead of doing something, she just stayed on her couch and looked around for an open window while absently rubbing her prickling skin. Her crappy apartment wasn't big, so that took all of two seconds. No open windows.

The reason she was distracted was right smack in front of her. Harsh Marit. Dr. Harsh Marit, actually. She'd spent the last ten years of her life believing her brother was dead. Only guess what? He wasn't. He'd just taken a call on his cell and was now standing with his back three-quarters toward her. Like that was going to make it harder for her to overhear.

She totally wasn't over the shock of him being here. Alive. She still had the shakes. Her emotions continued to seesaw between elation and disbelief, interspersed with a humiliating urge to cry. While he was on the phone, an iPhone for crying out loud, she was trying to calm herself down and not succeeding.

"Yes," he said into his phone.

The chill hit again, rolling along the surface of her skin. She resettled herself on the couch and put on one of those *I-am-politely-not-listening* faces. Of course, she heard every word her brother said. But Harsh wasn't doing much talking. He was listening mostly.

He kept talking and listening on his iPhone. The talking part he carried out in a low voice: very cryptic because, doh, she was sitting right there with functioning ears. He did the listening intently. She got another prickly roll along the back of her neck and up and down her arms. This time—third time being the charm?—she realized her goose-pimply skin had nothing to do with an open window somewhere in her apartment or with being stunned to have her brother here.

Her reaction was something else entirely.

Alexandrine's stomach fell to her toes. Why now? Like she didn't have enough on her mind already.

Harsh glanced at her once while he talked into his phone, and the odd prickling along her arms stopped, as did her feeling of uneasiness. That was strange. Her premonitions didn't usually come and go. They were unpredictable as hell, but when she had one, her physical reactions remained until the situation resolved itself. One way or another. So the fact that she now felt perfectly normal made her wonder if she'd gotten it wrong.

Her brother went back to listening, and her goose bumps returned, crawling along her arms to the nape of her neck and down her spine. The back of her head felt cold. From the inside. Which pretty much cinched things. No mistake. Something bad was coming her way.

"Fine," Harsh said into the phone. He disconnected his call and for about ten long seconds stared at the icons on the phone's screen. God, that phone was gorgeous. The chill in her head didn't go away. In fact, it got worse.

*Oh, shit*, she thought.

One time, several years ago, when she was a teenager and still living at home, she'd spent several minutes talking with an older guy who had seemed perfectly normal. But as they talked—and admittedly, she'd been using half her brain to decide whether she wanted to flirt with him, which was probably why she'd missed the signs at the outset—she'd met his gaze, and whoa. One look into the guy's eyes and she'd just known. Rock solid: *He wants to kill me.*

That time she'd had all the symptoms at once. He was trolling for a kill, and if she didn't leave—now—she'd be next. So she'd left. Pronto. Two days later, a girl's body turned up about a block from where she'd met the guy, with all the usual media hoo-ha over women killed in brutal fashion. Nothing happened, though, because the murdered girl was a runaway and poor and turning tricks to support a habit. For three weeks afterward, she'd had nightmares about would have happened to her if she hadn't lit out.

Premonitions were her thing. If there was anything reliable about her limited ability to use magic, that was it. Some things she just knew. It wasn't any big deal to look into someone's eyes and realize sanity was lacking. Any loser with half the empathy doled out to regular folks could do that. Her premonitions started out with prickling skin and an uneasiness that curled into her gut. And then sooner or later, she'd know she had to do something. Like don't go to the store after all. Or don't take the shortcut.

Now, just like that day with the killer and a dozen times since, Alexandrine knew something bad was going to happen and that the bad thing involved her. Always did with her premonitions. Harsh Marit was back from the dead, and her life was facing a bifurcation. Go one way and she was dead. Go the other way, she stayed alive. A binary set of possibilities. Zero or one. How she would get to the point where she knew which way was dead and which way wasn't was anybody's guess. This wasn't one of the more useful that-guy's-looking-to-kill-me kind of premonitions where her course of action was perfectly clear.

Something bad was going to happen. But she didn't know what. Not yet. She didn't even know if Harsh, specifically, was involved or if it would happen today or a week from today.

"Alexandrine," Harsh said. Like her, he was adopted, so they weren't genetically related and didn't look anything alike. He was tall, dark, and exotically handsome, and she was tall, platinum-blond, and probably a little above average in the looks department. She and Harsh might not have a blood relation, but everything else that mattered said they were brother and sister. They'd lived enough years in the same household that she loved him like the big brother he was. That hadn't changed even if he had let her think he was dead all this time. Harsh tucked his phone into his front pocket. "I'm sorry about that."

She tried not to let her awareness show, but it wasn't easy, and from the look in his eyes, she wondered if he sensed on some level how she'd gone cold inside. She was practically shivering from it. She didn't think he was the reason she was freaking out like this. But she'd bet real money he was the catalyst for whatever was coming at her. The question right now was whether her brother had any idea what she was. If he didn't, she'd really prefer to reveal that later. Much, much later. If ever. Preferably never.

"I need you to do something for me," Harsh said.

"Like what?" The icy chill in her head went off again, but it wasn't bad. Just enough to know the choice was still out there.

"Does it matter?" he asked. His shoulders tensed up.

"Yeah," she said, "it does."

"Don't be difficult about this, Alexandrine. I don't have time to explain." His eyes went hard. "Just do it, all right?"

"Just do it?" she said. "Who the hell you think you are? 'Just do it.'" Actually, that was a pretty good question. Who the hell was he? Didn't every adopted person eventually ask that question? She had.

Harsh folded his arms across his chest. He didn't look like he'd been dead at any point during the last ten years. Ergo, he must have been alive the entire time, including all those times she was crying about losing him. Which, come to think of it, kind of pissed her off.

"I'm your brother," he said. The set of his mouth softened, but his eyes stayed hard, and that was downright creepy. "What else could I be, Alexandrine?"

The question was softly put, even fondly. But she didn't doubt there was more to his question. She wished Maddy were here. Maddy would know what to do. More importantly, Maddy would probably know what not to do. Her best friend knew a hell of a lot more about this stuff than Alexandrine did.

The security doorbell buzzed and shocked the hell out of her, because she thought it didn't work. They both looked in the direction of her door. Then his phone went off. Again. This ringtone was a series of sonar pings.

"Don't answer, Harsh." She knew him. He was her big brother, and she just couldn't believe he'd hurt her. If he was here to kill her, her premonition would almost certainly have been more specific. Wouldn't it? It was also possible, she had to concede, that her premonition had nothing to do with Harsh. This could be one big coincidence. Only, she didn't think so. "Please, don't. Just this once."

"I have to." He slid the phone out of his pocket, touched the screen, and said, "Five minutes." Then he touched the screen again, looked straight at her, and said, "I am your brother, Alexandrine. Nothing has changed that." He met her gaze straight on. "Nothing."

"My brother," she said as he touched the iPhone again. Another series of icons appeared on the screen. "Right. My brother." All of a sudden, she felt like she was six instead of twenty-six with all the emotional maturity that implied. She tried to get a handle on herself, but so far her evening had been a bit too stressful for that.

"Alexandrine . . ." He gripped his phone. Hard. "I'm not here to hurt you. You have to believe that."

She did believe that. She really did. "Where have you been all this time?" she asked. He didn't answer. "Mom and Dad had a service for you. It was nice. Very refined. You would have liked it. Lots of crying. Tears. Emotion."

At the time, Alexandrine had been, what, barely sixteen? The age of attitude. With a capital *A*. But she sure as heck remembered missing her only brother. After the police decided he must be dead, even without a body, their lives just . . . stopped. Losing Harsh like that broke the family into little tiny pieces. None of them had ever really recovered.

"I'm sure it was very nice," Harsh said in a voice that was just a little too flat.

Alexandrine jabbed a hand in his direction. Since she'd know if she was in immediate danger from him, she decided they ought to get on with the surface business of him reappearing in her life. "You can't just drop back in without a word of explanation."

He sighed, but when he spoke, his eyes were just as hard as before. "I'm trying to save your life, Alexandrine."

"You're about ten years too late to be saving me, Harsh." Wow. That came out a lot more accusatory than she'd intended. But, then, she was upset. And unnerved.

"Full credit for surviving," he said.

"No thanks to you."

His eyes went far away. About a million miles. He hadn't told her yet where he'd been all these years. Why not?

The last time she'd seen her brother, he'd been wearing a suit and tie, and his hair had been short and neat. Ten years ago, he'd had a beeper surgically attached to his waist, and the damn thing used to go off all the time. Now? The professional look of the newly minted doctor of medicine was gone in favor of some kind of uncool grunge look. He wore faded jeans, a ripped T-shirt, and battered leather work boots. They didn't fit like they were his. His hair was down to his shoulders, and judging from the size of his arms, he'd been spending quality time in the weight room. Harsh had never been a gym rat. What new doctor had time for that? He'd barely had time for a kid sister once he went off to California.

Someone knocked on her door. Loudly. She lived in a crappy apartment building with broken security, so it wasn't any surprise that someone could get upstairs without getting buzzed in. The hair on the back of her neck stood up, though, and she wasn't sure if it was because she was startled or if it had something to do with her premonition. For the count of three, she and Harsh stared at each other. Interesting. He didn't ask if she was expecting anyone. And he didn't look surprised.

His iPhone did its sonar ping again. Harsh looked to see who was calling, and, boy, did she get a flashback. Thirteenth birthday. Beeper going off. Beloved older brother visiting from Harvard Med—it wasn't far, the Marit family lived in Brookline—leaving the party before the cake was out. Again.

"Just like old times, isn't it?" she said under her breath. Except not, because in the intervening years, Harsh had apparently turned into something scary. Different from what she'd become. Louder, she said, "Save me from what?"

He touched the phone's screen and told the caller, "Not now." Then he hung up. She got the feeling he wanted to shake the gadget. He didn't. Harsh had always been in control of himself. He looked at her and said, "From yourself."

"Huh?" Whoever was at the door knocked again.

Three times. Very slowly. Very loudly. Jerk. "Should I get that?" she asked.

He frowned. "I'm trying to save you from yourself, Alexandrine."

Right. He wanted to save her from herself. What a laugh that was, if only he knew. "Too late, bro. I'm a big girl now. All grown up."

"Alexandrine—"

"I'll be twenty-six in three months. More than old enough to have a job, pay taxes, drink hard liquor, and vote for president. At the same time if I want."

"I understand you're no longer a child."

The last time she'd seen her brother, she'd still been living at home in Brookline, Massachusetts, without any pressing need for a brassiere. Massachusetts was three thousand miles away from the City by the Bay, where her brother had gone to do medical research at the University of California at San Francisco. Her big brother the doctor. Mom and Dad were so proud. And then he disappeared. Dropped off the face of the earth. Presumed dead.

Right.

Not so dead after all.

"Things do change, don't they?" she said.

Harsh's phone pinged again. He answered it with, "I told you, five minutes." He touched the screen to disconnect the call, and by coincidence, Mr. Impatient outside her apartment bammed a fist on her door. Great. The neighbors were going to love that. They were probably calling the landlord now.

"I don't need protection," she said. And the minute she said it, she got a sick feeling in the pit of her stomach because, hell, maybe she did. "I've been on my own a long time, Harsh."

He stopped pacing. She didn't remember his eyes being such a piercing brown. She couldn't dismiss the creepy thought that something more was living behind her brother's eyes. That gave her the shivers, legitimate shivers, not premonition shivers. "When was the last time you talked to Mom and Dad?" he asked.

They'd been so busy reestablishing their relationship that she hadn't gotten around to catching him up on family news. "Talked to Dad two years ago." True statement. Harsh understood there was more and that she was baiting him. But he refused to step in it. Killjoy. "He's dead. Heart attack."

"I didn't know." He closed his fingers around his vibrating phone. "What about Mom?"

Yeah. So where the hell had her brother been that he didn't know anything at all? Turning into a freak didn't stop you from using Google or reading the paper, did it? Or getting on the phone, for that matter. The parents who had raised him and put him through college and medical school, which they would probably have done for her if she'd been a genius, too, had been destroyed, because they thought he was dead. "She's gone, too, Harsh. About eight years ago now."

For half a second, his expression was the Harsh Marit she'd missed every day for the last ten years of her life. Her chest went tight, and she had to concentrate to keep the tears away. They'd missed so much of each other's lives, and now that he was back, she didn't want him to leave again. Harsh was all she had left.

He opened his mouth, then closed it again. Finally, he asked, "What happened?"

"Cancer." She let out a breath. "Ironic, wouldn't you say? Her son, the brilliant oncologist, wasn't around to save her life."

He didn't say anything to that, and she felt rotten for the low blow.

"Look," she said. She scrubbed her fingers through her above-the-shoulders-length hair. "I'm sorry. That was unfair and not very nice. I didn't mean it."

"You're right." He fisted a hand. "I wasn't there." He was quiet for a bit, then said in a much lower voice, "I wish I'd been there to help her."

Alexandrine waited for him to tell her where he'd been all this time. He didn't. Again. "So, like I said," she said. "I've been on my own a long time. And nothing all that bad happened." But then, *bad* encompassed such a wide and varied spectrum. Bad included skipping meals to make the rent. Or getting evicted. Or hanging with a very rough crowd and wondering if you'd make it to twenty-one. "I left home, banged around a while, saw the sights. Did some stuff. Went to college."

She'd done things she wasn't going to talk about with anybody. "Now I have a job. I make shit money, but they let me telecommute two days a week." She held his gaze. "I rent this lovely hovel in the most beautiful city in the world." She tilted her head back and looked around her Mission District apartment. Ugly one-bedroom for four-teen hundred bucks a month, and she was lucky to have something that cheap. She brought her attention back to her brother. Ten years was a long time to vanish from someone's life. "I'm not a virgin anymore."

Harsh was taller than she was, which, considering she was five-eleven when she slouched, meant he was tall. Tall. Handsome. Doctor. Where the hell had he been for all those years when she could have used a big brother?

"I didn't imagine you were," he said.

"Where *have* you been, Dr. Marit?" Sarcasm was her specialty. A useful skill in her opinion.

He walked from her crapola analog television to her jam-packed bookcase and back. "I can't tell you." Mr. Impatient knocked on the door, and Harsh's cell phone rang. At the same time.

"Golly, Harsh, why don't you tell the guy to go get a life?"

He looked at her. Very unsettling, that piercing look. The skin on her arms prickled again. "I can't tell you where I've been." He frowned in the direction of the door. "Can we just leave it at that?"

"The land of Oz? Siberia? Witness Protection? Off to find your birth parents like me? Timbuktu? No, wait, that was me."

"You went to Timbuktu?"

"Uh-huh. And you? The Arctic? Prison?" That got her a poisonous look. "You don't have any tats. If you were in prison, you'd have the body art." Which she knew on account of the fact that for longer than she cared to recall, her bosom buddies were felons, complete with homemade tats. She cocked her head. "You were in the military, weren't you?" Who else had the ability to make a person completely disappear? "Government something. Am I right?"

Harsh stared at her. She didn't think he was going to answer, but instead, Dr. Harsh Marit, her adored big brother, clapped a hand behind his neck and said in a dark, raspy voice, "Prison would be a more accurate description of where I've been."

The desolation in his voice popped her angry-as-a-bee's-burned-behind balloon. "What do you need from me, Harsh?"

His damned phone went off again with a different ringtone. This time he answered with, "Harsh speaking." She watched her brother listen to whoever was on the other end. "No. I'm here. Yeah." He darted a glance at her. She didn't recognize the man behind those eyes. She rubbed the sides of her arms, but it didn't make the goose pimples go away. "Not yet. He's outside. Yes. Yes. I know. I will." Then he lost it and burst out with, "For Christ's sake, Nikodemus, she thought I was dead. Cut me a break, would you?"

Alexandrine rose. Her pulse thudded in her ears. The nervous feeling in her stomach refused to go away. Nikodemus? Now there was a name to make a girl sit up. Especially if she was a witch.

"Yes," he replied more easily, still talking into the phone. His eyes were hard again, flat-out pitiless, and Alexandrine wondered what horrible things her brother had endured while he'd been gone. A motorcycle engine revved outside. One of those loud, obnoxious bikes driven by jackass men in leather pants.

Harsh disconnected his call, lifted his head, and then touched his phone again. After a bit, he said, "Don't you dare leave." He was staring at her. "You want Nikodemus on your ass instead of just me?" he said into the phone.

Well, shit. That gave her another jolt and a half. Him saying a name she'd read about in the books she'd managed to scavenge. Nikodemus? No effing way. She got an all-body chill like you would if you found out Jack the Ripper not only wasn't dead but also lived next door.

"Park the damn bike and come in. I'll open the door for you."

"News flash, Dr. Marit." She sure as hell didn't want to meet any of his friends. "I can take care of myself. I've been doing it since before you disappeared."

Harsh closed his phone and drew a deep breath. "Not against these guys."

"What guys?"

The motorcycle cut off.

"The guys who don't give a shit if you die as long as they get what they're after."

"What?" That happened to be the only word she could find to say, and it came out sounding like smart-ass disbelief, which wasn't what she intended at all. It was just that this was too perfectly timed with her premonition for her not to be thinking, *Here it is.*

"This is what I want from you, Alexandrine." His gaze pinned her. Gloves off, metaphorically speaking. "I want him to stay here."

"I don't need a babysitter."

Harsh laughed, only without actually laughing. "With him here, no one gets to you."

Her brain froze up. Pure ice between her ears. The moment of decision was here. Ringing her doorbell, actually. This really was it. The decision, only she still didn't know which way she needed to go. Was the guy on the other side of the door a one or a zero?

After Harsh went to let in his employee from Human

Protective Services, there wasn't any sound in her shitty apartment. If she closed her eyes, she could pretend she was alone. But she wasn't. Harsh was at the door, making goo-goo eyes at it for all she knew. She addressed his back. "I found my biological father."

He turned around just as Mr. Impatient and I Have a Motorcycle knocked. His eyes lasered her. "You did not."

"Yeah," she said, "I did. In Turkey. A little village about two hundred kilometers north of Ankara."

Harsh opened the door and said, "Not in Turkey you didn't."

He was right about that. "I found out who he is when I was in Turkey." She waited a beat. "Seems I was born in Turkey. But my dad's Danish. Go figure. His name is Rasmus Kessler, in case you're interested."

He kept his hand on the knob. The door was about an inch or so open. It was impossible to see who was on the other side. "You didn't meet him. You couldn't have."

"How do you know?"

In the light where he was standing, it looked like his eyes changed color. Not possible, but that's what it looked like. "Because if you had, Alexandrine, you'd be dead."

# CHAPTER 2

Alexandrine watched her front door swing open. Harsh was facing away from her like he'd never said her biological father would want to kill her. Great. Just really great. As if he knew anything at all about her real father. He hadn't even known their adoptive parents were dead. And he didn't know anything at all about her. Not anymore.

The door opened enough for her to see past her brother. She got a chill in the pit of her stomach a hundred times worse than before. One thing was profoundly clear to her: Her brother had just let a killer into her apartment. She was too frightened to notice much besides black clothes and a pair of freakishly blue eyes that had to be a trick of the light outside her door. No way. Just no way, ever. The human eye didn't come in that color. Alexandrine brushed past Harsh and stuck out a hand, palm out. Perfect timing because Blue Eyes walked smack into her hand. He stopped; she'd gotten to him just inside the doorway.

"I'm Alexandrine Marit," she said. Her stomach roiled. Shit, this was worse than anything she'd ever felt before. And the freaky thing was that she didn't know what she was supposed to do. The crisis must be huge. Life changing, of that she had no doubt. But whatever it was hadn't hit critical yet. When it did, she'd know what to do. She hoped. She always had before. "This is my place you're barging into."

He stared down at her, and her blood froze solid. If she hadn't been so mad at Harsh, she wouldn't have gotten within six feet of this guy. She knew bad when she looked it in the eye, and she preferred not to. God knows she'd lived with that kind of bad after she left home. Gave a girl some painful lessons. Harsh's buddy was scary-bad. Scarier than Harsh. She wasn't at all sure it was a good idea to have Harsh in the apartment, let alone another man just like him, only worse.

"So?" Blue Eyes said. One word and it was golden. The man had a beautiful voice. *The better to take your soul, my dear.*

She had to tilt her chin to look into his face, and that didn't happen to her often. He wore leather pants, black gloves, black boots, and a zipped-up leather jacket. Black, of course. A motorcycle helmet was tucked under one arm. Ah. The jackass on the bike. Up close, his eyes remained a freaky neon blue. "Nice to meet you, whoever you are." She gave him a fake smile and hoped he didn't notice she was trembling. "But I don't want you here. I'm sorry Harsh wasted your time. Go home."

Nothing happened. No change whatsoever in her

premonition state; no sense of relief at having done the right thing. No diminution in her physical reactions. And no sense of what it was she was supposed to do to avoid the bad. But nothing was worse, either.

"Alexandrine," Harsh said from behind her.

She glanced over her shoulder. "You are *not*," she said without smiling, "the boss of me."

Harsh shook his head. One of those secret communication head shakes. Not directed at her but at his Painful-Death-is-my-middle-name buddy. She whipped her head back to the man in front of her.

Blue Eyes stared at her hand on his leather jacket like she'd just slimed him, and then he stared at her. She had time to register the fact that he was gorgeous. The way a tiger is gorgeous. Not one in the zoo, either, but a wild one. One who hadn't eaten in a week and thought she looked like dinner in an easy-open package. He stood a head taller than her without even trying. "Fuck off, witch."

Well. That sure let the cat out of the bag, now, didn't it? How the hell did he know that? Or maybe he was just lucky in his choice of name to call her.

"O-kaaay," she whispered.

He sidestepped her and headed for Harsh. She turned around and got a view of him from the back. Right. Black leather. There weren't many guys who could pull off black leather. His leathers had a lived-in look, and he totally pulled it off without looking like a doof. He and Harsh did some complicated hand thing with each other. All very male bondingish.

"Did you hear what I said?" she asked.

Blue Eyes turned his head to look at her. "Yeah." His

gaze traveled up and down her in a slow, half-curious, half-insulting sexual examination. "And then I said fuck off. Maybe you should go do that."

Alexandrine started a silent count to ten. She got to three. "Get him out of here, Harsh."

Harsh took a deep breath. "Alexandrine, this is Xia. As you may have guessed, he's a barbarian. Xia, my sister Alexandrine. She's off limits."

She made a face at them both. "Charmed, I'm not. Get out."

Harsh gave her a poisonous look, but Xia got one, too. At least they were even in the deadly glare department. "Both of you need to behave. Please."

Xia threw his helmet on her couch and then threw his very large body after it. She was damn lucky he didn't break anything. He picked up one of her purple silk accent pillows and tossed it at the opposite end of the couch. Apparently, purple offended him. Then he unzipped his jacket and draped his arms along the back of the sofa. Was her couch too girly for him? Black velvet with purple and turquoise pillows wasn't manly enough? Come on. She hoped her girly couch was killing him. His T-shirt was plain white and tucked into his pants. As far as she could tell, there wasn't even the tiniest bit of excess anything protruding over his waist. Single-digit percent body fat. The guy was seriously scary.

"Make yourself at home," she said. "You have five minutes."

"Xia," Harsh said. He tugged on his long hair. "For just once, could you pretend to be civilized?"

"What for?"

"Are all your new friends this nice, Harsh?" Alexandrine asked.

Xia glared at her. She looked at her brother for a bit. No help was coming from him. She studied Xia, hoping for some inspiration about how to dislodge him from her couch. The hilt of a knife stuck out of a dull black sheath clipped to his waist. A shiver of fear rolled down her spine at the sight of the weapon, and, creepily, Xia smiled like he could taste her reaction.

Another shiver jellied her knees. She knew in her bones he'd used that knife to kill people and wouldn't think twice about doing so again. She needed every ounce of her nerve to turn her back on him. "Okay, Harsh. You need to explain this." She held up her hands. Thank God they didn't shake. What the hell kind of trouble was headed her way that Harsh wanted someone like Xia staying with her? "You need to tell me exactly why you want Killer here to stay. You owe me that much."

Harsh sat on her favorite recliner. Also black velvet. "You e-mailed Álvaro Magellan."

"So?" What witch worth her soul didn't want to meet the great Álvaro Magellan? Not that Harsh knew that. Except, he knew about Magellan, and he knew about her e-mail. Her stomach got tight with tension.

"And you sent a photograph."

"It wasn't a kinky shot." Her joke might as well have been attached to a lead balloon. Ka-thud. She itched between her shoulder blades, but she didn't check to see if Xia was staring at her back. He was. She felt his stare in her bones the way you feel the one from a psychopathic axe murderer sizing you up as his next victim. But he wasn't an axe murderer. If anything, he was a knife murderer but not intending, yet, to use his on her. "So?"

"So, Alexandrine, there are people who know about you now." Harsh leaned forward with his forearms on his knees. He blew out a breath to get his hair off his face. Another chill ran down her spine. For the first time since he'd decided to pop back into her life, he was telling her the unvarnished truth. "People who won't hesitate to kill you for that amulet."

"Oh, shit," she whispered. No wonder she was having such a hard time with her premonition. The danger was twofold, the events unfolding because she'd contacted Magellan and because of Xia the Barbarian. True, she had sent a picture of a stone amulet to Álvaro Magellan. She'd needed an in, and since part of Magellan's cover was his expertise in such things, she'd gone to the trouble of getting a reference from a Berkeley prof who specialized in the subject. He had, naturally, given her Magellan's name. Her prof friend was an expert in trinkets of ancient Middle Eastern origin. Magellan was The Expert. If anyone could identify what her amulet was and provide a clue as to its provenance if it turned out to be the real deal, that person was Álvaro Magellan. So said her friend the professor.

Heck, yeah, she thought. All she wanted to know was whether her amulet was the real deal and whether she was wasting her time trying to use it. She didn't see the big deal with that. "It is valuable, then," she said.

"Valuable enough to kill for," Harsh said without any change in his expression.

"You're not joking, are you?"

"The way I'm not joking about Xia staying with you."

God, what a thought. "I am absolutely not letting Killer stay here."

"He's the only one I trust to keep you alive."

"But why? Magellan isn't going to come after me," she said. Damn, but she was still getting chills. "In case you didn't hear, he's dead."

Total silence. The silence behind her was deepest of all. Killer Boy was taking the quiet and making it bigger. On purpose.

"You are *not* sitting here telling me someone wants to kill me over a bit of carved rock. Hell, I don't even know for sure if it's real."

"It's real," Killer said.

She felt the weight of the amulet's cord around her neck. "Real schmeal. It doesn't do anything, so I guess it doesn't matter." She put that out there on purpose, and neither man looked even a little confused about what she meant.

She wanted Xia gone, but she hadn't flashed on getting him to leave as being her course of action. Usually once she'd identified a source of danger, she also knew what to do. In this case, there were two causes for her premonitional heebie-jeebies; Xia himself and whatever had been set in action with Magellan and her amulet. It was possible that those inciting events were setting off conflicting resolutions. Great. Just great.

"How long have you had it?" Harsh asked.

She wanted like anything to sit on the couch, but Xia was there taking up all the room. She stayed on her feet. "Since Turkey." Harsh's eyebrows rose. "Nine months, give or take."

"Can I see it?"

Instinctively, she reached for her magic to protect herself if they tried to take it from her. Like that would do any good. Xia let out a growl. An honest-to-goodness wolf in-the-wilderness growl. He sat up straight, and the back of Alexandrine's head turned into a block of ice. Her magic sputtered out. No surprise there, unfortunately. Damn, that man was scary.

Harsh narrowed his eyes at her. Xia was sitting up, his back ramrod straight, staring at her with pure hate in his eyes. And that didn't set her off. It should have. A look like that directed at her from a guy she knew was about as bad as they come? She ought to have reacted.

"Alexandrine?" Harsh said.

"What?"

"May I please see the amulet?"

The thing was, she didn't want to show anyone her amulet. Not out of distrust exactly, but more in an unpleasant, *precioussssss* sort of way. She sure as hell hoped she wasn't turning into Golem from *Lord of the Rings*, all wigged out over the Ring. And if she was developing that kind of sicko relationship with her amulet, wasn't that a freaking creepy thing to discover? She balled her hands into fists to keep herself from touching the cord. She knew, objectively, that showing Harsh her amulet was no big deal. He wasn't going to steal it or refuse to give it back. But her hands refused to cooperate, and what came out of her mouth was, "What for? Seems to me you two know all about it. Why do you need to see it?"

Harsh shrugged. But his eyes did that flicker thing

again, which was seriously unsettling to watch. Trick of the light, right? "Just curious."

She crossed her arms over her stomach. "I don't have it with me right now."

"She's wearing it," Xia said.

Alexandrine turned around. "What, you think you know what color underwear I have on, too?"

Xia stared at her with his neon blue eyes. The center of her chest frosted over. Her vision must be going off, because it looked to her like Xia's eyes were changing color, flickering between shades of blue, gray, and white. Xia mouthed the words *fuck you* at her.

Harsh said, "Cut it out." His phone went off again.

"She's lying," Xia said. "I can feel the talisman. She's wearing it."

"Harsh speaking."

"You know you're a jerk, right?" she said to Xia. "A major, A-one, top-of-the-line, first-class jerk. Your parents must be so proud."

He gave her another fuck-you look. "I'm the jerk who's going to keep your head attached to your neck."

"You're an asshole."

"And you're a fucking witch." He took off his jacket and threw it on top of his helmet. Yes, single-digit body fat. "And a liar."

"Yes," Harsh said into the phone. "In about an hour."

"Oh, no," she said. She put her hands on her hips and gave Xia her Black Glare of Death. Didn't do much but, then, she hadn't thought it would. He stretched his arms along the top of the couch. His skin was two shades darker than golden brown, total turn-on there. She liked them tall, dark, and drop-dead yummy. He had muscles that looked like they worked hard and often. They weren't there for show, she thought. Whatever he did required ruthless use of his body. "Don't be getting comfortable," she told him. "You're not staying."

He leaned back and smirked at her. "Oh, yes, I am, baby."

# CHAPTER 3

Witch or not, Xia thought as he watched Alexandrine
Marit stare down her brother, she was his type. Tall.
Long-legged. Nice chest. Didn't mind wearing clothes
that showed her body. Hip-hugger jeans; he was a total
fan of the fashion. He liked blondes just fine, and she was
way blond. Practically white-blond. He could do without
the short hair—that gave him the creeps—but to be fair,
the cut did good things to her cheekbones. The way her
shirt did good things to her chest. Maybe her boobs could
be bigger, but she wasn't deficient or anything like that.
All in all, Alexandrine Marit came in a nice package. Be
righteous to have a piece of that. If she weren't a witch,
he'd be all over her.

"He's not staying," she told her brother.

"Yes, he is."

Xia stuck out his legs and crossed them at the ankles.
This was fun, watching the two of them face off. He'd say
this about the witch—she wasn't afraid of Harsh.

She put her hands on her hips, and that lifted the hem of her shirt just enough to give him a view of pale skin. He wondered if she was wearing a thong. He sure as hell wasn't seeing any panty lines. "No. He's not."

"You're the one who let Magellan know you existed, Alexandrine. They know about you now."

"They? Who the hell is *they*, Harsh?"

"Who do you think? The mages. Real ones," Harsh said. "People who make you insignificant."

"Thanks." She took it pretty well, even though anybody could tell that hearing Harsh talk about the mage-kind had set her back a step or two.

"Your goddamned biological father knows about you now. Trust me, you weren't safe the minute you sent Magellan that e-mail. You little idiot. Now they know you have a talisman, and they're all going to take a shot at taking it from you." Harsh was close to losing his cool. Be interesting to see what that was like. "If you think for a minute Rasmus Kessler isn't coming after you for it, you're a fool. And an even bigger one if you think he cares he's your father."

Xia shot to his feet, but Harsh ignored him. His sister took a look at him, but Harsh was going off, and that had her attention at the moment. "Are you fucking insane?" Xia said.

"Shut up, Xia. This is between me and Alexandrine."

"Were you even going to tell me who her father is? Fuck, Harsh. How can you even stand being around her knowing what she is?"

Harsh ignored him. "Rasmus Kessler gave you away, Alexandrine," he said. "You didn't test out as someone whose magic would amount to anything, so he sent you to live with us normals." He spat out that last word. Harsh was hardly normal, no matter how you looked at him. "You were three years old, and he didn't want you. He didn't want you then, and he doesn't want you now. The only thing he wants from you is that talisman."

"I know that," she said, all chilled and calm.

Xia's head about exploded. He swung himself around to face Alexandrine, pulling enough magic to make the air around him spark. "You're Rasmus Kessler's daughter?"

"So?"

He should have known. He should have known the minute he saw her goddamned hair. Just like her father's, the bastard mage.

"Xia!" Harsh tried to get between them, but Xia was so pissed off, he reacted on pure emotion. He pulled hard on his magic and threw a block of energy that set Harsh hard on his ass. One thing he didn't get was that even though he'd pulled enough magic to fry the witch to hell and back twice, she didn't pull any magic of her own. No retaliation.

"Drop dead," Alexandrine said.

Harsh was on his feet now, and he was shouting. Xia tuned him out. *Blah blah blah.* Bad Xia. *Blah blah blah.* Nothing new there. His knife appeared in his hand, and he lifted it between him and the witch, imagining the scent of the blood she shared with Rasmus and watching it spill bright red from her body. His arm trembled. Her eyes got big and wide, and he could feel himself falling in. "Fucking witch," he said.

"No." Harsh got a hand on him, and the freak managed to pull enough to put a dent in the magic he had ready to strike. In the middle of all that, he felt Alexandrine pull, but what a joke that was.

"What do you think you're going to do to me, witch? Tickle me to death?" He took a step closer. This near to her, he could feel the talisman's pulse. Her magic, pitiful as it was, amped him up even more. Gave him a hell of a hard-on, too. "I eat witches like you for breakfast."

She aimed a knee straight at his balls, but he stepped out of range just in time. Her magic cut off. The witch had nothing going.

"Get away from her, Xia. Right now." Harsh moved between them, his fingers squeezing Xia's knife hand. "Now. Or you're dead."

He looked at Harsh, and he could tell from the other man's flinch that his eyes must be going off something serious. "Try it," he said. His body twitched and buzzed with the magic flowing through him. "Just try it and we'll see who's dead when it's over."

"Let her go, Xia." The asshole had one of those voices that got calmer and calmer the more things went wrong. "If I don't kill you, Nikodemus will." Harsh's magic cycled like crazy, but the threat of Nikodemus's reprisal was enough. Xia had sworn fealty to Nikodemus, and if he killed Harsh, Nikodemus would kill him. Painfully, no doubt about that. Harsh drew his sister away, and Xia closed his eyes and took a deep breath. And then another. Relax. Jaysus, she was nothing. Nothing to him. He didn't care. Not about her. When he opened his eyes, he was under control. Mostly.

"You should have told me who she was," he said.

"I didn't know until five minutes ago."

"What is the deal with you?" Alexandrine said to him.

She was all pissed off, practically spitting. He didn't give a shit about her mood. She came in close before Harsh could stop her and jabbed a finger to his chest.

"Get her away from me," Xia said. The skin across his back started twitching again.

"Maniac," she said. Her magic sputtered up again and then cut out.

He bared his teeth at her. "I'm what your kind made me. If you don't like the result, that's just too goddamned bad."

"Xia." Harsh was so calm he was freaky. "She doesn't know her father. She may not even be right about that."

Xia stuck his fingers in her hair and raked through her short cut. He didn't see a single dark root. A natural platinum blonde. "That's her daddy's hair," he sneered as he let her go.

The witch looked shocked as hell, and when she answered her brother, her eyes were still smack on Xia's face. "Oh, I'm right about that, big brother. He's my father, no mistake."

"Fuck this, Harsh," Xia said. How the hell was he going to manage this? Rasmus Kessler's daughter. "Do I have to do this?"

She blocked Harsh's view and faced him, giving him the finger so her brother couldn't see. "Drop dead, okay?"

Harsh had his iPhone out again. "Yes," he said to Xia. "You have to do this. You want me to call Nikodemus so you can hear it from him?"

"Fuck off."

"If anything happens to my sister, Nikodemus will hold you personally responsible. And so will I. You have my guarantee." He walked toward the door, his phone in hand. "I have to get going. We're due in Paris tomorrow morning."

"Fuck the others, too," Xia said. Harsh was going off to help Nikodemus and Carson negotiate with the other warlords. Personally, he didn't think the warlords would ever work together well enough to keep the kin safe from the magekind, but he was in no position to fault Nikodemus for his rosy outlook.

The witch narrowed her eyes at her brother. "Paris, France, or Paris, Texas?"

Harsh smiled and looked just like the human doc he supposedly used to be before he got all turned around. It made sense that Harsh's sister turned out to be Rasmus Kessler's daughter. Being a freak ran in the family.

"Paris, France," Harsh told her.

"Paris would be a safe place for me, don't you think?" Xia felt the panic underneath her words. "I have a passport. And enough money for a ticket. Won't take me ten minutes to pack a bag, I swear. Je speak français muy bien."

"You can't come with me."

"I don't want to stay here with him."

"He won't hurt you. Will you, Xia?"

He curled a lip at Harsh. No. But he wanted to. Be fun to spill a little witch blood. Or a lot.

"Why don't you just take the amulet, then?" Alexandrine said, all paniclike. Yeah, she ought to be afraid of him. "If it's that important, just take it."

Xia rolled his eyes. "Sure," he said. "Go ahead. I want to see this."

She whipped her head around to him. "I'm not talking to you."

"You can't do it," Xia said. He made sure she saw him looking at her rack. "Not in a million years, baby."

She put her hand to the cord around her neck. All she did was grip it, though. Didn't take it off. He doubted she could. Not with the way that thing was leaking magic into her. "An old Turkish woman gave it to me. I had to hike three hours to get to her village. She said my father made it." She touched her cheek. "She said I looked like him."

"Except for the hair," Xia said, "not that much."

She turned on him. "Would you please butt out?"

"Xia," Harsh said. He sighed. "That's enough. Really."

"Relax," Xia said. "I'm not going to do anything to her. I just want to see if she can take off the talisman."

"Why wouldn't I?"

"You're a witch, lady. And the magekind don't give up objects with that kind of power." He held out a hand and lifted his eyebrows. "Go on, give it to me, baby."

"Fine."

He and Harsh watched her fingers tighten on the cord. "In my lifetime, maybe?" he said.

She stared at her brother, and while she did, her pupils dilated until there was practically no iris left. She wasn't pulling, per se, because that implied some level of control, and by now he knew she didn't have any control of her magic. No wonder Rasmus threw her away. Without control, she was worse than useless.

"I told you," said Xia.

"Of course I can." But she was whispering. Her fingers tightened on the cord.

"Oh, yeah?" Xia said. "Then do it already, why don't you?"

"In a minute." She licked her lips, but she didn't move.

"Alexandrine?" Harsh exchanged a glance with Xia, who just shrugged. Point made. She couldn't do it.

"I will. I'm going to." Her hand shook.

"How long have you been wearing it?" Xia asked.

She looked relieved by the question. Sure she did. Because the question deflected the conversation from the fact that she couldn't take off the talisman. "A few weeks."

"Liar."

She put her hands over her mouth and took a deep breath. Her eyes got all big and scared. The witch should have been scared the minute she touched the thing. She dropped her hands to her sides and addressed her answer to Harsh. "Since I got back from Turkey. Maybe nine months. A little less. What difference does it make?"

"What if you just showed us?" Harsh said. "Can you do that?"

The room got quiet. Perspiration dampened the hair at her forehead and temples. "What's wrong with me?" she asked.

Harsh shook his head at him, and Xia ended up keeping his opinion about that to himself. "Try, Alexandrine," Harsh said.

She lifted the hem of her blouse. The thong was long enough that the talisman hung nearly to her navel. Xia was impressed she could do that much. Harsh made a come-here gesture in his direction. "Take a look, would you, Xia?"

Xia came around to Alexandrine and knelt at her feet,

because he was too tall to get a look any other way. He leaned in close enough that his breath made her skin twitch. Without needing to look hard, he knew both sides of the circle were carved; the front had a panther with a snarling mouth and extended claws. The reverse was the panther's body from the back, including an about-to-twitch tail, with the sole difference that this side also had a carved face.

"Well?" Harsh said.

"I don't know," he said, because he didn't see why he should make this easy for her. He knew what he was looking at. He squinted. "I can't really see." He looked up and winked at her right before he addressed her chest. "I think she needs to take off her top."

"Perv." She jerked down her shirt, but Xia's hand shot out and grabbed her wrist. She yelped, and Harsh lunged.

"Chill," he said, leaning in. "I'm just going to take a closer look. That's all."

"Xia. It's the condition of the talisman that matters, not the shape and depth of my sister's navel."

"I don't think it's cracked." Not yet.

"Don't *think*?" Harsh said, and he didn't sound too happy. The freak knew firsthand what could happen when a talisman cracked. If you weren't prepared or didn't have the magic to control the process, people died, and it usually wasn't a pretty thing to see. An unstable talisman was dangerous. Flat-out dangerous.

Xia reached for the carved panther. If he hadn't been holding her wrist, she would have jumped back. His fingers tightened on her. She didn't want him touching it. The reaction, her need to get away, burned through her to him as clear as the freaking rain in Spain. Shit, that was unexpected. He blocked the mental contact with her.

"No!" The protest burst from her. Xia couldn't help it. He enjoyed the fear coming from her. Nothing wrong with making a witch afraid.

"What?" Harsh asked.

"Something's wrong," she said. "It's nothing but a bit of carved stone. It doesn't work the way it's supposed to." Her voice was tight and breathy. "If it worked, if there was anything to it, I'd be able to do something with my magic, and I can't. So why can't I take it off?"

Xia ignored her panic, because why the hell did he care what happened to a witch? He sure as hell didn't want another slipup that would connect him to her, though. He used the hilt of his knife to move the carving to one side.

Harsh said, "What's that?"

"What?" She looked down. "Oh, that." Where the amulet rubbed against her skin, there was a blue-gray impression of the carved surface. Not a bruise, more like a shadow. A perfect impression of the panther. "Right. I know. Bizarre, isn't it? My skin reacts to something in the stone. You know, the way skin reacts to cheap metal jewelry. No big deal. It'll fade when I take it off." They looked at her, and it was obvious she totally didn't get the absurdity of what she was saying. "What? I assume there's a lot of iron oxide in the stone."

"Mark of the beast, baby," Xia said.

He kept the amulet to one side by letting it rest against the hilt of his knife. He moved the blade to one side and touched the discolored skin on her stomach. She happened to be looking down when he did. He got another jolt, and for a minute he didn't see anything but white. When his vision cleared, he was looking directly into Alexandrine Marit's eyes. In the expanse of time between their gazes locking and her blinking, he saw into her, a moment of flawless, infinite clarity. He could have touched her magic if he'd wanted to. She blinked, and everything went back to normal. Or almost normal. He rocked back on his heels with the snap of coming back to his own mind.

"Fuck," Xia said. He shook his hand like it hurt. It didn't. What he was feeling was an echo of the pain she'd felt the first time she'd put the amulet on.

"You okay?" Harsh asked his sister. Not him, and he was the one reeling.

"Sure," Alexandrine answered. "Why wouldn't I be?"

Xia turned his head, and their gazes collided. She didn't look away. She knew what had happened between them. She knew it, and she wasn't going to say a thing. "Fuck off and die, witch."

"You first."

"When was the last time you took it off?" Xia asked. He deliberately made the question sound dirty, and that got a reaction from her.

"For you, never."

He smiled at her. "Wanna bet?"

"Could you be any more of an asshole?" She yanked on her hand. He didn't move even an atom. No way was she going to budge him if he didn't want her to.

"Answer him, Alexandrine." Harsh paced between her chair and the couch. "When was the last time you took off the talisman?" he asked.

"I don't know." She watched her brother. That helped the agitation that was making Xia jumpy as hell. He hadn't released her wrist yet, and his fingers were tingling, bordering on painful. The sensation was moving up his arm, too. He was filling up with a twitchy energy, fed by contact with the witch. "A month?"

Xia snorted.

She swung her head to look at him. "What?"

"Liar."

"Okay." She yanked on her hand again. No good. He liked making her crazy. "Six months."

Xia rolled his eyes, but for a moment, their gazes met, and he got that crawling feeling again in his head. Her eyes dilated, and his brain flashed hot. A glimmer of magic bubbled up from her but not enough for her to do anything worthwhile. She couldn't pull. Magically speaking, she was a complete loser. Xia's fingers tightened on her wrist, accompanying the growl rumbling from his chest.

"Maybe seven or eight. What difference does it make?" Harsh stared at her like she'd confessed to eating puppies for breakfast. "I like wearing it. For crying out loud, Harsh, the damn thing doesn't even work. Not for me."

Xia released her wrist, and she stepped back. His twitchiness faded almost immediately. "It doesn't matter," he said to Harsh. "It's too late. Even if she could take it off, I'd say the consequences might not leave her in good health, if you get what I mean."

His sheer certainty that she wouldn't remove the talisman pissed her off, which was funny as hell to him. "Of course I can take it off. It's a necklace; that's all." She reached up and pulled the cord over her head, hard and fast, and kept on going until the amulet appeared at the neckline of her shirt. With a grin as fake as it was stiff, she held it out to Harsh. "See?"

Xia stuck out his hand. "I'm impressed," he said.

"I told you." Which would have impressed him even more if her fingers hadn't tightened on the cord.

"How about you give it to me? Or let Harsh if you don't want me that close," he said. "He'll keep it safe."

This time, he wasn't even touching her, and pain ripped through him. His knees wobbled with the force of the magic flowing through her, and it wasn't witch magic. It was coming from the talisman. His vision blurred. Oh, shit. He was going to barf. But she backed away, and the sensation eased up and then faded entirely.

"I can't," she whispered. "Oh, my God. Why can't I?"

# CHAPTER 4

*F*orty-eight hours after Xia's arrival, Alexandrine opened her eyes to darkness. She didn't know what made her wake from a deep sleep, but she was instantly alert, and that scared her. Her skin was nothing but goose pimples. Again. She sat up in bed and listened hard. It was bad enough having him constantly around, but ever since Harsh had let him into her apartment, she'd had a pretty much constant sense of impending, infuriatingly nonspecific disaster. The guy was a damn trigger for setting off premonition-like reactions without her ever getting so much as a hint about what she ought to do to head it off.

She really, really hated that.

The night Harsh left, Xia had sprawled on her couch listening to music or watching videos on an iPod. He'd been quiet last night, too. Yesterday, he'd lurked at her job where he demonstrated an eerie ability to appear from nowhere. Everyone thought she was sleeping with a male model, including Noah in legal, who she'd been crushing on for months. Two days of this crap, and he was ruining what little love life she had. All afternoon he'd been a constant pest. She'd been counting on him being quiet tonight, too.

And he was. Only now the silence sent a chill roaring down her back.

Her bedside clock glowed 1:24. Traffic went by outside. The apartment building was quiet. Nothing abnormal for the time of night, yet goose pimples rippled along her arms and down her spine. She tried to figure out if she was reacting to Xia or whether this was something else.

*Get out.*

Definitely something else.

She slipped out of bed and grabbed the first items of clothing to come to hand. Jeans, a button-down shirt. There wasn't time to find her bra.

*Hurry. Hurry. Hurry!*

She fastened the middle two buttons and left the rest. Sneakers without socks. She didn't smell smoke, but one of the buildings next door might be on fire. Maybe she ought to be gathering her most irreplaceable possessions.

The floor creaked outside her bedroom. She froze, her heart banging against her ribs. Something bad was out there, and given the way she was reacting, she wasn't sure if it was Xia or someone else. And here she was, trapped in her room.

Pulse racing, she grabbed her purse off the floor and dug for her cell phone. She was clumsy, though, and didn't find it as fast as she wanted. She listened harder. No question about it. There was someone out there. Moving around. One person or two? She'd put Xia on her

couch because that was the only place for him to sleep.
Bad enough they had to share the bathroom and the
kitchen. They didn't talk to each other unless it couldn't
be avoided, so she didn't know if he had plans for the
night that someone who wasn't a monumental jerk would
have mentioned. That had to be him skulking around out
there. Freaking her out. But the creepy-crawly sensation
didn't go away, and her stomach was a block of ice, and
her head still screamed, *Get out!*

What if that wasn't Xia making that noise?

Cell phone in hand, she inched open her bedroom door.
She didn't see anything, so she slipped out. She crept,
sneaky quiet, because if whoever was there wasn't supposed to be there, she didn't want him—or her—to know
she was awake. Duh. But wouldn't Xia know? Wouldn't
he protect her the way he'd promised? With his special
utter lack of charm. He might also have decided to hell
with that protection stuff; it was time to use that wicked
knife of his on her.

She froze and assessed her state—mental, magical,
and physical. *Get out* still pulsed in her blood, buzzed her
so hard her skin went twitchy with it. There were other
possibilities to consider. Xia could be dead. Seemed difficult to believe a big, mean SOB like him could go down,
but Rasmus Kessler was a full-on mage, and she'd heard
mages like him did things with their magic that less able
magicians, especially self-trained ones like herself, could
only dream about. She inched down the hallway, because
that was the only way out to get to either of the exits:
her front door or through the kitchen to the laundry room
downstairs.

She didn't see anybody. The couch was empty. No Xia

watching a movie or doing a silent sing-along to whatever his favorite music was. Her extra pillow was on the floor and so were the folded blankets. His helmet was a dark, round shape next to them. His jacket was slung over her recliner. The slob. A nylon bag was open on the floor. Killer Boy was in residence, all right. Just not here, and she didn't see anything that looked corpse-shaped. On her way to the kitchen, she checked the bathroom, just in case. No one there, either. He'd left the toilet seat up, though. Inconsiderate, selfish jerk.

So, where the hell was he? Out partying while she hung around convinced she was going to die any minute?

She stayed quiet because that persistent tingle down her spine had turned into a streak of ice. The idea of crossing her living room to the front door was not appealing. She'd be in plain sight. Whatever was after her would have a clear shot the minute she left the hallway. Outside the bathroom, she crouched and pressed 911 on her phone, then rested her finger on CALL. Footsteps came nearer. Quiet ones. A shadow passed the window by the front door. A very tall and muscular shadow. A tall, muscular, irritating shadow.

Xia.

She stood up and hit the disconnect button on her phone. "What the hell are you doing?"

The tall shape walked to the beginning of the hallway and stood there, lurking in the dark. Not saying anything. Her vision hadn't adjusted to the level of dark in here, and she couldn't see him very well. Still no acknowledgment of her.

What if it wasn't him? Her spine froze. She was a dead woman, that's what. "Xia?"

"What are you doing up?"

Well, that answered that question. Sweet as ever, wasn't he? Alexandrine brushed past him into the living room. Ice skittered up and down her back. The cold built up in the back of her head and started a slow freeze down her spinal column. Prince Charming followed. By the couch, she stopped and stood with her arms crossed over her chest. He stared. Below her chin. His intent gaze reminded her she'd only buttoned the middle two buttons of her shirt and that her stance must be giving him an eyeful. She dropped her arms by her sides. "I was trying to sleep and—Oh for the love of God! You pervert."

Xia held his knife in one hand. And unless you counted the knife, he wasn't wearing anything. Not a stitch. The shadows hid a lot of detail, but not enough for her to miss that he seemed to have muscles everywhere. As for his, ahem, manly equipment. Oh. My. God. *Do not look there.* A package to make a girl faint of heart. He wasn't the least embarrassed at being caught nudie-style.

"Where the H-E-double toothpicks are your clothes?" she whispered. Why whisper? Because it was dark. Because her spine was still ice. Because something bad was coming, and she didn't know what it was yet.

Naked shadow man cocked his head. "Did I wake you?" Not that he sounded sorry or anything.

"Yes." She kept her focus on his face. No staring at his ripped torso. Or muscled legs. Or anything else. Jesus, he was sex on a stick.

"You heard me?" He sounded incredulous. He didn't whisper, but she noticed he kept his voice low, too. He put his hands on his hips, knife still in his hand. "No way."

"Way." Not looking. Absolutely not looking.

"No."

"Look." She didn't bother keeping the irritation from her voice. "I woke up and heard you skulking around out here. Ergo"—she jabbed a finger at him with the hand clutching her cell phone—"you woke me up."

He took a step toward her, and she backed up. "Why do you have your phone?"

"In case I needed to call the police." The back of her knees quivered, but she refused to retreat another step.

"Did you think you needed to?" Xia advanced on her. A blink, and there he was, right in front of her, and she was seeing him clear as day. His hand circled her upper arm. "This is important," he said, keeping his voice low. "Did you think you might need to call for help?"

She tried to twist free of his grip, but that just wasn't happening. He had a knife, for God's sake. Terror bubbled up at the thought that this was the event that had awakened her—being in danger from Xia. He was going to kill her, and she'd walked right to him. "Let go of me."

"Answer me." His hand on her was warm through the fabric of her shirt sleeve. Like he was running a temp.

Her pulse pounded, but if he was going to kill her, wouldn't he have done it already? Why wait? As for his question, she'd learned a long time ago, before she knew anything of her peculiar heritage, that most people didn't react well to someone who claimed to know things before they happened. The ones who did tended to believe in astrology and tarot cards and tea leaves, all of which, in her opinion, were utter crap. "I heard a noise out here. What was I supposed to think?"

Xia put his free hand on the wall just above her shoulder. On the way up, dim light gleamed off the blade of his knife. "If Rasmus sends magehelds after you, I'm not going to know until they're inside. On top of us."

"Magehelds." She grabbed her arms and rubbed, because, shit, he was talking about magehelds like there really were such things. The world would be a damn scary place if there were such creatures.

"Yeah. Magehelds, baby cakes."

"It's true?" The question came out sounding completely genuine because, well, it was. But he made a face, and she hurried to add, "Magehelds. There's really such a thing?"

"Yeah, baby," he said in a low voice. "There is." He used his index finger to trace a line from her forehead to her chin. He didn't touch her, but her skin sizzled as if he had. "What's with you, gorgeous? You been living under a rock your whole life?"

Oh, shit. Magehelds were supposedly fiends or demons controlled by mages, powerful mages, obviously. Their existence was a matter of hot debate among the practitioners she knew. The really powerful mages didn't have anything to do with people like her, self-trained in magic. Mages like that were an insular elite, and to be honest, there was a lot of disinformation out there. Even her best friend, Maddy, who knew more than any of them, thought magehelds were most likely fables, like basilisks, ogres, and swamp monsters. Alexandrine's heart dove straight to her toes at the idea that magehelds were real. "Are you sure?"

"For fuck's sake." His voice was low and mean. "Am I sure. You're shitting me, right?"

In her attempt to educate herself about what she was, she'd come across references to magehelds more than once, but she just couldn't believe something like that really happened. Magehelds had to do whatever they were told. They were, in fact, magically compelled to do so. No matter what their instructions were. According to the versions of the legends she'd read, back in the Dark Ages and beyond, when demons were running amok in the world, mages kept innocent humans safe by killing or controlling the demons. Hence, magehelds, for a demon magically held by one of the magekind. They were stories. Legends. Not real. "How do you know they're real?"

Xia leaned toward her, and it was sheer nerve that kept her from shrinking back. His expression was bland despite the tension in his shoulders. "How do I know?" When he spoke again, his voice was hard and bitter. "Because I used to be one, witch."

She did a mental free fall through the implications of what Xia was telling her. Disbelief, denial, and horror were the main ingredients when she landed.

Xia rasped, "Why do you think I hate your father so much?"

"My father is dead," she replied. "My real father is the man who raised me, and he wasn't a mage."

"Kessler is still your daddy. And the apple don't fall far from the tree, if you get what I'm saying, witch."

"No," she whispered.

"Let's get clear, Alexandrine Marit. If you woke up feeling like something was going to happen, I need to know about it. Because I don't believe you don't have any magic on tap. You're a witch." He bent his head to her ear and whispered, "Now, Alexandrine." Damn, his voice was gold dripping with honey. "I need to know right now. Did you wake up thinking you needed to call for help?"

"I didn't think it." She lifted her chin to stare into his eyes. "I knew it."

He let go of her. "Fuck." But he wasn't cursing at her so much as expressing a general observation on the state of the world right now. If there was even the slightest possibility that real-deal magehelds were coming after her, she agreed with him.

The lights went out. Only, the lights in her apartment were already off. The glow from the streetlights disappeared without a sound, none of that electric buzz that sounded in the split-second before an outage. The room was darker than it ought to be. None of the electronic gadget lights in her apartment were glowing. The difference between closing her eyes and opening them became minuscule, which was disorienting to say the least. She was sick to her stomach, and her legs were jittery.

"Listen up, witch." She shifted in the direction of Xia's words. Did his voice sound like it was coming from higher above her head because he'd straightened up? "I've proofed the place against shit-head mages like Christophe or Rasmus, but it would take longer than I've had to make it solid. What I did isn't going to keep magehelds out for long."

"You heard something, didn't you?" she said.

"I didn't hear shit. But it's my job to make sure nothing gets in here."

"I think they're trying to get in now."

"Give me your mobile."

She obeyed without hesitation. He opened her phone. In the screen's glow she saw his determined face. The light made his eyes look white. He punched in a number and handed it back to her. "If you see me go down, or if you feel like you need to call for help, get into the bathroom and lock the door. Then call that number."

"Why not 911?"

Without the glow of her phone, they were enveloped in darkness. "Because," he said after a pause, "that's not the kind of help you're going to need. Whoever answers, you tell him you're Harsh's sister and you need help, now."

"Okay." Swear to God, Alexandrine thought she saw a neon blue glow in the place where his eyes ought to be. And then there was nothing. Either he'd blinked or looked away, or she was just seeing things.

*Get out. Get out. Get out!*

"Xia," she said. Her legs did not want to hold her up right now.

"Shh."

If anything, the darkness got deeper. The temperature dropped to an icy chill. Her skin crawled and the muscles in her legs twitched. "We have to get out of here," she said. "Right now."

Glass shattered somewhere in the building, in the direction of the kitchen, where a back door led to the apartment house's laundry room, garbage area, and garage. She jumped, but Xia clamped a hand over her mouth. His other arm snaked around her waist and held her tight, face-to-face with him. His body was unyielding. Her head clamored, spinning out of whack. A solid block of ice.

Xia put his mouth by her ear. "Quiet. You got that, witch? Not a word unless I ask you something." She nodded, and he slid his hand off her mouth. His lips were right by her ear. "Feel anything?"

She turned her head to use the same soft voice. "Like what?"

"Concentrate." He said the word like he meant *fuck off and die*.

"I don't know." Her head was pounding, and everything wavered in front of her, going in and out of focus.

He was still holding her tight. Her shirt had flapped open at the bottom when he grabbed her, and her bare belly was pressed hard against his, the amulet between them. His arm tightened around her, and her head spun. "How many?"

Wood broke this time. The sound came from the rear stairs that led from her kitchen to the laundry room. Whoever or whatever was here wasn't in her apartment yet, but they would be soon. They were going to get in. She pushed at his chest. Oh, dear God. Naked skin. Hardbody naked skin. "I don't know!"

"Guess."

She guessed. She was good at guessing. "Four."

"That's all?" Xia laughed. "Piece of cake. Here." He let go of her and handed her his knife, hilt first. "Take this. Watch the blade; it's sharp enough to take off your head. Something bad happens, you make the call first. But use this if you need to."

The knife was much heavier than she expected. And it made her fingers prickle with numbness. "I don't want it."

"Use it," he said.

And then Xia headed for the kitchen to face whatever was creeping up the back stairs in order to get into her apartment and kill her. Alexandrine stayed in the hallway, chill air pressing against her. Her knees shook. She tightened her fingers around the hilt of Xia's knife. She felt a little better. Very little. Having a weapon was good.

More wood broke. They were here. Inside. Right now. In the kitchen, something screamed.

# CHAPTER 5

$X$ia came back into Alexandrine's kitchen from the rear stairs where he'd kicked the little freak who broke the door. His buddies were farther down the stairs, waiting. They'd gotten in where there were lots of shadows to hide them from vision-poor humans. Windows to climb through. A narrow staircase to sneak up. Whatever mage was responsible for this attempt—and Xia still had his money on Rasmus even though he hadn't recognized any of the attackers—he'd let his magehelds do the dirty work. No surprise there. That's what mages did, right? They sent their enslaved fiends to kill or be killed. He figured one or two other magehelds had likely died breaking through his proofing outside the building, leaving four survivors to smash the laundry room window once the way was clear. Poor fucks. They hadn't gotten far. At least their deaths had been less painful than the ones who'd died outside.

He didn't think there'd be more right away. He knew

the drill. The ones he hadn't killed would slink off and talk about what went wrong and why, and either wait for further orders from their mage or bring on reinforcements. And if that was the case, they'd be in already. Which meant they were waiting for Rasmus to tell them what to do next. He figured he had twenty or thirty minutes of peace and quiet.

Xia rolled his shoulders and stopped at the sink to wash his hands and face. It felt good to fight with complete freedom. Without the aching, bone-deep pain of compulsion. Without hatred burning through him. The difference unsettled him. Until now, he'd not realized, not completely, how alien his freedom was to him. Talk about messed up. He'd done nothing but dream about freedom, and now that he had it, he didn't know how to live. In a sick way, he was grateful to be babysitting Harsh's sister, because it gave him something to think about besides what he was supposed to do with his freedom now that it belonged to him again.

The lights were back to normal, but he didn't turn any on. He liked the dark, and besides, he didn't have any problem seeing. He ran the water extra long, waiting until well past the time when it was hot. Extra soap for him. The smell of copper echoed in his mouth, a sweet tang of blood on his tongue.

While he waited for the sink to clear of blood, he found a glass and got a drink of water from a bottle in the fridge. Cool and wet down the back of his throat. Whenever he was coming down from high alert, he was hyper-aware of his surroundings. His proofing was back in place and felt good and solid, given the time he'd had in which to work. First-class proofing took days, and he'd had less than an hour to redo what he'd managed to put in place in the time he'd been here. Not to mention the limitation of having to wait until the witch was asleep before he got to work.

He returned to the sink and let his senses expand. None of the free kin were around besides him. Carson and Nikodemus were tucked away in the back of his head, and it was comforting to feel them. If he cared to, he could reach out to Kynan or Iskander. He could even touch Harsh, who sometimes stank of magekind.

He'd always been sensitive to the magekind, witches in particular. If Alexandrine Marit's place was full of vanilla humans, he'd still know exactly where she was. Right now, she was in the living room, about a yard from that sissy couch of hers. She made his skin itch. But there was something else here, too. Besides the stink of witch. He concentrated. Given his current sensitive state, which he expected would last another hour at least, he could make out more than before.

For sure Harsh's sister was coming into some power from the talisman, but she was still a lot more human than witch. Not that it mattered to him. Practicing or not, she was a witch, and he felt the power in her whether she could use it or not. The Marit woman wasn't stable. Not anymore. The talisman was fucking her up but good. She deserved what she was getting.

For a while, he listened to Alexandrine breathe. She was a good-looking woman, and it wasn't long before his thoughts wandered off in inappropriate directions. His body reacted predictably to the stimulus of thinking about her without her clothes. Man, he could smell her blood from here. Pulsing. Sweet with magic. She backed away from the couch and went back to her bedroom. Yeah. Run, baby, run, because he was feeling a bit frisky. Totally not down from his high. A little one-on-one with the delectable Alexandrine Marit would be a nice topper for the best evening he'd had since Carson cut him free.

He rubbed his rib cage, but his bruises were already fading. The magehelds hadn't put up much of a fight. Pity. Harsh's sister was coming back. He smiled to himself. Nikodemus did the nasty with a witch. Why not him? Physically, Alexandrine Marit was his type. At this point, he thought he could put aside his feelings about witches long enough to get laid. Hell, it'd been weeks since the last time he'd done it. Didn't want to get out of practice, did he?

Yeah. Right. He laughed to himself. Like that would ever happen. His hatred of witches was the stuff of legend. Hell, it predated his association with Rasmus. Which was why Nikodemus let Harsh pick him for this job over Kynan or Iskander. None of them figured he'd so much as breathe near a witch unless he was planning to kill her.

Now Alexandrine was heading this way. Given what she was, she probably knew she was safe for the present, but he flipped on the kitchen light just in case. The switch by the sink turned on a shitty fluorescent above the stove. The rest of the room stayed nice and dim. "S'okay," he called out.

He listened to her walk—now, why she did go back to her room, he wondered?—but stayed facing the sink in order to keep his back to the door, both hands gripping the counter because he was hyped up from the change and the fight, and he wasn't sure what that might be doing to his eyes, let alone the rest of him. Freaking out the witch was against his instructions. He stood there at the sink while two competing instincts went to war. Kill the witch or get laid. Harsh would eviscerate him if he put so much as a pinky on her with sexual intent. Same if he killed her. Only slower and more painfully. He could handle the first. Not so much the other.

He could smell her. Woman. Witch. Warm-blooded. And totally his type.

This was going to be interesting.

"Are you all right?" Alexandrine Marit asked from the doorway.

Only the one mageheld had made it into the kitchen. And he'd cleaned up the mess downstairs. He hadn't left any bloody footprints or anything disturbing on her clean kitchen floor. "Yeah. I'm all right."

She crossed to him and set his knife on the counter. "Here."

"Thanks." He picked up his glass of water and turned on the tap so he'd have an excuse not to look at her.

"Ahem."

"What?" Did he dare look at her? Slowly, he turned his head. He braced himself for a reaction. But she didn't freak. Nah. She wasn't the type, anyway. Must be his eyes were okay. She was holding out a bath towel. A fluffy pink one.

"I don't have a robe that will fit you."

"So?"

To his surprise, she reached out and brushed his hair over his ear. He gripped the counter hard, because, man, having her touch him was giving him urges he shouldn't be having. Her hair glinted silver in the light, and she smiled at him like she cared about his condition. "Beautiful as you are, Xia of the fantastic"—her gaze swept down and then back to his face—"eyes, we just don't know each other well enough for you to be naked in my kitchen."

Just like a human to be hung up over nudity. He took the towel from her. He wasn't hard or anything, but hey, he wasn't that far from a boner, and there wasn't anyone controlling his responses anymore. If he wanted to act on his impulses, he could. So, she was right. The towel was a good thing. He concentrated on her face even though he would have preferred to concentrate on those two lonely buttons holding together her shirt.

"Thanks," he said. He hadn't had consensual sex with a witch in too many years to count, so there was no telling what he'd do if he got a hard-on for her. In the process of wrapping the towel around his waist, he increased the distance between them. No way was he back in control. And it was up to him to keep what control he had. Freedom could be a bitch.

"You're welcome." She headed for the door that led to the back stairs, but she turned around before she got there. "You know, you're not so bad when you try to be nice."

"It's not easy." He looked down as he brought the end of the towel around his hip. "Damn thing's pink."

The corner of her mouth twitched. "You're man enough to carry it off. Or are you afraid you aren't pretty in pink?"

"Baby, I'm so pretty in pink, I'm worried you won't be able to help yourself." He tucked in the top of the towel and stood with his hands on his hips. "I don't mind not wearing it." He waited a beat. Sure enough, she was looking at him again, but he couldn't tell if she was pissed off or trying not to laugh. When she didn't come back with a smart-ass put-down—mages and witches didn't tolerate much shit from his kind—he said softly, "For you, baby, I'll take it off." He braced himself for the smack-down that was coming for sure.

"But my clothes stay on, Xia, so where does that leave you?"

"Same place as ever, I guess." He shrugged. "All alone with your pink towels."

"Don't go making me actually like you."

He walked over to her and didn't even care that he was feeling her and the talisman both or that it was cranking him something fierce. She was standing near the door that led downstairs—the kitchen was so small, just about anywhere was near the door—and Xia put his hands on either side of the frame. He leaned in until she practically had her back to the wooden surface. "You did good tonight. Kept your head on straight."

"Thanks."

"You get any more of those feelings, you let me know."

Slowly, she tilted her head back until it rested against the door, and then she smiled and his blood about boiled. "What feelings would those be?"

His stomach did a little flip. "The ones where you're okay with me not wearing this towel." To his amped-up vision, the shadow panther on her belly glowed a soft gray. And, uh-oh, she did not have on a bra. What would she do if he reached over and undid those buttons? His head was so full of the fantasy of reaching in and unfastening her shirt that well, hell, he reached in and—she went completely stiff. "What?"

"Something's coming." She spoke at the same time he heard the kitchen window crack.

He lunged for his knife on the counter where Alexandrine had set it down. He had a grip on the hilt when the proofing around the back staircase door gave way. The magic tearing away scraped like sandpaper over his heart. A split second before the door burst open, Alexandrine threw herself to the floor. Her evasive action was why the mageheld who came through didn't kill her with his first strike. But she was on her back when the fiend jumped her. Her knee in his crotch barely slowed him. She gave him a damn hard strike, too.

With the window rattling like a train, Xia launched himself at the mageheld and grabbed the thing by his chin. He had one clawed hand on the leather thong around her neck and was tugging, but Alexandrine went wild. Fucking wild. Hell, she practically threw the mageheld off her. Magic burned in his bones, and as Xia crouched down and drove his knife into the fiend's lumbar spine, he recognized a mix of magekind and demon in what she was pulling, and all of it was focused on the thing on top of her.

The mageheld went down hard on the kitchen floor, and Xia wasn't at all sure if he'd killed him or if Alexandrine had. The window stopped rattling. Silence fell.

She scrambled out from under the body, eyes big, breathing hard. There wasn't a mark on her, but her shirt was completely shredded. No need to wonder anymore what she looked like without her shirt. "You okay?" he asked.

His towel was on the floor, and he stooped for it so she could cover herself. But she just stood there, taking deep shuddering breaths and staring at the dead mageheld like she thought it would get up and try for seconds.

"Alexandrine," he said.

No reaction from her.

He went to her and awkwardly draped the towel around her as he tried not to look or touch. He wasn't exactly having pure thoughts. She wasn't aware of much, and she continued to radiate that weird mix of power. He didn't think that could be doing anything but getting her even more tightly wound up with the talisman. A similar process had nearly killed Carson Philips when she got on the wrong side of an unstable talisman. "Baby," he said, keeping a hand on her shoulder so the towel wouldn't fall completely off her. "Sit down, okay?"

She looked at him. "He was going to kill me."

He adjusted the towel, but she wasn't helping, and he was seeing more than he should. "I know, baby." He touched her cheek, and she let him. So he kept doing it. Her skin was shockingly soft. "He didn't have any choice. None of them do."

She leaned her face into his fingers. "That isn't right," she whispered.

"No," he said. Her eyes were big and wide, and Xia didn't mind so much looking into them. He was actually kind of liking it. Physically, he wasn't too far from changing, and there was magic and some pretty freaking raw lust flowing through him right now.

"If it weren't for you," she said, "I'd be dead."

"Nah." He stepped away. He had some things to take care of to make sure they didn't get overrun again, and besides, he didn't think she'd appreciate him putting his hands all over her, which is what he wanted to do right now. "I think you offed that one yourself."

Her gaze swept over him, and when she got back to his face after maybe a little longer than was safe for either of them, he cocked his head and shrugged. She held out the towel to him, and a bunch of stuff happened all in the space of a second or two.

He looked. And jaysus, she was just gorgeous. He had wet dreams about women who looked like her. He said, "Fuck," because he felt like a jackass for looking and getting off on it.

Alexandrine looked down at herself, then turned bright red and said, "Oh." She covered herself with the towel. "Well, that was embarrassing."

He tried a smile. "I guess we're even, then."

"I guess so." And she smiled back a little, and they were actually kind of okay. Amazing. He figured that wouldn't last long, since they were on opposite sides of the species fence, but it was nice for now.

"Look," he said. "I need to clean up here, but I could use your help, if you don't mind. Mostly to let me know if you feel them coming on again." Hell must be covered in ice about now: He was actually asking a witch for help. "If you don't mind."

"No, I don't mind."

"Be with you in a minute, all right?" he asked. He answered her unspoken question by looking at the dead fiend. Gotta take care of the dead. She nodded and walked out, with him looking at her naked back all the way.

Damn, he really, really wanted to get in her pants. And he really, really hoped his case of the hots for Alexandrine Marit came to a quick end. Because otherwise he was fucked.

# CHAPTER 6

$A$lexandrine walked out holding the damn towel across her chest, wigged out by Xia's silence and his reason for remaining behind. She didn't want to know anything about what was involved in getting rid of a body, so the faster she got out, the better. Her back itched the whole way from the kitchen to the living room: little icy-crawly fingers skittering up and down her spine. Other than that, she was numb.

In her bedroom, the lights were still off, but gadget lights were back. Light from the street filtered down the hall through the front windows. One quick check showed the clock by her bed glowing 3:13. She dropped the towel and went to her dresser for a bra and a fresh shirt. Her shirt was ruined, in complete tatters. *Oh, my God.* She'd flashed Xia. More than a flash. She'd stood there like a dork, handing him the towel and giving him all day to look. To be fair, he hadn't taken advantage or been an enormous jackass about it, but he'd definitely looked. No pretending he hadn't.

New shirt on and safely buttoned, she sat on the edge of her bed and bent over, holding her head in her hands. Xia the Jerk had gotten an eyeful of her, and he hadn't been a jerk about it. Go figure. And then there was the attack and nearly getting killed. She was shaking, but she wasn't feeling any emotion. That couldn't last. The crash was coming; the only question was when.

"Hey."

She jumped because she hadn't heard Xia walking toward her room. Damn, that was creepy the way he could move without making any noise. The man—or whatever he was, and Alexandrine was now very sure he wasn't a human male—made a very large darkened shape in her doorway. "Yes?"

"I'm done." She watched him put a hand up high on the doorjamb. And, yeah, still naked, and he still didn't care. She couldn't see much in the darkness, but she could see enough. After a bit of silence, he said, "I could use some help with the rest, if you don't mind."

It was probably killing him to sound so nice. She shook her head. "All I want is a nice calm life where my biggest challenge is practicing magic that almost never works. That's all. Really."

"Yeah, well, good luck with that."

He wasn't looking at her like he was remembering her flashing him, which she appreciated a lot. "They're going to come back, aren't they?"

"Sometime between now and dawn, I'd guess."

She pushed herself off her bed. "Rasmus Kessler

doesn't know who I am. He doesn't know anything about me. I doubt he even remembers he gave me away."

"Number one, yes, he does. Number two, so what? He wants that talisman, and he's coming after you for it, whether you're Alexandrine Marit or Mother Theresa."

"Mother Theresa is dead." She was cracking up. Totally losing it. Inside she was nothing but one huge hollow. Nothing left. Inside, she needed something to keep her from falling apart, but she couldn't find a crutch to get her around this. She had a permanent sense of impending disaster that just wouldn't go away. No matter what happened or what she did, apparently her life was in the toilet. Right now, though, she was stuck walking a high-wire without a net. "Okay. My dad the infamous mage Rasmus Kessler, who you hate worse than poison, who you hate probably more than even me, doesn't care if I die as long as he gets my amulet."

"Talisman."

"Fine. Talisman." She plopped back onto the bed and grabbed a handful of her comforter. "Heading for the hills sounds like a good idea about now. There's a way to the garage from the garbage area. We can go out the back, and no one will know we even left." Xia remained in the shadows, but she was seeing better now. He clenched and unclenched his fists. "I don't have a car, but we can walk out the side door and get a cab or jump onto the bus."

"It's not safe out there."

"And it's safe here?"

"Safer than if we're outside," he said. "I can control what happens in here. Outside . . ." From the doorway, he shook his head. "Not as easy."

What a thought, that there were magehelds out there

just waiting to crunch on her bones and spit them out. In her head, Alexandrine imagined monsters squatting in alleys and doorways, salivating and rubbing misshapen hands over the prospect of catching her first. "What are we going to do, then?"

"Do some cleanup and sit tight."

She looked at her clock. Three twenty-one in the morning. She was going to be a wreck when her alarm went off. If she lived that long. She hated feeling powerless. The fact that Xia believed he could handle this didn't help her at all. No way was she going to rely on someone else to save her ass. Not happening.

"Sit tight?" she said. This was stupid, talking to each other across the room. She let out a breath and walked to the door. She didn't look. Much. He moved aside and followed her to the living room. She turned around and put her hand on her hips. "You think I don't get that you're hoping my father will show up and give you a chance to kill him. Well, get real, Xia, because one thing I'm not is stupid. You want to kill Rasmus Kessler, and you're hoping I'm the bait that gets him here."

He wasn't bothered in the least, was he? "Until it's full-on daylight, it's safer in here than out there."

"So," she said calmly. Or tried to speak calmly, anyway. She was dimly aware that she did not sound calm. "You're no different than Rasmus Kessler."

"Oh, yeah," he said with a straight face. "Me and Rasmus. Practically twins." He was surly because she was being a bitch to him. She knew she was going off on him for no good reason, but she couldn't stop herself. She was on overload and looking for a way, any way, to release the fear and tension of the last hours. Fighting with Xia was an easy, chicken-livered out.

"You are," she said. "Neither of you give a shit if I live or die. I take that back. I think if you slip up and I get killed, you'll be doing the happy dance. Whoopsie there, Harsh. So sorry about your sister, may she rest in peace."

From where she stood, his eyes looked like they were glowing. Pretty unsettling, that. "I wouldn't wish for you to rest in peace," he said in a low, honey-spiced voice. "And I wouldn't slip up, either." He sneered. "If it weren't for my promise to Nikodemus and Harsh, you'd be dead already, baby."

"Thanks so much for sharing the love."

He glared at her. His eyes were definitely glowing. "I keep my promises."

"Goody for you." Inside, she was standing on the edge of a bottomless pit, about to fall over. "Why don't you go do whatever the hell you want, and I'll take care of saving my own skin. Really. I'm used to it." Her voice rose. "I've been taking care of myself for a long time. I don't need Harsh, and I don't need you, so just get the hell out, the way you should have the first time I told you."

"I promised Nikodemus and your brother I'd keep you alive. It's something I did tonight, in case you didn't notice."

She knew that, but she was in self-destruct mode and unable to stop. Alexandrine stepped up to him. She was tall enough to look into his eyes without tilting her chin. Much. "Did you happen to mention your little conflict of interest to them?"

"They know all about me and Rasmus."

"Fine." She threw her hands up, but they were shaking

so hard she was afraid he'd see and realize she was losing it. She wanted to strangle her brother for this. She really did. This was all his fault. All of it. Why hadn't he stayed dead? "What's your plan for keeping me alive, then? Let's hear some brilliant strategy, because that thing that jumped me, it wanted to kill me."

Xia shrugged. "Whoever comes, I'll take care of them."

"That's it? That's all you've got?" Now she wanted to strangle Xia. The lights were still off, but the streetlamp outside shone through the side windows and cast a yellowish glow on everything. She could see him just fine. He was standing, naked, with his arms crossed over a chest you could use for an anatomy lesson. "I feel safe and snug. There's an unknown number of crazed magehelds out there who think my heart is their target for the night, and you're just going to take care of them. Pardon me if I don't get much comfort from that."

He made a noise low in his throat that sounded an awful lot like a growl and made the hair on the back of her neck stand up. "Quit arguing and listen up, why don't you?"

"Fine." She glared at him. "I'm listening."

"I can take care of them when they get here." He touched her cheek with the tip of a finger. "Seriously, Alexandrine. I can and will. You can trust me about that much. But since I can't feel magehelds, it'd be nice to have some advance warning." He waited a minute. "Stay close and tell me when you feel them coming, and we'll be just fine."

Tension curled in her, choking her. "How am I supposed

to know something like that? I mean, what if it doesn't work? My magic. It doesn't always, you know."

Xia shrugged. "I don't know what you mages feel." There was enough light for her to see his muscled chest and the quite noticeable bulge of his biceps, not that she was staring, and below his belly button, she noted he had an innie, a narrow dark line of hair descended south, and . . . No. Not looking. "You knew to get the hell away from the door before it blew."

"I'm not reliable that way."

He rolled his eyes. "All I'm asking is that you tell me when you feel the urge to book it out of here."

"Believe me," she said. "I feel the urge right now."

He tensed, and it wasn't just your average tension but a state that telegraphed his readiness to engage and fight. For her. She got another chill. This was the real deal, she thought, him flipping from standard pain in the ass to combat-ready in a blink. This just couldn't be happening. "For real?"

"No," she said. Great. He was all business, and she was jerking him around. "I'm sorry." She about choked on the words, but, damn, she owed them to him. "That was juvenile of me." She stared at her feet. "I know this is serious. That was stupid. I shouldn't have made light of it."

He was silent long enough to make her uncomfortable. At last he said, "I still need to proof this place. You on board with that?"

"Proof my apartment." She shook her head. "What does that mean, exactly?"

"You really don't know anything, do you?"

He didn't say that like he thought she was stupid. "No, actually, I don't."

He didn't answer right away. "Okay," he said at last. "Proofing means I make a place or a room less prone to getting broken into by a mage or a mageheld. Using magic. There's not time to make it much more than difficult for them to get in, but the sooner I get it done, the safer we'll be." He strode toward her, his knife gripped in one hand. She stared at his knife. Was the blade actually glowing? "Relax," he said, rolling his eyes. "I'm not going to off you."

"I didn't think you were."

"Then I'm losing my touch." He was near enough now that pretty much nothing was lost to shadow. *Oh, my Lord, the man is gorgeous.* Flat-out gorgeously made. He put down his knife and crouched by his gym bag. She managed to look away instead of staring. He rummaged around inside until he extracted a pair of sweats. "Listen," he said while he stuck one leg, then the other into his sweats. "By now, Rasmus, or whoever the hell sent those magehelds, knows someone is here protecting you, since his boys didn't come back." He checked the tie at his waist and didn't do anything to it. "Next time, he's going to send someone who can get the job done for him. More than one." He bent for his knife. "We need to be prepared, witch, because when those guys come, it's not going to be as easy for me to take care of them as it was this time." His gaze seared her. "Now," he said, "you going to watch my back while I proof this place or not?"

Alexandrine nodded. He didn't answer, but after a tense silence, he nodded and headed back to her room.

She waited a beat before she called out, "Stay away from my underwear."

He was already down the hall. "If it's pink, baby, I'm all over it." But he was laughing, and it was actually kind of comforting to know they could joke at a time like this.

While he was off doing whatever the hell he was doing, she walked to her bookcase and pulled out a box hidden in the back of one of the middle shelves. She was getting jittery again, probably from whatever Xia was doing in her room.

She opened the box she'd taken out and removed a jagged metal blade lashed to a wooden handle. Both pieces were handmade. One of the felons she used to hang with had taught her how to make a shiv. Back in her wild days, this had kept her alive, and it would again if she had anything to say about it. She was *not* going to be caught unarmed around a mageheld again. No way.

She sat on the couch with her legs pulled up and one arm around her shins. The tension in her started to fall away, and what was underneath was shaky as hell. She wrapped one hand around the smooth wooden handle that was just long enough to stay hidden in her palm. For months after she'd made it, she'd polished the wood until the surface was shiny and smooth. She rested her forehead on her knees. Every few seconds, her skin goose pimpled. Her stomach was cold and empty. And on top of that, any minute she expected to hear someone breaking in or maybe just have someone grab her from behind. That was just normal twitchiness, because waiting was a bitch. This wasn't a premonition like the one that woke her up tonight or the one that made her throw herself away from the back stairway door.

She remembered the mageheld falling on her, but what she remembered most after the feeling of pure ice down her spine was the smell of heat and sand and the rage that vibrated from her attacker. When he'd grabbed for her amulet, something inside her had snapped. She hadn't just been fighting for her life. In fact, she was pretty sure she'd have traded her life to keep the amulet—the talisman, or whatever the hell it was. And that, she knew, was not a normal rational response for someone being attacked.

Xia came down the hallway and into the living room, and she jumped about a foot and a half, because, once again, she hadn't heard him coming. She tried to cover the reaction by standing up.

"I did the bathroom, too," he said. He came to the front of the sofa, and the first thing he did was stare at her shiv. "What's that?"

"Protection." She didn't have to hide what she was from Xia. No pretending. No leaving out big chunks of her past because she could hardly deal with it, let alone someone she was interested in dating. If finally occurred to her as a solid fact that she wasn't looking at a human man. He'd said himself he had been mageheld. So, what did that make him? She knew the answer. A demon of some kind. The kind of creature mages thought were too dangerous to go free.

"You make that yourself?" he asked.

How the hell did you tell the difference between a demon and a normal man? He looked human to her.

"Don't worry. I know how to use it." She cocked her head, daring him to make a crack. Her knife might be ugly, but the blade had saved her life and kept her out of trouble. More than once. "I've used this before. I can do it again."

His eyes settled on her with unnerving intensity. "Can I see?"

"No." Like she wanted his ridicule.

"What'd you use for the blade?" Hell if he didn't look genuinely interested. Not that she trusted him. No way. He was probably faking. Most men were when they wanted to sleep with you.

"Scrap metal I found at a construction site." Where *found at* might possibly be the same as *stole from*.

"Magic?"

"I tried a few times. It didn't work that I could tell." She shrugged. "My magic hardly ever does."

"I don't know," he said with a tilt of his head. "You're alive, aren't you?"

Was he serious? Nah. Not possible.

She nodded, and his face got thoughtful. "When was the last time you sharpened that?"

"A while," she said.

He drew his knife from his scabbard and held it up in the light. The blade definitely had some sort of bluish aura. "I made this, too."

"No shit?" His knife was a work of deadly beauty, with a carved hilt and that gorgeous glowing blade that looked to have some interesting shadows now that she could see it better. Was the thing completely carved?

"I worked on it for years. Still working on it even now." He reversed his grip on the weapon and presented it to her hilt first. "Trade you. Just for the night."

"Why?"

"I like yours." He didn't laugh or anything. The guy

looked dead-on serious. "You don't have time to sharpen yours. Not the old-fashioned way." He extended his knife to her again. "Mine's already sharp. And if you need to use a weapon, you'll have a better chance with mine."

She nodded because all he was doing was stating a fact. His blade was wicked sharp. And magic. And hers was pathetically not.

She took Xia's knife in her right hand, keeping hers in her left, and figured she wasn't imagining the tingle in her palm when she held his. Was that how she could tell the difference between human and not human? That chill in her body? The blade was made up of dozens of smaller blades that twisted around and under and over each other so that every surface was a cutting edge. "It's beautiful." And ghastly. Fearsome, like its owner.

"Thanks." Xia reached out and clipped his scabbard to her jeans. As he did, his fingers brushed over her bare skin. Heat flashed through her, and this wasn't of those freaky sensations she'd been getting from him all night. The heat was nothing but pure sexual reaction. Damn it. She gasped, and that made him glance up at her. Their gazes collided. Hard. "What's the matter, witch?" he said in his low and golden voice. His fingers feathered over her belly, a light enough touch that, if she was into self-delusion, she could call it incidental.

"What's up with that, Xia?" she said. She didn't move away and neither did he.

They spent some time standing there with his thumb brushing across her navel, just below her amulet. He was big and strong enough to hurt her, but she knew he wouldn't, even if he wanted to. The thing was, he didn't like her but he *liked* her. And she was thinking she liked him that way, too.

"Nothing's up," he said. But his thumb pressed gently over her navel while his fingers spread out, pulling her forward oh so slightly. Alexandrine bit down on her lower lip, not wanting to be the first one to admit she was turned on.

"Nothing, huh?" She looked into his eyes. "That's good. I thought maybe you were coming on to me."

"Baby," he said, and God, did she want to melt at the way he made the word sound so wickedly rich. She wanted to hear that voice when he was about to come inside her. "You worried you might like a fiend's dirty hands on you?"

"Not worried at all," she said. His slid his thumb up the midline of her torso, and this time she took a step forward. "I just think it's funny how you can't stand having the hots for a witch."

"Are you saying this doesn't bother you?" He used his thumb and index finger to pop the bottom button of her shirt. His mouth curled in a tiny smile.

"Does it bother you?"

He shook his head. "Maybe. But it's been a while since the last time I did it."

"Me, too, actually," she said. She waited. After a bit, his palm flattened over her, sliding under her shirt. She took another step forward.

He kept his hand on her belly. His little finger dove underneath the waist of her jeans. "Beautiful witch like you? That's hard to believe."

"Believe it."

"Maybe this doesn't bother me so much after all." He

did a little more exploring, and Alexandrine enjoyed her reaction. And his. Then, just when she was about to turn into a puddle at his feet and let him do whatever the hell he wanted, her chest turned to solid ice. Chilling certainty froze her to the marrow.

"What?" Xia asked.

She grabbed his shoulder. "Something's here."

He was all business in less than a blink. "How many and which direction?"

She concentrated and had to work at not letting fear get in the way. "Three, I think. Kitchen and there." The minute she pointed to the front door, it clicked twice. Once for the dead bolt and again for the regular lock. "Shit," she whispered.

"No worries, baby." He took her knife. He passed a finger over the edges, and swear to God, she saw sparks shimmering between his fingertip and the metal surface. Cold air drifted in from the direction of the kitchen. The back of her head got cold, too. They'd gotten through the back again without making a sound. Her front door swung open. "It won't be as easy as they think," he said, smiling at her from over the irregular tip of her knife.

She took her eyes off the door and stifled a scream. Something was coming in from the kitchen, and it wasn't human. "Another one just came in the back."

Then the air started burning, and the creature coming out of the kitchen went down with a thud that shook the floor even though nothing had touched him. Another one stood framed in the front door. This one was human in form, but his eyes flamed brilliant green. The lights went out again. No sound, no smell, no streetlamps or glowing gadgets, but with the fire arcing in the air, Alexandrine could see just fine. The third one engaged Xia. His attacker went in close, whirling, and she saw Xia's fist collide soundlessly with the monster's torso. Xia slid behind him and broke his neck.

She didn't have time to react to that, because the one coming in the front leapt for her. Time slowed. She saw and analyzed trajectory, size, and relative strength. The thing was going to land on her, and if she didn't do something, she'd be dead shortly afterward. That knowledge was certain in her head. She didn't have any choice but to use Xia's knife. She knew from brutal experience how to defend herself. All her old instincts kicked in.

The thing coming for her looked human, but she knew it wasn't and that it intended to kill her. Smell and sound continued to be dampened, but that didn't stop her arm from feeling Xia's blade slide through skin and muscle and then grate against bone. Blood spattered across her face like tiny embers. At the same time, she dropped to one knee and thrust up with the knife. No sound. No scent of blood. And no emotion, either. But her body vibrated with the force of their collision. As hard as she'd stabbed, the thing wasn't dead. It kept going for her. Her head snapped back.

With a clap that sent her stumbling, everything returned to normal. A shriek of agony echoed in her ears, and the smell of blood and exposed organs choked her. Breathing. That was her, sucking air. Her front door slammed shut, the locks engaging on their own. She blinked and saw Xia standing over the fiend who'd attacked her with his hand around the monster's forehead, pulling back. The point of his knife—well, her knife—protruded from the front of its throat.

He yanked on the knife handle and released the fiend with a sideways twist. The body fell hard. The other two magehelds were down and not moving. Alexandrine stared at the creature lying at her feet. She wiped a hand across her face and smeared blood into her eyes. Her gorge rose.

"You hurt?" he asked. He reached for her, probing along the top line of her cheek.

"No," she said, moving to avoid the contact with him. She could hardly talk; she was so hyped up. She looked at Xia, who was looking at her, and then she crouched beside the fiend she'd stabbed and closed its staring, glassy eyes.

"For a witch," he said in a low voice, "that was decent of you."

"Xia," she replied without looking at him, "I'm not your enemy." Alexandrine turned her head in his direction, and she could see every atom of his doubt. "I'm really not."

"Sure you are," he said. But he didn't sound convinced. "You're a witch."

When she got up, she left his knife on the floor. Blood dripped from her hand onto the fiend, and she just wanted to be sick—someplace where Xia wouldn't see her. "I'm taking a shower. Is that okay?"

"You tell me."

"I don't feel anything right now."

He shrugged. "It's probably too late for Rasmus to send anymore. Go ahead. I'll clean up in here."

"Thank you." She was a few steps away when he spoke in a voice that rippled down her spine like warm silk.

"Witch?"

She didn't turn around. "Yeah?"

"You all right?"

Hell, no, she wasn't all right. She wasn't ever going to be all right. She turned to face him. "No, Xia. I'm not. Right now my life sucks. I'm tired. I'm crabby, and I don't want any of this to be happening."

Mr. Sensitivity shrugged. "Leave the door open, Alexandrine."

# CHAPTER 7

Alexandrine figured there wasn't any point to locking her bedroom door. Anyone who wanted in would get in, including Xia. Especially Xia. The guy was scary. And not exactly human. At all. And now he was out there just on the other side of the door. Knocking softly.

She considered her door and the knock. After her shower, taken with the door open, she'd gone to her room and totally lost it. Big, huge crying jag with her face scrunched into her pillow so Xia wouldn't hear her and see her shaking like a natural-born coward.

She wasn't inclined to acknowledge Xia's knock. In fact, her first instinct was to pretend she was asleep. Her bedroom light was on, but hey, she could have fallen asleep with the lights on, right? It was going on five-thirty in the morning. Nearly dawn. She was entitled to fall asleep. Childish but tempting nevertheless. He probably knew she wasn't asleep. She called out, "What do you want?"

Silence. Then, "We need to talk. Okay?"

She slid off her bed and opened the door. "Talk about what?"

He managed to look threatening just standing there. Like her, he'd showered and changed his clothes. His gray cotton sweats followed the shape of his hips and thighs, and his T-shirt had the same incidental clingy effect over his chest. His knife was clipped to the waist of his sweats, the carved hilt protruding from the sheath. He'd put on a pair of ratty canvas sneakers, too, the kind without any laces. It wasn't like his clothes were form-fitting or anything. There just wasn't any disguising his insanely fit body. Clothes flat-out draped better on a physique like his. Water glistened in his black-as-sin curls. Not wavy curls but tiny, perfect corkscrews of wicked black.

When he wasn't snarling at her, he was stunningly beautiful, in an extremely manly fashion. Who was she kidding? He was gorgeous when he was snarling, too. Could he be any more appealing? She kept her hand on the door so he'd know she wanted this over with quickly; even with the perfect body so in need of feminine adoration. Now here was a distraction she could live with. Boy, she did like a man who could put her mind in the gutter. Of course, he wasn't exactly a man, was he?

"About us. We need to talk about us."

"There is no us." And as gorgeous as he was, there wasn't going to be any *us* to talk about, ever.

He quirked his eyebrows at her. "All right. Then we need to talk about the reason Harsh sent me here."

"I don't think I feel much like talking," she said. "I'm tired, and no offense, I'd rather be alone right now." She started to shut the door, but he caught it. Not many men could look down at her like she was practically short. Xia was what, six-five? Six-six? Taller than her, and that's all that mattered. She pressed on the door, but he pushed back, and nothing happened except she realized he was a lot stronger than she was. He sighed and pushed hard enough on the door that she had two choices: let him win the contest or stand aside. She stood aside, but he stayed in the doorway.

"I told Harsh this wasn't going to work."

He was trying hard to be nice, or at least as polite as he could be. Considering what he'd been like before, she appreciated him leaving out the part about how much he hated her for being a witch. "Yeah," she said with a shrug, "I know. Trust me, this isn't fun for me, either."

His eyes lost their hard glitter. "He thinks you don't need to know anything. He thinks I can just . . . do my thing to keep Rasmus from offing you and taking the talisman, and in the meantime, Nikodemus will work out what to do, and Carson will sever a few more magehelds for us."

"You could leave. I wouldn't blame you if you did. I have some friends out of town I can stay with."

"Baby, you don't really think that would keep you safe, do you?"

"No?" What a horrendous thought that was, getting her friends killed on account of her.

"You haven't got a chance against a mageheld. Not without me. No matter where you try to hide. After tonight, you should know the truth right here." He touched his chest in the area of his heart.

After a bit, she said, "Yeah, I guess I do."

"I promised your brother. I'm not leaving."

She gave him a smile, but it wasn't as bitchy as it could have been. "Sucks to be you, doesn't it?"

He actually smiled back. "Not as much as it used to." Xia leaned a shoulder on the doorjamb and brought out his knife. He examined it with a critical eye. A draft lifted the hair on her arms. With his attention on the knife, he said, "You're right about me. I do want to kill Rasmus Kessler."

"Right about now, I'm thinking me, too."

He looked up from his knife, and she got a shot of Xia and his sexy mouth that rubberized her knees. She had a terminal case with him, didn't she? "He's going to come after you again; you better believe that."

"Sucks to be me."

Xia frowned and shifted his weight from foot to foot, then ended up leaning against the doorjamb again. "I'd like us to get square."

"You think we can actually get along? I mean, come on." She lifted a hand and let it fall back to her side. "What with me being a witch and all that?"

"You're not the worst witch I ever met, okay?" He drew a finger along his knife, and she got more shivers up and down her arms. He smiled, and hell if she didn't get a tingle of arousal as a result. Rats. She wanted to find out if his mouth was as soft as it looked. Probably not. He was probably a terrible kisser. He was too selfish to be a good kisser.

She studied him. To be fair, he didn't look like he was lying. Not to mention he'd saved her life tonight. She owed him the benefit of the doubt. "If you're willing, so am I."

"All right, then." Xia nodded. "Fuck what Harsh

thinks you need to know, which is jack shit. Let's get a few things straight between us. That work for you?"

"Okay."

His eyes sparked that freaky blue again, like they were glowing inside. He put away his knife, and oddly enough, the rippling along her arms stopped. He lifted a hand above her head, pushed the door the rest of the way open, and walked in. The way he moved reminded her of a cat. All easy grace packed with the promise of death. He stopped halfway in and glanced around. He cocked his head to one side. "Why no pink? I was expecting pink when I was in here before. If you don't mind me asking."

She laughed because he was just so curious and surprised. "I like pink all right." Her room was black and gold. Mostly black. With burnt orange and green thrown in for accent. She might live in a dump, but there were things you could do to relieve even the dreariness of a cheap and unsafe home. "But not as a major statement."

He laughed, too, and sat on her bed. Hard enough to bounce a little. "Okay, here's the deal," he said, scooting himself back until he was leaning against one of the walls she'd painted black. Two others were gold. He linked his hands behind his head.

"Make yourself at home." Was he working his way up to something besides talking? Sheesh. This was going to drive her crazy. She considered propositioning him and seeing if they couldn't just bypass the yakking and get her past this state of constantly noticing him. He looked human, and that made it hard to remember he wasn't.

"Thanks." He tilted his head back, his gaze focused on the ceiling. "Right. Okay. I've been . . ."

Alexandrine shook her head and pulled out her desk

chair and sat on it. No way was she making the first move. Not yet. Not until she had at least one solid reason to think he intended to start something seriously physical with her, as opposed to him setting out to make her crazy, which she could totally see him doing. His gaze met hers. Her stomach took a dive. Damn, there was chemistry between them.

"Away," he said so softly she almost didn't hear him. "I've been away a long time." His voice fell into a monotone, and Alexandrine got a prickle of apprehension down her back. It was as if he was holding back so much emotion he couldn't afford to unleash any of it. "Out of the loop of normal people. Up until the last couple of months, my life wasn't my own."

Because of her father, she realized.

"I haven't been around normal . . ." He gestured and ended up letting both hands fall to his thighs. "But now . . ." He slid his knife from its scabbard and, blade held horizontal, stared at it. "Now I have my freedom." She saw just enough of his eyes to see the dead black lashes come down. "I don't do much right when it comes to getting along with people. The kin or normal people."

"People like me, you mean?"

He laughed and looked at her without moving his head. Neon blue full-on. Her stomach dropped to her toes. He had some serious sexual heat, and he wasn't even trying. "Baby," he said, "you aren't normal."

She shook her head, but honestly, it was a relief that he knew. "I see what you mean about not getting along. You need a warning label that says *Does not play well with others*."

"Everything's changed." He drew up his knees. Something in his eyes clicked off. He was a million miles away. "This isn't my world. Not anymore. Not the one I remember from before."

"Before Rasmus, you mean?"

He nodded. "Yeah. Before him." She didn't like this reflective Xia. It meant he had depth, and it was much easier to dislike someone you thought was shallow and egotistical. "I don't know the rules anymore. If I ever knew them. And if there are new ones, I'm not sure I want to follow them."

"I'm sorry."

He drew a long, slender finger along the blade of his knife. The gesture was oddly loving, and yet she didn't care to know what thoughts were in his head while he did that. She could practically see sparks leaping between the tip of his finger and the bluish surface. "I know. But you're still a witch," he said softly. "Your kind murder my kind, and if you don't kill us, you enslave us."

"You're wrong," she said. There was a lot she didn't understand about the world he and Harsh lived in, but she knew herself and she knew others like her, and none of them had ever dreamed of anything like that. "I don't do those things."

He looked at her with eyes that were a little bit sad. "You're a witch, Alexandrine."

"That's not fair." She was annoyed to be lumped in with slavers and murderers when she'd never, never do something like that. Not even if she had the ability. "I'm not like that."

"Believe what you want." He looked up. No trace of a smile remained. "You have a goddamned talisman. So pardon me if I don't bow down to your bleeding heart, lady."

She pulled her legs up so she sat cross-legged on the chair. "I can't do that kind of magic, Xia."

"Like that makes any difference."

"We're sharing, right? You tell me some stuff, I tell you some stuff?"

"Yeah."

If he was ex-mageheld, then for one thing, he wasn't human. Was Not Human. And then there was that whole enslavement thing. Given that, he must have seen and done some awful things. That would screw with someone's view of the world. Talk about some baggage. They had a lot in common. She could cut him some slack. If her biological father really did want to kill her, the plain fact was she needed more friends like Xia.

But she didn't imagine he'd like what he was going to hear.

# CHAPTER 8

When I was a teenager," she said, "barely a teenager, really. I guess it wasn't long after I turned twelve, a lot of strange things started happening to me. I got my first premonition about then. I thought I was going crazy, and I was too scared to tell anybody. My folks were realists. Stone cold. They didn't believe in ESP or any of that crap. I tried to tell my mom, but she said it was all in my head and took me to the first of many counselors. My folks, the family that raised me, I mean, they didn't have any magic. Complete normals, you'd say."

"Vanilla." Xia nodded and gazed at her. "Typical age to start training up a witch. Twelve or thirteen. That's when the magic really comes on." He clasped his hands behind his head. "Magellan started messing with Carson's magic when she was younger than you were then, but even Rasmus thought that was sick."

He talked about Carson like she was special to him. A girlfriend, maybe? But he also made it sound as if Carson was with Nikodemus. Even worse, then. Unrequited love. They were miles and miles apart, she and Xia. "I still have nightmares about what it was like back then. I really thought I was crazy."

"Yeah?"

Their gazes met, and for a while there, she thought she might end up trapped in his eyes and never get free. A shudder went down her back. She had to remind herself he wasn't human. Much as he looked human, he wasn't. He was something else entirely. Her inability to interact with him as a nonhuman was a disadvantage. He didn't have trouble making that distinction where she was concerned. "I got worse, and Mom hauled me off to doctors, psychiatrists, therapists, and counselors, and then Harsh disappeared. I found out that when I stopped talking, everyone liked that better. So I stopped talking about it. Everybody was happier that way. But none of it went away. I was still a freak."

Xia continued playing with his knife. He probably wasn't interested in hearing about her life. Why would he be? Better not to talk, right? Not talking made everyone happy: able to get on with their lives. Besides, there wasn't much more to say that she was willing to share. The problem was, she wanted Xia to understand, and that meant she had to keep talking. Even if she didn't want to.

"Go on," he said softly. "I'm listening."

If he'd spoken with even a hint of a smirk, she wouldn't have said another word. But he hadn't. "There are mage-kind who aren't like Rasmus or Magellan. People like me who got discarded when we didn't pass whatever the hell test they give when we're three. Farmed out to normal families or given to relatives who don't know what we are.

Only we're not normal kids, and some of us have more magic than you'd think."

"Yeah, well, a mage is a mage is a mage is a mage, baby. You're all the same inside."

Her stomach clenched hard. She didn't want Xia to keep hating her. "You're wrong. Not only that, but there are also more of us than there are mages like Rasmus or Magellan. Mages like my birth father don't mix with the proletariat; that's for sure. We weren't even sure mage-helds weren't all a big fable. And—"

He lifted his head to stare at her with an expression she couldn't begin to decipher. "How many?"

"Of what? Oh, you mean like me?"

"Like you," he said.

"In San Francisco, five or six that I know about. Maddy—she's the strongest of us—she thinks there's more who never find out what they are. They either go insane or they go on living normal lives and everybody's happy."

"Jesus," he whispered. "That's a fucking scary thought. That there are more of you out there." He shook his head. "How'd you find out what you are?"

She made a face at him, but he was smiling, at least a little, so she didn't put any attitude into her grimace. "I found my birth certificate in my mom's stuff. I wasn't getting along too well with my dad back then. I left home for good not long afterward. When I got out here, I started looking for my real parents. My biological mother is dead." She let her head roll back. "So I went looking for my birth father."

"That so?"

She snuck a glance at Xia to see how he was taking

this. Hard to tell. He looked thoughtful. Maybe. "I found the adoption agency—it was here in the City—and they told me I was born in Turkey. That's where I found out who he really is." She hung her head. Talking about her past connected her with feelings that were rawer than she'd expected. "I came back with the amulet, and here I am."

Xia didn't say anything, and she had no idea how to read his expression. She returned to her semi-lotus position on the chair and touched her middle fingers to her thumbs. The pose was a trigger for her. Helped her relax. He didn't say anything, just kept staring at his knife as if he was imagining himself cutting out her heart. What a cheery thought.

"In the spirit of getting along," she said, "how about you tell me about the other half?" Every time she looked into his eyes, she got a shot of heat through her, a tingle at the back of her head. Chemistry? Uh-huh. Some serious chemistry. Didn't that just blow chunks that she was totally hot for someone who thought hate wasn't a strong enough word to describe his feelings for her?

"You can't trust me. Except for not letting you get killed, you can't trust anything about me. Everyone who knows me thinks I'm a fucking bastard, okay?"

"Thanks for the heads-up."

He got the point of her dry tone and smiled enough to make her toes curl. Total asshole, but in the looks department? He was exactly the kind of guy she went for. Tall. Dark and wicked as all get-out. If she was really lucky, maybe he was the kind of guy who didn't talk much when he had sex, because then they could do it, and she could pretend he didn't hate her guts and neither of them would say something to ruin the moment. He waved a hand. "About the talisman you're wearing."

"You keep calling it a talisman. Why?"

"On my side of the world, witch, that's what it is." He pressed his lips together and ran his fingers through his still-damp hair.

"Okay, okay, I'm listening."

He lifted his head, and she was hit once again by the unnatural blue of his irises. Damn, but he was good-looking. She wondered if beings like him were into meaningless sex. Seemed like they ought to be. Did that mean they could have some meaningless sex without him blowing the don't-let-Alexandrine-get-killed part of his assignment?

"For the magekind," he said, "the ones like Rasmus or Magellan, their words have power when they're said just right and with the right magic pulling them along." He frowned at his blade. "Especially when you give a gift of blood. Say the right incantation over a human and a mage can absorb his life force. The human dies, in case you wondered, and the mage, instead of dying at eighty, dies at eighty-one. Kill one of the kin—that's monsters like me—and the mage lives a whole lot longer." He glanced at her, and Alexandrine was careful to keep her expression noncommittal. "That's why your father's still alive." The corner of his mouth quirked. "After all this time."

Alexandrine didn't reply to that, because what Rasmus Kessler did was not her fault. It was creepy to hear Xia accuse him of such evil. "I thought you were going to tell me about talismans."

He looked away, but she saw his fingers tighten around

the hilt of his knife. When he looked back, he said, "Do you know how a talisman gets made?"

She shook her head. He held her gaze, and she recoiled from the blaze of hatred in his eyes. So much for keeping herself in a calm, relaxed state.

With a quick gesture, he brushed his curls off his forehead. "I had to watch when Rasmus got himself a mageheld—a freshly taken one, which he prefers and laid him out so he couldn't move." Xia closed his eyes. "But he can hear and feel and think, and all of us mage-helds felt what was happening. Rasmus pulled as much magic as he could, as hard as he could, and then he cut the fiend here." He touched his sternum. "Sometimes, he'd kill another fiend first. To prime his magic. Without blood, he can't focus the magic right. The whole time the fiend's body is dying, and all of us feel our kin's life and magic being siphoned into some object like that carving you're wearing."

Alexandrine closed her eyes but opened them again when the images in her head were too hideous to bear. She didn't want to believe him, but what little she'd read about mages and fiends paralleled what he'd told her so far. From a different point of view, sure. That just made it all the more sickening.

"When it's over, he's alive in there. Trapped without a body. Separated from the kin." He brought his hands together, slowly at first and then quickly until his palms met with a gentle slap. Xia's eyes were looking inside himself. "You feel the screaming in your bones for days," he whispered. "You live with it forever." His focus snapped back to the present. Alexandrine recoiled again. "And then

Rasmus learned Magellan's trick of taking our power directly, and it got even worse."

Horror at what he was saying froze her in place. What the hell did you say to something like that?

"I've seen that done, too. I've been there, at your father's side, while he murdered one of my kin so he could live a few more years. And I've been there when he cracked open a talisman for what's left of the magic inside." His fist clenched and unclenched on his thigh. "Wondering if one day it was going to be my turn."

Alexandrine didn't say anything. How could she? She had no idea how to respond to someone who'd just laid generations of atrocities at her feet. All those years wondering about her heritage and this was it: evil. She touched the amulet around her neck. "You're telling me this thing's alive?"

"There is a life inside."

Her stomach turned.

Xia kept talking. "Talismans don't last forever. The life dissipates, finds ways out through flaws in the container. Magellan figured out he could crack one and make the magic his. Do that often enough, and you're not going to die from natural causes. Ever. I was there when he taught Rasmus."

Still Alexandrine had no words. None at all. No wonder he hated her. No wonder.

"When one of the free kin finds a talisman, we take it back if we can. And we crack it open. They have no body, so we give whoever it was our bodies." His tongue came out and touched his lower lip. "It's never easy to assimilate with what's left. It's impossible to know its condition until it's too late. But if we live through it, we honor the one whose body died. Their magic lives in us. With us."

"You've done that?"

He laid his knife across his lap, and his gaze unfocused again. The pit of her stomach turned cold. He stroked the knife from hilt to tip. "No."

"But you intend to." With her amulet. She realized she was stroking the carving through her shirt.

"Yes."

How did she even begin to address this? "I . . . I didn't know. I didn't know what this was."

"I know," he said.

She felt about an inch high. "Even if I wanted to, Xia, I couldn't trap someone's magic in a can of tuna fish."

His head swiveled until they were looking at each other again. "You're still a witch."

"My magic doesn't work."

He gave her a dismissive look. "The talisman is changing that."

"No, it's not."

"That thing's working on your magic. I can feel it. Sooner or later, you'll be pulling just like Daddy."

"No," she said. Her heart shriveled to dust. "I refuse to accept that. For me, it's just a bit of carved rock. That's all. It doesn't do anything." That was a lie, though, wasn't it? The talisman had done something to her. Or did she have a nonmagical explanation for her inability to take off the amulet? She pulled the amulet from under her shirt. The stone leopard stared at her with lifeless eyes. "Rock," she said, more to herself than to Xia. "Nothing but a carved rock. Maybe there used to be something in there, but there's not anymore." She was rationalizing, and that made her feel dirty. Actions had consequences, some-times, oftentimes, unintended ones, and consequences ought to be faced. "Whatever it was, it's gone."

She knew as well as he did that she didn't believe that. Not really. He leaned toward her. "Take it off."

"Bet you say that to all the girls."

"Come on, Alexandrine Marit." He gave her a look. She knew better than to think he meant anything sexual by it, but she still had a sexual reaction. "If it's just some carved rock, take it off for me, baby."

Denial rose up, swift and hot and burning. The damn thing wasn't magical, if it ever had been. And yet she couldn't make her hands move to the cord that held the talisman. Right now, this minute, she believed to her core that taking it off meant she'd die. And that was just plain crazy, because she hadn't thought that thirty seconds ago. Alexandrine slid off her chair but grabbed its top rail when her legs wobbled. "Why is that?" she whispered. She hadn't felt any of this happening to her. "Why can't I take it off?"

"Because you're a witch," he said. "The talisman has been leaking into you for months. Changing you so slowly you never noticed what was happening."

"No." With anger and terror mixing into sheer nerve, she yanked on the thong. The leather bit into the nape of her neck, cutting her. The pain was a relief that cut into her panic. The leather broke with a faint snap and a scrape along her skin. She heaved it at Xia with everything she had in her.

She watched the talisman arc through the air. And she saw Xia catch the leather thong. The amulet spun from the end, dark then light, dark then light. The breath in her lungs froze. Her skin prickled. Fire flashed in her head, and the heat grew until she was convinced she was going to go up in flames. Every inch of her body burned. A shudder ripped through her, and on its heels came more searing heat. Just like that, the amulet was back in her hand.

From the bed, Xia said, "Don't ever tell me again you're not a fucking witch."

"I didn't do that." But there the amulet was, on her palm, with the two ends of the broken thong dangling toward the floor.

"Put it back on," he said.

"I don't want it." Her voice trembled. "I don't want it near me. It's horrible." She fought back a sob, but it didn't work. God, what a pathetic noise that was. "I can't live like that. Knowing the truth about what it is. I won't."

Xia slid to the edge of the mattress and extended a hand to her. "Come here."

"What for?"

He made a face. "Just do it, all right?"

She put her hand in his, and he pulled her onto the bed. Alexandrine knelt on the mattress, talisman in her hand while he grabbed the broken ends of the thong and tied them together. He put the thong around her neck.

"I don't want it." But she was still gripping the carving like her life depended on her holding it.

"It's going to take some doing to get that off you without damaging you." His palm lingered on her nape. "I can't do it here. Not now. That kind of magic takes preparation. You understand me?"

"But you'll get it off me, right?"

"Yeah," he said. "I will." He pried her fingers open. "I'm just going to look at it, all right?"

"Okay." She felt like her mind was being split in two. Half of her wanted to stop him from even looking at the amulet, and the other half, apparently the weaker half, wanted him to take it off her, because she knew she didn't have the strength to do it by herself. Not again.

She ended up putting her hands on his shoulders for balance. He went still. Statue still. Then, after a bit, he tilted back, taking her with him so that the amulet swung away from her body. He slid two fingers behind the carved stone.

The very minute his hands touched the amulet, she fell into his mind. God, it was crazy insane. Things like that didn't happen. Couldn't happen. People didn't leave their bodies and go visit someone else's head. But the world dropped away. She was touching Xia's mind, and what she found there brought a scream to her throat.

# CHAPTER 9

Alexandrine fell and fell without hitting bottom, and when the whirling sensation stopped at last, Xia's mind surrounded her. He wasn't doing anything about it, not yet. In the first instant of their touching, she knew him immediately and intimately. His hatred of her went bone-deep. He hated her for what she was. For being a witch. For being Rasmus Kessler's daughter. But he wanted her, too, and that was scary, feeling all that hatred and desire coming at her. At the center of what he was, there was a cold, deep universe that pulsed in time with the beat of her heart. Magic. His magic. Narcotic magic.

As her dizziness receded, she got flashes of his physical experiences. He gripped her amulet so tight the edges cut into his palm. The sharp bite of the stone hurt her, too. His other hand was in contact with her. Or maybe that was her touching him.

Disoriented by her inability to separate his sensory information from hers, she swayed. The motion helped her separate herself from him. She tried to right herself but couldn't, because she didn't know which way was up or down, left or right. Fear vibrated through her with a low bass tone so subtle she almost didn't recognize what it was. It was Xia's power flowing through her.

*This can't be happening.*

She flattened her hands over her ears. "Get out of my head."

"Alexandrine."

He was so achingly beautiful. His voice was so beautiful; she wanted to listen to him forever. Especially if he said her name like that, slow and soft. Her head cleared a little. Not much. And when it did, her stomach rolled up. She pried open her eyes and found herself looking into Xia's neon blue gaze.

"Alexandrine," he said again.

Her dizziness faded enough for her to realize she was still kneeling, still gripping his shoulders, and that he was on his knees, too. He had an arm around her waist. Underneath her shirt. An accident, that. He only meant to keep her from falling backward off the bed. Nevertheless, his fingers splayed over her bare back. He clutched the amulet in his other hand, and she could still feel the pain in his hand.

"Breathe," he said.

Oh, God, she had no idea if he'd spoken out loud or directly into her mind. She inhaled. The world settled, but nothing was the same. Icy air rasped in her lungs. Her eye sockets hurt. Xia's irises were big, wide pools of electric blue.

"Better?" he asked.

"So," she said, pushing him away, well aware that he

moved because he wanted to, not because she was strong enough to budge him. He let go of the amulet, and with a jolt, the connection ended. "Was it good for you, too?"

"Fuck off, witch." They were both unnerved, then. "That wasn't my fault."

"Well it sure as hell wasn't mine." She'd read about the dangers fiends allegedly posed to humans. Right about now, she was thinking maybe the warnings weren't far off the mark.

"I don't go in without permission," Xia said. "I swear, I don't know what just happened." He pushed her shoulder. "You wanna whine about what happened, go do it to your magekind friends about how fiends need to be taken down and killed or made into slaves. Maybe you can team up with all your lame-ass mage buddies and see if you can pull enough magic to get a mageheld of your own." He reached out and poked the amulet, pressing it hard into her belly. "You could kill this and live a little longer."

She got all mixed up again, when without warning she was staring into her own brown eyes. Honey-brown, she thought. Her eyes. Cheeks. Nose, chin, mouth. None of what she saw registered with her. It was like looking into a mirror and not recognizing her own face. Pure lust lanced through her. Sharp and needy. "What is this?" she whispered. She was having trouble breathing again. "What's happening?"

"Hell if I know." He took back his hand, but in the instant before the stone fell, cool and sweet against her body, she knew he was lying. The connection between them wasn't gone, just minimized. But it was there, a high tension wire just waiting for the circuit to complete.

"It's the talisman." She took his hand—amazed that he

let her touch him after everything he'd told her about what her father had done—and opened his fingers, expecting to see blood. There wasn't any, and she was mysteriously and vaguely disappointed by that. Her room seemed very small now. Intimate. Her thoughts and feelings were all mixed up with a desire so intense she hurt, and that, too, was mixed up with anger, puzzlement, fear, arousal, and curiosity. To her bones, she knew some of these reactions were not hers. She couldn't tell which ones belonged to him and wasn't sure it would matter if she did know. She brought his outstretched palm nearer. Xia took a breath.

"Well look at that," she whispered. "Now you have one, too."

On his palm was the gray impression of a panther. Just like the one on her stomach, except the obverse side. She traced the outline of the creature, then followed a line down his wrist to the crook of his elbow. She pressed the tip of her finger to the purple bump of a vein. "Which one of us," she softly asked, "wants the taste of blood? I can't tell."

A corner of his mouth twitched. He pulled his hand free of hers, though his other remained splayed on her back. If she knew he wanted her, then he must know how she felt about that. He touched a fingertip to the back of her neck where the leather thong had cut her skin. The salty sting of his finger touching the spot made her suck in air.

"Baby," he whispered. "You hurt yourself." His voice was low and sweet and full of desire. "How bad is it?" he asked.

"Not very."

"I can make it better." He stayed close to her, and in

her belly she felt an echo of his desire to touch her. And to taste her, too. That would do something to him, she thought. For him. Tasting her blood.

She wasn't herself; she knew that. Though she no longer felt like she was in his head, the connectedness hadn't faded. She lifted her gaze from his hand and, whoa, head rush. She got caught in his eyes all over again, and she was dizzy and losing her sense of physical and mental boundaries. How the hell was she supposed to know where his thoughts ended and hers began? His body was the same as hers. Her body was the same as his. She knew him intimately, so how was she supposed to keep the barriers up when she couldn't find them? Or, and this was a poser, how was she supposed to know when she was getting his thoughts and desires? Or both. Or maybe she was hallucinating all of it.

He pulled her nearer, and her palms ended up against his chest, against warm skin and unforgiving muscle, and she turned her head to the side. He brushed her hair off her neck. Arousal zinged through her. His knife was in his other hand, but she took it from him and set it arm's length away on the mattress.

"I shouldn't want you like this," Xia said. "I don't want to. You're Rasmus's daughter." He touched a fingertip to her nape again and bent his head, inhaling softly. "But I do. I want you so bad I hurt."

Alexandrine thought she'd melt right now, right into a puddle for him to do with as he would, except for when she was doing as she would. He slid a fingertip along the abrasion left by the leather thong. Then his arms tightened around her, and softly he growled. The sound came from deep in his chest, un-human. His lips brushed her nape and then opened, pressing down on the back of her neck. His tongue slipped along the cut, tasting, touching, and then became a kiss, moving around to her throat.

She tipped her head back, and his hands brushed down her arms, urging her closer. No problem whatsoever. The closer she was to him the better. She ran her palms down his torso from his breastbone to the top of his sweats, while he helped her keep her balance with his hands spread over her back. Somehow he ended up with his hands cupping her ass. She trailed a finger down. All the way down. "You have a fantastic body," she whispered.

His eyes flickered, and a sizzle of energy went up her arms. She leaned in and kissed the side of his mouth. They connected again. Mentally. Without the disorienting trading places. Her breath stopped. Xia threw back his head and groaned, hands clutching her. His arms shook and he stopped. Everything. All of it. He set her back. Too far away for her to touch him.

"Alexandrine . . ."

She didn't feel any steadier than he looked. Leaning back, she looked at him. "What?" she said. "That felt good. You know it did. So what's the matter?"

He drew up his knees in line with his shoulders and tipped his head back. His expression went blank, and then Alexandrine watched while the emotions that came from him—lust and hunger, and then anticipation and desire—appeared on his face. He kept his gaze on the ceiling. "That got out of hand. I'm sorry."

"I'm not. Well, I am right now, but I wasn't before."

He lowered his chin and looked at her from under a veil of dead-black lashes. A direct look. "You know what I want right now," he whispered.

"Yes."

After a bit, he said, "I know what you think you want."

"It was fantastic, Xia. Why wouldn't I want that?" She was still getting flashes of his feelings, and she supposed that meant he was getting hers. Their eyes met. Collided. Connected.

"So," he said in a low voice, "what the fuck are we going to do about that, Alexandrine?"

She scooted closer, a finger sliding along the bare inside of his forearm.

He lifted his panther-marked hand and set his palm on top of her shoulder, pushing aside the fabric of her shirt in order to put bare skin to bare skin. For a minute there, she had the eerie sensation that the mark on his palm was moving, tickling her skin.

"I need you to tell me you're going to let this happen," he whispered.

"Yes," she said. "I'm going to let this happen."

He brought her toward him, and she instinctively exposed the side of her throat to him again. His breath warmed her skin. He touched his finger to her, drawing a line that burst with cold and then heat. Somehow he'd managed to open a cut. It stung but she didn't care. Blood trickled down her skin. His mouth opened over her skin, and he tasted again. More this time. Deeper. Harder.

Colors whirled behind her closed eyes. Amethyst, violet, emerald, streaks of ruby across endless black. She fell into him, joining with the pulse of his power, a reservoir of magic so dark and deep and wide she'd never find the end. He lifted his mouth. Alexandrine was aware now that she was in his embrace, that one of his hands cupped the back of her head and that his forearm pressed against her upper back, keeping her close to him.

He took a long breath, and her body flooded with a sensuous anticipation that burned with an edge of hunger. The warmth of his lips on her skin startled her, and then she felt his tongue, moving along the cut he'd made. He felt so good. So right. Lord, but she wanted to touch him.

Xia released her and, making a fist, stretched for his knife with the other and used the blade to nick her wrist. She flinched and then watched, fascinated, at the welling line of red. Her blood was so very red. Blood scent rose to her, the tang in her mouth already. The sense that he was in her head doubled. Or maybe that was her in his head. She couldn't tell. Did the desire to taste belong to her or to him? His eyes flashed through several shades of blue.

"What are you waiting for?" she asked.

He brought her wrist to his lips and gently, slowly, touched his tongue to the drop. The taste exploded in her mouth, transmitted from him to her. Whatever she'd expected, it wasn't this shivering of connection through her, pulling her deeper into Xia's mind, into the center of his magic. When she lifted her head, she had trouble getting her bearings. She sat on her haunches, trying to make the room stop spinning. Xia steadied her.

"I fucking hate witches," he said. His hand, big and warm and more than capable of killing, followed the upward indentation of her spine. He brought her head to his and kissed her, hard, and Alexandrine returned his kiss with unrestrained passion. With one quick motion, he grabbed the top of her shirt and pulled at the buttons until they either came free or popped off.

The minute his finger brushed the curve of her breast,

she leaned in and kissed him; she'd been dying to kiss him since forever. He let her. He even kissed her back. His hand slid around, unfastened her bra, and covered her breast. He pulled back to take a look.

"You've made it clear what you think of me," she said. "You sure you want to see where this leads?"

"Yeah. You?"

"Oh, yeah." She grabbed his wrist and spread her fingers up and over the back of his hand, pressing his hand over her breast. "I want you to touch me."

He spread his thighs and pulled her forward. Off balance, she tipped toward him. She got a hand up just in time. Her palm hit the wall beside his head and kept her upright. The scent of lavender soap came to her, faint but rising from his skin, like the clean smell of his hair. Her amulet swung forward, dangling between their bodies. She watched it move.

He said he hated her, but that wasn't what he was feeling. Not by a mile. She didn't move. He raised his eyes, too. His hand on her back tightened. And his other hand, his panther-marked hand, touched her belly. She sucked in a breath. She kissed him again, and yes, yes, he kissed her back, and damn, he was good. His mouth was soft, and he was a monumentally good kisser, with an edge that promised she could make him lose control without much more effort. His tongue slipped into her mouth, and Alexandrine flat-out melted for him. Wherever he was taking this, she was right there with him.

She wanted to touch him. Had to. She drew back, pressing kisses on his mouth. "Shirt off," she said, tugging upward on the hem of his T-shirt.

He stopped her. "Alexandrine."

"What?"

"No." His hand gripped her wrist. "Not that I don't want you—you're effing beautiful—but . . ." His eyes flashed white, which startled her. "I'm sorry," he said in a low voice. "I can't do this. We can't."

"Why?"

He let go of her and rolled onto his back, one arm over his eyes. He had an impressive erection going, so there wasn't anything wrong in that department. Fully functional. God, but she wanted him. "I can't."

"Because I'm a witch? We've been over that." She sat beside him with her knees drawn up to her chin and her arms wrapped around her shins. "You knew that when this started. Why chicken out now?"

One neon blue eye appeared when he moved his forearm. "Because I didn't think you'd make me this hot." He moved his arm off his face and stared at the ceiling. "I haven't done this in a really long time."

"That's hard to believe. You must have women lining up at your door."

"I get plenty now," he said. "All the vanilla I want. I meant doing it with a witch."

"And?" She was dying to touch him. Dying for contact with him. She wanted to feel his arms around her and feel her naked skin against his. She wanted to touch his body everywhere and find out what made him fall apart.

"When I was mageheld," he said softly, "Rasmus didn't let me have sex. Not often, anyway." His eyes stayed focused on the ceiling, where she'd stenciled a stylized golden sun on the black portion over the bed. "When he sent me after a witch, he usually explicitly forbade me from doing her."

She reached for his near hand, which happened to be the panther-marked one. For whatever reason, he let her twine his fingers with hers. Her palm tingled. Maybe he didn't notice the contact; he was pretty far into his memories right now. "Like that would have been the same as sex I wanted to have. It's different when you want to hurt everything and everyone. And it's different when you're compelled." He raised his knee and glanced at her. "Rasmus Kessler is one of the magekind, and that means he's a vindictive bastard. A couple of times he told me to do it. Some witch he wanted dead. So I had to. Not that I minded. Killing mages and witches like you was my favorite thing to do. He liked to be in my head during those times so he could feel everything I did to them. You understand what I'm saying? He knew I was mean and a fucking nasty bastard."

"Xia, I know," she whispered. She wished she didn't, though. "It's all right."

"Killing one of the magekind was the closest I ever got to feeling like I was free. I lived for those orders."

Alexandrine squeezed his hand. "It's all right. I understand." And too bad she did. No wonder he didn't want her.

"It's not like I never got laid." His lashes hid most of his eyes at the moment. "A mageheld is always looking for loopholes, always looking for ways to rebel. But it didn't happen often. Most of the time, if I had sex, it was because Rasmus wanted it, too."

"I'm sorry."

"I got taken because of a witch." He sat up, sitting cross-legged. Their hands stayed clasped. "Betrayed by a witch. She didn't have any impressive power—enough to make a living, but she couldn't pull like Rasmus or Christophe. She was with Rasmus, too, only I didn't know that until it was too late."

"And I'm a witch." Not the one who betrayed him, but Xia understood that. He just didn't like witches. With good reason, unfortunately.

He let out a breath and brought their interlinked hands to rest on his thigh. "You're a witch with no control over your magic. And that makes you dangerous. There's no way"—he looked straight into her eyes— "no way, I'm putting myself into a situation where I could get taken again. No matter how bad I want my dick inside you."

The thought of that took her breath away for a moment. "I couldn't, Xia. You know that. Not even if I knew how."

His eyes narrowed, but they remained neon blue. "You don't have any idea what would happen to you if you did it with someone like me—and I don't, either." He draped a hand over his raised knee. His fingers were long and slender. "You think that talisman came back to you because the laws of physics just decided to take a vacation? You pulled, Alexandrine. Magic. And it worked for you. Considering that when I come, I won't be thinking of protecting myself from you . . . Well, there's only one way I'm doing a witch."

"Oh." She studied his face. He was serious. And what's more, she realized, he wasn't saying no, was he? He was setting out parameters that worked for him. "What way is that?"

"If I'm in complete control."

She tried to make sense of that. Some fun images popped into her head, which meant that couldn't be what he was talking about. "I assume you don't mean tying me up."

Xia released her hand. "What the hell have we been talking about all this time? Fuck, Alexandrine, you're not an idiot. I mean *in control*." He tapped his index finger on her forehead. The contact zinged through her. "Totally and completely in control of you and your magic."

"You can do that?" She'd read about it, of course. Talked about it with others like her who were trying to learn on their own and sift out the lies from the truth in what they'd heard or read. But she'd never believed it could be done. Hell, she hadn't believed magehelds existed, let alone that there were free beings like him.

He rocked forward, pressing his fists into the mattress until she ended up on her back with him stretched over her. Her reaction to him went from zero to completely turned on in the time it took her to inhale. He slid a hand under her chin and pressed a finger just under the edge of her jaw. "Baby," he said in a low voice, "you'd be amazed what I can do." His gaze burned into her, gorgeous neon blue. And his mouth. Wow. So incredibly kissable. "Want a sample?"

She put her arms around his shoulders. Lord have mercy. The man was nothing but muscle and warm skin. "Maybe."

"Yes or no?" He settled his pelvis against hers, and his voice was all low and spicy dark, and that was just so unfair. "I need permission for this."

"Fine, then." She arched up, feeling his erection. All of her—mind and body—longed for that. "Yes."

He touched her forehead again, and this time the tap became a hum and then a sense of pressure on her skull, and then he was in her head. Really and truly there, and it wasn't what she'd anticipated. This was different from before. She was suffocating, panicking, because she existed in one tiny corner of her mind and no more.

Xia had the opposite reaction. "Alexandrine," he whispered. His eyes cycled through a million shades of blue, ending with white irises with the faintest of blue streaks in them. "That's good. You feel so good."

He lowered his pelvis to hers again, and though she knew her body was aroused, Xia had control of her reactions. As he eased up, she was more at home in herself. Yet not alone. If she could act on what she was feeling, it was only because he allowed it. The thing was, he liked it; that was obvious. He liked being in control, and she wasn't comfortable knowing he could make her do anything at all without her deciding to go along. Anything. He withdrew his psychic presence from her, and she fell back, shuddering with the aftereffect.

"Oh, my God," she said. He went in for a kiss, and this time it was her putting up her hands to stop things. "No, that's . . ." No way. No way could she take even five minutes of that. "I don't . . . I can't."

He moved away. "Let me know when you're ready to do it like that, and I'll risk Harsh killing me for daring to lay a hand on you."

"Why?" She sat up. Her arms trembled, and she tried to cover it by wrapping them around her raised knees. "Why would it have to be like that?"

One corner of his mouth curled. "I'm never letting a witch get that close to me ever again. Never." He raked his fingers through his hair. "I don't care how fucking turned on I get. If you want us to do this, it's on those terms or not at all."

She rolled off the bed on legs that hardly held her upright.

"I thought so," he said under his breath.

Her heart shrank. "I'm sorry, Xia. Really sorry."

# CHAPTER 10

$I$t was Friday now, if Xia had the calendar right. He didn't follow human time unless he had to, so he wasn't always sure what day it was. He lay on the couch staring at the ceiling, his feet hanging off the opposite end while he tried to center himself. None of Alexandrine's furniture accommodated a six-and-a-half-foot man, so he wasn't very comfortable. What a fucked-up week this was so far. Ever since the fighting ended—for now—all he thought about was getting Alexandrine underneath him again with him in her head and her magic wide open to him, and him doing her hard while she begged for more. Not a fantasy likely to come true.

About eight in the morning, he heard her on the phone, calling in sick to work. She made another call after that, but by then he was in the kitchen, looking for something to eat and really trying not to listen. There wasn't any food that he could find. Seriously. Total food haul: one can of butter beans, a dusty box of rice, and two shriveled carrots. That was it, and in his human form, he needed to eat now and again.

By one o'clock, Xia was starving and out of ways to keep his mind off last night's near disaster with the witch. Hunger only added to his unpredictable psychic and physical state. Since Alexandrine wasn't going in to work, there wasn't any way he could get a quick bite, and he couldn't leave her alone while he went shopping. He didn't hear her in the shower until one-thirty, and when she was done, she went straight back to her room. By two, he was ready to lick glue off the walls. He thought about calling Iskander or even Kynan to get a connection going, because he was just not in a good state of mind for dealing with Harsh's sister.

A hour of Dropkick Murphy at full blast didn't help much. He kept thinking about helping Alexandrine get naked and how he'd slip into her head and get them both extra juiced before they did it. His stomach rumbled. He turned off his iPod and tuned the television to a channel showing *Cops*. His favorite show. Damn, but he needed a drink, only he knew from looking that her fridge was a total stranger to beer. There wasn't so much as a bottle of wine. How the hell did anyone living two hours from the wine country not have even one bottle of wine in the house?

He needed to relax and stay on his game. He needed to stop thinking about having sex with a witch and start thinking about how he was going to keep her alive when he didn't have any of the kin around to help him recharge or bring him down off his high from last night's business. He grabbed his bag and rummaged through it until he found a custom-folded envelope of glossy white paper small enough to fit on his palm. He was unfolding it when Alexandrine came out of her room.

"Is that *Cops*?" she said, all perky and shit.

"Uh-huh."

She had on jeans, a ratty blue sweatshirt, and no shoes. Her hair was styled away from her face, but a few platinum strands dangled down her forehead. Despite the banging-around clothes and untidy hair, she managed to look blistering hot. She'd never let him lay a hand on her again, and even if he did get lucky that way, like maybe if she lost her mind or had some kind of temporary amnesia that also turned her into a nympho, she'd recover and Harsh would cut his balls off. He wasn't getting laid anytime soon.

"I love *Cops*." She came close enough to see him and stopped dead. Her gaze focused on his hand. Specifically, on the envelope there. He should have known a witch would react this way. Her expression went blank. "No drugs in my house," she said.

"I noticed that." He kept unfolding the paper. He wasn't in a great mood, and now he was face-to-face with the witch who was cranking him. "No alcohol, either."

"Absolutely not, Xia." He got a shot of magic from her that sent his heart racing. But she sputtered out pretty quickly. Hell, she faded so fast he didn't even need to pull to make sure he stayed safe. "Not here." Her voice was low and intense. "Not around me. And not in my house."

Her magic rippled the hair across the back of his neck. The way she looked, you'd think he'd just told her he ate babies for breakfast and was about to truss one up and slather on some butter right now. "It's not cocaine, if that's what your deal is."

She crossed her arms over her stomach like it hurt. "What is it?"

"Nothing you need to care about." If she was pretending not to know, he'd find out pretty quick.

"I do care. This is my house," she said. The way she kept her voice so freaking calm bugged the hell out of him. Just like her brother. Ms. Calm and Rational. "There's no drugs here. Ever."

"It's not a drug." He kept the paper creased and shook three dime-sized yellow triangles onto his palm. "Not that kind of drug, anyway."

She sat on one end of her sissy black velvet couch with one leg curled under her and one foot touching the floor. Tapping her toe on the hardwood. He crowded her on the sofa. He could tell she didn't like him being so close to her; witches never did want anyone to get close when they weren't sure they had the mojo to control someone like him. He ought to know. He was an expert in that department.

"Stop staring at me," he said.

"Is that hashish?"

Gave him the creeps the way she sounded so serious and shit. Well eff that. He didn't have to do what a witch told him to. Not anymore. Not ever again.

"It looks like hashish to me."

"I told you, it's not a drug." That wasn't exactly true. She grabbed his wrist just as he was about to take the first pill. The contact burned. If she felt it, she didn't show it. He pulled but kept his magic on tap. "What the hell do you think you're doing?" he said. All along his back, his skin rippled. His dick got hard, too. "You keep touching me, and you might just end up with me inside you."

She didn't let go of his wrist, and now he was getting tingles up his arm as a result. Her gaze was so intense that his skin itched from the base of his spine to his head. No way was she stable. The problem was, he was quickly reaching a point of instability himself.

"Baby," he whispered, and he didn't think he sounded entirely nice. "I want it bad. You ready for that with me?"

She let go of him, but his case of the hots didn't diminish nearly enough. "In case I didn't mention it last night, I was pretty messed up for a while."

"I remember." He plucked one of the pills from his palm and held it up, watching for signs that she knew what it was. "It's copa."

"Copa." Her mouth moved as if she were tasting the word. She looked relieved by the strangeness of it. "Never heard of it."

"You sure about that?" He needed to get himself relaxed, or he was going to find himself on a high ledge with no way down. He didn't exactly have a record of making the best choices when he was at the edge.

"I saw drugs every day of my life back then." The tip of her tongue did a rapid swipe along her lower lip. "Coke. Meth. Dope. All the pills you can think of. You name it, I saw people killing themselves with it."

He put back the pills and stared at her. "You use, too?" He grabbed her arm and turned her palm faceup. She didn't stop him from pushing up her sleeve. "No scars."

Her eyes stayed on his face. "Wanna check between my toes, too?"

"You weren't a junkie. No way were you a junkie."

Alexandrine pulled both legs underneath her and kept

her gaze on her lap. "No. Not a junkie the way you mean." More unfocused magic bubbled up from her. He was sure she didn't know she was pulling, but he was getting a buzz on from her all the same. If she did know, then she didn't know what to do about it. Lucky for them, he did. "But I was headed for serious trouble." She shrugged. "Practically a given when you live like that. My friend Maddy found me and introduced me to other mages. Mages like me, I mean, and I got myself straightened out."

Xia turned on the couch to face her. He tried to imagine her as one of those magekind kids on the streets, throwaways manifesting without any guidance and ending up prime bait for kin who couldn't control themselves or for mages who wanted to pull out what magic was left. He'd been sent after a few in his day. Some dirty, drugged-up teen abandoned by his own kind for not measuring up or just some street mage unable to deal with the magic. If she'd slapped him, he couldn't have been more shocked. "For real?"

"What you decide to put in your body is your business, Xia, but please." She left her sleeve up when he released her. "I would really, really appreciate it if you didn't use in my house." She licked her lips, and Xia got some really disturbing images about what he'd like her to do to him. "I can't be around that." She met his gaze straight on. "I don't want to be around that. Not anymore."

"Does Harsh know what you were like then?"

"He wasn't around." She tugged on her hair and wrapped white-blond strands around a finger. "I thought he was dead. So, Xia, if you're going to use, you have to leave. I think even Harsh would back me up on that."

He unfolded the envelope again and stared at the pills.

He knew he could be a jerk. Hell, he managed to piss off his kin often enough. But there was another hole in the wall of hatred he had for Alexandrine that hadn't been there two minutes ago. Resisting that kind of life. He was almost in awe, as a matter of fact. He shuddered a little at the knowledge that any of those times Rasmus had sent him out for some fucked-up, immature mage, he could have snatched her just as easily as any of the ones he'd actually brought back. "More information for you, okay?" he said. He hoped he wasn't making a mistake telling her this. But, shit, he really needed something to take his mind off all the things he wanted to do with and to Alexandrine Marit.

"All right."

"The kin . . ."

She looked blankly at him.

"Fiends, okay? Demons if you want to be lazy about it. People like me. We need to connect with each other." He touched his temple. "Psychically. If we don't or if we can't, things get rough on us. It's harder to focus and stay controlled. Harder to do everything, and sooner or later everything just . . . hurts." He met her eyes. He needed her to understand what was going on with him. "There's a cost for me staying in human form. And for damn sure I'm paying for being around your magic. There's no kin here, Alexandrine. No one to help me down, and it hurts. If I'm going to keep us both alive, I need a way not to be so fucking uptight."

She gazed at him like she was trying to read his mind. "I had no idea."

He let his head hit the back of the couch. "I know that." He drew in a breath. "That's why I'm telling you."

"You're hurting now?"

Xia turned his head to look at her. "Alexandrine, I am way too uptight around you."

"I can't help that. And I'm not going to let you blame me for it, either."

"No blame, baby." He sat up and damn near touched her. No touching the witch. Touching the witch would be bad. Very bad. "It's not your fault that I want in your pants and that I'm cranked because I can't have what I want."

"I appreciate you telling me." Alexandrine crossed her arms over her stomach. He gave her a look, and she flushed. "About the copa, I mean, not about your state of sexual frustration. I thought you were trying to get high." She gestured at him, then returned her arm to her waist. "How bad is it for you?"

"Not that bad. I can get along." Lie. Major lie. But what was the point of telling her that? He'd deal because he had to.

She gave a tight shake of her head. "If you need to take that, you should, Xia."

"You sure?"

"I don't want to die. Do you?"

"Well. Since you put it that way. Thanks." Xia picked up the envelope and took two of the pills, quickly, then refolded the envelope and put it back in his bag. Please, let the stuff work fast. Really, really fast.

"Does it do anything to humans?"

Xia gave that careful thought before he answered. "If you're vanilla, no."

She narrowed her eyes at him. "And if you're not?"

Guess there wasn't any way of dodging the bullet speeding straight for his forehead. He decided to get it over and done with. "Mages take it, too," he said. He was already feeling the effects of the pills—a faint and pleasant sense of well-being. But not nearly enough to cut into his heat for Alexandrine Marit.

"But we don't connect psychically the way you do," she said. "Why do they take it?"

"It's different for magekind than it is for us. For a while, it lets a mage pull more than he might otherwise."

Her attention was all for him. And here they were, sitting on the couch, all cozy, and he was feeling a whole new respect for her. She had totally turned around her life, and even a monster had to respect that. He brushed a thumb along her eyebrow and got a sexual sizzle from the contact. She drew back, but not far. He knew she wanted him. On a purely physical basis, they both wanted the forbidden. How screwed up and sick was that?

"Magic is unpredictable for humans," he said. "Even for us, it takes time to learn how to pull and then to know when you've pulled too much or when you haven't pulled enough. Mages having trouble that way, well, copa can get them regulated so they can pull. But most of them take it so they can pull more."

"There's always a downside," she said.

He tucked a stray lock of her hair behind her ear and left his hand cupping the side of her head. Oh, yeah. He was getting hot for her all over again. "A lot of the more powerful mages abuse it; they want the extra jump it gives them. And some of them keep taking it until it kills them. Rasmus smokes it. I kept hoping he'd overdose, but he's always careful about when and how much and how often."

"Like I said."

"S'okay, Alexandrine. I should have told you from the start."

"Thanks." She put a hand on his wrist again, and the sizzle was definitely there. And then she leaned toward him. He wasn't an idiot. He knew an invitation to get down and nasty when he got one. And, yes, he was on board that train. With just one condition.

"You know how it has to be, Alexandrine."

"I don't understand why. Aren't you relaxed now?"

He stood up before he could do something stupid. Really, really stupid. He headed for the kitchen. Fast. The sooner she was at his back, the sooner he wouldn't have to look at her long legs or think about how much he wanted them wrapped around him with her panting and begging him to get on with doing what they damn near did last night.

She followed him. Mary's little lamb, for Christ's sake. He didn't want the reminder of what he wasn't going to get. And if she was going to offer, he didn't trust himself not to accept. He made it to the table with her right behind him. The first thought in his head when he turned around was that she needed to be naked, and he needed to be naked and taking care of her heat.

"What's the problem, Xia?"

"Nothing," he said. He opened a cabinet he knew would be empty. "I'm hungry and there's no food in this place." He was trying. Really trying not to go off on her, but he wasn't having much luck. And that was with the copa. Without it, she'd be flat on her back and he'd be driving hard. "Fuck," he said to another empty cabinet. "Just fuck this whole thing."

"Has anybody mentioned you have a major attitude problem?"

He glanced at the ceiling like he was calling on the heavens for patience. Would it hurt for him to hope the ceiling crashed on her? "All the time, baby."

Jaysus, he wanted out of here. Away from her magic and her long legs. Either that or he wanted in her pants. Either one worked. But she wasn't saying yes to the one thing he had to have consent to do with her.

"What happened to Mr. Nice Guy?"

"He died of starvation about an hour ago." His retort just came out, no stopping by his brain to check whether it was a good idea.

"What is your problem? I thought that stuff was supposed to help you. If you ask me, you're worse."

He looked at the floor and then looked at her. "What's my problem? I'm hungry for one thing."

She lifted one eyebrow. "And?"

"And I want you so bad it hurts. Your magic is getting to me."

She went quiet, and hell, her silence cut. The skin down his back rippled. Pissing off a witch wasn't smart. She took a step toward him, and he could feel the magic boiling up in her. From long habit, he braced himself for her retaliation. But nothing happened.

"I'm sorry," she said with a shrug. "I wish it was different," she said. "I really do."

His day was just getting better and better, wasn't it? He had a witch feeling sorry for him. "Can we just shut up about this now?"

"I know there's no food." Alexandrine went to a cabinet and got down a bag of popcorn, the old-fashioned kind, which gave him a great view of her ass. Nice. He amused himself by imagining her naked ass against his naked groin. With his naked dick up inside her naked— maybe that wasn't a safe image. Alexandrine got out a heavy iron pan and a bottle of canola oil. "There hasn't exactly been any chance to go shopping." She turned on a burner and poured oil in the pan. "I hate to cook."

Xia knew he'd been an asshole to her, so he manned up. "I'm sorry if I sounded like I was bitching at you. Not your fault."

"Thanks," she said.

"I thought you didn't like to cook."

She leaned against the counter to keep an eye on the four kernels she'd thrown in the pot with the oil. "Making popcorn isn't cooking."

Come to think of it, he hadn't seen her cook yet. The day he'd tagged along with her to her job, she'd stopped to pick up something on the way home. Well, shit. He got that one wrong, didn't he? "I'm sorry."

She sighed and waved him off. "Never mind."

"Look. I'm used to being told what to do and when to do it." Her eyes got big when he said that, and he didn't know what that meant, either. Was she pissed off? "This freedom thing is new for me. I mess up all the time."

One of the kernels popped, and Alexandrine turned back to her pot of heating oil. She had one bare foot braced on the arch of the other. Long, long legs. He didn't know what to make of her silence. His spine tingled—not from her pulling but from him expecting her to. That's what the magekind did. They fucked over the kin whenever and wherever they could. All she did was pour in the rest of the kernels and cover the pot.

They didn't say anything while the kernels started popping. She got out a sissy bright red bowl that said *popcorn* on the side with fluffy white popped kernels dancing along the rim. "You have got to be kidding," he said.

"I'm a perfectly likeable woman, I'll have you know." She checked the popcorn but replaced the lid. "We all have days when we're not in such a great mood, but any way you look at it, I'm not the wicked witch you think I am."

Man, five minutes of trying to be nice, and he was up to his eyeballs with stress. "Witches make my skin crawl." He poked a finger in her direction. "Maybe it's not your fault, but my skin's crawling right now."

She leaned back, her arms folded across her chest. "Fine. I'm a scary witch who can whoop your ass just by crossing my eyes." She crossed her eyes at him. "You're not writhing on the floor gasping for air." Her eyes uncrossed. "Gee, what went wrong? Could it be I can't do magic worth a damn?" Her voice rose. "Or maybe I don't believe in hurting people just because they have a personality disorder."

"You're still a witch."

Her eyes went all big and hurt again. This was *not* going well. She ought to know the kind of danger she was in, being on the wrong end of Rasmus Kessler's interest, only she didn't really, truly get it, and that was just freaking fucked up. Hell, Iskander would have been a better choice than him for guard-dog duty, and Iskander was a complete psycho. And he still wanted her, too.

"I can see we're going to have a real fun time this weekend." She took the pot off the burner, filled the sissy red bowl, and sprinkled some salt on it.

"What? No butter?"

"Fresh out of butter." She ate some. "Besides, butter is bad for you."

Xia stood up and snagged a handful of popcorn from her bowl. Even without butter, it was the best popcorn he'd ever had. Beat the microwaved shit by a mile. Jaysus, but he wanted her. Right now. On the table.

"You know," she said. She didn't have any idea what he was thinking. "You're not the only one with issues. I've been trying to convince myself last night was more about the long drought between boyfriends than it was about you."

"But?"

"I've never met anyone who can deal with what I am. You can, and you just can't imagine what that's like for someone like me. People have been calling me crazy practically my whole life. But you . . . you're not going to find out about my witchiness and dump my ass." She held out the bowl to him, and he grabbed more popcorn. "Oh, I know, you hate witches, but at least I don't have to pretend with you. So I keep thinking, 'Hell, yes, I should sleep with you.'"

Xia looked at the table. Looked sturdy enough to him. "Works for me."

"I've been wondering if I can handle your restrictions. Maybe. Probably not. Maybe. Who the hell knows."

He ate more popcorn. "And?"

She gave him a lingering look. "And I want my friend Maddy to meet you."

He about choked. "What?"

"I invited her over for dinner tonight." She gave him a fake bright grin. "I hope you like Thai."

"Cancel it."

"It's not like she's a normal person, Xia. She's the strongest and smartest of us, and I need to talk to her about what's going on. I'm going to go crazy if I don't."

"She's a witch." He walked to her refrigerator and yanked it open. Then he opened both the bins. The shriveled carrots were still there.

"Not like Rasmus, Xia. She's not like that. We're not like that."

He stared into her fridge for half a second longer, then shut the door hard enough to rattle the interior. "I don't want her here."

"I think she should meet you," she said.

Talk about getting uptight. "I'm not a pet for you to show off."

"I know that. But—"

He opened her cabinets one after another and found mostly dust or her dishes and glasses. In the last one, he grabbed the can of butter beans. "Are these any good?"

Alexandrine shrugged. "I dunno. Can opener's missing."

"I have no duty to protect any witch besides you."

"I know that, too." She looked down to gather herself. "She's still coming. You don't have to see her if you don't want to. You can stay in the bedroom."

"Ashamed of me?" he said.

"You're being a jerk again. Why is that?"

Xia stood in the middle of her kitchen, glaring at her. "If there's trouble, she's on her own."

"Fair enough," she said.

He went back to searching for food he might have missed before. "There's nothing to eat here. What kind of person lives like this? Why the hell don't you have any food?"

"What the hell is freaking you out? I haven't been shopping in a while, all right? And now I'm under house arrest, so it's not like that's going to change."

He put his hands on his hips. "You went to work. What makes you think you can't go grocery shopping?"

"Oh, I don't know." She sat down, legs splayed out. "Fiends beating down my doors and trying to kill me?"

"As long as we go while it's daylight, we'll be fine. We've got three more hours at least before it's iffy. Even the magekind are careful about exposing themselves to normals. They'll stay low during the day." Getting the hell out of this tiny apartment was the best idea he'd had all century. "Let's go."

She leaned back on her chair. "We can always order in."

"They can't deliver enough food to keep me happy. I'm starving. Let's go."

"Okay, okay."

Alexandrine went off to find her shoes while Xia put on his leathers. They went outside without saying a word. She adjusted an empty backpack while Xia produced an extra helmet for her. She gave his Harley a doubtful look while he started it up. "I've never ridden on one of these." She had to raise her voice over the engine noise.

He revved the motor. "Baby, all you have to do is hang on for the ride."

# CHAPTER 11

Alexandrine got on behind him with the motor roaring loud enough to vibrate her entire body. She put her arms around him and held on. Thank God he couldn't see her close her eyes in terror as they got moving. And thank God he couldn't read her mind about having her arms around him. The man turned her on like nobody's business.

Once they got to the store, it was obvious his mood hadn't really improved much. Xia made himself a really large, annoying shadow that didn't say a word; he just followed her everywhere and from time to time threw something in her cart and dared her to take it out. She didn't. Lots of pasta and meat, she noticed, and no junk food. If the guy needed to eat to keep himself on an even keel, then she wanted him to eat. She hoped she had enough money in the bank to cover the bill.

There was another problem besides his mood and appetite. He was seriously hot no matter what. In his leathers, he was to-die-for sexy. Women and men gave themselve whiplash looking at him. A whole lotta staring going c in the soup aisle.

She should have expected this, but she hadn't. An oh, the humiliation. Alexandrine was jealous of everyor who drooled over him, because, hey, pick one at rando and she, or he, had a better chance of getting him in th sack than she did. Unless she agreed to be locked down

Her head filled with images of a plain T-shirt stretche across a lean, muscled chest, and now she was imprinte with the recent recollection of her on his motorcycle wit her front plastered against his back and her arms aroun his no-fat middle. He clomped after her, keeping so clos she bumped against him every time she turned around.

"This is dumb," she said when she'd had enough c him tailing her through the store like he was glued to he butt. "Dumb, dumb, dumb." She faced him and pushe him in the chest with both hands. He didn't budge. "La off, would you?" She lowered her voice. "No one's goin to attack me in the vegetable department. And if the do?" She picked up a zucchini and waved it at him. "It the vegetable of doom for them."

He didn't laugh. He just stood there staring over he shoulder, looking like he'd stepped out of the pages c *Bad Boy Magazine*. He was just too freaking hot for her t live. Those black curls of his were killing her. Right nov a few dangled over his forehead, and golly, didn't she jus want to run her fingers through his hair?

Maybe she'd be okay doing it his way. Or not. Probabl not. Mostly.

Xia scowled. "We need to get the hell out of here."

"I thought you said we'd be safe."

"Probably. But I'm getting a bad feeling about this."

She shrugged. "I'm not." She pushed him again. Natually, he didn't move. She grabbed a pineapple and put it her cart. "I'm shopping for you, too, you know." A bag f potatoes. Some grapes and a can of the fake whipped ream sitting by the ersatz strawberry shortcakes, beause, well, hell, she was an eternal optimist, wasn't she? /as she really considering agreeing to his terms? What e needed was a distraction. A reason not to be looking him so often.

"Are you finished?" he asked. He'd just dropped two rge bags of baby carrots into the cart when his attention ot to her left. She rolled her eyes and looked to the right, here a tall man with a military haircut was heading into e produce section. Whoa. He was probably stopping by fter work; he was dressed in black trousers and a gray weater that draped like cashmere. Very European of im. The way he walked reminded her of Xia. The man ripped an empty basket in one hand as he headed for the ok choy.

Their gazes met the way that sometimes happens in tores, in an impersonal friendliness. A draft rippled the air on the back of her neck. She smiled, and so did he, nd he moved on with his shopping. She followed his rogress. Wow, he was good-looking, coming and going. 'alk about an excellent reason to be distracted. Totally ot. Not as hot as Xia, in her opinion, but a damn good->oking man. Too bad Maddy wasn't here. He was her /pe. Sophisticated. Probably had money and a penchant r spending lavishly on the woman of his dreams. As for er? She went for big bad boys in leather. Who thought he was the scum of the earth. Sigh.

She glanced at Xia. He was looking at her, and it wasn't one of his I-hate-you-you-fucking-witch looks. He looked at her like maybe her getting the whipped cream was a brilliant idea. Her stomach dropped to her toes. What the hell, she thought. You only live once, and if she didn't like what he needed, well, they could stop or she could just say, *Honey, never again.* She gathered up her nerve, kept looking at Xia, and said, "Okay. We'll do it your way."

At first he didn't get what she meant. Then he did. His gaze went from intense to scalding hot. Her heart did a few extra beats as she waited for him to say something. But all he did was touch her shoulder while she was standing there clutching a cauliflower. His fingertips lingered. Alexandrine melted. And then, holy cow, he slipped a hand behind her, into the curve of her lower back. Like they were a couple or something.

*Oh, my God.* They were going to sleep together, with no sleeping involved. She was going to strip off his clothes and touch his naked skin and explore his body. His finger worked under her shirt and stroked up her spine. And then he would do his thing, and, well, whether she'd be able to do anything was a question yet to be answered.

"Nervous?" he asked.

"No."

"Liar." His mouth twitched. "I won't hurt you," he said. "It'll be okay."

He kept his hand on her back, caressing her with his fingertips. And, boy, she was ready and willing to do it right here. In the interest of avoiding a scene likely to end in their arrest, she headed for the spinach. The good-looking guy was nearby, too, and he gave her a once-over that did nothing for her now. She shivered, though.

"What?" Xia said, but it wasn't a nice, easygoing in- quiry. He sounded intense, even for him.

She frowned. "What, what?"

"You shivered. Why?"

"I got cold."

"Listen to me." He bent his head close to hers and kept his voice low. "If there was another mage here besides you, I'd know. A mageheld is another matter. I can't feel a mageheld. They're cut off from the kin. But you"—he crowded her even more—"you can."

"I didn't feel anything."

"You shivered."

"People shiver all the time." She lifted her forearm to- ward him. "We're standing right by the spinach misters, Xia. I got cold. That's it." She stopped short. Really, was he sure? Really sure? She got a hollow feeling in her chest. "At least, I think that was it."

"Tell me what you felt. Where, when, and how."

"Cold. Along my arms." Now that he was making her tell him, everything sounded so much creepier than it had felt at the time. "The back of my neck, too."

"Not in your head or maybe your chest?"

She thought about it. "Maybe. I'm not sure. It didn't last long." She thought about how she'd felt. "Like a draft of icy air along my skin."

He frowned. "Is it possible to tell who set you off?"

Right. She was going to tell him she was ogling a com- plete stranger five minutes after she'd told him she'd have sex with him on his terms. "Seriously, Xia, I thought it was the misters."

"This isn't a game, Alexandrine. I need you to be straight with me."

"All right." She threw her bagged spinach into the cart and looked around. They probably wouldn't have ended up doing it, anyway. He'd find some way out of it, or his terms would turn out to be too much for her to handle, and she'd find a way out. "That guy." She nodded in the direction of the hottie with the buzz cut who happened to be standing by the string beans. "I'm not even sure I felt anything. I'm not having any premonitions, Xia. Nothing bad's going to happen. I'd know if it were. I was just looking at him, that's all, and I got a chill."

Xia looked in the direction she'd nodded. His eyes flickered, and she got another ripple along her arms. "Not good," he whispered.

"Well, yeah. He's a major hottie. I was thinking of giving him my phone number. But that was before, I swear."

His attention went back to her. "Are you an idiot?"

"No, I don't think so."

He took her by the upper arm and came in close to speak in a low voice. "He's mageheld, Alexandrine."

"How can you tell?" She turned her head. The hottie was watching them, no doubt about it. But then, lots of people were watching them on account of Xia being even hotter than this guy. In her humble opinion.

"Number one," Xia said, "short hair. We all get shaved when we're taken." His fingers tightened on her arm, and his eyes did that flickering thing as he walked her to the Pink Lady apples. "His name's Durian. Until recently, he was Nikodemus's right hand. And, baby, you don't want to be on his bad side, because back in the day, any fiend who crossed the line against humans got whacked by him." His voice rasped. "I'm on his bad side, seeing as I'm the one who helped Rasmus take him down."

Alexandrine's heart turned cold at the abrupt reminder of what Xia had been to her father. Meanwhile, Durian walked away from the beans and examined a butternut squash. His attention flicked up, and their gazes met. He smiled at her, and now he didn't seem as friendly. Goose bumps rose on her arms.

"All right, then," she said. She kept her tone deliberately calm despite feeling anything but. "What now?"

"He won't try anything here; too many humans around." He seemed to realize how close he was holding her and released her. "Bag up your vegetables of doom and let's see if we can get out of here without him interfering."

"Right." The truth was, they'd been attacked three times last night, and if Xia hadn't been there, the magehelds would have gotten in the first time, and they would have destroyed her place. And probably have done worse to her. Much worse.

They walked to the checkout line. Durian headed for the front of the store, too, but he didn't get in line. He dropped his empty basket and disappeared. Alexandrine got in another line, paid a numbing $281.92 for her groceries, and headed for the parking lot with Xia on her ass again. They got her overflowing canvas shopping bags into the side panniers on his bike. The rest was stuffed in her backpack. Alexandrine didn't see Durian anywhere, but her arms and nape were cold. Xia was getting on the bike when Durian, swear to God, appeared from nowhere, just the way he'd disappeared inside.

"Xia," the magickeld said.

"Come on, Alexandrine," Xia said. He handed over her helmet. She got on, arms tight around his middle while

Xia backed the bike out of his spot. Durian followed, smiling a wolf's smile he directed at Xia. Alexandrine's heart was banging a hundred miles an hour.

"Rasmus sends you his best wishes," Durian said.

People went in and out of the grocery store the whole time, blissfully unaware. They pushed carts, carried bags, herded their children.

"Carson's going to come after you." Xia touched some gizmo on the motorcycle, and the engine roared to a start.

Through the faceplate of her borrowed helmet, Alexandrine saw Durian's eyes flash an improbable deep purple. "Not anytime soon," he said over the sound of Xia revving his bike. He pressed a hand to his chest and grimaced. Ice shot down Alexandrine's back. She tightened her hold on Xia. The air in front of Durian coalesced. Sparks shimmered around the forming edges in tiny purple flashes. The nape of her neck got colder. Xia's body tensed, and the cold in her head spilled down her spine.

"Just try, assassin," Xia said. The air rushed toward them, faster, spinning, gathering force. Xia did something, and the whirling mass of air dissipated. "You know better than to try that shit with me," Xia said.

Durian acknowledged that with a shrug. "Maybe it's time we stopped hiding from humans." He looked at Alexandrine, who was damn glad the helmet hid her face. "Your little witch will take you sooner or later, fiend." Her hearing was muffled with the helmet on, but she saw the venom in his face. "Or have you forgotten she's Kessler's brat? It's in her blood."

"All you have to do, mageheld, is hold on. Nikodemus and Carson are coming after you." Xia put his helmet on and directed his bike out of the parking lot. When he made the turn onto the street, he gunned it, and Alexandrine held on for dear life.

They parked half a block from her building. While she got off the bike swearing she'd never ride one of those again, Xia hauled out her bags. He set them down, leaving her to pick them up on her own. He had his knife in his hand, so she didn't complain. That whole scene with Durian had shaken her. She wanted Xia free to take care of whatever needed handling. When she was ready, she headed for the entrance with her keys dangling between her clenched teeth. And then she stopped.

Her heart beat double time. Not fast, but doubled, like she had two hearts in her chest. It was hard to get a breath. She put down one of the bags and let her keys fall onto her palm.

"What?" Xia asked.

She had an odd feeling in her upper chest, a tickle to go along with whatever the hell was going on with her heart. She concentrated on the sensations and lost them both. The amulet felt hot where it rested against her belly. "I don't know," she whispered. "Something's wrong."

Xia grabbed her arm. "Like last night?"

"No." She shook her head. Just like that, everything went back to normal. She was disoriented now. Her heartbeat was back to normal, and the frost along her arms was gone, but she wasn't so sure she was back to normal. "It's not that. I just . . . It was nothing. It's gone now, anyway."

"You sure?" Xia frowned.

"Yes, I'm sure." She walked to her building's front door. The throbbing in her chest returned, and she must have slowed down or paused or something, because Xia stopped her with a hand to her shoulder. She longed to be safe at home where she'd never go out ever again.

"If you think something's off, don't ignore it."

"You're making me paranoid."

"Good."

"I have no idea what to think anymore." She shifted her bags again. "I'm getting a cramp. Can we just get inside so I can put this stuff down? It's heavy."

"Give me your keys." She dropped her keys onto his outstretched hand. "Thanks," he said. He turned the key in the lock, and even though she knew everything was fine, thank you, she felt inordinately glad that Xia was big and mean. "You feel anything?"

"No."

They took the stairs up to her floor, where he unlocked her door, and she set down the heavier bags. "Stay here until I tell you it's okay."

"And if it's not?"

He glanced over his shoulder while he opened the door. He wasn't smiling. "Leave the bags and run."

"Okay." But everything was okay, right? She felt normal. No magic, no premonitions. She was, as Xia would say, vanilla. And that, she realized, was not normal. Not for her. There wasn't ever a time when she felt completely and utterly normal. Shit. She stopped him with a hand to his arm. "Xia, wait. Something's wrong."

He glanced at her and while he did, she looked past him into her living room. Through some trick of the light, the interior looked oddly gray and empty.

"Stay put," he said.

Knife in hand, Xia went inside. Geez. It was like he vanished into the gray. A moment later, he appeared in her line of sight, light on his feet despite his clunky black boots. While she stared inside, normal fell away. Her throat closed up, and she quivered with the certainty that she and Xia should never have come inside the apartment. Ice swarmed up and down her spine. Something was in her apartment. Something dangerous. "Xia!" she called out.

He turned his head and looked right at her. His gaze burned neon blue and connected with hers with the disorienting dizziness of last night. "Run," he said.

# CHAPTER 12

$\mathcal{A}$lexandrine dropped the rest of her bags at the same time she saw a twisted quasi-human form leap at Xia's back. Light as air, Xia turned. He moved with a dancer's grace as his arm slashed upward. The man—animal? Thing?—who'd thrown himself at Xia screamed and hit the floor in a boneless heap. With sickening horror, Alexandrine realized Xia had killed his attacker and was turning to a second intruder with the same fluid grace. She didn't need to see more. Heart pounding in her chest, she bolted.

She didn't get far. At the top of the stairwell, she collided with a hard body. The impact sent her reeling backward, but a large man caught her by the shoulders and kept her upright.

"Whoa there," he said.

She looked into Durian's face, and her stomach turned. There hadn't been any warning. None at all.

"Are you all right?" His fingers tightened on her shoulders. A lovely, slow smile curved his mouth. "Is there a fire somewhere?"

"Let go of me." She whipped away, scrambling to get her backpack around to the front so she could grab her phone. He didn't release her. "I said let go."

"Rasmus doesn't want you hurt," he said. He smiled again, but there was something off about it. Something unreal. Unsettling. "If something's wrong, maybe I can help. I can protect you from Xia."

She didn't like him touching her. Her skin flashed cold, and the talisman, swear to God, she felt it moving. Her belly crawled with the sensation. Alexandrine used her backpack as a weapon. He didn't even grunt when her heavy, can-filled pack hit him. He got a hand on one of the shoulder straps and yanked her pack from her hands. So fast she didn't see him move, his hand curled around her throat, his fingers digging into the back of her neck, his thumb pressing on her windpipe.

"It won't take much for me to kill you," he said. This time, he didn't try to hide his eyes or the malevolence in them. "Don't think I can't, witch. I know a hundred ways to kill you with a twist of my hands. Rasmus doesn't want you hurt, but he understands reality sometimes intervenes with his wishes. I have dispensation for circumstances such as that, little witch."

Alexandrine went still.

"Much better." He walked her backward, toward her open apartment door, scooping up her backpack on the way. "Inside, Ms. Marit, if you please." Durian pushed her inside and shut the door after them. Her backpack landed on the floor with a thud. He released her throat and spun her around with his forearm jammed underneath her chin.

His other hand held her wrists behind her back. He pulled back hard enough to threaten her air supply.

"Thank you, Durian," said an accented voice. Two bodies lay on the floor, and they were dead; there was no question of that. She smelled blood and something acrid underneath. But the room was so crazy wrong with light and color she couldn't tell if one of the bodies was Xia.

Durian turned her toward the kitchen. Where her television used to be, Xia had a tall platinum-blond man pinned to the wall. His arm seemed to have stopped its downward thrust just in time. Despite the knife at this throat, Rasmus Kessler was unruffled. "If Xia does not release me," her father said, "terminate her, Durian."

Durian's arm tightened around her throat. "With pleasure."

Rasmus lifted his hands. Everything about him shouted rich as all get-out, from his suit and tie to the heavy gold ring on his thumb. The faceted red stone flashed in the light. Impossible as it was chronologically, the mage looked about thirty, maybe thirty-five, with hair the exact same color as hers. His eyes were blue, though. Not brown like hers. "Alexandrine Marit, you see I am defenseless."

"Fuck you, Rasmus," Xia said. His body trembled. He looked at Alexandrine. "Don't believe a word he says."

Rasmus Kessler smiled, and the effect wasn't at all pleasant. "Durian. Proceed."

Xia lowered his knife and took a step back from the wall. He didn't look very happy about it, either. Rasmus straightened his coat and moved forward. Particles of gray dislodged from the wall and trickled to the floor. Everything around them was gray. A strong scent of ashes hung in the air. Her living room was more or less empty. The walls and floor were covered with a fine gray dust that clouded around Xia's feet when he took another step back. He was breathing hard and looking totally pissed off.

Rasmus shook his long hair behind his shoulders. "That's better." He stared at Xia, twisting the ring on his thumb. She'd bet money the thing was magical. "Just like old times, isn't it?"

Xia gave him the finger.

"Still a savage, I see."

Rasmus Kessler wasn't just youthful. He was young. Too young to be her father. Except he was. He was a handsome man, startlingly so, but not normal. Not a normal man at all. His accent wasn't strong, and his English was otherwise impeccable. "Durian," her father said without taking his eyes off Xia, "bring Ms. Marit to me."

Durian's arm eased up on her throat as he propelled her across the room. Whatever was all over the floor crunched like sand under their feet, and yet a fine dust rose. The smell of ashes choked her. When she was standing before him, with Durian gripping her upper arm, Rasmus nodded at Durian. "Please subdue Xia, Durian. Do not kill him."

"No!" Alexandrine shouted when Durian let go of her. Farther in the room, Xia let out a growl. He crouched, his knife held loosely in one hand. From where she stood, his eyes looked white. Her chest froze solid. She was deathly afraid Xia would be so focused on her safety that he'd get hurt or killed or even taken.

Rasmus watched Xia with unsettling avarice. Her father was a mage, the man who hadn't wanted her when she was a baby and who didn't want her now. The man who had once enslaved Xia and who had sent magehelds to kill her. She didn't know what was safe to say around Rasmus, what he knew and didn't know about her, Xia, or the amulet. She wasn't going to give him any information unless she saw a benefit. His thumb ring, set with a large ruby that, if real, must have cost enough to buy a place in San Francisco, pulsed with magic. She'd bet her own money he'd used it to disguise his presence. Not that tricking her would be difficult for someone like him.

"Ms. Marit," Rasmus said in his calm voice. "You don't know what Xia is. I do, and I assure you, you have had a narrow escape. You are fortunate to be alive."

"Yeah, right," she said. "That must be why you broke into my place and did this to it."

He brushed gray dust off his coat. "You mustn't think that, Ms. Marit." The gemstone in his ring, the size of her middle fingernail, was set in a beveled mount. She didn't doubt it was real. For mages, the ruby had special power, and he was using it right now. She could feel it. "Quite the contrary. I am trying to keep you alive."

With a look in Durian's direction, she said, "And you told numb-nuts over here to kill me because . . . ?"

"A verbal feint. I was confident Xia would not allow Durian to kill you when he wants to do that himself. In a most painful manner, I assure you. Such is his speciality, I fear." He looked her up and down. "Xia has killed more women and children than you can count on your two hands. And, alas, I know how each murder was carried out. His reputation, deserved, I promise you, is . . . unsavory." His eyes narrowed. "He hasn't hurt you, has he?"

She studied his face, trying to find a resemblance to her. They were of a similar height, both of them six feet.

hey had the same hair, and maybe there was a similarity
the shape of their faces. But her eyes were brown, and
s were blue. He was also too young to have a daughter
er age. No one would ever believe he was her father. She
lt sick, remembering what Xia had told her about how
asmus achieved his apparent youth.

"I'm afraid Xia, like most of his ilk, has no great af-
ction for our kind." He gestured like he was Jesus in one
' those cheesy icons pasted onto vases and tins in the
usewares section of the grocery store.

"What do you want?" she asked. She knew the truth
fore he replied, which meant that when he finally an-
vered, she knew he was lying. She'd be an idiot to think
r a second that he cared about being her father.

"You are wearing a necklace, no? A carved panther."
e cocked his head. "Surely, even you with your so very
mited powers must have guessed by now what it is." His
tention shifted to Xia again, and the greed in his eyes
illed her heart. Oh, she knew what Rasmus Kessler
anted most of all, and it wasn't her amulet. He wanted
ia back in his control. Rasmus twisted the ring on his
umb. "An object of such power as that cannot fall into
e wrong hands." With a glance toward the center of the
om, he said, "Durian, do take care of our little problem.
should like to have him in hand within the minute. Have
made myself clear?"

Maybe Rasmus did want her amulet, she thought, but
e wanted Xia more. He hardly gave a damn about the
lisman compared to how badly he wanted Xia back
der his command. Alexandrine glanced at Durian and
ia, who were circling each other warily.

"Fine," she said. "Take the damn thing."

Durian lunged at Xia, but Xia sidestepped him and
brought the hilt of his knife down on Durian's back. Durian hit the ground hard enough to shake the floor but was
on his feet in a flash. "Nikodemus wants you," Xia told
Durian. He drew back his clenched hands and struck Durian again. The air around Xia wavered. Durian doubled
over. "He's going to send Carson after you, and that's a
promise."

She pulled the leather thong over her head. Her insides
felt like they were being ripped out as she dangled the
talisman in front of her. Rasmus reached for it, but just
before his fingers touched the thong, Alexandrine took a
deep breath and threw it across the room. It landed with
a dull thud and skidded several inches, sending a cloud of
dust into the air.

Rasmus backhanded her. After all these years, her
survival skills remained intact. She went down but
didn't make a sound. She knew how to keep quiet when
she was hurt and how to fight dirty, despite her desperate, stomach-killing need to have the talisman back. She
kept moving, raising a cloud of ash. Eyes closed and
breath stopped against the choking dust, she threw her
leg up and caught Rasmus in the side of the knee. She
heard and felt a satisfying crack. The mage roared with
pain, but he headed for the talisman. Relentless bastard
wasn't he? Alexandrine rolled and pushed to her hands
and knees in one motion. She tackled him around the
ankles. Rasmus went down, and Alexandrine kept moving through a billowing cloud of stinking, gritty dust.
Her compulsion to regain the talisman worked in her
favor. She wanted it more than Rasmus did.

To her left, Rasmus staggered to his feet. The air

ound her turned to ice. She was frozen there on the
round, breathing in the dust, choking on the stench. Her
st sight of the world was going to be of her father about
kill her. "Go ahead," she said, connecting with his eyes.
Kill me, Dad."

"Durian," Rasmus called, "the woman is yours when
ia is mine. This must be done. End it now."

Across the room, there was a horrendous crash. The
oor shook. Dust rained from the ceiling.

Rasmus bent for the talisman. When he came up,
 held it clenched in a fist. Alexandrine screamed and
apped her hands to her head. Her eyes burned like hell-
e. From the corner of her eye, she saw a shape mov-
g toward them. She didn't know whether it was Xia or
urian, because they were all covered with ash by now—
r, Rasmus, Durian, Xia.

The energy coming from Rasmus's ring shivered her
ones. He was saying something she couldn't make sense
. A moment later, she couldn't breathe. Even as she
ruggled to draw air that wasn't there, she saw deep into
asmus, connecting with him in a visceral, terrible pulse
at was nothing but raw emotion. She saw his magic as
 it were a living thing. She also felt his rage at having
st Xia and his utter conviction that Xia was a danger
 them all if he remained free. And under that certain
lief there was also greed. He wanted Xia's power under
s control.

Every word Xia had said about him was true. Ras-
us Kessler, a killer many times over, was now intent on
enslaving Xia. She could feel it happening. The sheer
gliness of his intent made her sick.

Xia collided with Rasmus, knocking him to the ground.

She heard the clink of the talisman hitting the floor, and at the same time, her connection with Rasmus ripped away. Burning white heat blocked her vision and, *bam*, she was in Xia's head, looking out of his eyes at her, on her knees, gasping, and there wasn't anything she could do to stop it. She didn't know how to make her body move when she wasn't inside it. The pain coursing through her belonged to Xia, and she didn't see how anyone could survive it. Someone shouted, and then she fell out of Xia's head and back into her own body. Xia had the amulet now, the thong clutched in one hand so he wasn't directly touching the carving. Her burning need to have her amulet back overwhelmed everything else. Something in her chest went *pop,* and just like that, the amulet was back in her hand. She clutched it hard.

"Alexandrine!" a woman cried out.

She pried open her eyes and saw Maddy standing in the doorway with two plastic bags of food and a bottle of sparkling water tucked under one arm. Maddy dropped her bags but, absurdly, not the bottle of water and rushed to Alexandrine. "Are you all right?"

"Maddy, get out." Alexandrine got to her hands and knees and shook her head, trying, ineffectually, to push her best friend away. Pain streaked through her. She pushed herself upright in time to see Xia get blown off his feet. A gash across his shoulder bled profusely. Horrified, she saw Durian put Xia in a headlock while Rasmus advanced on him, touching the ring on his thumb. The room sizzled with magic that sent her stomach into revolt.

"So, Xia," Rasmus said, "it seems you're to come back to the fold."

"No!" Shit, but her head burned like it was on fire.

She tried to pull but got nothing. Magic never worked for her when she tried. "Xia!" She stretched out a hand, but he was too far away and too late. Rasmus had reached Xia and was touching his chest. Her throat choked with panic. She didn't have the kind of magic that could stop this from happening. She headed for Rasmus, intending to do something. Anything. But Maddy grabbed her arm and brought her up short. She whirled on her friend and shouted, "Maddy, do something! Stop this, please."

Her best friend stared at her, eyes big. "All three of them?" she asked.

"Stop the blond guy," she said. Then she grabbed the bottle of water from Maddy and went after Durian, because if magic failed her, then all she had left was a plain old physical fight. She felt Maddy pull, and that diverted Rasmus's attention. She heard him say, "Subdue the fiend, witch," and then Alexandrine was behind Durian and swinging hard.

The water bottle smashed into the back of Durian's head at the same time Xia kidney-punched him. With a grunt, the mageheld crumpled over. Xia clasped his two hands into a hammer and swung at Durian's spine. He was doing his best not to kill Durian, but it was compromising him, just like his promise to protect her had compromised his ability to protect himself from Rasmus. His knife was on the floor, the blade glowing as it disappeared under a layer of ash.

Rasmus shouted again. "Witch!" He plainly meant Maddy. With Durian in a heap on the floor, Rasmus retreated from Xia. "It's the fiend we need taken down," he told Maddy. "Before he does irreparable harm, please."

"I'm trying," Maddy said. She sounded calm, but then

she always did when the pressure was on. Alexandrine felt Maddy's magic flowing from her, distinctly, if not completely, different from Rasmus's.

Xia whirled in Maddy's direction. His eyes flashed from neon to blue-streaked white. He looked ready to spit fire.

Alexandrine lunged for the spot where Xia's knife had landed. Low to the floor, the ash was still hot. She swept her hand through the stuff until she had the knife. One of the edges of the blade sliced her palm, but she ignored the pain. By the time she had the weapon safely in hand, a river of ice formed down her back. Xia's eyes were now pure white.

Rasmus stumbled and then slowly dropped to his knees. His eyes bulged while Maddy turned pale with the effort of whatever it was she was doing to the mage. It didn't last long. Rasmus whispered to himself, and the air exploded over their heads. Xia threw Alexandrine to the ground, landing so he covered her with his body. Sparks fell, hissing and popping as they landed all around them. One burned into the back of her exposed calf. The floor rumbled beneath them and knocked Maddy off balance.

Alexandrine rolled over when Xia let out a howl. Maddy crouched on the floor, her hands covering her bowed head. Durian was on his feet, the back of his head dripping blood. With a snarl, he launched himself at Xia, who brought up a leg and gave the mageheld a thundering kick in the chest. In the same motion, Xia whirled and shoved Rasmus hard enough to send him sailing through the air. The mage hit the wall with a crack.

"Come on," Xia said. He wasn't even breathing hard.

He grabbed Alexandrine's hand and hauled ass for the exit.

Maddy followed them into the outside hall, where she turned and slammed the door closed. She pressed her palms flat to the surface and muttered to herself. "Maddy," Alexandrine said. "Come on!"

Maddy turned her head and looked directly at Xia. "Get her out of here. Now."

Beside Alexandrine, Xia nodded and yanked on her arm.

"Maddy!" Alexandrine cried.

As Alexandrine and Xia ran for the stairs, Maddy called out, "If anything happens to Alexandrine, fiend, I will find you."

Xia laughed while they hauled ass away from her destroyed apartment. She tried to put on the brakes when she got a look at his back. His T-shirt was bright red with blood. "Oh, my God, Xia." She still had his knife clutched in one hand. He wasn't slowing down at all. "You're hurt."

"I'll live," he said.

They kept running.

# CHAPTER 13

At the second flight of stairs, Xia headed for the back stairs, where their footsteps banged on the wooden steps. Alexandrine's brain wasn't fully cooperating with her body yet, but Xia had a firm grip on her upper arm as they raced through the laundry room. Someone had left clean laundry in a basket on top of the dryer, and as they flew past, she snagged a black shirt from the top.

They kept going until they were in the building's underground parking garage. Only then did Xia stop moving. He stood at the entrance, scanning the vehicles. Alexandrine grabbed the hem of his ruined T-shirt and yanked up. Xia looked at her like he thought she'd gone insane, but she flapped the black shirt, and he got what she was going for. He stripped off his shirt in favor of the one she'd "borrowed."

"Thanks," he said. During the shirt transition, she got a good look at his back; it was covered with tiny pinpricks of blood. But, call her crazy, they seemed to be healing before her eyes. The slash in his shoulder didn't look as bad as it had upstairs, but that didn't mean it looked good.

"We need to get you to a hospital," she said.

"I'm fine, baby." He draped his uninjured arm over her shoulder and started walking toward a beat-up red Toyota Corolla. "This should do."

"What should?" she asked. Xia was radiating some strange vibes that sent prickles up and down her arms. He put a hand on the car door, and the back of Alexandrine's head got cold. There was a *click* as the locks disengaged.

He opened the passenger side. "Our ticket out of here."

She stared at him while he walked around to the driver's side and got in. "We're stealing this car? We can't steal a car."

"You stole a shirt." Which, by the way, was on the small side for him. He slid the driver's seat all the way back, put his hands on the steering wheel, and ducked his head enough to give her a look so hot she just about melted. She was pretty sure she wasn't imagining that his eyes were changing colors.

"I didn't steal it," she said. "I borrowed it."

"Get in, Alexandrine."

"Xia. Stealing is wrong."

"Staying here to get killed is even more wrong. Get in." He grinned at her. "Besides, we're not stealing. We're borrowing."

Somewhere inside the building, someone roared. She got in, closed the door after her, and snapped in her seat belt. "Feels like stealing to me."

Xia grabbed the steering wheel. "God, I love these old cars." He patted the dashboard. "We're only going far enough to make it past Rasmus's magehelds. Then we'll ditch the car someplace the police will find it, okay? No harm, no foul."

She shivered once—right before Xia started the car without the key. "Nice trick," she said.

"Nothing to it." He backed the car out of its space and tuned the radio to a classical station. A song from Bach's *Anna Magdelena Notebook* came out of the speakers. At Alexandrine's look, Xia scowled. "I hate this classical crap, but it'll help with the illusion that it isn't me."

"What music do you like?"

"Vampire Weekend, all the way." He headed the car out of the garage. "One more thing before we go."

"No more crime. Please."

"I saw Nikodemus do this thing once."

"What?"

He braked and looked at her. "Chill, okay? I need to try hiding your magic, which means I need in your head." He lifted both hands from the wheel. "Just long enough to get you past the magehelds, all right?"

A scream of rage reverberated from the interior of the apartment building. Shit, she hoped Maddy had made it out. "Do it."

He was there before she was ready. Just a tap of pressure on her temples and he was alive in her head. The sensation was similar to what she'd experienced before, but she felt even more cut off from the world this time. Inside, she was turning into pure ice.

"It's okay," he said in a low voice. "You're fine. We're fine. Doing good." He released the brake, and they drove out of the garage to the sound of Bach. She was surprised to see the sky was dark. Had that much time really passed while they were dealing with Rasmus? A couple of times as he maneuvered in traffic, she got a prickle of ice along her arms. Xia invariably reached over and patted her leg. "We're cool, baby. Totally cool."

At South Van Ness Avenue, he merged onto the main thoroughfare and draped an arm along the top of her seat. They drove vaguely north and west until they ended up in Presidio Heights. Only then did he release his hold on her. She slumped on the seat afterward, taking deep breaths while she readjusted to being alone in her head. "That wasn't so bad," she said.

"Baby," Xia said. He put a hand on the back of her neck and massaged her tight muscles. "You fucking rock."

They left the car parked on a street near the Presidio, the former military base with million-dollar views now converted to residential and commercial uses, and they started walking. With the fog in and a bitterly cold wind whipping past them, she was shivering enough to be more than happy to keep close against Xia's body. He ran hot, and right now she was glad.

"Where are we going?" she asked.

"My place," he said. Xia had his arm around her shoulder. Yes, it was true they had completely different strides, but still, he was surprisingly uncoordinated as they walked. He stumbled once, and Alexandrine had to tighten her arm around him to keep him steady.

"You okay?" she asked. They were walking downhill at the time, nothing too bad for San Francisco. Even though this wasn't her neighborhood, she knew the area well enough to know eventually they were headed for a steeper downhill.

"No," Xia said.

They passed a streetlamp, and she got a good look at his face. He looked like shit, pale and haggard, and that terrified her. "How much farther?" she asked.

He stopped walking. His arm tightened around her, and she threw her hip toward him so he wouldn't fall over. "I was going to borrow another car, but I think we need a cab."

"You go to jail if you get in a cab without the money to pay," she said.

"I have money."

"Okay, then." She swallowed hard. She didn't like the thought that something was wrong with Xia. "Then we need off this street and on to one with more traffic. Can you make it?" He nodded, and they started walking again. She got the third cab she hailed. She and Xia climbed in, and he gave the driver an address in Sausalito before he went limp against the seat, with her holding his hand and keeping a finger pressed against his pulse.

Sausalito was the first town on the north side of the Golden Gate Bridge, and she held her breath while they drove, praying he'd be all right. She kept expecting something would prevent them from getting there, but nothing did. They made pretty good time. Traffic was light on the bridge, and thirty-five minutes later, they pulled up to a blue house right on the water. Alexandrine tugged Xia's wallet from his back pocket and was relieved to see enough cash to pay the amount on the meter plus the tip. Barely. Oh, unfair. Xia's driver's license photo was fantastic. He looked like a cross between a rock star and a movie star. He wasn't smiling, not Xia, but he could have sent this photo to a modeling agency and gotten callbacks.

"He all right?" the cabby asked as Alexandrine fished

out bills. She had to fork over extra money because of the dust that still covered them when they'd gotten in the cab. A layer of grit now covered the backseat. The driver wouldn't have let them in if she hadn't promised him a whopping big tip.

"What? Oh, him? Sure." Halfway to Lombard Street and the approach to the bridge, Xia had passed out completely, and she'd gotten what felt like a lightning bolt to her head. "Jet lag," she told the driver. She had the talisman back around her neck, which was why she was better off than Xia at the moment. He was better now, too, but she viscerally understood what *fevered eyes* meant. He was burning up. "We just got back from Japan."

"That's a long flight," said the driver.

"It's murder, I tell you." She leaned over Xia. "Look," she whispered without handing the driver his money yet. "I really think you need to go to the ER."

Xia's eyes went wide open. His hand gripped hers. Hard. "No."

"There a problem?" the cabby asked.

"No," Alexandrine said. "No problem." She handed over the promised fare before she opened the street-side door. She got out while Xia peeled himself off the seat. He shuddered when they stood outside. The taxi drove off, and Alexandrine couldn't help feeling like she was alone in a world she didn't understand anymore. "This the house?" She nodded in the direction of a 1960s structure with no front yard and stairs that led down to the front door. The water looked to be about twenty feet away. Gulls wheeled overhead, flapping their wings on air that smelled like the ocean. Sausalito was on an inlet of the bay, so this wasn't the Pacific proper. Still, the ocean wasn't far, and the view of the bay from here was spectacular. Multimillion-dollar homes around here.

"So?"

"Great." Her stomach was queasy from the attack at her apartment, not to mention the effect of having the talisman yanked off her. Ever since she'd put it back around her neck, she'd been feeling heat coming from it, a constant tingle of magic that made her tense and antsy. She ignored it and headed for the front door.

Xia grabbed her arm and steered her away from the stairs. "We go in the back."

"Like tradesmen?" His palm was hot on her skin. To be honest, she wasn't feeling so great herself. At least they weren't switching back and forth between minds anymore. That was enough to make a girl barf. "What, I'm not good enough to go in the front door?"

He was already leading her around the side of the house. "The front is for losers."

"All right, then." A wooden gate barred the way to more concrete steps that also led down. Where you'd normally see a latch, there was a wooden disc carved with a frowning face. Xia touched the disc, and the gate opened.

"I said no more crime. Really."

"No crime," he said. "I promise."

"You are aware that breaking and entering is a crime in the state of California?"

He looked at her over his shoulder with a bracing display of the Xia that irritated her to no end. Thank God. "Yeah?"

"Do you even know whose house this is?"

"Uh-huh." He held open the gate for her.

"Okay, whose?"

"I told you we were going to my place. This is it."

When she'd gone through the gate, he closed it, and they continued down the steps to a flagstone patio with a metal table and two metal chairs. There were more painted wooden discs around the back door. Xia did something with his hands that made her head throb. They weren't sharing their mental space anymore, so her headache was a coincidence. Had to be. Right? Right.

He opened the door and walked in with her behind him. She saw a mud room with a laundry room across a short corridor to a bathroom. He didn't do anything like turn the lock when they were safely inside. He did, however, take off his shoes and socks.

To be polite, she did the same thing while he opened the back door and dumped what looked like a gallon of gray sand from his boots. He flapped his socks out the door, too. She followed suit. When she turned around, Xia was shirtless and working on his leathers. He threw his wallet on a shelf.

"Hey!"

Practically before the word was out, he was naked. He shook out his clothes, then bent over and scrubbed his hands through his hair. Gray dust rained down. "You better do the same," he said. "You don't want this crap on you longer than necessary." He walked into the bathroom and started the shower.

"I'm not taking my clothes off in front of you."

With one arm still in the shower adjusting the taps, he looked at her. "Why not?" He seemed genuinely baffled by her objection. "We're going to do it later, anyway." He smiled at her, and really, he must be the only man in existence who could make a beautiful smile terrifying. "Or are you taking that back?"

"I'll just call you Mr. Romance from now on."

He shrugged. "Whatever. I'm still not letting you in my house covered with that crap. You can shower in here or go hose yourself down outside. Your choice."

"Fine." The truth was, she wasn't taking it back. Why should she? Plus, her skin was starting to itch. "Hand me a towel, please."

He reached out of her line of sight and came back holding a black towel. Still naked, he grabbed his discarded clothes and dumped them into the washing machine. "Put your things in when you're ready," he said.

He got in the shower.

Alexandrine turned her back and stripped. Dust floated in the air and onto the floor. She threw her clothes in the washer with his. Now what? Was he expecting her to wait out here until he was done? Or something else? What did a girl do with a naked man?

The shower door was glass, and aside from a bit of steam, it was crystal clear. Xia had his back to her with his head bowed while he washed his hair. And what a lovely back it was. If he'd ever been injured, you sure as heck couldn't tell now. She dropped her towel and got into the shower with him.

# CHAPTER 14

Xia turned when she closed the door after herself but kept soaping his washcloth. Water dripped down his face. He blinked a couple of times, and Alexandrine smiled at him. Why, yes, she was a little nervous about making the first move. She could so easily crash and burn. What if he threw her out? "You're not going to tell me you don't take showers with witches, are you?" she asked.

His gaze traveled from her head to her toes, lingering on the bits in between. "Fuck, Alexandrine," he said. He made room for her under the water. "You're all legs, aren't you?"

She looked down, partly for the sake of tweaking him but mostly to hide her smile of relief. "I'm okay, I guess." There was, of course, nothing wrong with her body. She worked out hard, and that, combined with some lucky genetics, gave her something to flash at a naked hottie in the shower.

"Baby," he said, "you are way more than okay." He

put away his washcloth to grab the shampoo. With a littl
adjustment and some deliberate clumsiness, they got he
hair washed and grit-free. The soapy water around thei
feet ran less and less gray. There was a constant zing o
magic between them, too.

She'd be lying if she said she wasn't a bit giddy a
touching him. Not the slightest ding marred his skin
Those thousands of bloody pinpoints were gone. S
was the nasty cut on his shoulder. Best of all, he wa
aroused, his penis thick, and that was actually a relief
She didn't think she'd ever been so turned on in he
life, and judging from the evidence, he didn't feel muc
different.

Then Xia put aside the soap and the washcloth an
propped both his hands on the shower wall well above he
shoulders while he leaned in. Closer and closer until hi
torso pressed against hers. They both ignored the fact tha
he was keeping his erection away from her. They wer
walking a fine enough line as it was. When they finall
did do it, she didn't want them to be in a shower. No
with the limitations he was placing on the act. Probably
Unless he started doing stuff like this, in which case, oh
God. She tilted her head toward his. She did like a ma
taller than she was. He kissed her and proved the spec
tacular first time was no fluke. The man knew how to kiss
a woman senseless.

He leaned closer until his belly touched hers, hi
erection, too, and she about dissolved. The talisman wa
trapped between their bodies.

The stone flashed hot. Burning hot.

Alexandrine saw stars. Not the good kind. Her hearing
and vision went out and then flashed back from a differen

erspective and a different body. The pain was incred-
ble. Everything inside her was on fire. She saw and heard
erself say, "Crap."

Everything winked back, and she landed in her own
ead, her own body. Her sensations instead of his. Only
ow she was hypersensitive to everything. The sound of
e shower hurt her ears; water hit her skin like boiling
ain. Xia's back was flat against the opposite wall, his
rises were red-flecked white, and then back to neon blue.
Iis knees wobbled. She would have helped him, but she
vas too dizzy to manage much besides turning off the
vater.

"Are you all right?" she asked. The amulet lay ice-cold
n her skin.

Instead of answering, he put a hand to the shower door
nd bowed his head like he was praying for patience.

She felt pressure behind her eyes. "Are you doing
nagic?" she asked.

He rested his forehead against the door. His shoulders
lumped, and then he tensed like he was getting a full-
ody cramp. "Fuck," he ground out. Alexandrine put a
and to his shoulder, expecting him to shrug away the
ontact. He didn't. He fumbled with the door and stum-
led out.

Alexandrine followed. Gently, she closed the shower
loor. Unlike Xia, she grabbed a towel and wrapped it
round herself. "What happened?"

He shook his head. Water dripped off him, and she
anded him a towel, too. He scrubbed his face dry. "We
ave got to do something about that goddamned talisman.
t's dangerous."

"Agreed," she said. She felt more than a little

apprehensive about the talisman, but she wasn't deluded enough anymore not to recognize the way the thing worked on her—drawing her in, making her feel like she wouldn't survive without it. "But how?"

"We need to crack it." He met her gaze. It seemed impossible that two minutes ago they'd been about to become extremely personal with each other. Now he was all business. "What's inside needs to come home."

She took a step back and wrapped her towel tighter around her. The amulet was hers. It belonged to her. It wasn't for Xia to decide what they should do with it. She understood how twisted and even evil her sense of possession was, but that didn't stop the reaction. She made a tight fist and forced herself to ignore the creepy-crawly way the talisman made her feel. Xia was right. Whatever was in there needed out. No matter what it did to her before or after. She swallowed the lump in her throat. "I know."

Xia rubbed himself dry. How like a guy to be so freaking low maintenance. He headed into the laundry room and threw his towel into the washer. He grabbed a box and measured out detergent. "Bring me your towel, would you?"

"I don't have any clothes." At least he didn't seem to be angry with her.

"So?"

She gave him a look, and he relented.

"All right, all right. Here." He snatched a T-shirt off a shelf behind him and tossed it at her. "That's all I've got for you until our clothes are clean."

The shirt was plain white, and when she had it on, the thing hung halfway down her thighs. Long for a T-shirt.

short for anything else. Great. So much for modesty. She gave her hair a quick rub before she took her towel to the washer and dropped it in. "I need a comb, if you have one. Some moisturizer would be good, too."

He twirled some dials, and the washer started. The man had no shame whatsoever. Every muscular cut he had was on view. Thank God, because the sight gave her something to think about besides what it would mean to crack the talisman. "Cabinet above the sink."

Sure enough, back in the bathroom there was a comb, along with a moisturizer so expensive she had to wonder about the woman who'd left it behind. Jealousy was not a pretty thing, but, yes, indeed, she was jealous. She sat on the john and worked on her hair. Didn't take long seeing as how her hair was so short. Now for the moisturizer. Cucumber scented. While she put it on, Xia walked into the bathroom. He'd put on a pair of jeans, and he stood in the doorway with a thumb hooked through one of the front belt loops. No shirt. She tried not to be obvious about looking at him. Golly, though. He smiled at her. The sort of smile that acknowledged the sort of look she was giving him. What if they never managed to work out this sex thing? By now they both knew they'd be hot together. They just had to find a way around this. Please.

"A lot could go wrong," he said. "There's no guarantee it will work. And if it does, it might not work right. I might not survive." His gaze stayed steady on her. "You might not."

She put the tube of moisturizer on the floor. "I know the truth now, Xia." She pulled the amulet out of her shirt and let the carved panther lie on her open palm. Inside her, a dark and unpleasant voice whispered that she could hide the amulet or say she dropped it somewhere, and while he was looking for it, sneak out of the house. And it was telling her that if she ran, she could keep the talisman forever. She waved her other hand. "I used to look at it and imagine the person who carved it and think, wow, what a talent to make something like this out of a lump of rock." She shook her head. "I don't think it's beautiful anymore."

Hell. Was she even getting through to him? From his tense expression, no. "Now that I know what it is, I can't live with this." Inside, she was nervous and jumpy and a bit sick to her stomach. "I don't care what it does or doesn't do to me or what happens when you take it back." She hung her head for a minute before she continued. "Okay, I do care, but I can't have this around me. I just can't. There are some things, Xia, that are just wrong." Her stomach clenched. "And this amulet— talisman—is one of them. I'd rather be dead than tied to something like this."

"Just so we're clear about the risks, baby."

She blocked off her panic about what would happen to her without the talisman. "From here, my future looks bleak no matter what. So let's just do what needs to be done. Now."

Xia reached behind him and pulled out his knife. He did that whenever he was upset or in the process of making a decision. He drew a fingertip along one of the surfaces. It was a relief to know she didn't have to hold back with him. She didn't have to pretend she was normal or hide what little ability she had. She didn't have to omit details about her past or lie about it, either. A flare of light between his finger and the blade fluctuated through the colors of the rainbow, and the back of her head got cold. Magic. That was his magic she was feeling. She waited to hear what he'd say.

"The problem," he said without looking away from his knife, "is that with you wound up around the talisman like you are, you're going to need to pull in order to help keep you safe." He lifted his head, but only enough to see her. "You understand?"

"Not really. I mean, I'm not sure," she said. The toilet seat wasn't comfortable. No matter how she shifted, her butt was cold and getting numb. "It's better if things are perfectly clear. Especially since we both know I can't pull reliably."

"Copa solves that for you."

Her heart headed for the floor, taking her stomach along with it. "Copa."

"You're going to have to pull, Alexandrine." A frown quirked at his mouth. "I know how you feel about taking drugs, but it's the safest way to do this. If we do it. Otherwise it's like I'll be in there with a machete when what I need is a scalpel."

Alexandrine rocked forward. "You said it's addicting to mages."

"Yeah. Eventually."

"But not so much for mages without much magic?"

He shook his head. "No exceptions that I know about. But it's only addicting when you keep using."

Alexandrine took a deep breath. "What's it like? Taking copa."

"You're magekind, Alexandrine. I'm not. I don't know

what it'd be like for you. All I know is taking the copa will help you pull enough magic to make this safer."

There had to be another way. But as the panicked thought clamored in her head, a voice in there whispered, *You could use magic. Real magic. At last.* "That doesn't mean it would work on me."

He rested his head against the doorway. "It's not about whether you have much magic or not, Alexandrine. You have plenty. It's just you can't use what you have because you didn't get taught before it was too late." He frowned. "It's like this. Rasmus has an open door between him and his magic. You have a pinhole. Every now and then, the talisman widens your access, and if you knew anything about what to do with your magic when that happens, you could probably take Rasmus's head off. The copa will make your pinhole wider. Give you better access and allow you to pull more than otherwise."

She stared at him. Great. Just great. "You sure there's no other way?"

"Nothing that isn't way more risky than this."

From somewhere deep inside her, a place she knew could never be buried deep enough, she felt a buzz of anticipation. She would feel what it was like to have the kind of magic that mattered. She'd be able to do things. Create fire from atoms in the air, turn on a light when she was nowhere near the switch. Hell, she might even be able to impress her father. She could pull magic and change her reality with a thought or a word. Her throat closed off. She refused to blink for fear she might cry. It wasn't fair to want this so bad and have it be for all the wrong reasons.

"You could keep the talisman," he said. "We could wait for Nikodemus to get back and see if he can't do something to help." He drew a breath. "He saved Carson from something similar. Maybe he could save you, too."

"There's no way of knowing how much longer it's going to hold together, right?" she asked.

Xia nodded. "It could crack in you, Alexandrine, and I don't know if I could bring you back from that."

"So," she said softly, "we wait. Or we crack the talisman now. Either way it's risky."

"Pretty much."

"But the longer we wait, the more unstable the talisman gets." He nodded. She traced a line on the floor with her bare toe. There was another side to this they were both avoiding, and it was time to get it out in the open. "The longer we wait to do something," she said while her stomach turned to lead, "the longer what's trapped inside suffers. Isn't that true?"

He ran his tongue around the inside of his mouth before he answered her. "Yeah," he said. "That's true."

"All right, then," she said.

He touched the side of her head, taking a lock of her platinum hair between his fingers. She wondered if he was thinking about Rasmus. "I'll throw it away afterward," he said.

"The talisman?"

He gave her a look. "The copa."

It didn't matter, but she didn't tell Xia that. The real danger wasn't that she would steal some copa off him afterward. Maybe she would, maybe she wouldn't. The real danger was the bone-deep hunger for magic she'd lived with all these years. If she fed the hunger now, after starving for so long, she'd spend the rest of her life knowing there was a way to have the magic back. No wonder mages abused the stuff.

"Whenever you're ready," Xia said. His hand slid around to her cheek.

"Now," she whispered. Her heart pounded in her ears. "Let's do it now, okay?"

He inclined his head. "There are rituals," he said, "that can make this easier. For us both."

She knew he meant easier for her. "Rituals." She licked her lower lip. "What kind of rituals? Do I have to do something disgusting to you?"

"Well, it helps," he said with no change in expression, "if I've had a mind-blowing orgasm beforehand." He ogled her. "Two or three would be even better."

"Pervert." She was grateful that he'd tried to make her laugh. That was really very sweet of him. And coming from him, that meant something. Her heart kind of twisted up. Here he was being decent to her, thinking of her when he hated her because of her father and because of what she was and what had been done to him by people like her. She resisted the urge to throw her arms around him and hold on tight.

"So?" he said.

"I'm not giving you an orgasm." Maybe she'd be okay. Maybe the copa wouldn't work on her the way he thought. She wasn't much of a witch, after all. She was practically vanilla. Maybe it wouldn't work on her, and she wouldn't have to spend her life knowing what it was like to use real magic.

"It was worth a shot. You sure?"

"So tempting," she said, and this time she didn't resist the urge to touch him. He didn't shift away from the contact. "But, no."

He left the doorway. "Come on," he said. "Let's get this done."

# CHAPTER 15

Xia's living room was stunning. While he organized a few things and got ready for the big event, Alexandrine stared out the floor-to-ceiling windows, trying to get a handle on her nerves. The view of the cove flat-out took her breath away. She gave up trying to relax and just let herself fall into the beauty of the moon on the water while nerves churned a hole in her stomach.

When she got around to noticing anything else, she had to adjust her assumptions about the man who owned this house. *Elegant* wasn't the word, but *striking* came close. One wall was dark blue, the others stark white. Contrast was everywhere. Nepalese rugs in various shapes and sizes accented the bamboo floor. He favored the more austere designs, but one of the rugs was a riot of color and pattern. A bittersweet-orange couch angled toward the windows on one side. A smaller couch faced a gas fireplace built into a wall perpendicular to the windows. Tibetan and Nepalese masks hung on the walls; some of them were garishly painted devils while others were animal faces carved of dark wood. There were framed photographs, too, all of them black-and-white nature scenes. Carved animals cavorted on the mantel, some abstract, some disturbingly real.

Xia came in with an armful of items that he arranged by the fireplace. Alexandrine's stomach tightened. He laid out a small brazier and poured oil into the bowl on top. He did something with his hand, said a word, and a flame appeared underneath the bowl. He laid out several other items by the fireplace—his knife, unsheathed; a stoppered glass bottle; and a wooden box, which he opened. She recognized the pills he took from it: copa. He crumbled one into the oil, and she swore she saw sparks dance over the surface.

Alexandrine walked to him. She didn't trust herself to speak without betraying her anxiety. Part of her wanted to run away, to make a mad dash for the door. As she stood there, inhaling the scent of warming oil, she composed a speech about why she had to refuse the ritual. The amulet was hers. Hers. Hers only. She couldn't give it up or she'd die. And the copa, a really bad idea.

He held up another of the pills. "It'll be different for you than it is for me. Sometimes a mage gets disoriented his first time taking copa. I've seen that happen."

"Disoriented how?"

"It depends." His eyes flickered between neon blue and aquamarine, and she wondered what memory he was dealing with. The witch who'd betrayed him to Rasmus? The paler his eyes, she realized, the more stress he was feeling. "I'll be here with you, Alexandrine. I won't let anything happen to you."

Two distinct compulsions went to war, one new, one old. The first and newer one was the impulse to keep the talisman to herself by any means necessary. The second and far older reaction was her indescribable longing to be able to do something with her magic that wasn't trivial. She stared at the pill on his palm.

"Does it last?" she asked. "I mean, does the effect fade away, or is it something permanent?"

Xia walked to the larger couch. He held out a hand and waited for her to join him. She did, pulling her T-shirt down and underneath her butt as she sat. "You have to be a serious abuser for the change to be permanent," he said. "Most of the mages I've seen who were addicted died before they reached that point."

"And the others?"

"If they don't stop, they all die from it." He settled in on the couch. "Sooner or later, copa will kill a mage."

"Great."

"Don't worry." His southeastern view of the water was completely dark. "You won't go that far tonight. This being your first time and all, you aren't going to have some instant-death moment. Besides, if you take only one, the change will fade pretty quickly." He put a hand on her thigh. Very nonchalantly. "You have what it takes not to let it go that far, Alexandrine."

"What if you're wrong?"

He lifted one shoulder. His fingers curled around her thigh, though. "I'm not."

She torqued her upper body to put her forearms on the back of the couch and got her legs tucked under her, with her torso facing Xia. "Thanks for believing in me."

"Why wouldn't I? Now, the first sign it's working is

our eyes change. From what I hear, you'll feel the physi-
al effects later." He shook his head to get his hair off his
orehead. "Don't be surprised if the copa changes your
rises dark gold."

"Gold, huh?" She was nervous about this whole thing
nd feeling shaky. "That sounds kind of pretty."

His fingertip brushed beneath her eye. "Your eyes are
retty just the way they are."

She touched his hair with her near hand. His curls
vere soft. "The feeling's mutual. Have I told you how
orgeous your eyes are? Women probably tell you that all
he time."

"Actually, they don't," he said. He settled a hand on
he top of her shoulder, stroking gently, and Alexandrine
eaned toward him.

"Maybe we should have sex now. In case something
ad happens, you know?"

He cupped the side of her face. "I won't let anything
ad happen to you. When we get there, Alexandrine, I
vant to take my time."

"I'm okay with that." She felt a light pressure in her
ead, the way you do when you're in an elevator that's
oing too fast. Did that mean he was pulling magic?

He held out his hand. One triangle of ochre yellow
ay on his palm. She took it from him. "I'll be right here.
Okay?"

"Bottom's up," she said. The shit was awful. Disgust-
ng. The copa had an earthy, mildewy taste, maybe a little
itter. "Gaghhh."

"Don't chew it, Alexandrine. Just swallow fast."

"Now you tell me. Yuck." The stuff went gritty on her
ongue, but she got it down. "What about you?"

"Me?" He leaned toward her. "I'm getting hot, looking at you in my shirt and thinking how you don't have anything on underneath."

"Perv."

"Yeah, I know." He sidled closer to her.

"Are you going to take any?" In answer, he took out three and tossed them down like they were his favorite kind of gumdrops. She raised her eyebrows at him.

"I'm bigger than you," he said. "It takes more to get going in me."

She frowned at him. "Your eyes haven't changed color."

"Baby," he said softly, stroking her arm between her wrist and the sleeve of her T-shirt, "I'm not a witch."

"Me neither," she said. She resisted the impulse to tug on her sleeve. "Not to speak of, anyway. I'm just a plain old nonmagical mage. Of the female variety." She stayed where she was. Her pulse was going hard, but that was just anxiety with a little bit of horniness thrown in. At least she thought so. "I don't feel different yet. How long do we have to wait for something to happen?"

"Not long. A couple of seconds more."

"That fast?" She put her chin on her forearm. So, was she relieved or disappointed? She wasn't sure. A little of both, maybe. She didn't feel anything at all. Nothing different. No altered state of consciousness. No magic bubbling up just waiting for her to pull. What a disappointment. The copa didn't work on her. "Guess that means I'm not a witch after all. The stuff doesn't work on me."

"Baby." He drew a finger along the underside of her right eye. "Guess again."

By the time Xia said *guess again* in a voice that was

x on tap, the taste of the pill she'd taken was gone. She ill didn't feel any different.

Xia got off the couch and pulled her to her feet to lead er to a bathroom off the living room. Everything in here as black. Everything. The tiles, the walls, the ceiling, e fixtures. He even had black soap. Black towels and and towels, too. He got her facing the mirror above the ack granite vanity. "Take a look."

She looked. And blinked. Then squinted and took closer look. Her eyes weren't the familiar brown she w every day. Her irises were darker, deeper, almost old. "Whoa," she whispered. She put a hand on the all by the mirror and hung her head, shaking it as if e motion would toss out the color and put everything ck to normal. Slowly she opened her eyes. She looked her right. He hadn't found black toilet paper. She d no trouble distinguishing the toilet paper from the all. Everything else blended in. She looked in the mir-or again. Her eyes were still gold instead of brown. he raised her gaze and saw Xia's face reflected in the irror.

Not that it mattered. His eyes weren't normal, either, it that wasn't any different. His eyes had never been nor-al. "Now what?" she asked.

He scooted closer to her, peering at her eyes in the irror. "Can you pull?"

She turned around, and they were so close they were ractically touching. "I don't know."

"Try." He slipped a finger under the leather thong round her neck and lifted up. Not much, but enough to ake her anxious. He let go, and she went back to feeling ormal. "Can you?"

She tried to access her magic. But, as usual, there
was nothing there. "No," she said. "I can almost never
pull on purpose. It's mostly been accidental. You know,
premonitions. Or else stuff that happens that I never
expected."

"Damn," he whispered. She shrugged in response. Xia
dug into his pocket. "Here." He gave her another pill, and
this time she dry swallowed. The taste wasn't nearly so
bad that way.

"What if this doesn't work? This will suck if I get addicted to this crap for nothing."

Xia put a hand to her cheek, and Alexandrine went
still. His touch electrified her. "It's going to work. I can
feel your magic, Alexandrine, and it's seriously turning
me on. So believe it, it's working, baby."

"Then why can't I do anything?" She knew she'd let her
frustration echo in her voice, because his hand smoothed
her cheek. "I'm a failure at this. I always have been."

"You're not. The mages who survive learning to use
their magic were raised knowing what they are. They live
it. Breathe it. They study and practice for years before
they go out in the world."

Her head throbbed, and she rubbed her forehead to
ease the tension. Didn't do any good at all. Her vision was
going, too. The corner behind Xia refused to register in
her head as a corner.

He slid his fingers up to her forehead and pressed gently. "You grow up to kill monsters like me."

She pressed her spine against the wall next to the
vanity, with her hands trapped between the wall and the
curve of her backbone. He looked away, and her eyes were
really doing funny things, because his profile vanished

le vanished. He turned his gaze back on her, and there
e was. Big as life. She brought up her hands and pushed
im away.

"I'm not a killer." Her stomach went all jumpy. "I've
ever killed anyone, and I'm not about to start now."
he stumbled past him, but the room disappeared.
verywhere she looked she saw black, yet at the periphery
f her vision, rainbows arced off angles that weren't there
hen she looked. Her brain couldn't parse out what she
as seeing and assemble the information into an image
he recognized. "What's happening to me?"

Xia's voice in her ear was the only thing that made
ense to her. "I've got you." His arms anchored her in the
oom. "It's all right. Be calm, and in a minute everything
ill settle down. I promise."

"Is this going to go away?" Her stomach stopped
witching and got tight and queasy.

"Yes."

He put a hand on her shoulder and guided her forward.
t least she thought it was forward. The lines of the room
lted off in crazy directions. Everywhere she looked she
aw brilliant color. Some of the colors she'd never seen
efore in her life.

"Sit," Xia said.

She did and recognized the brighter orange of the sofa.
hey were back in the living room, then.

"Close your eyes." She did, and Xia's voice continued.
Concentrate on something you like. Puppies. Or uni-
orns or whatever girly crap turns you on. Turn off the
anic and concentrate on your magic."

She thought about Xia in the shower. Before everything
vent crazy. When Alexandrine opened her eyes, there was

Xia, sitting beside her. Next to the fireplace. In his perfectly normal living room. No rainbows. No walls that refused to meet at right angles. "Are we going to do it?" she asked. "The ritual, I mean. Not the hot monkey sex."

"Soon," he said. "Focus like that if you start to lose it again, and you'll be fine."

"What the hell is in that crap you gave me? And how come you're not bouncing off the walls, too?"

"I'm not like you."

"Vive la différence," she whispered.

"Lie back. Yeah, like that. With your head relaxed." He shifted closer to her and leaned over her. She got a full-on dose of his neon eyes when she opened her eyes. He put his fingers on either side of her face and massaged her temples.

"Oh," she said. "That's heaven."

"Just relax. Think about puppies and fluffy bunnies." She rolled her eyes. His fingers were magic. She found herself relaxing in spite of herself. "Feeling better?"

"Yes." Her thoughts expanded out, and gradually she became aware of Xia in a different way. Not just his physical presence, but also his mental presence. She could touch his mind if she wanted to. What an odd sensation. To think you could get inside someone's head. She knew that happened—heck, it had happened to her. But to think that sort of thing could be deliberate gave her the chills. His fingers moved from her temples to the sides of her head, rubbing circles in her scalp. Heaven. She'd seen the man naked. Touched him. All six-foot-and-something inches of him. An awesome body. What would it be like to make love with him? His hands had been on her, so she had a clue that he'd put her in orbit.

ia stopped massaging her head. "Don't stop. That feels ivine."

"This is getting dangerous," he said. He stood and, rabbing her hand, got them both to the rug in front of the replace. The earthy smell was stronger here, so close to he brazier. She was tempted to inhale and hold her breath n case the stuff worked like weed.

Lazily, she opened her eyes. Her eyes met his, and it vas like free-falling and landing someplace alien. She vasn't sure what happened, but whatever it was, she got dose of Xia so intense she felt like she was inside his houghts. "Wild," she said.

He moved just his head. Oh, great. His eyes were oing that glowing blue look again. He tossed some-hing else into the shimmering oil and leaned in to ake a deep breath. He gestured for her to do the same, ut she was already on her way. In close, the scent of erbs was sharp and intense. And then the lights went ut. The only illumination came from the fireplace. hadows flickered on the floor and on the planes of Xia's face. Hers, too, she supposed. Xia wasn't star-led by the power outage. But, then, nothing seemed to righten him.

"What did you do with the lights?"

"Concentrate, would you?"

"On what?"

"Whatever you want. Just pick something and concen-rate on it."

"Fine." She chose the little brass bowl, because she'd lways wanted a bowl like that, but all the ones she saw vere too expensive. Several minutes passed in the dim ight. The scent of the herbs grew sharper and took on a

bitter undertone. She was hideously aware of Xia beside
her, sitting with his hands on his thighs, his head bowed.
Like he was praying.

Her mind didn't feel connected to her body anymore.
Yes, the copa was definitely having an effect on her. She
took a breath and oddly caught a whiff of heat and sand
and an ancient desert. From the herbs Xia had thrown
into the oil? She didn't think so. The scent seemed to be
coming from Xia. Her throat was parched, too. She didn't
want water, though. She wanted the taste of copper sharp
on her tongue.

"Yeah," Xia whispered. "Me, too. But I need you to
pull, Alexandrine. And then hold, you understand me?"

"Gotcha. Do magic but don't do any magic."

His eyes flared. "Do it, would you?"

"You won't be too disappointed if this doesn't work?"

"Would you just pull?"

"Fine." She reached into herself, prepared for nothing
much happening as a result. Only, her magic was there.
Ridiculously easy to reach. She could pull and have magic
flow into her in a river instead of a drip.

He drew a hissing breath and whispered, "Alexandrine." She watched him reach for his knife and hold it in
his left hand. He tipped his head to one side and brought
the tip of his blade to the skin above his collarbone. He
made a deft nick. He didn't flinch. The smell of blood
came to her so abruptly her head swam.

Xia said something low and soft that didn't sound like
English, because it wasn't. The meaning danced at the edge
of her mind but eluded her, of course; whatever language
he'd used, she couldn't even identify it, let alone hope to

understand it. He shifted until he was facing her. "Alexandrine." He gestured her toward him. "You first," he said.

"First what?" she whispered. But she knew what he wanted to do. His blood welled up from the nick, deep liquid red, and that drew her attention and stopped her thinking about anything but that welling scarlet. Her head felt feverish.

"Alexandrine," he whispered. "Now."

She put her hand on his shoulder and leaned toward him. *Just get it over with.* If she didn't do something now, his blood was going to be wasted.

"Keep holding your magic," he said.

Her mouth touched his skin, and then the taste of his blood burst over her tongue, thick and dark and better than anything she'd ever tasted. She pressed her fingers into his shoulder, half expecting him to shift away. He didn't. He remained still. Not a flinch. Not even an extra-deep breath. He tilted his head more to give her better access, and she moved in, rising up and slipping her other hand around the back of his neck. Pressure built in her head and focused in the center of her forehead, a tap almost. Her tongue touched his skin and came back. She was dizzy, and she must have swayed or maybe just tightened her fingers on him, because his hand went to the back of her head, steadying her, holding her there.

His skin was smooth beneath her lips, warm, and he smelled good, of soap and a faint undertone of heat. His hair, soft and warm, fell across the back of her hand. Was the rest of him this wonderful to touch? She wanted him. She couldn't deny that his body and his beautiful eyes and his face did something fatal to her. Xia tightened his hand on her head and pulled back.

When she looked up, they were closer than she expected. Both of them kneeling, torsos touching. She was pressed against his chest. Xia didn't let go of her head. He raised his knife, and in the shifting light, rainbows shimmered along the blade. He pulled back her head, twisting to expose the side of her neck. The sense of pressure around her head increased.

"Keep holding," he said. He spoke softly, again using words she didn't understand.

Their gazes met, and she blinked as she lost sight of his face. Her mind was filled with an image of her face, as if she were looking down at herself. Her body thrummed with sexual heat and Xia's desire to penetrate. To be inside heat and damp and to feel the softness of a woman's body. Which would be her. With Xia.

*Fuck, Alexandrine.*

She had no idea if the words were spoken out loud or not. She blinked again and managed to reorient herself. Xia's eyes burned blue, flickering with something else that lived in his head. She saw the blade move toward her, then lost sight of it as he came closer. She felt the sting of the touch. Icy cold. Or burning hot. She couldn't tell. And then his head descended.

As kisses went, well, this wasn't. His mouth was on her throat, and he was holding her tight in his arms, and she was too dizzy to think straight. It was as if a brilliant, sizzling line connected them, and there was magic zinging along the connection. Then he was there. In her head. And he reached into her core. Through her and into her magic, where the talisman's power had entwined with hers.

# CHAPTER 16

*F*uck.

Xia thought the word straight into Alexandrine's head. She was whacked out on copa, to the point where her body and mind whirled with the drug. And, man, did she feel good. Prime grade-A witch at her most compelling goodness, exactly the kind of magic the kin craved. The talisman was there, too. Enough of that magic was in her that she could long for the taste of blood as if she were one of the kin. Very unwitchlike of her, that, and one hell of a turn-on for him. Like Carson had been, only even more with Alexandrine.

One of her arms circled his waist, holding on to him for dear life. As if he wasn't holding her tight already. Because he was. The smell and the taste and the texture of her blood had his senses on high alert. All of them. And there was the matter of her being in his head and him being in hers. They shared mental space even though she was pulling magic.

That made him vulnerable to her. Yeah, he was taking a risk. But the possibility that she'd take him mageheld was pretty damn remote.

At the moment, they were both in deep, dark trouble if he didn't get this shit with the talisman over with soon. Part of him didn't give a rat's ass about anything but keeping his connection with her going. The rest of him understood he needed to act before he lost her and the talisman. He maintained a fierce grip on her head. She couldn't have moved if she'd wanted to. Even with her taking up residence in his head, without a clue about what was happening to them, he was perfectly clear whose thoughts and urges belonged to whom, which he knew from bitter experience wasn't always the case when fiends and mages went at it like this.

Swear to God, he wanted to go back to her throat for more. Her blood tasted even sweeter than it smelled. He opened his eyes. Just a little. Enough to see the top of her shoulder. She tipped her head back, and their eyes connected with an intensity that sucked the breath from him. His head went spinning, seeing through her eyes a thousand emotions, colors melding, angles refusing to coalesce into shapes. Feeling the incredible high and needing it. Wanting to be cranked higher. Already worried that she was coming down and losing her ability to pull.

He forced himself to focus on what they had to do. His hand slid down the back of her head to her shoulders, and he took his connection with her deeper yet. He found where her magic surrounded what was, for her, the alien power of the talisman. Way more power than he wanted there to be, way more. The thing had been leaking into her for months. This wasn't going to be a slice-and-dice procedure the way he'd hoped. He couldn't just rip away the points of contact between her magic and the talisman's. With the way she was all tangled up with the talisman's magic, he'd permanently damage her if he tried that, if not kill her outright.

He sent his magic into the core of hers, where the power from the talisman had settled in. All those months she'd been wearing the thing, its magic had been affecting her from the inside out. Eventually, the talisman would have completely assimilated with her, and who knew what she'd have ended up like. Dead? Or like her father? More like what had happened to Carson after her run-in with a talisman? Or something else? His money was on dead. He went to work, slipping his magic in, getting around what didn't belong.

Because the copa in her system allowed her to pull significant magic, Alexandrine got what he was doing. She mirrored his actions where she could, retreating at times, pushing sometimes until, after what felt like a year and a half, he'd isolated as much of the talisman's power as he could. Outside their connection, in the physical world he'd practically forgotten, he put a hand around the carved stone that had imprisoned one of the kin and cut the thong that kept it around her neck.

He drew the talisman's magic away from her. At first, nothing budged. But they both felt the reaction in her. Power flared from the core Xia had encircled, blazing hot. He pulled again, and the talisman's magic separated from Alexandrine. Not easily, not smoothly as he'd hoped, but in a sticky, smoky flow. Reluctant. Her magic fluctuated, focused one minute, completely unfocused the next. Fighting him, and then not. The way she seesawed between full-on mage and vanilla reminded him a lot of Carson Philips before her encounter with a different talisman. If Alexandrine shut down now, she was fucked, and he'd be afraid to try again.

Shit. This had to be finished.

Alexandrine shook with the effort of keeping control of her magic. Through the haze of the magic he was pulling through them both, he reached for her physically. Her skin was clammy, and her pupils were pinprick small, her pulse thin and erratic, all classic signs of a mage about to bottom out. Worse, he was getting a lot of interference now, because the copa was fading from her system and she was having trouble holding the magic she had. If this went on much longer, she'd crack apart before he finished; give her more copa, and he was pushing her that much closer to addiction.

Rock and a hard place. Did he do nothing and wait for her to die, or did he give her more copa, get the talisman out of her, and then hope to hell he hadn't overdosed her? He didn't see that he had much choice.

He flipped open the box and fished out another pill. "Come on, baby. Almost finished. One more, and we're done."

She looked at him with her golden eyes fading to brown. "I don't feel so good. I used to feel good. I don't now."

"You need to take this." He held out the pill. "You're going to shut down otherwise, and I need you able to pull."

"More magic," she said. "Sure." She smiled, but it was a smile that broke something inside him. "Why not?"

Goddamn if his heart wasn't ready to shrivel into dust.

And for a witch. She couldn't check out on him. No way. He wouldn't let her. "If you can't keep pulling, Alexandrine, this is going to fail, and you'll die."

She nodded and took the pill he gave her.

The copa had an immediate effect. Her eyes went back to pure gold. Not the adulterated crap they called gold today, but the rich, deep true gold from hundreds of generations past. She stopped cycling high and low. Her magic went hot and stayed there, and that left his way to the talisman clear. He wanted to take a swim in all that power.

He went back to work. Alexandrine pulled so much magic that the air around them sparked. But she had the balls to keep all that power on tap despite knowing he was going to sever her from the talisman. He was well aware that if she let go of that much power, the backwash could kill them both. He sliced his palm with his knife and took the talisman in his hand. The power inside needed an easy path into him, and blood was the perfect conductor.

No time to waste. He started jimmying the rest of the talisman's magic loose. Heat seared the palm of his hand, hotter and hotter until a raw scream teetered at the top of his throat. Alexandrine's body bowed away from him, and she gasped. Magic surged from her, but she held it back. A rainbow of electric light flashed over them. He gathered himself and punched in hard, taking over her and her magic to prevent her natural inclination to fight this. Sweat stung his eyes. He wanted to stay here, enfolded in her magic and her. But he didn't.

The talisman's magic came loose all at once, rushing into the stone that had imprisoned it, and when he felt the magic looking for a way out, he pulled so hard he thought his body would explode. His blood provided the conduit between the prison of the carved panther and him. Fire ripped through his veins as the foreign magic burst from the carving and shot into him—magic of the kin, old, unfocused, and full of the pain, rage and despair that had attended the last moments of the living fiend's physical existence. His scream erupted.

Assimilation took time; that's what he'd always heard. Hours or even days before the process was either complete or failed. But this . . . this was everything at once. Total cohesion, propelled in part by the push of Alexandrine's magic and the pull of his. The world crashed into him, and he shattered.

When it was over and he was back in his mind and body, Xia sat back, barely able to keep himself upright. Alexandrine was on her knees, and she stayed there, head down, hands hanging at her side. Still flying high from the copa and yet spent. His hand flamed with pain. His heart beat triple time while he struggled to maintain control of his physical body. He was disoriented from the ride and not sure he was in the clear yet. One thing was for sure, though—he wasn't dead. It didn't hurt to be dead.

Alexandrine reached for his hand. The leather thong that had held the talisman was nothing but a pile of oily ash on the floor between them, scattered on his thighs and the lower front of her T-shirt. Gently, she pried his fingers open. Transparent sand was all that was left of the carved panther that had imprisoned an ancient fiend's life and magic.

"It's gone," she whispered. He caught the edge of grief in her voice and wanted to pull her into his arms and tell her everything was going to be all right now. "It's really gone."

Xia extended his hand over the oil in the brazier. His arm shook as he let the material cascade down. For several minutes afterward, tiny flashes of black light glittered over the oil. The smell was pleasantly bland.

"Yeah," he whispered back. "It's gone." He took a breath. "You all right?"

"No." Her copa-altered eyes were bleak.

She knew, he realized. She'd known all along that she'd come out of this totally messed up. Not because of the talisman, but because of the copa. He should have seen that himself, what she was putting on the line for him. With the amount she'd pulled and held close, how was she going to give that up?

"You?"

"No." Xia stroked a hand along her face and around to the back of her neck. He wanted to hold her, but what if she didn't want that from him?

"What happens now?"

"We wait and see if I assimilate with the talisman or if it kills me. Could go either way right now." He frowned because she was looking like she was about to bust out bawling or something. "Hey," he said. "You're not crying, are you?"

"Absolutely not." She managed to look offended, so maybe she was telling him the truth. "I never cry."

But when he brushed the side of his thumb underneath her eye, his skin came away wet. "Hey," he said.

"I don't want you to die, Xia."

"Don't go crying over me. I thought you hated me, anyway."

"I do. I swear I do."

He curled his hand around the back of her neck. "Good," he said. He liked the way she didn't pull back from him. "We're in total agreement, because I don't want me to die, either."

"God, you're an asshole, Xia." She wound her arms around his neck, and the next thing he knew, she was kissing him without it being his idea. And she was good at this. Butterflies exploded in his stomach. Her tongue came into his mouth, and they went into overdrive.

He curled his fingers behind her neck and pulled her to him. His butterflies turned into liquid heat. The copa augmented her magic in a way that was totally turning him on, but hell, she'd turned him on before the copa. Witch magic. The spice that made sex kinky hot. He couldn't wait to know what she was like. Hot. All soft and sweet. Curves where he needed them to be. He kissed her with everything he had in him; he didn't want her to change her mind, and he was losing it over her. He wanted her to be as wild for this as he was, to be desperate for the physical and mental connection.

She worked a hand between them and went straight for his groin. He reacted, hell yes. Hard as a rock, balls tight, spine getting the heat from the sexual tension that happened between mages and fiends. She got her fingers on the top button of his jeans. Her presence in his head flared hot. Totally shared, baby. Totally hot.

She popped the button.

Sparks rained down on them, and she turned her face to the ceiling. With eyes closed, she let them land on her skin. She didn't have any idea what she was doing, but he felt the magic in the sparks that hit him. "So beautiful," she murmured.

He was hard. Really, really uncomfortably hard. But he didn't want to rush through this. Not if she needed something different from him after what she'd been through for him. She got his zipper down and her hand around him, her body shifting under his the way a woman did when she wanted more contact. He lost his ability to focus on anything but the certainty he was about to get what he wanted, which was hot, hard sex with Alexandrine Marit.

"Fuck," he said on an indrawn breath.

"Xia, you read my mind," she said.

"You know how it has to be." Jaysus, her fingers were doing some magic all their own.

"I understand." She gripped him harder on the up stroke.

"Alexandrine . . ." Whatever else he was going to say got lost as she closed the distance between them, and they were kissing again, only this time she didn't hold anything back. She was a talented woman. And, sure, he knew she was maybe a little vulnerable right now, but he was vulnerable, too, come to think of it. With every second that passed, he was that much closer to knowing which way the assimilation was going to go. Wasn't that a reason to let things happen? Hell, they might both be dead in a couple of hours.

They were on the floor, with the fire warming one side of them, his body sprawled over hers, and he was kissing her and touching her and trying to get closer. He had a hand on her ass by the time they came up for air, and then her thighs parted and his hand went between her legs, and his fingers did what he wanted his cock to do. Hell, he was brainless with lust. Lust for sex with Alexandrine and a lust to touch her magic with her there to mirror him the way she had when he was separating her from the talisman. She looked at him with copa-enhanced eyes and just about made him come with the heat he found there.

He slid his free hand around her waist and brought her to him while he got up close and personal with her magic. She was still holding, and, damn, it was a rush. He could also feel the remnants of the talisman in her, too, and he liked that even better. Witch with a hint of fiend. She put her hand down his pants and cupped his balls while her thumb stroked up and down.

"For one of the magekind," he said, "you're not so bad."

She laughed, a low, sexy sound he liked a lot. "For a whatever the hell you are, you're not so bad yourself. And," she said, stroking him until his eyes rolled back in his head, "for a witch hater, you're a fantastic kisser."

"Oh, yeah?"

"What would it be like if you didn't hate me?"

"A lot like this, I think." He kissed her again, long and slow, and by the end, he had both arms around her, his clenched fist pressed into the small of her back while his other hand went everywhere else. He stayed in her head, and they kissed some more. Just when he was sure he was going to lose his mind if he didn't get inside her, she moved over him, straddling him and reaching for his fly all in the same movement. He took control of her magic, and she tensed a bit. They waited to see how this went down. Because the totally crazy thing was he didn't want this if she wasn't okay with him holding her magic.

She took a deep breath and moved her hand. He prepared himself for bringing this to an end. But then she found his fly. Oh, yeah. All the way unzipped. He caught her hand. "You sure you're okay with this?"

"Xia, don't you dare ruin this." Her eyes were bright with tears. "Don't you dare."

He groaned, loud and long, when she took him in. He knew even in his human form he was bigger than most men, but she didn't have any trouble with him. She was wet. Totally wet and hot for him. A perfect fit. What a lucky bastard he was. All she had on was his T-shirt. His insides clenched when he got a hand under her shirt and over her breast. She grabbed the bottom of her shirt, pulled it off, and flung it away. Holy hell, she was gorgeous. He nearly, but not quite, forgot about her magic.

She was so tight around him he started thinking he was going to come way too soon. She arched her neck and let out a low, soft sigh that ended in a moan, and he lost it. The only thing on his mind was physical in nature—the way she was tight around him, so wet and hot; the way she swiveled her pelvis on his, getting what she needed from him. He lay back and let her take the lead. Already he was wound up tight, feeling his climax coming on.

He didn't think he'd ever been with a woman, human or otherwise, who took such complete control of the physical act with him. Usually he was the aggressive one, because usually he was doing what Rasmus told him to. Not this time. He was doing a witch, and nobody was telling him how to touch, where to touch, what magic to use, or how much to hurt her before he killed her.

He loved this. He loved her body, he loved the way her copa-darkened eyes went all soft and wild at the same time, and most of all he loved the way he was rapidly approaching a mind-blowing orgasm. She put her hands on his shoulders and leaned down. He pushed up.

"I need you to do me," she said. She looked into his eyes. And, damn, but she was moving her hips the whole time, bringing him deep inside her. "Hard. Please, Xia. Do it hard."

As if he'd say no to a request like that. He rolled them over, and, jaysus, the minute he was on top with his dick harder than granite, he found himself on a whole new level of sensation. Her legs went up and around his hips, and he did what she asked. He pushed himself into her hard and kept going until sweat ran down his temples. She needed hard. He gave her hard. His specialty, in fact. Hard sweaty sex that crossed some lines was just what he liked. He held back his climax somehow, because she wasn't there yet, and he was determined to watch her come.

In the back of his head, he was aware his magic was mingling with hers, not a little, which sometimes happened when the sex was really good, but a lot. A way lot. Not just his magic, but the talisman's, too, wild and out of control. He shouldn't let that happen, but damn, the touch of his magic with hers sent his brain straight toward nirvana. He just didn't give a damn.

"How hard do you need it?" he asked.

She threw back her head, exposing her neck to him. "Oh, God, Xia."

His gaze focused on her pulse. She had no idea that made him even hotter for her than ever. He might as well offer himself up right now. He could see the place where he'd nicked her earlier and could smell the smear of blood left behind. He slid a little closer toward climax.

He leaned down and bit her, and hell if he didn't change. Not completely but enough that his teeth easily cut her skin. A growl rumbled from deep in his chest. He wasn't sure if she was aware of him being different, but so what if she was?

He went the rest of the way. All the way. He welcomed the ripple down his back, the flash that meant he was something new for her. Bigger and harder, and wasn't that just what they needed? Hard. Fast. Hot. She arched into him, but her head stayed back, her throat remaining exposed to him. He licked at the cut. The taste of her blood filled his mouth. Sweet, coppery salt. Out of control.

Their eyes met and they connected through the gaze. He had her magic, all of it. He was in her head, feeling her high from the copa, sharing her rocketing trajectory toward orgasm. She pushed toward him, looking for more, her breath coming in deep gasps. He reached down and slid his taloned hand around her thigh to draw her leg toward him. Her hands gripped his body. No way could she not know, but even seeing what he was, knowing what he was, she was totally hot for him. For this. For what he was.

His magic went deep into hers, and he just flashed out of control at the exact same time that she convulsed around him. His balls went tight, and he hit a wall of pleasure that took him away from everything but this. He came a second later, and he just knew—oh, shit, there was a hollow feeling in the pit of his stomach the size of the Pacific Ocean—he'd done something to her magic he shouldn't have.

# CHAPTER 17

*T*he best sex ever was apparently a life-changing event. Alexandrine kept her eyes closed and took stock. The postcoital glow was definitely on. Besides that, though, she felt different. Very different. No surprise there, since Xia had done the talisman-ectomy. She felt the lack of it, a kind of ache, but it wasn't as bad as she'd been dreading.

Xia withdrew from her physically but maintained the psychic connection. He wasn't human just now, and she decided she liked it. He was gorgeous like this. They shifted their bodies, but she held on to him for moment, reluctant to give up the closeness. He was a lot bigger than her, but she wasn't worried he'd hurt her. He wouldn't. There were blue highlights in the shadows of his body, and she stroked him along the line of his flank.

He didn't move away even though she half expected him to. Instead he stayed near, moving a taloned hand from her shoulder, down her midline, around to her hip, and along her thigh. His palm was hot and didn't feel human.

"Alexandrine," he whispered, and the low, rumbling sound sent a shiver through her.

"Mmm," she said. She let go of him, sorry to give up his warmth and let the lingering sensual heat fade away. Xia rolled onto his back but kept a hand on her belly. He groaned once, and then the air around him shimmered and he was human again. Interesting. She felt his magic in a way she hadn't before. Awareness of him tingled in the back of her head and made her awake and alert. In an odd way, the talisman wasn't gone. A part of Xia now drew her the way the talisman had. Wasn't that strange? She wanted to have him near because he reminded her of her amulet? Crazy. She sat up and spotted her T-shirt an arm's length away. She grabbed it and put it on.

Xia bent his knees and groaned. The magic in him whirled, surprisingly chaotic. She didn't expect that of him. He sat up, too—all those delicious muscles flexed—and there they were, looking at each other. Pure killer-boy. Her belly got tight and hot. He leaned toward her and kissed her sweetly. Tenderly. As if he'd stopped thinking up new and painful ways for there to be one less witch in the world. She was such a sucker for tender. With the contact, the heat in him flared in her. She was touched by his kissing her when he didn't have to.

"You all right?" she asked.

His hand rested on her shoulder, gripping gently. "No."

"I didn't know you could change like that." She looked over at the wooden box that held the copa. Ebony wood with a white pine inlay of zebra stripes. No difficulty recognizing that again. Already her edge was fading. She wanted it back. She wanted to stay in that perfect place where she had magic that would make her father take notice, where she had the power to do anything. Where Xia wanted her because of what she was.

He reached around her to close the lid on the box and fiddle with the catch until it clicked. "You didn't freak out," he said. "When I changed."

"No," she said. Even though his changing to something else had been freaky, she'd been in the mood for freaky just then.

He locked gazes with her. His eyes were neon at the moment, no flickering through shades of blue. "You didn't mind?"

"No," she said. "You were . . ." She struggled for the right words. "Bigger. Dangerous." She touched her neck, sliding a finger along the breaks in her skin. Teeth marks. His image was burned into her head. Lapis skin. Talons. Sharp teeth. His eyes were white streaked with blue. She'd taken him hard, and that dark scary edge when he was like something from a book on medieval demons was, well, hell. She liked it. She better than liked it. "It was good, Xia. Way more than good."

Xia got to his feet slowly and looked around until he found his clothes. They weren't far away, yet he swayed when he walked to get them. Near the fireplace, the brazier sputtered. "It's the copa that made you feel like that, Alexandrine. Maybe you don't know for sure what you saw." The muscles in his back and ass flexed as he put on his boxers and then his jeans.

"Like hell. I know what you were like, Xia. Don't try to tell me I don't." She stood up and found she was remarkably steady. Unlike Xia. His magic was going all unbalanced again. He turned around. And this time his irises flickered through shades of blue. "You were beautiful," she said. "The most terrifyingly beautiful creature I've ever seen." He grabbed his hair with one hand, and she stiffened. "Checking to see if it's still there?" she asked.

He glared at her. "I'm trying to get my head around what we just did; that's all."

"We had sex."

Xia's mouth tightened. "Let's go get your clothes, all right?"

"Sure." They went to the dryer, where he retrieved her clothes and tossed them at her. She got dressed. "So, Xia," she said while she was buttoning her shirt. Her fingers were shaking. "How come I feel like I'm being punished?"

"I lost control with you."

"I liked it," she whispered. He was withdrawing from her, and she didn't want that to happen. Stupid, needy Alexandrine.

"You don't get it." He threw out a hand and caught his weight on the wall. "Fuck."

"Maybe you should explain it to me."

"I'm fertile when I'm like that." He grabbed his hair again. "I should have known better, Alexandrine. I did know better. And I did it anyway, because I have never been that hot for a woman in my life."

"That's what got you so worked up?" She let out a sigh of relief. "Relax. I'm on the pill."

He turned his head to look at her. "Like that matters."

"I'm not going to get pregnant," she said. Xia closed his eyes as if he was going to barf. "Hey, maybe you should sit down."

"I'm fine." His hand on the wall fisted as he opened his eyes. "The kin don't reproduce with each other," he said. "We have our offspring with humans. Or the magekind. Not only am I fertile in that form, Alexandrine, but it's damn likely I made you fertile, too. It's how our bodies and our magic work. Whether you're on the pill or not."

Alexandrine got a chill down her spine. "Okay." Now she was thinking she was the one who needed to sit down. She got cold right down to her heart, and this time magic had nothing to do with it. "Right. So, I'm going to end up a single parent. Is that what you're telling me?"

"Hell, no." Xia swayed on his feet. His eyes unfocused and his legs wobbled. "The kin don't abandon their children like the magekind. They are loved no matter what. And if it happens, you will be taken care of."

She went to him, afraid he was going to fall if she didn't hold him up. "Maybe you better lie down. Jesus, Xia, you're burning hot."

"It'll pass."

"When?"

He laughed. His eyes were unfocused, and she was getting dizzy from the way his magic was going all freaky on him. He threw out a hand, and she caught him, bracing him against her. "Hopefully before I die."

No way. She was not going to let him die. "In the meantime, Xia, where's your room? How about we get you flat on your back?"

"With you on top again?" His eyes flicked to white with streaks of ice blue. And stayed that way.

"You are so bad," she said. But she was thinking, *Hell yes.* "Bedroom?"

"Upstairs. Second door on the right." He wiped his forehead on his arm.

"Let's go, then." She put her shoulder under his, and he draped his arm over her back. His entire body quivered while they walked. She got an echo of his pain in her own body. "Maybe you need to see a doctor."

"No doctors." His fingers gripped her hard. "You understand me? No doctors ever. It's not done."

"Fine," she said. A bit sensitive about that, wasn't he? "No doctors."

The upstairs room was standard enough. Pretty normal, actually. Bed. Dresser. A smallish walk-in closet. A bedside table with a lamp and a stack of books on it. The view of the water was even more spectacular than the view from downstairs. She got Xia over to the bed. His knees crumpled and they landed on the mattress, with her partially underneath him and his elbow digging into her side. He rolled off her and lay back with his eyes closed. Magic surged from him, just about frying her eyebrows off. This connection between them was just freaky.

She perched on the edge of the mattress and stroked his face. His skin was dry and hot, and she didn't know what to do for him. Heck, she didn't even know if it was safe to give him aspirin. While she was touching him, trying to figure out what to do, he changed. Instead of gorgeous Xia the bad boy, she was looking at a creature of lapis-lazuli blue, with fingers that ended in deadly talons and cheekbones that slanted too sharply to be even remotely human. Her gut clenched with an instinctive, primordial fear. With his eyes closed, his lips drew back as he let out a low growl. His teeth were sharp. All of them. Especially his canines and incisors. She didn't run.

She wanted to, but she didn't because he wasn't well. Xia wasn't well at all. His skin was soft under her fingers. Not skin, really. His hide was soft and burning hot.

He lifted a hand and circled his taloned fingers around her wrist. His magic flared hot again, chaotic and completely and utterly compelling. A rainbow of fire arced over the bed and vanished with a sizzle and pop that seared her ears. Xia changed back, and his eyes flickered open. Pure white irises streaked with ice blue. "It'll be all right," he said. He threw his arm over his face and shuddered. "I'm good now."

She slid off the bed, sick to her bones. She didn't want Xia to die. He couldn't die. But a tiny voice in her head whispered that if he did, she wouldn't betray him by turning herself into the kind of copa-addicted magekind he hated so passionately. Alexandrine had no doubt whatsoever that if she gave in to the compulsion to drug herself in order to have real magic, she and Xia would be done. "You sure about not seeing a doctor?"

"The only doctor I'd trust near me right now is your brother." He lifted his arm off his eyes enough to glare at her. "And he's in Paris with Nikodemus. Why are you crying?"

"I'm not." She brushed at her cheeks. Crap. "Fine. Go ahead and die on me, then." Her voice edged up the register. "See if I care."

"Downstairs." He shivered, and her skin goose-pimpled from head to toe. What on earth was the deal with that? "In the fridge. There should be a plastic jug. Get me a big glass of what's in it."

*"Ja, mein commandante."*

"Just do it," he whispered.

On the way out, she kept getting bizarre flashes of what he was feeling. No fun. At all. For either of them. A headache throbbed behind her eyes, and she didn't know if it was a headache of her own pounding away at her cranium or if it was coming from Xia. A quarter of the way down the stairs, her heart sped up. At first, she thought the reaction was due to her being about thirty yards from a box full of copa. Because, yeah, she was completely aware of that. A full-body shiver of apprehension went through her. The problem with that theory was that the refrain stuck in her head wasn't *More magic!* but more like *What if something happens to Xia while I'm downstairs? What if he goes away? What if somebody takes him away from me?*

She slowed, a hand pressed to her upper chest, which vibrated with an achy hollowness. True, she didn't know the house, and she figured some level of anxiety about the unknown was to be expected. And she sure as hell wasn't forgetting about the copa and the way touching her magic was getting harder and harder. But the panic rising in her about Xia wasn't normal. In fact, the feeling was reminiscent of how she felt when she tried to take off the amulet. Anxious. Resistant. Paranoid. Wigged out and Golemy.

She forced herself to continue down the stairs, and everything got worse. Her stomach hurt, and her pulse drummed in her ears. At least the pain distracted her from that zebra-striped box in the living room that held the best dream of her adult life to date. Inside that box was her ability to use real magic. By the time she found the kitchen, she was trembling, with sweat beading along her forehead. It couldn't be withdrawal. From what Xia had said, a mage had to be using for a while before he was addicted. But geez, coming down from the magic was going to be a hard landing. Nothing to do about that but suck it up like a big girl.

In the kitchen, she rummaged around and found the plastic jug Xia had told her about and a selection of cups made of black glass. Her hands shook hard enough that she had to worry about spilling while she filled the glass with the contents of the jug. The stuff smelled like crap. There wasn't much food in the house—now, wasn't that ironic?—a six-pack of beer with a guillotine on the label and a half-empty bag of tortilla chips. Nothing here but stuff to get cranked on. Beer. Copa. Chips. And Xia. She looked around and didn't see a phone anywhere. No land line. Just great. Her mobile was in her backpack. In San Francisco.

Unless Xia had his phone with him, there was no way she could call for help; by now, she was thinking one or both of them was in serious need of an intervention. She didn't have anything against drinking; it was just she didn't like not being in control. A beer would taste good about now. Maybe a beer would help her forget about copa and tiny little Xias running around at her feet. But what she needed more than anything was to be upstairs with Xia.

Cup in hand, she headed back to the stairs. At the bottom step, she stopped. The brazier was still burning in the living room, giving off a smoky scent. The oil was going to catch fire and burn the house down. With them in it. She put the cup on the bottom stairs and walked in, feeling the trembling start up worse than before.

The zebra-striped box was there. Filled with copa. She had the shakes, but she couldn't help feeling they didn't have anything to do with copa or her magic. The metal bowl holding the oil was scorching hot. She felt the heat even before she knelt to figure out how to douse the source. The problem was immediately apparent. She was going to need magic, and she was on magical low tide. "Great," she muttered. "Just great."

She pulled and got next to nothing. The zebra-striped box taunted her. A little more copa would take care of her problem. A quarter of a pill was all she needed. Maybe half of one. He'd never notice one missing pill even if he bothered to look. She picked up the box with trembling fingers. Panic bubbled up. She pulled again, and this time she caught the upswing of the ebb and flow of her magic. The oil stopped smoking.

She was okay. She'd done actual magic without drugging herself. She clutched the box so hard her fingers hurt. What if Xia needed her magic, and she was back to her usual pathetic might-as-well-be-vanilla self? She fumbled with the box, but it refused to open. "Shit."

She turned her back on the living room and headed for the stairs, still working at the box. Hands shaking, heart pounding, jittery with the certainty that if she didn't get back to Xia, she'd die or worse. *Chik.* The lip of the box lifted. Golden yellow flashed in her vision. Copa. She stopped and opened the box the rest of the way. The pills crumbled easily, she remembered. When Xia had taken some at her house, they were wrapped in paper. She headed back to the kitchen, fighting panic the entire way. In the garbage, she found an old receipt reasonably clean and big enough to serve her purpose. She opened the box again and took out two of the pills, and when it didn't look like too many were missing, she took out three more. She folded the receipt around the pills and put them in her front pocket.

She felt like utter shit. She was a liar. A betrayer. A deceiver. How long had she lasted? Half an hour? Forty-five minutes? And here she was, in trouble already. She was better than this, wasn't she? Alexandrine turned on the water in the sink and flipped the switch for the garbage disposal, then upended the box over the sink. The copa dissolved almost immediately. For good measure, she used the sprayer attachment until there weren't even any crumbs left. She did the same with the pills she'd put in her pocket. Problem solved.

Alexandrine left the zebra box on the counter. Open and empty.

Her panic stayed with her.

She retrieved the cup and started up. Each step reeled in her panic. The higher she went, the closer she got to Xia, the less jittery she felt. By the time she reached the top, her panic vanished. She dimly remembered what she'd felt like downstairs. Xia was half sitting on the bed, struggling with the top button of his jeans, a testament to bad living and insane amounts of exercise. He looked up when she came in, and oddly, she had the impression he was relieved.

She gripped the plastic cup of stinking swill she'd brought upstairs with her. "Here, I brought that stuff from the fridge."

"Thanks," he said. Xia took the cup from her and stared at her long enough to make her feel a bit odd with the silence. What if he knew what she'd done downstairs? He closed his eyes and emptied the cup in one long swallow. When he was done, the cup slipped from his fingers and fell to the floor. The fact that it didn't break had to be a miracle.

"Help me," he said. His breathing was shallow, like he was holding back some major hurt. "I need to get out of my clothes."

She swatted his hand away from his fly. "Let me, okay?"

He leaned back on his elbows, and boy, oh boy, did that do something to his abs. She tugged on his zipper.

"Hurry up, would you?" he said.

"I'm hurrying. Quit moving around, and maybe I can get these off you."

He stretched out a hand and touched her cheek. Heat zinged through her, and behind that was a bone-deep pain. They both winced. His pain flowed back into her. His fingers spread over her cheek. "It's better when I touch you."

"All right," she said. She pressed his palm to her cheek and braced herself for the flash of pain. And, man, she did get pain. Fire burning right through her. The contact also brought her waning magic closer. Her head buzzed, colors flashed, and she felt Xia's magic, her magic, and the talisman, too.

"Baby," he said. "Don't stop. Please."

"I won't."

The tension went out of his face. He went back to working on his pants. Right. He needed to get undressed. She unzipped his jeans the rest of the way. His shivering increased. His skin was hot. Burning hot. She yanked down his jeans and took his socks off, too. When she straightened from that, he was flat on his back, wearing nothing but a pair of black boxers that he was pushing off. He shoved his thumbs in the waistband.

His eyelids vibrated. "I need to be naked, Alexandrine. Have to be." His eyes flashed. In her head, his imperative echoed. *Have to be.*

Xia struggled to sit, and Alexandrine put an arm around him to help him take off the rest of his clothes. The internal chaos that was sending him off the deep end flowed into her with the contact. She felt him relax. Her magic mirrored the pandemonium going on in him. As naked as the day he was born, he passed out, and the chaos in her ramped down. Just like that.

"Xia?" She leaned over him, a hand to his forehead. She got a sense of deepness settling in on him. Whether that was good for him or not, she had no freaking idea. He was still warm to the touch, but not scorching hot like he had been earlier. With some degree of pushing and prodding and pulling that was by no means easy, she managed to get him under the covers. Afterward, she picked up his jeans and boxers with the intention of folding them. Ms. Domestic, she was. She set his knife and scabbard on the bedside table.

His magic was wide open to her. And she could still pull. More now than when she'd been downstairs trying to figure out a way to put out the brazier. Way more. Being around him cranked her magic. Which didn't make any sense at all. She let his magic flow over her, through her, around her, in her.

There was a bathroom down the hall, and she went in to wash her face. Her body ached with a less acute version of the anxiety attack she'd had downstairs. Bizarre. Once again, the sensations put her in mind of how she'd felt about being separated from the talisman. She washed her face and scrubbed her fingers through her hair. There was a new toothbrush in the cabinet along with some Tom's of Maine peppermint toothpaste, so she brushed her teeth. Much better. No expensive lotions in here. Thank goodness. Ms. High Maintenance hadn't made it upstairs, then.

Back in the bedroom, she sat on the edge of the bed and stared at Xia. Pain etched his face, and his body moved restlessly. Once, he hissed, baring his teeth. But he maintained his human shape. Sleeping, if that's what he was doing, didn't look soothing. She remembered him saying he felt better when she touched him. Based on the way she'd kept transitioning into and out of Xia's mental and physical experience, she guessed that when she touched him, some of his pain siphoned off into her, thus providing him some measure of relief.

She touched her fingertips to his cheek, and immediately an echo of pain washed over her. The longer she touched him, the more vivid his reactions felt. Swirling chaos from his magic, amidst which she could occasionally distinguish the talisman, seeped into her. Physically, his body was taut with pain that slammed into her like a rogue wave. With the contact, Xia's expression eased, and his body relaxed.

Alexandrine, however, found herself floating in nightmarish pain.

# CHAPTER 18

$K$ynan Aijan glared at the cell phone on the coffee table. The ringtone was "Linus and Lucy" from *Peanuts*. He wished he'd picked some other ringtone for these calls.

"Are you going to answer that?" Iskander asked. Considering their respective reputations, one crazed killer and one psycho, Kynan thought the query reasonably and politely put.

Iskander was a psycho, sure, but he was a psycho who knew how the hell to have a good time. Whatever the event, Iskander was always fully charged and intent on the experience. He didn't reach out to his fellow kin often, but when he made the psychic link, he burned. Sometimes during an exchange, when the kin were connecting, casually or otherwise, Kynan felt Iskander's sexual desires, his affinity for the male form. For example, he knew Iskander thought Nikodemus was hot, that he'd been with Nikodemus and Carson both, in a manner of speaking, and that he had erotic memories of Harsh. How the hell was Iskander, with his personal dose of craziness, keeping himself under control? It would be nice to know how he was doing it. Kynan wasn't having as much success himself.

Right now, Iskander was gaming with a white-hot passion and didn't bother to take his eyes off the wall-sized media screen in front of them. On-screen, he caught another animated fish. Lucky bastard. Without pausing, he said, "Your phone is ringing, Warlord."

"I'm not answering it." What Kynan needed was to get laid. Despite his current disinclination for the act, he sometimes thought if he didn't get someone else to work him, he'd go as psycho as Iskander. He was having some serious fantasies about making it with a human, especially with Carson Philips. Too bad she was off limits. And these days, calling her *human* was stretching things a bit. There weren't many women who'd be down with what was going through his head these days.

"My friend," Iskander said, "your phone is very annoying."

"That's the ringtone for numbers I don't recognize. Whoever it is will give up, and it'll go to voice mail." As if on cue, the phone stopped ringing. "See?"

Kynan was not in a good mood. Some would say he was in a permanent bad mood. Yes. He was. So what? Even this was better than the hell his life used to be. Fact was, he wasn't getting past his need for Carson Philips. As ordered, he'd killed her parents when she was three and brought her to Magellan. He'd watched her grow up isolated and lied to and smarter than was safe for her. He'd watched Magellan poison her and had even dosed her himself. He'd watched her turn into a beautiful young woman and had constructed elaborate fantasies in which he worked out a way around Magellan's strictures on him in order to get Carson into bed, where he'd either take hours to kill her or bind her to him permanently. He'd come closest to fulfilling the first. After everything he'd done to her, she'd severed him from Álvaro Magellan. Killing Magellan didn't begin to repay his debt to her for setting him free. He'd sworn fealty to Nikodemus, but so what? He owed his debt to Carson Philips, and she wasn't ever going to be his.

"Please, next time answer the phone," Iskander said. The cobalt stripes down the left side of his face got brighter.

"You looking for a fight?" he snarled.

"Not with you, Warlord." Iskander pulled, and that got Kynan cranked up. A little violence might just take his mind off his troubles. "What I want is for you to answer your phone when it rings."

Kynan looked at his mobile, which was sitting there all innocent and quiet. He cocked his head like he was considering the request. "Nah."

"What if that was Xia calling you on some other phone?"

A good point, but Kynan couldn't bring himself to care. "If it rings again, you answer it."

"With all due respect, Warlord, I don't take orders from anyone but Nikodemus." Iskander had the cojones to back up that kind of talk. Few of the kin cared to cross a warlord, which Kynan was, whether he'd sworn fealty to Nikodemus or not. For a psychotic, Iskander was even-tempered, slow to take offense. He lived in a world with different rules. And yet, Kynan had no doubt Iskander didn't give a shit about making his displeasure over ringing phones known in a physical manner. A fight with Iskander would take off the edge that was killing him.

"Like you should talk." One thing he liked about Iskander was the way he was nuts. His mental instability came out in all kinds of interesting ways without regard to time or place.

Iskander shrugged. You never could tell exactly where you stood with a blood-twin. Even a former blood-twin. Maybe the phone thing was going to push him over the edge.

Bring it on.

He and Iskander were supposed to be waiting for word of whatever the hell had happened to Xia. Not so privately, Kynan thought Xia had gotten into a fight with Harsh's sister and then offed her. Considering Xia's attitude about witches and the rumor, backed up by the evidence Kynan had seen at her place when he went looking for Xia the other day, he liked the odds of finding out Xia had killed Alexandrine Marit. It might be a while before Xia decided it was safe to show himself around here. Nikodemus wanted answers, though, and Harsh was ready to come home to kill Xia with his own two hands.

He clenched his Wiimote. Lucky bastard. If anybody got to kill a witch, it ought to be him. He needed it more than Xia.

Iskander slumped on the couch, working his Wiimote for *Legend of Zelda,* intent on fishing as only a psycho former blood-twin could be. Kynan's cell went off again. Iskander stared at it for several seconds. Oddly enough, the phone did not explode or melt. The call went to voice mail, and they went back to fishing. Five minutes later, the phone rang again.

"My friend," Iskander said in a low voice that didn't sound friendly at all, "answer the phone."

"No." Whose idea had it been to play *Legend of Zelda*, anyway? He couldn't catch enough fish, and besides, his shoulder was getting sore.

Iskander grabbed the phone and started squeezing. Kynan didn't doubt he could crush the phone without pulling magic. The guy was seriously strong. They all were, compared to a human. "Say good night, Gracie," Iskander said cheerfully.

Kynan held out a hand for the phone, and Iskander dropped it onto his open palm. He flipped it open at what had to have been the last second before the call would have been sent to voice mail for a third time. He held it to his ear and said, "What the hell do you want?"

Dead silence on the other end.

Kynan's finger went to the disconnect button, but something stopped him. The silence gave him itchy skin. It wasn't Nikodemus. Nikodemus would have taken his head off for answering the phone like that. Harsh would have found a way to freeze him over the airwaves, and Carson wasn't ever going to call him. What woman wanted to call the freak who'd tried to rape her? "Who is this?" he asked.

Through the phone, someone cleared his throat. Her throat. Definitely a female. "I think I have the wrong number. I'm so sorry."

Crap. He didn't think this was a wrong number at all. "Who is this?"

"Um." Another itchy silence followed. "Alexandrine Marit. Harsh's sister?"

Okay, so Xia hadn't killed her yet. Kynan sat up. He

let Iskander feel the mental charge that zapped Kynan through and through. They got a connection going, and that was just what he needed, wasn't it? A psycho's thoughts leaking into his head. Like he wasn't disturbed enough all on his own. "I know who you are," he said into his mobile.

Iskander turned off the Wii and slipped the Wiimote strap off his wrist. The three blue stripes tattooed down the left side of his face started to glow. Yeah, that felt good and twisted. The burn of psycho magic. Kynan got the urge to go out and do some harm.

"Who am I speaking to?" Alexandrine Marit asked. She spoke as if she was afraid of being overheard. What the hell had Xia done now? Or maybe she thought he could reach through the phone and rip out her heart. He wouldn't mind killing a witch about now. Might be a nice way to improve on his shitty day. "Is this Nikodemus?"

"Nikodemus is in Paris with your brother." He wasn't sure how much she knew about Nikodemus and Harsh, or the kin, for that matter. They were better off if he didn't say more than what she seemed to know already.

"Yeah," she whispered. "I know." Another silence stretched out. So. She wasn't a stupid woman.

"This is Kynan Aijan. Put Xia on the phone."

"I can't." She hesitated, and this time Kynan waited out the silence. "Something's wrong with him." She was supposedly Harsh's sister, but she didn't sound anything like what he expected, which was overeducated and bossy as hell. Her voice was calm, but a quiver of anxiety underneath cracked at the end.

"What's wrong?"

He could hear her swallow. "I can't wake him up."

Kynan's body flashed hot. Seeing as how the kin didn't sleep, at least not the way humans did, either she was lying to him or something had managed to take down the meanest bastard Kynan had ever met. Besides him. "Where are you?"

"North of San Francisco. I don't know the exact address."

More points for being smart under pressure. "Sausalito, right? Blue house? On the water?"

"You know it?" Relief filled her voice.

Kynan decided he wouldn't mind the drive to Sausalito. He needed to get away from Iskander and all his psycho energy, anyway, and besides, he wanted to know what the hell had happened to Xia. Maybe he could pretend Alexandrine Marit was Carson. On the other hand, *he* hadn't promised to keep the little witch alive. Maybe he could do Xia a favor and off the witch to get him out of guard duty.

Now, wouldn't that be a fun way to pass some time?

# CHAPTER 19

*K*ynan snapped his phone closed and stood, smoothing wrinkles from his jeans as if he were wearing a five-thousand-dollar suit. At Magellan's insistence, he'd lived in Italian suits for years. For him, custom Brioni. Now, whenever he was reminded he wasn't wearing tailored wool, he got a jolt, especially now that he was back where Magellan had fucked him over every minute of every day. Denim instead of superfine wool under his fingers disoriented him. Sometimes he'd catch himself reaching to straighten a tie he wasn't wearing.

He seriously wished he could kill Magellan again, only slower this time. Make it last. Make it painful.

Now that Magellan was dead, a suit meant one thing and one thing only: enslavement. Anything else, on the other hand, meant freedom. The day he stood in his old room, in possession of his own life at last, Kynan's instinct had been to burn every goddamned suit Magellan had ever forced him to wear. So he did. He'd gotten a nice little fire going after a bit.

He incinerated fifty thousand dollars' worth of Italy's finest menswear, and then he went grunge. Totally out-of-fashion grunge. Old jeans. Cargo pants. T-shirts and hoodies. And, naturally, he was growing his hair. He didn't do anything to it. At all. After all those years with a shaved head, he'd forgotten what color his hair was and whether it was curly or straight or something in between. Thick. Straight. Golden brown. Hell if he wasn't a pretty boy. Took vanillas by surprise when they found out he wasn't as nice as he looked.

"How will I know it's you?" Alexandrine Marit asked.

"I'll ring your cell right before I knock."

She thought about that. He wasn't sure what to make of her cautious question, which was a good one if she was on the level, or her long silence thinking about his answer.

"Okay," she said at last.

He figured she had to be trolling for more of the kin. Xia down, Kynan Aijan to go. The thought of killing a witch gave him a hard-on.

"Please." Her voice cracked with anxiety again. "Hurry."

Iskander turned off the rest of the equipment while Kynan tucked his mobile into the front pocket of his jeans. "You need me along?"

"No." This ought to be easy enough. Retrieve Xia. Give the Marit woman a reassuring pat on the head. Or maybe take her into a room and spend some time putting a period to her existence. Then come home. Text Harsh that his sister was either accidentally dead or that she'd left on her own on account of her being a pain in the ass. "I'll call you if I do."

Kynan took one of Magellan's three Jags out of the garage, and when he got to Sausalito, parked three houses down. He felt the mage about a hundred yards out. Creepy. Made him wonder that the hell Xia had gotten himself into. The fiend could handle any nastiness that came his way; he didn't doubt that. But still. As a warlord, Kynan's body ramped up for a fight whenever something felt off. And this situation felt off in a major way. Spilling some mage blood would improve his mood a hell of a lot, not to mention take off some of the edge he'd been living with lately.

What worried him as he got closer was that he didn't feel Xia. At this distance, given what he was and given what Xia was, he ought to be feeling the presence of one of the kin. Since he didn't, he was probably walking into a trap. Stupid witch didn't know who or what she was dealing with.

There weren't many reasons for him being unable to sense Xia. Everybody's favorite witch killer was too strong for Kynan not to feel him by now. Either Xia had somehow gotten himself taken by the mage inside or he was dead. The one or two other possibilities weren't worth considering, given the risk of walking into a house with a mage of unknown ability inside. He regretted not bringing along Iskander now. A psycho might be just the thing to have watching his back.

Well. He didn't have a psycho watching his back. If Alexandrine Marit had either killed Xia or taken him, she'd die a lingering death if he could do anything about it, and he figured he could. Another mage would be a sweet addition to his kill count. Harsh would just have to spend the rest of his life moaning about his late sister. Kynan spent an extra thirty seconds trying to catch any hint of what was going on in there. Even this close, he didn't get any sense of the kin at all. Damn. Nikodemus wasn't going to like losing Xia.

Payback for the witch was certain. And he had some sweet ideas about how to make her suffer for it, too. Predictably, he got turned on. Yeah, honey. Life for the witch was about to take a major downturn.

Xia's place was right on the water, a spectacular home that must have cost a fortune anytime during the last twenty years or so. For all he knew, Xia had bought it back when a house in Sausalito went for fifteen thousand, tops. He descended the narrow stairs to the door and got a tingle from some serious proofing. Xia was damned strong, enough to challenge his warlord status if he wanted to. With this level of protection, the witch hadn't come through the front door. When he reached the door, with some sort of climbing vine in his face, he found the last received call in his phone log and punched CALL. From inside the house, he heard a cell phone start a series of musical tones. He knocked and waited for the witch who may have taken Xia. Possibly, she was under duress. He didn't think Rasmus was inside, but it never paid to assume, did it? The guy got around like nobody's business.

The woman who answered the door was a knockout, if you liked them tall, leggy, and wholesome. He didn't. He didn't much like the platinum hair, either. He preferred little and delicate. Like Carson. But female sufficed. His body was definitely interested in some recreational hurting. If he was going to settle down for a night of fun with a human woman, he wanted a slut, and Harsh's sister wasn't a slut. Pity. Not that he wouldn't want some one-on-one with her if he was normal. But he wasn't normal. And neither was she; he was face-to-face with a mage about to flame out.

Her complexion was ashen, her forehead shiny with sweat. She must have been pulling some serious magic to be this close to collapse. Of course, it would take some serious magic to kill Xia. So her condition wasn't that shocking. She was wearing old jeans that showed off her long legs and a long-sleeved top that ended about an inch above her low-riser jeans. She had the body to pull it off. Bare feet, too. Her short hair was white-blond without a dark root in sight. She was leaking magic and something else that didn't feel right. Although there was no physical resemblance that he could see, Harsh sometimes gave off a similar vibe of magic that wasn't quite right.

Wasn't that interesting? Harsh Marit's sister was a witch. He wondered how long he could make it last before he killed her.

"Kynan Aijan?" she said. Her eyes were big and more than a little scared. A good act. On the other hand, maybe it wasn't an act. There weren't many mages who could take down a warlord, and one of the few who could was already dead. Another tic in the legend that was Kynan Aijan. On the other, other hand, if she'd taken down Xia, a warlord might not be much of a stretch for her. She looked like she'd been worked over, though he didn't see any bruises. Xia wouldn't have been easy to kill or retake, which would more than explain her looking like she'd run two marathons, back-to-back.

"That's me," he said. Kynan fucking Aijan. Mage-killer extraordinaire. A little blood and carnage anyone? He smiled at her. This was his whole problem, right here. Ever since Magellan, he wasn't really turned on unless he could look forward to dealing some pain.

"Come in."

As Xia loved to say, *fucking witch*. She opened the door and let him in. Once inside, every instinct he possessed screamed at him to kill the witch now and be done with it. If she had managed to take Xia, number one, that meant the kin's bond with Carson wasn't proof against another mage since it hadn't been for Xia, and number two, she planned to do the same to him, didn't she? "He still alive?"

"Yes." She drew in a trembling breath. Beautiful woman, if a bit ragged around the edges at the moment. He got a good close-up look at her eyes, and things just got more and more interesting. She was on the downside of a copa high. The better to take a mageheld with? "We better hurry." She gestured toward the stairs. "I managed to get him upstairs before he passed out."

"Sure," he said.

For a witch, she was remarkably unaware of the kin. She wasn't reacting to him the way the magekind usually did. Jumpy or greedy. Calculating and sly. Superior. Overconfident. Pulling magic to see what it would take to win. She wasn't pulling; he was sure of that. Maybe she had nerves of steel and an Oscar or two sitting on a shelf somewhere. Or maybe she was too high on copa to think straight. A dazzling flameout was right around the corner.

Kynan thought about that. If she started to go, he could

play a little with her before the process either destroyed her magic or outright killed her. He got hard just thinking about that. Hell, he could reenact Magellan's killing if he wanted. Only it would be the way he wanted it to be. Slow and painful. Fun.

She moved past him to push the door closed and shoot the dead bolt. That, he didn't like. He sure as hell didn't want a doped-up witch behind him. He faced her and turned with her as she left the door. "He said no hospital. Insisted, if you want to be precise about it. I should have ignored him, I think. But after he . . ." Her voice shook, and she bent her head for a bit. When she started up again, the quiver was mostly gone. "Well, anyway, I found the cell phone in a drawer and called the number Xia gave me in case something bad happened. And you answered."

There wasn't anything organized about the magic seeping out of her. She wasn't pulling, yet she reeked of magic. Hell if he didn't get a whiff of the kin from her. Strange. The skin across the back of his neck prickled. Carson had felt a little like that the night she severed him. His feelings got all mixed up between bone-deep lust and hot desire to see the witch dead. He could satisfy both, now, couldn't he?

"What happened?"

"I'm not sure." She glanced over her shoulder at him but didn't look him in the eye. "Rasmus Kessler came after us."

Oh. Major deception there. The liar. She was hiding something. She turned around on the stairs and used her fingertips to scrape her hair away from her forehead. The skin underneath her copa-hyped eyes was purplish.

"Harsh was certain I was the one in danger. God, he

was such a jerk about it. But Rasmus was after Xia, not me or even the amulet."

He narrowed his eyes and stopped thinking about having her naked and spread-eagled while he had control of her. The way Magellan used to like. "What amulet?"

She turned around, and he went back to following her upstairs. If she was going to try anything, it had to be soon. Unless she thought she could take him despite him pulling more than enough to snuff out her pathetic mageborn life. She was delusional if that's what she had in mind. Kynan would be more than pleased to tear her head off her shoulders. Might even be kind of fun. Grow the legend. Kynan the mage killer. He could break off from Nikodemus to start his own band of vicious, killing fiends. Their specialty could be killing the magekind and any humans who got in the way. Why, all on his own, he could probably blow the lid off any hope of Nikodemus bringing the kin together.

Apres Kynan Aijan? Armageddon. Had a ring to it, it did.

"Xia kept calling it a talisman." She looked at him over her shoulder again. "Does that mean anything to you?"

For the first time, though, he thought she might be playing him straight. He grabbed the back of her elbow and stopped her from continuing upstairs. His skin crawled from being so close to her poorly controlled magic. He reacted sexually, too. Normal for a fiend to get a hard-on for a witch, so he wasn't too worried. "Did Rasmus do something to Xia?"

She shook her head. "Xia kicked his ass. He was pretty much fine until we came here. More or less."

"I'm sure he was."

"He took the amulet."

More deception leaked from her. He sure as hell wasn't getting the truth from her, was he? "Rasmus?"

"Xia." She waved her other hand. "Amulet. Talisman, whatever the hell it is. Xia took it." Her voice shook. She wrapped her arms around her middle and bent over. Her entire body quivered, and he heard her bite back a groan. "I have to get back to him."

He pulled her upright. Nothing good ever happened to the kin when they were around a copa-addicted mage. She was ashen and shaking. Going into withdrawal, most likely. She was young to have been abusing long enough to be this bad off. Well, let her feel the pain. She deserved whatever she got for getting herself addicted to that stuff. "What happened then?" And then she killed him? Took him down? Murdered Xia in cold blood?

"And we were . . . um." Her cheeks turned pink. "He had the talisman in his hand, and then everything was just burning. Burning white hot." She leaned against the banister and took a sideways step up the stairs until she was as far away from him as his grip on her elbow permitted. "Nothing I did helped him. He was just, I don't know. Unconscious. I didn't know what else to do for him, so when I found the phone, I called. I can't believe I remembered right. And you answered."

"You're telling me Xia passed out?" He pushed her to the top of the stairs. "He's not dead?"

"I don't think so." Her voice got small.

"Uh-huh." He didn't feel a thing. Nothing.

Kynan made it to the bedroom door first. There was Xia, on the bed, flat on his back and under the covers, though he'd kicked off most of the blankets. He was breathing, but Kynan couldn't feel anything from him. Either he was mageheld again—and that circumstance was starting not to fit the facts, because right now Alexandrine Marit wasn't acting like a mage who could pull if her life depended on it, which at the moment it did—or Xia really was out cold. Not many things did that to one of the kin. A talisman was one.

He knelt at the side of the bed and tried to connect. Nothing happened. One of Xia's hands was fisted so tight his knuckles were white. He'd heard some of what had happened with Carson and the talisman she'd stolen from Magellan. His stomach knotted. According to Alexandrine, if he'd understood her correctly, she'd had a talisman and Xia had taken it. Not as in taken it away, but from the looks of things here, as in cracked it. Taking on the life inside.

Had the thing cracked on him without Xia being ready for it? Kynan took Xia's fist. His arm was limp. Completely nonreactive. He tried unfurling Xia's fingers, but that didn't work. They were closed too tight. He unleashed a little power. Nothing much. He tried a little more.

"Don't you dare." The last word came out of Harsh's sister low and venomous. She launched herself at him like she was rocket-propelled. She didn't pull. If she had, Kynan would have killed her on the spot. "Don't you hurt him!"

Now, she was by no means a delicate female like Carson, but in his human form, Kynan was six-four. A mage wouldn't have bothered running at him. A proper mage would pull magic and let him have it. But she didn't. She barreled into Kynan, arms extended, and caught him off balance because he was expecting magic, not a tackle.

At the contact, her magic came out of nowhere and shot through him, and it hurt. Bone-deep. He hit the ground and roared.

His worst fear sprang to life before his eyes. Her magic ripped through him. He wasn't going to lose his freedom again. He wouldn't. He pulled so much power the air over him ignited.

"Don't you touch him like that." Alexandrine bared her teeth and stood over him, fists clenched. Why the hell wasn't she going for the kill? He was down and momentarily vulnerable. "If you hurt him, I will rip off your arms and beat you with them. Do I make myself clear?"

"You and what army?" He was still free. Still in total control of his magic. Why wasn't she trying to fry him again? Why wasn't she doing to him what she'd done to Xia? She'd knocked him on his ass, getting the advantage long enough that any mage worth his salt would have tried to take him. And she didn't.

The answer, incredible as it seemed, was that she didn't because she couldn't.

He got off the floor, temper flaring. Whatever the hell her deal was, he didn't want a mage that close to him ever again. "Witch, I'm trying to help him, for crap's sake." She advanced on him, and he snarled, the sound right on the edge of human. She caught up short. "Touch me again, and your head's going to land fifty feet from your shoulders."

The woman flinched but she stayed put. "Don't you do that to him."

"What the hell is wrong with you?" Kynan stretched out a hand and touched the tip of his finger to Alexandrine Marit's forehead. He got a blast of magic, unfocused and not all that impressive. But he also got a direct line to Xia, which shocked him to hell. The woman gasped, and then her eyes rolled up in her head, and she hit the ground like a sack of dead rats.

"Oh, hell. No," Kynan said. Impossible as it seemed, he finally got what had happened.

# CHAPTER 20

Alexandrine came to with a pounding headache that threatened to turn her stomach inside out. Her head felt like mush, and her nose was getting a strong whiff of hot sand. Swear to God, that's what she smelled. A desert at high noon. Coherent thoughts came . . . very . . . slowly. She was almost—almost—content to drift in the soft heat of her head.

*Odd,* she thought through the mush that made up her brain. She didn't seem to be hearing very well. Her ears were stuffed full of the same pudding in her head. Another problem was that something held her tight enough to have her ribs in a painful squeeze, and that didn't feel so great. Her feet also didn't seem to be on the ground, and her torso was smashed against something else hard with her right arm trapped between. That didn't feel so great, either.

Ouch. Yeah. Definitely ouch. Her shoulder hurt. Her other arm dangled in the air. She remembered she could open her eyes and look. What a genius! She pried open her eyes and got a fantastic close-up view of . . . black. Not an inside-of-the-eyes black, but a cotton-fabric kind of grayish black. She ought to know what she was looking at, but her mush-for-brains couldn't come up with the information. The sensation that she was floating came back for a while. Ah, but what about moving? Was she capable of actual movement? How clever of her. Bodies move. She had a body. She could move and see what happened.

Wriggling didn't do any good. Whatever had her wasn't letting go. She concentrated on making sense of her situation and fighting off the desire to just float in the vast nothingness around her. Concentrate.

Held tight. Feet off the ground. Sandy scent. Cottony-black. People. No. Not people. Xia, who she needed to be near. That jogged her brain but not enough to know who Xia was except that she had to be with him. Out of order and jumbled, and terrifying. She stomped down her panic. The memory gates were switching on now.

She remembered a tall man bending over someone lying on a bed. She had a flash of herself in the shower with a man whose hair was dark and whose body made her ache with desire. But not the man bending over the bed. That shower scene played in her head like a movie. The image of a very large and dangerous man with brown hair, not black, filled her mind, too. Jesus, but her brain hurt. She'd rushed that guy, pushed him? She couldn't remember. Why couldn't she remember? Obviously, the guy on the bed had to be Xia.

*Pop.* Her hearing came back in a rush. For a few seconds, she was utterly disoriented. The noise hurt her brain, and nothing made any sense. All she heard was the ocean roaring in her head with some bizarre pattern of sound twisting through the waves crashing onto the beach. And then—

"—didn't pull, you asshole." The speaker's voice came from a million miles away. "What did you think you were doing, pulling on her like that? You could have killed her."

She was sure he was talking about her. How nice that someone wanted to keep her alive. She tried to speak, but her brain didn't seem to be connected to her mouth, because no sound came out.

"So?" someone replied.

The speaker was whoever was holding her—at last her brain connected some of the sensory dots swimming through her mushy brain. Someone was holding her tight. Too tight. And she didn't recognize his voice, either.

"So," said the nice voice, "she didn't pull, and this is Harsh's sister. Cut her a break."

"She attacked me," said whoever was holding her. Much as she tried, she couldn't make her memories come together enough to feel anything but disoriented. She kept her eyes closed and tried to remember again. Xia was hurt or sick or something else that was dreadfully wrong. A stranger had tried to hurt him, and she'd collided with him. That was the last thing she remembered.

Now, she needed to get back to Xia. Had to. Awful things would happen if she didn't.

"Bring her back here."

"Why?" said whoever had her.

"Jackass." The tension in the man's voice struck a familiar note. She knew him. Xia. She managed to move her head and got piercing pain in her eyes from the light hitting her retinas. She squinted. Her line of sight included a tall, strikingly muscled man standing about five feet from wherever she was. His hair was black and curly, which seemed like it ought to be familiar, yet she couldn't put a name to him. Shower. She'd been in the shower with him, and she needed to get to him. Her memories connected voice, appearance, actions. Their past. Yes. That was Xia. He was naked and holding on to a dresser with one shoulder hunched over like he hurt too much to stand straight. He wasn't looking at her. His attention was above her. On the man holding her. She could see Xia's eyes flickering a weird, impossible color of blue. Jesus, her head hurt. Her stomach pitched.

And then the memory floodgates burst wide open. Xia was naked. But she'd had sex with him, so that wasn't as embarrassing or alarming as it could be. A swift kick of panic sent pure energy into the man holding her. Xia was it for her. Just it. The only. No matter what. She had to be near Xia. Had to be near him. Had to. She had to get back. Because he was her talisman now, and she still had a connection.

"Hell," said the man who wasn't Xia. His voice wasn't entirely unfamiliar, but she couldn't place why she thought she knew him. Magic, she thought. She'd pulled magic and used it against her captor. To no effect that she could tell. She tried to speak again, but was unable to yet. The speech part of the mind–body connection remained nonfunctional. She was having trouble moving, too, on account of being squeezed. "She's coming to."

Whoever was holding her walked farther away from where Xia stood. Inside her, something tore. More pieces fell into place. She was Alexandrine Marit, and her brother's name was Harsh. She struggled and at least some of her parts worked, because the man's arms tightened around her.

"Let go," she said. Her words came out slurred, but he seemed to get the idea that she didn't want him holding her.

"Quit moving." He kept walking, heading downstairs.

Alexandrine lifted her outside hand and started flailing. She pulled as much magic as she could. Sparks showered overhead, then stopped. Pretty but not useful. Her brain was on fire, and the heat was consuming her from the inside out. He was heading downstairs, and she did not want that. The sensation was completely separate from her other feelings. Easily distinguishable and creepy as hell.

"I said, bring her back, Kynan," Xia called out.

The man who'd tried to hurt Xia was named Kynan Aijan, and he was the one holding her. Taking her away. She screamed, and this time her voice worked spectacularly. The back of her hand connected with the side of Kynan Aijan's face, along his jawbone; the contact hurt. Pain shot from her hand to her elbow.

He dropped her, and she rolled down a couple of stairs before she caught herself. She got her feet underneath her and stood on the last step, hunched over, hands over her mouth. The air around her pulsed, coming at her in crushing waves. She looked up and for a split second calculated what it would take to get past the freak on the stairs and back to Xia. Inside, she was nothing but shivery panic and burning down to her bones.

Kynan pressed a hand to his cheek and said in a low growl, "What the hell do you think you're doing?"

At the top of the stairs, Xia shouted. A roar. A deafening, soul-destroying roar. "Kynan, no!"

That's when she got it. What was going on with her and Xia. This wasn't like her previous attachment to the talisman; it was her attachment to the talisman exactly. One and the same. Xia had separated her from the carving but not from the magic. Now that the magic was in Xia, she was attached to him in the same way that she'd been attached to the talisman. "That's not good," she said to herself. "Not good at all."

"What is with you?" Kynan Aijan was big. Way big. And pretty, despite looking like he wanted to hurt something. The side of his face was red where her knuckles had connected. She recognized him, though. And she remembered who he was. She'd let him in the house, because Xia had told her he would help if something went wrong. Well, hello, big strong demon guy. Something had gone terribly wrong.

She struggled to regulate her breathing, but it didn't work. She sounded and felt like she'd sprinted a mile in under five minutes. Without the training. "It's all right," she told Kynan. "I just need to go upstairs, if you don't mind."

Kynan faced her with his arms crossed over his chest, his feet wide apart so he blocked the stairs. "Not until I know what the hell is going on."

She remembered more and more details about what had happened to her. "I called you. You came. I let you in. Because Xia cracked a talisman, and I think it's not going very well for him." She breathed through her mouth until her anxiety settled. "Something went wrong, and he needs your help to fix it."

"No shit." Under his breath, he muttered, "Goddamned witch."

Xia smashed a hand to the side of the door. That got Kynan's attention. She looked at Xia and for a moment saw white. Pure, burning white. She made a move for the stairs, but Kynan grabbed her arm. She managed to keep her cool. But it wasn't easy.

"She's not lying, Kynan," Xia said.

"I'm not letting her near you. Not in your condition. I only just got you back among us. I'm not giving her another shot at you."

"Kynan—"

"When she's not doped up on copa, maybe she can be in the same room as you."

Alexandrine tried to straighten up, but her insides were tearing up. Her legs buckled. She managed to get a hand out to keep her head from breaking open on the stairs. Sprawled on her stomach, she saw Kynan staring at her; his eyes were going all funny. From golden brown to amber and then black as sin, each color full of hatred.

Xia swayed on his feet, his face chalky. He was still hunched over, like his body hurt. From the doorway, Xia said, "She needs to be here. I need her here."

Kynan leaned down and grabbed her by the arm.

"Drop dead," she said.

"You learn the trash talking from Xia?" he asked. He pulled her up the stairs. The closer she got to Xia, the less she shook, the less her body felt like it was ripping up inside. The more normal she felt. By the time they reached the top, she was steady on her feet. She put out a hand, reaching for Xia. Xia stopped looking at Kynan Aijan and looked at her. Their gazes connected.

*Click.*

She saw herself through Xia's eyes. She looked like the worst day hell ever had since Satan moved in. He blinked, and she was back in her body. "Oh, my God," she whispered to him. "Xia, we are so messed up."

As an experiment, she backed away as far as the hallway. Her shakes started again. Close to Xia, she was fine. Normal. Not a care in the world. Away from Xia, the shakes came on.

"Alexandrine." Xia took a shaky step forward. Kynan's hand shot out to steady him.

Another two steps away, and her lungs couldn't draw air. Then she took five steps forward, and the sensation that she was suffocating eased. She closed her eyes, and all she saw in her head was Xia—not the amulet, which didn't exist anymore, anyway, but Xia. Her heart lurched. "Oh, shit."

"Get inside, both of you," Kynan said. He steered Xia back to the bed, leaving her to make her way alone. He put out a hand and blocked Alexandrine's path to the bed, where Xia was now sitting, cross-legged. "I'm not letting you get close enough to touch him," he said. "Hell knows what that might do to him." He grabbed a chair and swung it around to face the bed, gesturing to her. "Pull, and you're dead. Clear?"

Uh-oh. She didn't doubt for a second that he both meant it and could carry out the threat without breaking a sweat or suffering a twinge of conscience. In fact, she was pretty sure he'd think it was fun. "Sometimes it just happens," she said. "I can't stop it. Or make it happen."

Kynan looked to Xia for confirmation on that one. Xia nodded. "Fiend," Kynan said, "we need to have a little talk about you and your witch." He studied her next, and though she didn't have his attention for long, she felt raked over when he was done.

"You aren't going to talk to him about sex, are you?" she asked. "Because, lucky for you, I've already had the talk with him about your fertility thing."

Kynan turned on Xia. "Tell me she doesn't mean what I think she means."

Xia shrugged.

"Xia's a big boy, Kynan," she said. "He knows what goes where and why." She was feeling like she needed a chair, but she wasn't going to give Kynan Aijan the satisfaction. "So do I, as it happens. It was good, in case you're interested. Really, really good. Fantastic, actually."

"Sit down, Alexandrine," Xia said.

She stuck her tongue in her cheek and counted to five. "Xia, what you and I did and what either of us was like when we did it is none of his business."

Kynan touched the top of the chair he'd pulled to the side of the bed. The motion was a caricature of a gentleman assisting a lady to her seat. "I'm not going to pick you up if you fall over. In fact, if you do hit the ground, I'll count this as one of my better days."

She glanced at Xia and assessed whether she wanted to stay where she was and risk falling on her ass or sit down and risk giving Kynan Aijan even one iota more of satisfaction than he already felt. Xia's panther-marked hand was open and faceup. He didn't look so hot to her. If she touched him, she knew she'd feel a fever. She walked forward, but Kynan stopped her with an outstretched arm.

"You don't touch him." He backed her away from the

bed until she hit the chair. "I need answers from both of you." He gave her an ugly smile.

"Five," she said, crossing her arms over her chest. "You don't like that one? All right. How about . . . Constantinople? Or 1066."

"I don't care if you die," Kynan said. "I really don't. I'd be happy to make it happen right now."

"I thought you were trying to hurt him," she said.

"You're a witch. I was checking to see if he was alive."

"That's exactly what you'd say if you were trying to kill him, isn't it?" She kept her shoulders straight and looked him directly in the eye. "How do I know you're not on their side?"

His eyes flickered from golden brown to smoky quartz. "Whose side would that be?"

"One of the men Xia was fighting back at my apartment. A mageheld."

"You can't tell the difference between a mageheld and a free fiend?" he shot back. The air started to feel thick at the same time she got a chill in the back of her head.

"Kynan," said Xia. "She doesn't know what you are. She really doesn't."

"Honey," Kynan said. He had a sneer to go along with the endearment. Lucky her. "If I was working for Rasmus, you'd already be dead. And so would Xia." His eyes flickered again. "In fact," he said in a low, hard voice, "considering Xia's condition, I ought to be asking you that question. What the hell did you do to him?"

She rolled her eyes in Xia's direction. "Are all your friends this charming?"

"Yes."

She pressed her lips together. She didn't trust Kynan Aijan. Not an inch. Heck, not even half an inch. "With your attitude, pretty boy, I don't see much point in telling you anything. It'll be faster if you decide now that this is all my fault, because I'm the big bad wicked witch in the room."

Behind her, Xia sighed. "It's all right, Alexandrine. I promise you, he's a friend. More or less. Kynan, please, will you at least listen to what happened?"

"Go, Xia," Kynan said.

All of Alexandrine's energy evaporated. She hit the wall with no more strength to call on. She sat hard on the chair. If she hadn't landed on the chair, she'd have landed on her butt, and Kynan would no doubt have taken great pleasure in stomping on her while she was down. She covered the back of her head with her hands and started counting the lines in the hardwood floor at her feet. Her desperate urge to be near Xia was gone. She even wondered if she'd imagined her panic attack.

"She had an unstable talisman," Xia said. "Rasmus was after it."

Without looking up, she said, "Bullshit. He was after you. He wanted the talisman, but he was after you first."

"Sure," Kynan said, reasonable for the first time. "No mage can stand to lose a mageheld. Besides, take down Xia and getting the talisman is easy."

Xia kept talking. He left out details about the sex, thank God, because that really was none of Kynan's business, in favor of a boring explanation of how she'd agreed to take the copa so they could work together to remove the talisman.

Next, Xia went off on some theory about how the two

of them were linked, because the sticky parts of the talisman's magic had stayed with her, leaving her still linked to the magic that was now assimilating in him.

Kynan, meanwhile, had walked around the bed and was now leaning against the wall on the other side. The better to glare at her, she decided. He had his arms crossed over his chest. True, he was eye candy to rival Xia. She wasn't going to deny the man was seriously handsome. Maybe even spectacularly so. *Does he change, too?* she wondered. *And if he does, what does he look like? As gorgeous as Xia?* That didn't seem possible.

Whatever the answer to that, his scowl made him look dangerous. Xia had the same dangerous look, only with Xia, there wasn't any need to guess whether he would kill. He would. No question about it. With Kynan, she wasn't so sure. There was something off about him. Sure, he'd kill. She didn't doubt that, but she got the impression he'd rather leave you maimed someplace so you could die nice and slow. While he watched and took detailed notes so he'd do better the next time.

"That's all?"

His stare made her skin crawl. There was a quiet that lasted too long. She let go of her head and looked up. The cold sneaking down from her head to the back of her neck and along her arms was coming from Kynan.

During the silence, Kynan shifted his focus from Xia to her. "Witch," he said softly and very mean. "You shouldn't be here. Not here. Not with Xia. The last thing he needs is to be involved with a goddamned witch."

"Bigot," she said, shooting a look at Xia. But Kynan was right, wasn't he? She shouldn't be here. Well, too bad, because she was.

"Tell us what you did, Xia," Kynan said. "Because we all know there's more to this than just a talisman."

"I bound her magic to mine."

"What does that mean?" Alexandrine asked.

"It means he connected his magic to yours." Kynan shrugged. "If I had to guess, I'd say you two are the closest thing to being blood-twins without actually being that screwed."

Xia didn't react to that. No denial. No admission. Alexandrine didn't know what to make of the silence. She didn't know what a blood-twin was, other than what she could guess from the name.

"Hell. It just happened, all right?"

"Not really seeing that," Kynan said. "You're in so tight with her that it's hard to believe that happened by accident."

Xia clenched a fist and refused to look at Alexandrine or Kynan. "It wasn't an accident."

"What did she do to you?" Kynan's lip curled. "Stop protecting her and just tell me the truth, Xia. One way or another, there's a way out of this."

"It was me," Xia said. "Sorry to disappoint you, Kynan, but this whole mess was me all the way. I got her and the talisman separated, mostly, and then I went a little farther." Xia made a gesture that included his body from head to toe. "And not like this."

"You did her like that?"

"Yeah, Kynan. We did it. Like that."

Alexandrine waved a hand. "Can we please not forget that I'm right here?"

"She's a witch, and you fucked her while you were changed?"

Xia glowered. Black Glare of Death. "She was fantastic, Kynan. I've never had it better. If it had been you, you'd have done the same."

"I don't think so. And if I had, you can bet she wouldn't have lived afterward."

Alexandrine jumped up from her chair, and that brought Kynan off the wall. She speared him with a look. "Drop dead, why don't you?" she told him. She was trembling inside. She didn't understand everything Xia had just said, but she understood enough. She took a deep breath and addressed Xia. "Whatever happened, Xia, is there a way to fix it?" She looked at Kynan, resisting with all her might the urge to rub her arms, and then she looked at Xia, who was looking paler than ever. She was hollow inside. Completely empty. "How do we fix this? Can we fix this?"

Xia shook his head. And then he looked at Kynan and said, "Warlord?"

She peeled her attention from Xia to look at Kynan. "*Warlord?*" Oh, crap. If a mageheld was the second scariest thing a girl could meet, well, a warlord was supposedly the first. "He means you, right?" From what she'd read about warlords, much of it questionable, she was looking straight into a whole new world of trouble. Warlords were fiends with enough magic to fry a dozen mages without a sweat. Warlords commanded armies of fiends loyal to them, fiends who lived to do their bidding, whatever that might be.

"Yeah," Kynan said, obviously enjoying her realization of the skyscraper-sized hole she'd dug for herself. "He does mean me."

She didn't know all that much about the world mages

lived in—much of the information she had access to was incomplete and wrong—but she knew enough to figure that smart-assing her way onto a warlord's shit list was stupid beyond belief.

"That's what I am."

Ice formed around her heart, and yet the odd thing was, she had a glimmer of hope. If he had that kind of mojo at his command, then he wasn't all hot temper and talk. He could do something about this. "So, Warlord, how *do* we fix this?"

He smiled, but he wasn't trying to reassure her. "I don't think you'll like the answer."

"If there's a way to avoid this sinking ship, I'd like to hear about it." She sat back down on her chair.

"Easy," Kynan said. "It starts with your blood and ends with me taking control of your magic."

"Permanently," Xia added. "He means permanently."

# CHAPTER 21

$X$ia didn't give a flying fuck if Kynan had the magical muscle to fix this or not. The warlord wasn't going to play nice; Xia knew that for a fact. He kept himself still, staying in his cross-legged position on the bed. He was a bit in shock that he was thinking he needed to defend a witch without being coerced. But here he was, ready to defend Alexandrine Marit from Kynan Aijan. Rasmus Kessler's little girl. Shit. He'd spent too many years enslaved to her father to have anything but hatred for the magekind. They were vermin who ought to be wiped out, and as far as he was concerned, Alexandrine's father was public enemy number one. Right?

But he was determined to keep her away from Kynan. She was in this mess only because she'd put it all on the line for him. Giving up a talisman and calling Kynan when she was afraid he might die. Who'd have thought a witch would ever do that for someone like him? So, right, he owed her. That wasn't all, though; he was starting to worry there was more between him and Alexandrine than a debt. More than blow-his-mind sex. A lot more.

"What's the matter with you?" Kynan said. "You want to stay hooked up with a witch?"

"Fuck if I know." Big fat lie there. The world had changed without him noticing until it was too late. He was all hung up on a witch. He and Alexandrine couldn't stay like this, but he sure as hell wasn't turning her over to Kynan with his reputation for dealing out pain. Not going to happen.

Kynan faced him and deliberately blocked Xia's line of sight to Alexandrine. The warlord pressed the tip of his index finger to Xia's forehead, and Xia let him in, because connecting with one of the kin was normal, necessary, and in a situation like this, required if they were going to get clear on what was and what was not going down. The kind of mental separation humans endured every minute of their lives would drive one of the kin to madness. He accepted the connection and even took some level of solace from it.

"I can help you," Kynan said softly. "You know I can."

"I know, Warlord."

"Then why the hell do you not want me to fix this?"

The warlord's body filled his vision; Kynan's magic filled his head. Alexandrine was there, too, a presence that got them both worked up, because she was a witch, and her magic was arousing to the kin. Their downfall. Kynan understood a lot now. But not everything.

Xia gave him access to his memories of Alexandrine. All of them. From his initial meeting with her to their sexual encounter, and what he was when he finished. He gave Kynan what he knew about her past and her learning the truth about the talisman she wore, up to and including her agreement to dope herself with copa despite the risks and her personal feelings. And that was the thing, wasn't it? He didn't want to lose her, and he wasn't delusional enough to think that wasn't true even before he screwed up and linked them in both directions.

"Don't be an asshole, Xia," Kynan said. The sexual memories got the warlord jacked. Alexandrine was amazing, and when he changed? That was best of all. There weren't many free fiends these days who got down and dirty with a witch, and doing a human when he was changed was totally forbidden without all kinds of precautions, none of which Xia had taken. "We both swore fealty to Nikodemus." His hand now cupped the back of Xia's head, and there wasn't any mistaking how the warlord's sexual state of mind and body was fixated on Alexandrine. "I'm not letting you go down without help, Xia. Not to a witch. Not to Rasmus Kessler's brat. You need my help. Take it."

Xia leaned away, getting Alexandrine back in his line of sight. She was sitting on her chair, very quiet. Keeping a low profile, though he knew she'd gotten at least some of the exchange between him and Kynan. She was there with him.

"There's another solution," Kynan said softly. He swept his thumb across Xia's mouth and then down along his throat to the cut Xia had made for Alexandrine. His connection with the warlord felt good. He'd been isolated with Alexandrine long enough to want the link with one of the kin. None of his kind wanted to go long without connecting with other kin.

"Yeah?"

"Kill the witch."

Alexandrine's magic flashed but didn't do much, though she did drop out of the psychic connection. Neither he nor Kynan brought her back in. She pressed her spine flat against her chair, watching them with eyes wide and skin the color of white ash. Her eyes were losing that copa-induced gold, but her pupils were still pinpoint small. Killing Alexandrine was out of the question. He'd kill Kynan before he let that happen, and he let the warlord see that.

"You're messed up right now, Xia. You won't feel this way when she's gone."

"She's Harsh's sister," Xia said. He tipped his head, giving Kynan access to the knife cut in his neck. The warlord pressed a finger on the wound and sent a pulse of magic into it. He came away with his fingers smeared with Xia's blood. "You can't just off Harsh's sister."

Yeah, and if Kynan tried, Xia would kill him, warlord or not. No matter what Nikodemus might decide to do to him afterward.

Kynan licked the blood from his fingers, and Xia got a rush of connection between them. The warlord's expression reminded him that Kynan hated the magekind as much as if not more than he did.

"You're a worthy warrior, Xia," Kynan said.

Xia pressed three fingers to his forehead in acknowledgment. Kynan released him to stand in front of Alexandrine, head tipped to one side. She gripped the sides of her straight-backed chair like she was afraid she'd go flying off if she let go.

"I'll kill her for you," he said. He addressed Xia, but he was looking at Alexandrine.

"No, Kynan." He had a burning urge to walk over and plant Kynan a facer just for mouthing off like that.

"Kill me and be done with it?" Alexandrine laughed. "That's pretty pathetic if that's the best you can come up with."

Had to admire the woman's nerve, talking back to a warlord like that. Was Kynan thinking of Rasmus and his white-blond hair when he looked at Alexandrine? He didn't anymore. She wasn't anything like her father. Or any of the magekind he'd known. None of them would have put themselves on the line for him. But Alexandrine had.

"Xia doesn't like my suggestion." Kynan put a hand on Alexandrine's shoulder, drawing a finger up to the nick Xia had made in the side of her throat.

Xia forced himself not to physically react. He had a bad feeling about this. Really bad. The warlord pulled. He sounded all casual and shit, but Xia felt the excitement in him, and a definite arousal. He wanted Alexandrine. Her magic, her blood, and her body. Red welled around Kynan's finger. Not happening. Kynan Aijan wasn't going to get anything going with Alexandrine. No way.

"Killing you is the simplest solution for us all."

"Why don't you kill Xia instead?" she asked. Her sarcasm was lost on Kynan. "Wouldn't that solve the problem, too?" She put a hand to Kynan's wrist and pushed hard enough to break their contact. "Oh, right. But then you'd still have a witch on your hands."

Kynan turned his torso in Xia's direction, licking

Alexandrine's blood from his finger. Their psychic connection flared hot. "See? She doesn't care about you."

"You asshole," Alexandrine said.

"Do you want me to do it?" Kynan asked. "I'm not afraid of Harsh. I'll handle him. Right now, Xia, Harsh is planning how to take your head for this disappearing act of yours. If he finds out you kept her alive until I got to her, you can come back whenever you want. You'd be a hero, practically." He smiled, but it was a smile that reminded Xia of the kinds of things magehelds dreamed of doing to their mages. "She tastes good, Xia. Give me a spare room and an hour or two to get good and worked up to it, and the witch isn't a problem anymore. Guaranteed."

Alexandrine shot to her feet, magic coming out of her wild and scattershot. Her fear changed the balance of emotions between them. Not for the better, unfortunately. Xia got a charge of adrenaline, an instinctive reaction to strong emotion from one of the magekind. He wanted her locked down, under his control. His. Totally his. And Kynan wanted the same thing. Same means, different result.

She was staring at Kynan, her eyes wide open and face dead white. Xia's head filled with the image of him pulling himself on top of her, skin to skin, and biting hard enough to draw blood. Sweet, hot blood. Witch magic resonating in his bones. The problem was the image came from Kynan. That was what Kynan was thinking right now. And the warlord was a nanosecond away from making it happen.

"Get the hell away from me, you sick fuck." Alexandrine pushed Kynan away. Her attention shifted to Xia, and, *wham*, the connection with her was like a bomb going off in his head. She felt it, too. He *knew* it made her feel alive. *Bam* again. Three way. The minute Kynan was back in the connection, all three of them knew a part of her was turned on by the idea of the warlord touching her like that. She didn't like the idea—Kynan frightened her—but something in her wanted it. Bad. What a wicked witch she was.

Her magic echoed in Xia. Hell, he could feel her pulling, and that cranked him up. He and Kynan both responded. Kynan got a hand around the front of Alexandrine's throat and immobilized her before Xia could act. The built-in lure of her magic for his kind was tinged with a sense that she belonged to the kin. Worse than their desire to subdue one of the magekind, with her having that spice of kin in her, her challenging Kynan was like dangling fresh meat in front of a starving lion. Kynan was a warlord, and he wasn't made to overlook a challenge. Nobody challenged a warlord without a death wish or believing he had one hell of a good shot at surviving the consequences.

"You're very beautiful." Kynan brought Alexandrine closer to him. He was reacting on two levels now, his nature as a warlord taking care of a challenge from a lesser fiend and as one of the kin reacting to one of the magekind. Alexandrine was up on her toes, both hands clenched around the warlord's wrist. "We'd have some time first. Before I kill you. Several hours, even. I could make your last time good for us both." He ran his free hand through her hair, letting the white-blond locks spill through his spread fingers. "Would you like that, witch?"

"Let her go," Xia said. He was dealing with his own set of reactions to what Kynan was doing. His muscles rippled as the urge to crush Kynan flooded him. He crouched on the bed, ready to leap, a growl rumbling in his chest. He didn't care that he was dizzy or that he hadn't recovered from the mess after the talisman's magic had shot into him all at once. He wasn't reliable enough to take on a warlord and hope to come out alive at the end. But he was going to try.

"Come off it, fiend." Kynan stroked Alexandrine's cheek. "It's not like she won't betray you eventually. In your own immortal words, she's a fucking witch. She ought to be dead. Let me take care of this."

"You're not killing her," Xia said. On some level, he agreed with Kynan. Hell, yes, killing Alexandrine would solve their issue. But killing her wasn't going to happen. He was responsible for her. For her situation. And, anyway, she wasn't like the magekind who came after the kin. But most of all, he just couldn't give her up. She was his, and he wanted it to stay that way.

"Your funeral, fiend," he said. "No killing the witch. But that leaves only one way to fix this." Kynan's magic went full on, filling the room with power Xia couldn't help but respond to. Even Alexandrine reacted. Kynan set both hands on her face, tipping her head toward him while her hands curled around his wrists.

Her eyes darted to Xia, the whites of her eyes showing. "Is this really the only way?" she asked the warlord.

"Yes," Kynan said. "It is. If you want it fixed right." Alexandrine nodded, and Kynan smiled while he brought her closer. "Then let's go, witch."

The connection went hot and dark and right at the edge of going out of control. The three of them were hooked into each other, and the link was seriously, beautifully fucked up. No wonder Kynan Aijan was feared. He was a sick monster. The magic filling the room quivered. Xia didn't doubt the warlord could do just about anything he wanted to with it or that Xia and Alexandrine would be right there with him while he did.

Kynan leaned closer to Alexandrine, and the connection between the three of them went deeper. Jesus. They were throwbacks to the way things had been before everything went to hell between humans and the kin. Before the magekind started fighting back. Before assassins like Durian were necessary to put a stop to the kin's predation of humans when it seemed like there was still a chance to save the way things used to be.

Magic flowed between them, sharing, even soothing, the chaotic effects of the talisman's magic. Damn, but Kynan had some powerful shit going. Xia felt practically whole. Energetic, almost. And Alexandrine's magic was an alluring spice, amping him and Kynan. The warlord's hand moved forward, raking through Alexandrine's hair. Through their connection, Kynan felt her magic the way Xia did. An intimate bond of witch with fiend thrown in to make her irresistible. If Kynan was remembering the sex, it was without distinguishing the fact that he hadn't been her partner. The memories were shared and real to them all. Alexandrine herself might not be capable of making that distinction right now.

Kynan released Alexandrine. She tilted her head to keep looking at him, offering—if only she knew . . . well, maybe she did—her throat to a monster already smelling blood and high on power. Just to help a bad situation get worse, Kynan's interest level ratcheted up along with Xia's. Throw a warlord's power into a volatile mix and watch everything go boom.

Kynan set the tip of his finger to Alexandrine's forehead. "Ready, witch?"

Her mouth was open as she panted, but she reached up a hand and grabbed Kynan's wrist. Cords of sinew and muscle stood out in her forearm. The skin over Xia's back rippled, and he let the change take him, because killing Kynan would be quicker and easier if he wasn't burdened with his human form. "She's not agreeing. Get away from her, Kynan."

Kynan turned to Xia. "You're sure? I thought you didn't want me to kill her for you. There are two solutions to this that I see, fiend, and you know it. Kill her or I take her magic. That's it. There's no door number three."

"Get away." Xia was on his feet now, standing on the bed, ready to leap. Wanting to leap.

"As you wish." Kynan released Alexandrine, and once again, she dropped out of their connection. He kept a hold of his magic, though. "You two can stay like this, then. Have a long and happy life. All six weeks of it, if you're lucky."

"Shut up. Both of you." Alexandrine pulled in a deep breath. The room stayed silent while Xia and Kynan stared at her. "He has to do this," she said. Her eyes were hardly gold at all anymore. Back to nearly vanilla. "Think about it, Xia. I sure don't want to be following you around like a puppy until the day comes when you can't stand it anymore. Because let me tell you something in case you hadn't noticed: We can't be more than five feet apart before we both start getting the shakes." She looked at Kynan. "If you take my magic, Warlord, what happens to me? Would I still be able to pull?"

"No."

"Alexandrine—"

She lifted a hand in Xia's direction. "It's better this way," she said. "I never really had any magic, anyway." Alexandrine took a deep breath. "All right, then, Warlord. Do it."

"Fuck this," Xia said. He grabbed the front of Kynan's shirt and yanked the warlord forward. Kynan budged, a little, but he kept an eye on Alexandrine like he wanted something tender and human for lunch. And it seemed he did, having volunteered to take Alexandrine's magic and with her having just said that's what she wanted. Like hell was Kynan going to do that to her. She was his, and nothing was changing that. Kynan pushed Xia hard.

"Stop it!" Alexandrine's voice shook. "Geez, you two are like little boys. Can the macho shit, would you? I said let's do it. So let's do it, all right?"

"You don't understand," Xia said. Oh. Crap. Completely the wrong thing to say. Alexandrine gave him a glare that could have melted steel; she was that hot with anger.

"No, *you* don't get it, Xia." She leaned toward him. "You don't get it at all. Since the minute you walked into my apartment, you've been telling me what people like me do to people like you. Did you think I wasn't listening? Or not paying attention to what my father was trying to do to you?" She blinked hard. Xia didn't miss the glitter of tears. Kynan stayed close to her, and Alexandrine didn't back away from him. She threw a hand into the air. "I fall apart if we're twenty feet apart, and so do you. Do you want to live like that? Could you? That's twisted and sick." She closed her eyes for half a second. "We'll start hating each other for real, and I don't want that. I really don't."

"I'm not arguing," he said.

"Good. Since there's only one way out of this, and we all know it, why don't we get it over with?"

"It won't work out the way you think," Xia said.

The warlord gave him a look that said more than words could have about his opinion of fiends who stood up for witches.

"Nothing ever does, Xia." She turned to Kynan and met his gaze head-on. "Warlord." She touched her fingers to her forehead. Guess she had been paying attention. "Whatever you have to do to make this go away, do it."

Kynan smiled. "Sit down, fiend," Kynan said to Xia.

He did. But he stayed prepared. Xia was getting a hell of a wave from Kynan. The flow of magic through and around him increased, and it floated him as high as a kite. Kynan was shaping his magic, focusing on Alexandrine and bringing Xia along. He could feel her, close and real, her magic flaring hot. Alexandrine's fear rolled through him, and Xia edged off the bed toward her. Her eyes were losing their pinpoint status now. She was practically back to vanilla. He stretched out a hand, just close enough for him to brush her shoulder.

"I won't let Kynan hurt you," he said. "Not physically. This is going to be all about your magic. If you're really going to do this, I'll make sure you come out okay. I promise."

She licked her lips, and Xia and Kynan both followed the tip of her tongue. The connection between him and Kynan drew hard at him. The warlord was turned on by Xia's recollection of sex with Alexandrine. He wanted to do her like that, too. He wanted her long legs wrapped around him, hearing her moan while he was changed, going harder and harder.

Alexandrine touched the back of her head. "I'm cold here," she said. "Like ice."

"Kynan's pulling, and you're reacting to that." So was he. Reacting and pulling. The warlord had some twisted magic. His power flashed hot, then settled down.

She rubbed her arms. "Was that him?" she asked.

"Yeah, baby. That was him."

The mattress dipped as Kynan knelt on the end of the bed. He'd already pulled enough magic to incinerate the room. The air got hot, and Alexandrine, whose body wasn't adapted to this, broke out in a sweat. She knelt on the bed, too, rubbing her forearms.

"What's going to happen?" she asked. "Will it hurt? I want to be prepared, that's all."

Kynan leaned forward, looking down into her face. Her eyes were wide open and fixed on his. "I'm going to pull," he said. He put a hand behind her neck, cupping her nape. "You might feel it. If you do and you feel like fighting it, don't."

"How?" she whispered. "How do I do that?"

Kynan's eyes turned dead black. "Just don't, or I won't be responsible for the consequences."

"She can't promise that, Kynan." Xia slipped an arm around her waist. "I'll keep her under control, all right?"

"See that you do, fiend, or I'll fry you both."

"I can handle it, Warlord." Xia reached for the magic building in him. Alexandrine was familiar to him now, and getting himself settled in her head wasn't hard at all. He felt her mind join his and then theirs. He was far from stable, and he had to work hard to stop the chaos in him from boiling over. Despite Kynan being so near, Xia pulled Alexandrine into his arms. Her magic beckoned to him. Sweet and hot. Power rippled down his skin and along his spine.

The warlord returned his attention to Alexandrine with considerable intensity. "All you need to do right now, witch, is fall in. Like you did before when it was Xia. I'll do the rest."

She nodded, but she was stiff as a board and holding on to the bedspread so tight her knuckles were white.

Kynan released some of his magic into her. Alexandrine jerked back and cried out. He moved in, and Xia slid a hand under Alexandrine's chin, turning her head to the side to make things easier. Kynan pressed the side of a fingernail to her throat until blood welled from the cut. The warlord got a taste of her blood, and with that, Xia felt Kynan's magic go in. They both felt her resist. And struggle not to.

Xia had her under control. Only, as it turned out, he didn't have himself under control. Things got fucked up fast.

# CHAPTER 22

*K*ynan Aijan smelled like hot sand. His body radiated enough heat to make Alexandrine feel like she was in the Mojave Desert. In summer. At high noon. His mouth was on her throat, and the freaky thing was how she was losing her sense of where she was in space. She was afraid of what would happen to her when this was over but couldn't see how keeping things the way they were was going to be worth the shit her life would become. No way would Xia be okay with a permanent connection to a witch.

Xia was a familiar, calming presence in her head, but Kynan was there, too, and the warlord didn't calm her down. Her thoughts folded in with Xia's and Kynan's with so little separation she wasn't sure who was experiencing what. Maddy would find this experience fascinating, and Alexandrine tried to commit the details to memory so she could tell Maddy what it had been like. If she lived through this.

The taste of blood flowed in her mouth and down the

back of her throat, hot, sweet blood spiced with magic. Those sensations had to be coming from Kynan, and yet an alien part of her wanted more. She wanted more of the rich, deep taste of blood. Alexandrine reached out and touched. Who? She opened her eyes and tried to move her head. Someone was holding her, but he let her go, and she connected with black eyes: beautiful, intense, black eyes in a strong face. Kynan Aijan. How lovely he was. The image of Maddy she'd held in her head was still there, and Kynan was enthralled by it. She actually felt the warlord searching for more. With a growing horror, she realized her memories of Maddy were there for him to study and commit to memory. Just like his memories were open to her.

She moved toward him, touching his cheek, running a hand along his torso. His magic pulsed in her. He wasn't Xia. She wanted Xia, and this was Kynan Aijan. Warlord. Lover of Magellan, the man who'd enslaved him. In love with Carson Philips, the woman he'd been ordered to murder. A killer hundreds of times over. Because of people like her.

"We're not like him," she said. And she was thinking of Maddy most of all. "She's not like them."

"Xia," Kynan Aijan said. "You need to get her under."

"She is under," Xia replied. "You're the problem right now. Quit jacking off and get this done, Warlord."

The exchange brought Alexandrine's thoughts and perceptions into better order, discreet, individual. Discernible. Kynan Aijan and Xia. And her. Alexandrine Marit.

"You're a pain in the ass, Xia," Kynan said.

"That's what she tells me."

Her head flashed cold, and her blood froze in her veins

as Kynan reached for her magic with the intent to take. Every instinct she possessed screamed in protest.

"Baby," Xia whispered in her ear. His arms encircled her, held her tight against him, but they didn't stop Kynan from coming after her. "I'm sorry," he murmured. "So sorry."

She had to let this happen. She wanted to fight him, but if she did, God help her, she faced a life in which Xia would come to hate her. She'd probably learn to hate him, too. What kind of future was that? If she kept her magic, knowing what the copa would do for her, eventually she'd take it. And then take some more. Until she ended up like her father. Cold. Merciless. A slave to her magic. With blood on her soul. Or dead. Or both.

Kynan's will worked its way inside her. Fear sent her pulse skittering at his continued incursion. Alexandrine reached inside herself, quivering with fear, and let down her defenses; she wanted a different life than the one before her if she didn't. She wanted an independent life. And maybe most of all, she wanted a chance with Xia.

*Baby, it's okay. I won't let him hurt you.*

The process started with unexpected speed. She tried to shout that she wasn't ready yet, but the air around her compressed until it felt solid on her skin. *God, let it be over quickly.* The smell of heat and sand radiated around her. Sound roared in her head. Colors rainbowed behind her closed eyes. A tearing pain set in, continuing, inexorable.

Kynan was cutting her off from her magic. Meager though her abilities were, her magic was a part of her. She hadn't expected to feel like she was being ripped apart.

"No," she said. Out loud? In her head? She struggled to sit upright and then did, away from the comfort of Xia's embrace, sliding off the bed. The cacophony of sound and pain followed her. The major muscles of her legs slivered with pain, a rain of needles beneath her skin. She lurched, moving backward so that she continued to face the bed yet managed to keep her balance.

Kynan's magic came on, taking over her head again. Her vision was doing funny things. Nothing worked the way she expected. Colors bled together again; lines of perspective disappeared or took impossible trajectories. She squeezed her eyes closed and shook herself. When she opened her eyes, she could see again. But everything was different somehow, and she didn't understand why or what or if the world would ever be normal again.

On the bed, Kynan sat on his haunches, hands on his thighs. His eyes were pools of black. Ink black. Midnight black. Forever black. Xia stood at the side of the bed, not far from her, and her heart turned over in her chest at the sight of him. Loss overwhelmed her. She wanted, needed, respected, and maybe even loved Xia, crazy as that seemed, and it tore her apart to think that when Kynan was done, her connection with Xia would be gone. Even though it had to be this way.

Would he want anything to do with her when her magic was gone? Or would he think, *There's a witch well served?* Why would he care anything about her, once there wasn't any reason to protect her? Her legs gave out as Kynan's power surged into her again, enveloping, suffocating her. Ripping away from her.

Gasping, she bent her head down, touching her forehead to the floor, forcing herself to do nothing while this horrible rending of herself went on and on. She felt the moment when her magic became inaccessible. Not gone as she'd expected. Just inaccessible to her. It was as if she were trying to reach through to the other side of a mirror. She could try for the rest of her life, and she'd never be able to step through.

It was over then. Grief filled her. She was separated from her magic. Saved by a loss from which she'd never recover.

Alexandrine lifted her head, and the first thing she saw was Xia. He was close to her, as if he'd meant to go to her and then thought the better of it. If she wasn't in such pain, she could touch him. He was the color of lapis, nothing like his human form, and was beautiful in a way that both terrified and aroused her and reminded her she may have lost more than her magic. His eyes burned blue. Searing hot.

It was over. Everything was over.

Inside her, the tearing pain started again, burning in her, through her. Kynan was an enormous presence in her head, malign and evil. Her back shivered, and she didn't need any magic for the leap of intuition that shattered her. Kynan wanted more than her magic. He wanted her bound to him the way Magellan had bound him. Against her will. Enslaved. The knowledge took root and blossomed outward. If he succeeded, and she didn't die tonight, he'd make it happen eventually. His presence in her head grew, and Alexandrine fought the warlord with everything she had in her.

He was taking control. Making her whatever the fiend equivalent of a mageheld was. Kynan's magic suffocated her. A part of her that wasn't her magic but was still some essential part of her ripped away.

*Help me.*

She fought hard. Holding on with everything left to her. With her eyesight going out again, she was unable to focus on anything that wasn't smack in front of her. She saw Xia stand up straight. The air around him rippled, and then he vanished.

On the bed, Kynan's head snapped back. For half a second, Alexandrine was perfectly clearheaded. She and Xia had made a terrible mistake trusting Kynan. He was after more than her magic and her memories of Maddy. He wanted her to pay for what Magellan had done to him. And now that he knew about Maddy, he'd want the same for her best friend, too.

*Run.*

If she didn't, with Kynan Aijan owning her and her magic, she'd be dead within twenty-four hours. She didn't think for a moment he'd let her live long. No way could she survive the kind of things he wanted to do to her.

The warlord's magic came back at her in a whiplash effect. She screamed, but no sound came from her paralyzed throat.

Kynan Aijan hadn't moved from his kneeling position, though he'd relaxed. He was Kynan. She knew that. Brown hair past his ears, a face a woman would die to have looking at her in passion. And yet, though she saw the warlord, what she felt from him was pure Xia. An invisible wire ran between her and Kynan, but it connected to Xia, who, as far as she could tell, wasn't even in the room anymore.

Her throat felt raw, and when she managed to speak, her words were hoarse. "Xia?"

Kynan smiled, and that's when she noticed his eyes weren't black anymore. They weren't breathtaking golden brown, either. Kynan's irises were white, streaked with pale blue. "Fuck, yes," he said.

A shiver went down her back and lodged in her belly, because the voice was Xia's; everything except the way he looked was Xia. She pushed herself to her feet on hollow legs. "What happened?" she whispered.

The warlord slid off the bed and stood at his full height. Not as tall as Xia but longer legged. "Don't be going all boo-hoo on me, okay? We need to figure out what to do now."

"Xia?"

He strode to her and got up close, sliding his hands from her shoulders and up her throat to hold the sides of her face. "Don't freak on me, Alexandrine. Keep your head on your shoulders, and there's a chance we'll get out of this."

"How?" She put her hands on his chest and immediately snatched them away when his eyes changed color. Flickering from white to blue to brown to black and back to white.

"Kynan wigged out on us," he said. "He got your magic and then he just . . . lost it. If I hadn't taken possession, we'd both be dead."

Alexandrine backed away; she had no doubt in her mind that this was Kynan Aijan standing in front of her, touching her. And yet she felt a connection to Xia, and it came from the warlord who was looking at her with Xia's eyes.

"Babe, babe." Xia's voice again. "You're freaking. That's not productive."

"Is this permanent? Are you trapped in there? Xia?" She stepped close. "If you don't tell me what's going on, I really am going to freak."

His body went hot, and then Kynan growled, a sound that froze Alexandrine where she was. "I can't hold him much longer." His eyes flashed through shades of blue and, finally, back to white. "You can't be in here when I let him go, Alexandrine. You need to get the hell out of here."

"Bullshit," she said. "He'll kill you."

"Maybe."

Inspiration, or just pure desperation, hit. "Where's your knife?" she asked.

"Get out, Alexandrine."

She grabbed his scabbarded knife, shoved it in her front pocket, and dragged him down the stairs after her. The brazier was still hot. She pulled out Xia's knife, letting the scabbard fall to the floor, and yanked on Xia's hand. "Down. Now. On the floor."

Xia, in Kynan's body, stretched out on the floor. Alexandrine straddled his torso. Her hands shook as she pulled the knife from its scabbard. The blade glowed blue in the dimness. She let the scabbard fall to the floor and put the point of the blade under Kynan's chin. She touched his cheek. "Thanks, Xia. Now, let him out. Or you get out, however the hell that works."

"Watch out with that thing—it's sharp."

"Yeah, I know." She managed a smile. "Do what I said, Xia." She tightened her thighs around Kynan's rib cage and tensed. The air heated again, but she didn't feel any corresponding chill in her head. No prickling along her arms. She didn't dare look, so she sensed, rather than saw, Xia leave the warlord. She pushed the knife closer to his chin. His eyes flickered. Brown eyes, close to black. "You pull, Kynan Aijan," she said, "or try anything at all, and you're toast. We clear?"

# CHAPTER 23

$X$ia stayed in his nonhuman form once he let go of Kynan. Warlords had killed for lesser infractions than what he'd just done, which was break one of the kin's primary rules—possession without consent was forbidden. He expected Kynan would want to pound him down to the size of a brick. He was not, however, so contrite about what he'd done that he wasn't prepared for Kynan's retaliation against Alexandrine. Xia made sure he held enough magic to put some serious hurt on the warlord before he went down.

Only, Alexandrine managed to have thrown a major kink in things. She pressed a hand to the warlord's shoulder and kept the point of Xia's knife right above the knob of Kynan's throat.

"Don't even think about it," she said to Kynan. With her voice all hoarse, she sounded damned scary. "You pull, you even blink, and you're dead."

"Something wrong?" Kynan asked. For a pissed-off warlord, he looked normal enough, but Xia felt the power gathering in him. Alexandrine was oblivious. But he wasn't, and on more than one level. Man, that was fucked up.

"What the H did you think you were doing?" she snarled at the warlord. "You tried to kill me."

"You're a witch." He moved a hand.

"Nuh, uh, uh." Alexandrine put all her weight into pressing Kynan's shoulder flat to the floor. "This thing is sharp. I don't think you want to make any sudden moves when I'm not feeling very steady."

Kynan's eyes flickered through shades of brown and gold. He gave a fake grin. Right. Because Kynan was saving all that magic to take off Xia's head. Right now, the warlord didn't give a shit about Alexandrine. "You're cured, witch," he said. "No more magic. Go forth and re-joice. I won't stop you."

"Thanks. That's so touching." She shifted a bit but kept the knife under his chin. "Now, I want your word you won't harm Xia."

"I promise."

"Liar." Alexandrine moved the knife to the side of Kynan's throat, keeping the blade edges close to his skin. She nicked him, a little deeper than necessary for the oath she was going after, but she didn't know the knife the way Xia did; she didn't know its responsiveness, the way the charged metal reacted to living skin. He knew each and every lethal surface of each and every blade. Alexandrine didn't. Kynan was lucky she hadn't sliced his jugular, and the warlord knew it.

The portion of the talisman's magic that remained

in her flipped on like a light in the dead of night. She breathed deep, and so did Xia.

"Swear it, Warlord," she said, slowly, bending down.

Xia smelled Kynan's blood, too. He and Kynan both felt her desire to taste blood as if she were one of the kin. The warlord's blood was a rich, dark narcotic. No way could she resist. Not ever. Not with the talisman's magic in her. Not with this connection going.

"Xia's a lucky bastard to be free of you."

"Yeah," she said. "Right. I'm lucky, too. Being free of you and all that." She touched the blade to the underside of his chin. "Swear, Warlord. Or my face is going to be the last thing you ever see in this world."

Kynan's magic about boiled the room. Alexandrine twitched, tight with the talisman's remaining magic. She was pulling like she was one of them instead of a witch. Nothing very scary, but damned if she wasn't pulling magic like one of the kin. Which made a scary kind of sense. Kynan had cut her off from her own magic. The magic she could pull now could only come from the talisman.

"I swear, witch, I will not harm Xia."

"That's good." Her voice was soft, raspy still. Very sexy. She leaned over Kynan, clutching the knife, and sealed the deal with a taste of the warlord's blood. Kynan's eyes closed, and his hand came up to grab the back of her head and hold her there.

Xia felt every moment of it, the way she responded, Kynan's response, the oath taking hold. The warlord had it bad for her. The guy was hot for the witch. Xia returned to his human form and crouched by the two of them. He swept a finger through the slice in the warlord's neck and licked away the blood.

Kynan growled and rolled, crushing Alexandrine to the floor. Her eyes were unfocused, because she'd had a taste of Kynan Aijan.

Alexandrine already had the knife up. "No." There wasn't anything unfocused about her eyes now. "No way am I letting you touch me. Not like that."

"You poor bastard," Xia said to Kynan. He was getting a full-on dose of the warlord. "Witches do it for you, don't they?" He grabbed Kynan's shoulder and pulled him off Alexandrine. He got a flash of a woman's face—Alexandrine's friend Maddy—right before he cut off their connection. "Leave her alone," Xia said.

"What for? She's a witch." With a growl, Kynan got to his feet.

Xia reached down and offered his hand to Alexandrine. Which she took.

"I didn't promise not to harm your little witch, Xia," Kynan said. "Or any other witch."

"Get out of here, Kynan. Go home." He grabbed Kynan's upper arm. "Maybe I did something I shouldn't have, but I'll deal with the consequences, all right?"

"What's your witch going to say when she finds out?" Kynan asked.

"I said I'll deal with it." He leaned in. "Nikodemus won't be happy if he hears what you did, Warlord."

"He won't be too happy with you, either."

"I did what I had to."

The corner of Kynan's mouth lifted. "Given any thought to what that means, witch hater?"

Xia fought down the urge to clock him one and won. He

wasn't wild about ending up in a fight with Kynan Aijan. He pressed three fingers to his forehead and bowed. "You got out of control, Warlord. I made sure she didn't die."

Kynan touched his forehead, too. "My apologies, fiend." He said it straight up. Confessed his sin like the warlord he was. No excuses. Even though he had a good one. Just not good enough, in Xia's book.

All the former magehelds sworn to Nikodemus were major misfits, explosions waiting to happen as they coped with freedom and the weight of their past. Kynan had been Magellan's mageheld. His personal killer and fuck buddy. He'd lived with Carson Philips, snatched her from her parents, been with her every day, watching what Magellan did to her. Everyone at the Tiburon house knew Magellan had sent Kynan after Carson with a kill order and permission to do whatever he wanted in the process and that he'd gotten more than a start on that, too. Now Xia knew what Kynan had wanted from Carson and that he'd tried to get the same from Alexandrine.

Xia bowed his head again, three fingers to his forehead. "Warlord. You should go home."

Alexandrine didn't say anything until Kynan was gone, but she looked relieved when Xia closed the door after the warlord. Relieved to have him gone; then she tensed again. Right. With just the two of them here now, they stood in the living room in an awkward silence that kept getting bigger and wider. Xia turned on his heel and stalked into the kitchen. She stayed there, alone in the other room, while he opened the fridge and grabbed a La Guillotine Ale. He didn't get the shakes. No gut-wrenching need to have her near him. He kind of missed it, though.

He studied the inside of the fridge. He didn't have any

food, but he did have those La Guillotines. He grabbed another, one for him and one for her, and then remembered Alexandrine didn't smoke, drink, do drugs, or talk dirty. Well, sometimes she talked dirty. He stayed in front of the open refrigerator, staring at the remaining ale, his plastic jug of copa-laced infusion, and a shriveled orange. Shit. They were going to starve.

He heard her walking toward the kitchen. At least this wasn't that freaky tether like before. He wasn't panicking at being apart from her; sure, he was glad she was coming in, but not unnaturally so. Aside from the anticipation racing to his balls, he didn't give a shit that she was going to be here in a minute. Well, not really. He was looking forward to being in the same room with her, because she was hot. Aside from that, he was neutral about her. Shit, this was fucked.

Kynan was right. She was going to hate him when she found out what he'd done. To her. To them both.

Here. Now.

He put back one of the bottles.

"Xia." But his name came out in a raspy whisper, and the sound got to him. She cleared her throat and tried again. Louder. "Xia. I think we need to talk."

He shut the fridge and faced her with his La Guillotine in his hand. "This okay with you?"

"It's your house. I can deal with you having a beer."

He popped the top with his thumb and drank about half of it, feeling like a bastard the whole time. He shouldn't drink in front of her if she didn't like it. On the other hand, he really needed a cold one.

"So," she said when he walked to the counter and

leaned against it, his La Guillotine hidden behind him. "I'm not completely clear on what happened."

"You faced down a warlord, that's what." He didn't like what he was feeling. If there was anything about this he could blame on magic, he'd be the first one on that boat. But magic had nothing to do with him wanting her in his arms, and nothing at all to do with the way he wanted her to be with him. Rasmus Kessler's daughter.

"Yeah." She bobbed her head. "Yeah, I did. I'm clear on that. But my magic is gone." She frowned. "Not gone, but blocked off. I assume because Kynan did what he said he would."

"Uh-huh." He reached behind him for the ale and took another pull. Lying to her wasn't good. But how, exactly, was he going to tell her?

"But I still feel you."

"That so?" He was hot for her. More than hot. Shit. He had a lot of nerve giving Kynan a hard time about liking witches. He had his own little case of interspecies fraternization going on here, didn't he?

"Why is that?" she asked. She walked right up to him so that they were less than an arm's reach apart. "If Kynan has control of my magic, why do I feel you and not him?"

"Easy answer," he said. Here came the part where he had to break some bad news to her and lose any chance he had of being with her the way he wanted. He prepared himself. "Kynan doesn't own you; I do," he said.

"Hardy har har."

He drank more of his La Guillotine. He kept his fridge dialed extra cold just so he could feel icy ale slide down the back of his throat. "How about I put this in terms you can understand?"

"Why don't you do that?"

He looked into her eyes and waited until she was looking at him. "All your base belong to me, Alexandrine." She was enough of a geek to understand the hacker joke about a server being controlled by someone on the outside.

"No way." She shook her head. "You don't control me. I wasn't freaking out when you came in here. No shivers. Not sick to my stomach." She went back to the door, where she turned in a circle like she was showing off a new outfit. "See? Perfectly normal."

He crossed his arms over his chest. She did the same, which was kind of funny. Jaysus, he wanted to have sex with her again. "Kynan fixed that before he went off the deep end."

"Pretend I don't know anything, Xia. Spell it out for me. Baby talk if you have to. Tell me what else he fixed and how he did it."

He couldn't help but laugh. "He severed you from your magic and then tried to make you demonheld."

"The way you were mageheld." She nodded. Her shirt rode up, exposing an inch or so of her bare skin. "I thought it was something like that."

He nodded. "I got there in time to stop that, in a manner of speaking."

"Baby talk, remember?" She came back in. Her eyes were suspicious. She didn't trust him right now. Not at all. Smart witch.

"I took you from him. I went in without permission and took it all myself." The sound of the refrigerator ticking was loud in the silence that followed. He stared down the neck of his beer bottle. "He would have killed you, Alexandrine. I could feel what he wanted to do to you. Maybe not right away, but he's messed up worse than I am. Magellan fucked with him; you understand me? He's not normal anymore. None of us are."

"Yeah," she whispered. She pulled out a chair and sat with her heels on the edge of the seat and her arms wrapped around her drawn-up knees. She nodded. "I'm not the same anymore, either. Something's different." She released one hand to touch her forehead. "Here. Only I don't know what it is."

"It's me," he said. Hell, she wasn't going to want anything to do with him after this. "I own your magic. I own you."

"What does that mean? If you give me an order, I have to follow it?"

He shrugged. "I'm not sure. What Kynan did wasn't a ritual I ever saw Rasmus do. He's a warlord. He can do things I can't." Hell. She was going to hate this. "There's no question your magic belongs to me. I can feel it right now. Touch it if I want. If I want, Alexandrine, I can pull from your magic."

"Should be easy to find out, though. Right?" She gazed at him. "I mean, try ordering me to do something. If I was your mageheld or whatever you call it, I'd have to do it, right?"

La Guillotine in hand, he cocked his head to one side. The air shimmered like the floor between them was a miniature Sahara Desert. His spine tingled, and a cold sensation settled in the back of his head. "Take off your clothes."

Alexandrine touched the top of her shirt and unfastened the top button. She did a second and was going for a third when she burst out laughing. "Psych," she said.

He tilted back his beer and drained the contents. The buzz in his head didn't go away.

She laughed. "You totally thought I was going to do it, didn't you?"

He laughed, too. "I totally want to see you naked, that's all." He shrugged. "That kind of shit worked for Rasmus all the time. It was worth a shot with you."

"That's just heinous, no matter what."

She was still laughing, but Xia's chest got tight, and he didn't like what he was feeling. "You're right," he said. "I never should have done that. Not when it might have worked."

"Are you saying you care what happens to a witch, Xia?"

Their gazes met, and there he was in her head. Overwhelming her without meaning to. He was there and in control of her magic. Just her magic, not her will, too, which was a relief. He pulled and got her magic, not his, and he had no idea how to use that kind of power. Her magic wasn't like his.

"Like this," she said. And she did something he almost missed. But he saw how she would have pulled if she were able, and that was enough. He turned out the lights. With her magic. Alexandrine gasped once, and then he shut off his touch.

"Okay," she whispered. "I felt that happen. Whoa. That was just freaky as all get-out."

"Sure is."

The silence got deep there in the dark. Bottomless

deep. He owned a witch. One of the kin hadn't been in control of a witch since the years were counted in three digits. His mouth went dry, and he swallowed hard to compensate. Didn't help much. He grabbed his beer but the bottle was empty. Damn.

"Before I forget or chicken out," she said, "I want to say thank you."

"For what?" He knew he sounded bitter. "Ruining your life? Turning you into a demonheld freak?"

"Better you than Kynan."

"You think so?"

"Yeah, I do." In the dark, she rocked on her feet.

Xia said, "You okay with this?"

"More or less. Depends."

"Carson is cut off from her magic, too. But she came out okay."

"What happened to her?"

"Magellan." He shrugged. "Then she assimilated with a talisman, the whole thing. Even though you have a little of our magic in you, I doubt you can do what she does."

"Which is?"

"Sever magehelds from the mage who holds them."

"Wow." Her eyes opened wide. "Really?"

He got a little thrill, thinking about the implications. "I don't think you can sever a mageheld, but maybe I could—if you were close enough for me to pull your magic."

"You have something specific in mind?"

"I could go after Durian instead of waiting for Carson. We could. The two of us."

She was quiet for too long. Just when he was think-ing her silence meant no way was she working with him like that, she said, "The thing is, I've been standing here thinking."

"Yeah?"

"Mmm." Her voice stayed low. "I've been thinking, I don't want to live like this for nothing."

The cut he'd made on her throat hadn't healed yet, and she'd made some motion that got it bleeding again. His vision was on, because he was working close to the edge. Bright drops beaded along the wound in brilliant red. The scent hyped him up; it was his nature, and besides, he knew how good she tasted.

He held out his hand. "Come here," he said.

She did. He got his fingers around her shoulder and drew her toward him to lower his mouth to her shoulder and taste. It was even better when he was like this, halfway to changing and wound up over whether she'd agree to have sex with him again. And she smelled and tasted and felt so good.

"Fuck me, Alexandrine," he whispered. He meant to add *you taste good,* but the words didn't make it past his lips.

Alexandrine went still. So did he, when he realized what he'd said and how she must be interpreting him. He was pretty sure she was holding her breath. Interesting. She didn't pull back or scream or slap his face. "I don't own all of you," he said. She couldn't miss that he was turned on, considering he had her up against his body. "Just your magic." He buried his fingers in her hair. "And, baby, that means I don't need to be in control of you for us to do this. Not anymore."

"I can say no." She wasn't wondering out loud; she was stating a fact. No big deal at all.

"Are you going to?" He was more turned on than he'd been in ages. She knew she could say no, but she wasn't saying it. Not yet. So, how far did she want to go with him? He reached between them and popped the top button of her jeans. Did she want to have sex with someone like him? She knew what he was now and what was going to happen if she didn't say no. "This okay?"

"Yes," she said.

"That's good," he whispered back. He got his thumb and first finger on her zipper and pulled down. The sound was damn loud. Music to his ears. She stayed still while he unbuttoned her shirt. Two more buttons, and he was going to have her shirt off and his hands all over her. "So, tell me, Alexandrine. Am I gonna get laid again?"

Alexandrine drew in a breath. "Well. Yes. I think you are. Oh, my, Xia."

He growled, and she didn't even flinch. The sound was the kind of bloodcurdling growl that sent her ancestors fleeing to safety several thousand years ago. Shirt off. Bra next. He reached around her and fumbled the hooks. Shit. This was no time to be clumsy. He hoped she didn't notice. But then hooks popped and everything came free. Bra. Gone. She stepped close and put her hands on the counter on either side of him while he got his hands full of her soft breasts.

He leaned back and got a clear view of her body. His arm darted out and snagged her around the waist. She put a hand on his shoulder to keep her balance. Her skin was even softer than he remembered. "I'm going out of my mind here."

Her other hand got busy with the fly of his jeans. "That so?"

She pushed his jeans down, and he stepped out of them, taking his boxers along for the ride. His shirt went, too. He changed form, and hell if she didn't put her arms around him. Didn't even hesitate, did she? The feel of her bare skin against his was a fantastic kink. Human skin against him, soft and warm, and she was willing. She pressed her mouth to his chest, found his nipple, and licked.

He got her out of her jeans and then into his arms to walk her to the kitchen island and stretch her out on the surface. With one taloned finger, he traced a line in the air from the middle of her chest to her pubic bone. She groaned, feeling the magic move from him to her. After tracing a few more lines, he went straight for her core. Her hips arched toward him. She smelled good, tasted good, was wet for him and salty, and he worked her with his mouth, keeping one hand on her bent knee with a gentle outward pressure and using the other to brace himself against the island. He didn't let up until she came.

She didn't have her breath back when he bent over her and kissed her breast. She hissed and arched toward him. Her hands landed on his upper back, and he had to be careful not to scratch her. She completely let herself go, and he dedicated himself to finding out what she liked best about him touching her in this form. Just about everything, it seemed.

He pushed up enough to meet her gaze while he brought her hips closer to the edge of the island. "You know what this means," he said. She nodded. "There's no going back for either of us now."

"Xia—"

He slid inside her, and she adjusted herself until he was there, all the way, all of him inside her body. Heaven. The impulse to mate threatened his control. He was closer to his physical urges now, and when one of the kin was with a human like this, the instinct was all about reproduction.

"You know, right? If I'm in you like this?" He pumped once and about lost it. "Tell me now if you don't want the risk." He shivered from head to toe as he levered back. "I want this with you." In again. Slowly at first, then faster until he was inside her all the way and feeling the pressure of her around him.

"Xia, please."

"I want you. It's you, Alexandrine," he said. In this form, his voice was deeper, rougher. "You're the one." Because she was. Alexandrine Marit was the woman for him. She accepted what he was; hell, she embraced what he was. She got her hand between them again and stroked his cock. He grabbed her wrist and stopped her long enough to say something that not so long ago he'd have thought was impossible: "You're the only one I want."

He saw her smile, soft and a little sad, even, and his breath hitched, and that was it for him. He was gone, and the issue of risk became moot.

# CHAPTER 24

Alexandrine woke up with her face flat on the mattress. Not even a pillow. The bedroom was dark, and beside her the place where Xia should have been was still warm. Her connection with him was in place. This wasn't the same connection she'd felt when her dependence on the talisman was messing with them both. Her link with Xia came strictly from that left-behind magic, and it was as unmistakable as it was foreign.

According to Xia, she'd always feel an awareness for kin who weren't mageheld. Now that her magic was gone, she was realizing just how thoroughly even her meager ability had affected her. An entire level of background noise was gone from her life. The talisman's magic wasn't completely unfamiliar to her; it was just that without her magic, there wasn't any interference between her and what had been left behind. She had a lot to adjust to.

Without opening her eyes, she knew Xia wasn't far away. And yet, something was wrong. The air felt wrong as it came into her lungs and felt wrong on the way out, too. The center of her bones vibrated with a sense of the world being out of step. They hadn't resolved the issue of his big confession; that was one problem. *You're the one.* Human men said stupid things all the time when they were getting hot and heavy. She figured things probably weren't much different with Xia. He'd gotten worked up and out came words he hadn't meant.

She didn't want to put him on the spot by asking if he meant it. Assume the negative. That was much safer. So, she just hadn't ever acknowledged what he'd said. The tactic hadn't been a resounding success. They weren't square anymore. Maybe she should have made a joke so he would know she hadn't taken him seriously. They'd have been better off if she had. But she hadn't and now things were all messed up between them. She hated that.

Without moving, she opened her eyes. Her side of the bed faced the closed bedroom door, which meant she could make out Xia standing in front of it with his head tipped to one side. Through their connection—always on it seemed—she knew he thought something was wrong, too. There was a lot for her to learn with the talisman's magic. Not that she could do much with it, but she did have this unfamiliar and foreign link with Xia. That was something else to deal with, no lie. He took a step toward the door.

"Xia?"

He lifted a hand, a signal for quiet. But their connection got wider, richer. She knew his thoughts and even some of what he was experiencing. Her skin crawled, and the base of her spine turned to ice. She clenched her fists as, through Xia, one of the premonitions she'd been having her entire life shook him hard. She wasn't at all confused about this, even though the sensory information wasn't coming from her. She was getting it through Xia, who owned her magic and knew even less than she did about how it worked.

She sat up. In a low voice, she said, "Get away from the door, Xia."

Xia turned his head toward her. He was in human form, wearing his jeans and nothing else. A splendidly awesome sight, to be sure.

He replied in the same low voice. "Why?"

Was he pulling? Either he wasn't or she didn't know how to identify the signs of him accessing her magic. How completely bizarre to think she was having one of her premonitions but having it filtered to her entirely through her link to Xia. "When I feel like that, something's going to happen. Trust it."

"For real?" His eyebrows lifted and he nodded. Guess he was learning, too.

"It's not a joke, Xia." From Xia, the sense of urgency doubled. "Something's going to happen. Move it."

*Wrong approach,* she thought. Xia was prickly about being told what to do. So, no surprise, he didn't move. He just crossed his arms over his chest and went back to listening or whatever the hell he was doing. The flow of her premonition ceased.

"I'm ready for whatever it is," he said.

Alexandrine threw off the covers, and Xia turned just enough to give her an eyebrows-raised look. She ignored him. No way was she going to face whatever was happening when she was buck naked. She fished around in the dark for her clothes and managed to find her jeans and Xia's shirt.

"How can you tell what's going to happen?" he asked.

She shook her head. "How would I know? You cut me off." Her connection to Xia returned, and so did her ice-cold spine. Alexandrine concentrated on what she was getting from him. "It's hard, getting this through you. It's like trying to walk through a house of mirrors."

The magical spigot opened wider. Icy fingers squeezed her heart. She opened herself wide, and wow, it hurt her brain. She had a pinhole to her magic. Xia had the Grand Canyon. Impressions came at her so rapidly she couldn't process them fast enough. She concentrated harder on what she did recognize. The images and impressions coalesced.

"I don't know," she said. "I don't know how it works anymore."

Xia held up a hand. This time, she felt him pull. A thread of magic that echoed in her. At least this little amount didn't make her dizzy. Whatever he was doing, her premonition didn't go away. In fact, another chill crawled up her spine, a regular iceberg this time. Her fingers shook, but she got her jeans pulled up and fastened and his T-shirt over her head. She tied the shirt in a knot at her waist. Shoes. Where were her shoes? She found them and jammed her feet in her sneakers. Her premonition went off again, bigger. More intense. Something bad was going to happen any minute. If they weren't ready for it, the outcome was going to be dire.

Alexandrine walked to Xia and pulled his knife from

its scabbard. He pulled off his scabbard and handed it to her. "Don't hurt yourself, babe."

"I won't." She snapped the scabbard to her jeans and felt better. Not enough, though. Xia went back to listening and working with his thread of magic. If Xia was feeling anything like she was about the remnants of the talisman's magic in her, which was disoriented and confused, then he had no idea what he was feeling and, likely, had missed most of the information her premonitions could provide.

There wasn't a sound out of place. Nothing that didn't belong. No footsteps. No eerie creaks. But someone was breaking into the house; she was sure of it. Xia continued to pull just that strand of power, a wisp of energy that raised the hair on the back of her neck. He cursed softly.

Her inner ear went off kilter. It was here. Whatever it was, it was here, right now.

"Xia, get away from the door!" Her warning came in a low, harsh whisper. At the same time, she moved toward him. She lurched, off balance because she didn't know how to deal with the different kind of magic that flooded into her from Xia. She landed hard on the floor. So much for being quiet. Xia, however, maintained silence. The man was a total freak of ice-cold nerves. Her hand shot out and wrapped around his ankle. She yanked. Hard. Xia landed on his ass away from the door.

Which exploded inward, sending splinters of wood into the air where his head and chest had been.

"Damn," someone said. "I don't usually miss."

"Fuck," Xia said at the same time.

She was on her feet in one fluid motion, Xia's knife in hand. Light reflected off the blade with a dull blue sheen that wasn't natural given the lighting in here. She got a hum in her fingers that worked its way up her arm. Magic to which she hadn't been sensitive before. She stayed where she was with Xia's knife balanced in her hand. "Next time," she said, "listen to me, would you?"

"We have bigger problems now." Xia grabbed her arm and backed them both away from the door.

"Let's talk about this, Xia," said their as-yet-unseen visitor. "May I?"

Someone walked in. A tall, dark someone with a voice that shivered her insides. Once he was in the room, with the door blasted to slivers, there was enough light for her to see it was the man from the grocery store. The man who'd attacked them at her house. Her father's mageheld, Durian.

"Take another step and you're dead," Xia said.

Alexandrine shoved Xia behind her, or, more accurately, she pushed herself in front of him, because if Xia didn't want to move, he freaking didn't move. Instinctively, she judged the distance between her and Durian and what it would take to put the knife in his heart.

The other fiend took a step back, hands raised. "All I want is the talisman," the fiend said.

Of course. She was a witch, and magehelds were not allowed to harm the magekind unless ordered to do so. Like the shaved heads, that was a fact of their condition. Alexandrine's spine flashed hot, and this time she was able to identify the magic Durian held, though again, filtered through Xia. If she had her own magic, she'd be feeling Durian's power directly while Xia would feel nothing. Instead, she had this bizarre reflection of her magic. Xia pulled harder, which sent the air around them vibrating.

That she felt all on her own. By herself, she could only feel Xia pulling.

"It cracked, Durian," Xia said. "And assimilated. Your mage is shit out of luck. So how about you go deliver the bad news and leave us alone until we can get Carson after you?"

Durian's lip curled. "Rasmus will be so disappointed."

"Xia," she said. Her premonition fired off again, subtly changed because even with Durian right here in front of them, Xia's revelation had shifted the parameters of the danger. "It's you he's after."

Durian glanced at her once, then returned his attention to Xia. He looked menacing in black. Black jeans. A black sweater. Black Vibram boots. His black hair was shorn close to his skull. Of course, being six foot and then some with a dancer's lines kind of added to the elegant bad-ass mystique he had going. Hell, from what she'd seen so far, all fiends were physically gorgeous and scary as heck.

"Are you quite sure, Ms. Marit," Durian said, "that you don't wish to see your father again?"

"Not interested."

Xia turned his head. Damn him, he'd stepped aside so there was once again a clear line of sight between him and Durian. She didn't like this. Not even a bit.

"I'm not letting you take her."

With a chillingly dead smile, Durian cocked his head and said, "What a pity."

She concentrated on processing what she was getting from Xia. She had a new worry now. What would happen if her magic went off the way it sometimes did when she was stressed out? Even when her magic was hers, she wasn't any good at dealing with it, and Xia sure as hell wouldn't know what to do. The entire situation was too new for either of them to know how this worked or affected them.

"Perhaps you'll change your mind," Durian said to her. "Your father finds you far more interesting now than when you were a child. Xia may accompany you, if you like." He inched closer.

"Back off, buddy," Alexandrine said. She could tell Xia was working up to something big with his magic. He wasn't the only one. Unfortunately, Durian was doing the same thing. The pressure in her head kept ratcheting up, a sign, she figured, that her magic was close to boiling over. Durian was pulling; she was getting that from Xia, too, while he ignored what was going on with her magic. Her mouth went dry as a bone.

"It's a shame," Durian said, "that Carson Philips isn't here." He put a hand to his chest and grimaced. His gesture wasn't idle. He frowned and moved his finger up and down the midline of his chest. "Our meeting tonight might end quite differently if Magellan's little witch were here."

Xia lunged and Alexandrine grabbed his arm. "No!" She shouldered her way in front of him again, and he crashed hard against her back. She stumbled toward Durian. The air was so hot around them she practically fried. "Xia, it's a trick. He's up to something."

"Am I deceived?" Durian's eyebrows rose. "A witch protecting a fiend?" He laughed. "Remarkable."

"Fuck off, Durian," Xia said.

"You've gone to the dark side, Xia, haven't you? Letting a witch protect you." Durian put his hands on his hips. "Or has she so emasculated you that you can't take care of me on your own?"

Xia shook off her hand, and everything after that was a train wreck. Durian released his power. As she expected, he feinted at her. Xia stepped in front of her, and that's when Durian let him have it. Of course, she was caught up in it, too. A bonus for Durian.

She might not be able to directly feel the mageheld pulling, but she sure as heck felt his magic when it hit her. She reeled under a concussive shot that short-circuited her brain. A flash of light blinded her, but not before she saw Xia blown off his feet and Durian hurl himself after Xia. Magic lanced through her, bone-deep and so dark and terrifying a scream burst from her. She couldn't move. The world went black and soundless.

When she opened her eyes, or maybe when her ability to process vision and hearing came back, she was on her ass on the floor, facing the blown-out door and surrounded by slivers of wood. The doorknob was near her left shoulder, a mass of melted brass.

She got a deep breath, and her relief at breathing was replaced with panic. Her sense of Xia was gone and so was any echo of her magic. The lack of it knifed through her heart. She peered hard into the darkened room and saw Xia sprawled on the floor with Durian bending over him. Every muscle in her body protested when she tried to move.

Durian looked over his shoulder at her and said, "Don't you ever give up?"

"No," she said, hunched over and gasping for air. With Xia out, she didn't have a link to her magic, but she also didn't have any of the confusion, either. Right now, she figured her best hope was a reprise of what she'd done to Kynan. No magic and take him by surprise.

Xia's knife was still in her hand. With the effects of Durian's magical blast still bouncing around in her head helter-skelter, she was off balance and nauseous. But, hell, she'd felt way worse the time Kynan blasted her. Compared to that, she was in the pink. Even if she'd had her magic, she couldn't take down a mageheld like Durian, but she could slow him down. Sometimes brute force got you what you had to have. The hilt of Xia's knife burned her palm, and she rushed at Durian as hard and as fast as she could.

Unfortunately, Durian's mind was even faster than his reflexes.

She got stopped with the mental equivalent of running into a wall. Her arm froze before she started the downstroke to Durian's spine.

The mageheld's fingers gripped her wrist. He snarled. "Stupid girl."

Durian's magic churned in her, burning the inside of her head. She tried to focus on the talisman's power, because she wanted to blast Durian to heck and back, but nothing happened except that the inside of her skull continued to sizzle. The power to stop Durian remained horribly out of reach. Without Xia, she couldn't get to her magic, and she didn't understand the magic from the talisman, let alone how to use it.

"You're not taking Xia."

"Yes, I am." Durian laughed, but not as if he were amused. "This is your fault, you know. If he hadn't been so intent on protecting you, witch, I'd never have gotten him down." He put a hand on Xia's forehead. "Here's another one for you. Information free of charge. Rasmus doesn't give a shit about you." The fiend hauled an inert Xia to his feet as if he wasn't dead weight. He pressed a hand to his chest and grimaced. "What he wants is Xia back in the fold." The scent of blood welled up, sharp and intense. Was Durian bleeding or was it Xia? "I've been told to make that happen."

Her stomach clenched. "Take me with you, then."

"If you had enough power to make you worth training, Rasmus wouldn't have given you away all those years ago." He draped Xia over his shoulder. "Sorry, witch. But Xia's going back to his master."

"The hell he is."

"That's what all the mages say when they go up against Rasmus." He touched his chest again, and this time Alexandrine was sure the scent of blood was coming from him.

"You're hurt."

Durian sneered. "I'm mageheld, witch. Take my advice. Consider him lost to you. It'll be easier for us all."

"If Rasmus thinks he can make Xia one of his magehelds again, I want some of what he's smoking."

"I do what I'm told. That's it." He lifted a hand and kept it raised between them. "I imagine Rasmus has some thoughts about how to overcome whatever Carson did to Xia and your brother, too, or I'd not have been sent after him." He shrugged and walked out of the room with Xia over his shoulder.

Alexandrine couldn't move for what seemed like an eternity after Durian left with Xia. The more time passed with her mind cut off from her ability to use her body, the more her heart felt like it was being ripped from her chest.

The effect didn't wear off. It just ended. One minute she was frozen with Xia's knife clenched in her hand and the next, her arm slashed down at the point where Durian's spine had been. She was damn lucky she didn't end up stabbing herself. As it was, the blade went a couple of inches into the floor. Oops.

She yanked on the knife and arranged the slivers of wood to hide the hole. He'd probably never notice. Her hand shook when she was done. Her premonitions were still dead-on. Something awful had happened. Xia was gone, and unless she figured out what to do about that, her father might just figure out how to take him mageheld again.

Alexandrine sucked in a deep breath, but it didn't do much good. She remained teetering on the edge of despair. Her father lived in Berkeley, which was at least half an hour from here, provided she had a car and didn't hit any traffic on I-80. She didn't have a car, so it didn't matter if traffic was bumper to bumper or she could speed the whole way there.

Sitting around feeling helpless and sorry for herself wasn't going to help the situation. She clipped Xia's scabbard to her waist, put in his knife, and headed downstairs for the phone she'd used to call Kynan. She punched RE-DIAL. Straight to voice mail. "Crap!"

She left a message along the lines of, *Something awful has happened to Xia. Call me the minute you get this.* In between the words, she might have sobbed. She set the phone on vibrate and stuck it in her front pocket.

Time to take stock. She'd contacted the only person she knew who might be able to get her some help. Kynan wasn't going to want to help her, but he would help Xia.

She was pretty sure of that. But one phone call didn't mean she had time to waste waiting for a call back. If he called, and if he decided to help, it was going to be too late. What else? She doubted Google was going to be of any assistance, and no way was she getting any of her nonvanilla friends involved in this. Maddy was in enough danger as it was.

The thing was, she knew where Rasmus lived. She'd been to his house, and despite the fact that she couldn't touch her magic, she was still a witch. Durian hadn't killed her, and that meant her father hadn't lifted the stricture against harming the magekind. In sum, she knew where Durian was taking Xia, and it was a good bet any magehelds she met there couldn't hurt her. Not unless her father ordered otherwise. Not even Kynan Aijan could claim that level of protection.

She found the rest of her clothes and got dressed. Then she went downstairs and searched the house for car keys or money or maybe a gun—hey, one of those could do some damage. No gun that she could find, but there were twenty-five dollars in a desk drawer and a 1968 Chevy pickup in the garage. The heap of green metal looked like it was held together with chewing gum and bungee cords. No keys. Xia wasn't the type to leave his keys in the ignition, anyway. She found them hanging off a hook stuck to the side of the fridge.

Money, phone, a sharp knife, a broken-down pickup, and immunity from magehelds. What more did a girl need to go on a rescue mission?

She grabbed a black hoodie from Xia's closet to protect against the wind, which was whipping up whitecaps off the water. The Bay Area could get damned cold any time of year. The hoodie was too big, but in her old life, all she'd ever worn were clothes that were too big. She revved up the Chevy. Lucky her, a full tank of gas. At the last minute, she went back inside. She rolled a change of clothes for Xia into a blanket she stripped from the bed and then snatched his shoes.

Alexandrine hadn't driven a vehicle with a clutch since she had been a joyriding seventeen-year-old, but driving turned out to be a lot like riding a bike. A few lurches and a little grinding of gears, and she was on her way to the People's Republic of Berkeley. Since she didn't own a car and the one time she'd been across the bay she'd gone the Bay Bridge route, she didn't know the roads well. Mostly by accident, she found there was a way to the Richmond–San Rafael Bridge not so far from Xia's place. Once over the Richmond Bridge in the no-toll direction, she knew the way without having to guess. The driver's side window plunged into the door after she took the first Berkeley exit, which meant she drove into the Berkeley Hills with a hurricane blowing into the cab. Icy wind roared in her ears. Ah, refreshing.

Half an hour later, she parked the Chevy on Wildcat Canyon Road. The parking brake didn't work, which at last explained the triangular block of wood stowed on the floor of the cab. She got it jammed behind a front wheel before the car rolled too far. She walked up the driveway and was stopped by a security gate. Locked. Hmm. What the hell. She pushed the button on the gatepost. She wasn't going to surprise a mage and a houseful of his magehelds, anyway. Someone inside buzzed her in without asking who she was. They probably knew. What a friendly bunch they must be.

The one and only time she'd been here, she'd chickened out and never gone up the driveway. This time she did, with her hands shoved in the front pocket of her hoodie. Dear old Dad had a shiny dark blue Jag. The motor clicked as it cooled, and the obvious conclusion that Durian had transported Xia in this car kind of pissed her off. Xia got to ride in a Jag, and all she got was a rusted-out Chevy. She squatted down and used Xia's knife to deflate the back tires. Then she walked to the front door and rang the buzzer.

A shaved-headed man who looked like Vin Diesel opened the door.

She didn't feel jack shit from him. "Hi, there." She bobbed her head at him and kept her hands in the hoodie and Xia's knife in her hand. "I'm Alexandrine Marit, and I'm here to see my father. Rasmus Kessler." She stepped inside without waiting for an invitation. Wow. Her father had a damned nice house.

"He's busy," said the Vin Diesel look-alike.

She met his gaze head-on. "Tell him I'm here, please."

"No."

"What the hell is going on?" said a voice she recognized.

"Hey," she said as Durian came down the twisting marble stairs. Paintings, actual original paintings, hung on the walls. She recognized a Cézanne that had been stolen in Zurich. "Guess who?"

"You're a pest, aren't you?" The mageheld walked into the entryway and stood in front of her with arms crossed over his chest.

She grabbed her phone and hit REDIAL.

"Who are you calling?"

"The cavalry." She just hoped they were home and answering the damn phone this time.

"Go home before you get hurt."

She held up a hand. "Do you mind? I'm on the phone." The mobile stopped ringing. Somebody was answering. "Excuse me a minute, would you? This is a personal call."

# CHAPTER 25

*K*ynan waited outside the North Berkeley Peet's, holding his quad macchiato with foam only and kept an eye on the line inside the coffee shop. It was getting dark but not cold yet. His vision was excellent, and he didn't have any trouble seeing. Good thing he didn't wear suits anymore. He'd stand out if he still dressed that way, since everyone else was heinously young and university casual—shorts, sweats, jeans, and T-shirts. Instead, he fit right in.

He was wearing ripped jeans with a black T-shirt and black boating shoes, a beat-up denim jacket he'd borrowed from Iskander was draped over his arm. His hair wasn't long enough yet to put in a respectable ponytail, so he left it down. If he had a backpack, he'd fit right in.

From the sidewalk, he watched the woman get to the head of the line for coffee. She wore ratty blue jeans with pointy leather shoes that dressed up her look. Her hair was such a dark brown it looked black, and her ass was first class. Long legs. An inch of honey-brown skin showed between the top of her jeans and the bottom of her shirt. She had some kind of tat on the small of her back. A tramp stamp. What he could see of the swirling, interlocking pattern of green and blue looked impressive. She'd gotten a real artist to do her up. Most of the men in the place were giving her long, serious looks. Kynan didn't blame them. She looked even better than she had in Alexandrine's memories.

When the witch had her coffee and was heading for the street, he backed away a step and took the opportunity to stare at her some more. She was average height, maybe a little below that, and she was slim, with eyes that seemed to be the same color as her pupils. She had a mildly hooked nose and a full mouth. Native American, he guessed. Stacked, too. She was quite lovely. Perhaps not a raving beauty, but she was getting her share of attention from jerks looking to get in her pants.

He let up on his block so she'd feel his magic. Just a touch. Be interesting to see what she did. He sipped his coffee as she came out rubbing one arm. Her dark eyes settled on him, and he got a once-over. And then the do-over. Now that his hair was growing back and he found hours when he could relax, he was skewing young again. The better to pick up grad students with. Man, she had no idea what he was. None at all. She narrowed her eyes at him, and he smiled at her while he backed off the magic. Oh, yeah. He totally wanted some of that. He took a step toward her, smile in place, and she slowed down.

"Hi," she said.

"Hey. Good coffee?"

"Yes. Yours?"

"Very." He drank more coffee. He hadn't picked up a woman since the days when picking up a woman meant paying for the pleasure of her naked person. He was fairly certain offering to pay wasn't going to work with the delicious Maddy Winters. Kynan nodded in the direction of the sidewalk seating. "Want to sit down a minute and enjoy the evening?"

She thought about it and then nodded. They found a table, and she slung a heavy backpack off her shoulder and onto the sidewalk next to her chair. She stuck out a hand. "Maddy Winters," she said.

"Maddy." He smiled at her, and he clasped her hand. She looked directly into his eyes, and damned if he didn't get a tingle from her that was purely sexual. Nothing magical about it. "Kynan Aijan," he said.

She nodded. "Kynan. Nice to meet you."

Shit. She was seriously beautiful. He thought about putting some moves on the lovely Maddy, who probably didn't want her sex delivered with a side of pain. Pity, because that meant she wasn't going to like it much when they got personal. His phone rang and interrupted his train of thought.

Saved by the *Peanuts* song.

He pulled his mobile out of his jeans pocket. "Pardon me," he said to Maddy. He opened the phone. "Yes?"

"Kynan?"

Alexandrine. "I should have known it would be you." Well, he thought, once he'd gotten over his astonishment at her call, at least she didn't sound teary this time. He wondered if she knew he was sitting across from her friend Maddy. "My boy all right?"

She didn't answer right away, and when she did, she sounded phony. The deliberate kind of phony. "No. I don't think so, no."

He turned sideways so that Maddy couldn't see his face very well. She tilted her head and sipped her coffee. He smiled back. Damn, but she was pretty. Exactly what he needed tonight to get himself over his frustration. There could still be a dead witch tonight. "Where are you?" he said into his mobile.

"Um." Two heartbeats, during which he stared at Maddy's breasts. Nice shape there. "At my father's house."

He froze. "What the hell for?"

Again she didn't answer right away, and when she did reply, her voice dropped in pitch. "Because that's where Xia is."

Kynan's entire body flashed hot. He no longer thought the call was some stupidity on the part of an inept witch having issues with a fiend who hated her but who wanted to boink her. He lowered his voice, too, and that caught Maddy's attention. "What the hell is he doing there?"

"Yeah. Right," she said brightly on the other end of the call. "Exactly. Someone came and got him. Good old Dad."

"Someone took him to—" Shit. He bit back the mage's name. How much did Maddy know about Alexandrine's father? He grabbed a handful of his hair and held on hard. His heart banged against his chest. "Did he go there on his own?"

"No. This guy named Durian came to the house. In fact, I'm standing here looking at him right now."

Durian was bad news. You didn't fuck with a

mageheld of his power. "Durian can't be trusted." He glanced at Maddy, so gloriously and exotically lovely and interested in him, and of course she was listening. How could she not? He lowered his voice again. "He's not free. Capiche?"

"Yes," Alexandrine said. "Just a sec."

Maddy's expression altered slightly, and Kynan felt her magic. She wasn't pulling, not yet. But she wasn't vanilla anymore, either. Like he needed to be more turned on than he already was. Alexandrine's muffled voice addressed someone else. *I'll only be a little longer. Why don't you go tell Rasmus I'm here to see him?* Kynan heard someone laugh in response. A very male laugh.

"What the hell are you doing?"

"He's a bigger pain in the ass than you, if you can believe that. Hey, Durian?" Her voice got a little fainter. "You under any orders from my good old pops right now? Other than to be an ass, I mean. Hey."

Kynan could see her in his head, giving attitude to Durian. "He'll kill you," he said softly. "Without thinking twice about it. Don't piss him off, and get the hell out of there."

"I'm still a witch," she said. "No thanks to you. Durian can't harm me." That magelike attitude of hers was the only reason she was alive right now. Her voice got far away as she addressed someone else. "I'm giving you the benefit of the doubt here, Durian. What's the answer?"

He heard Durian say, "No."

"Great." Her voice came back louder. "Anyway, the thing is," Alexandrine said, "I need to get in touch with Carson Philips."

"She's in Paris." Kynan watched Maddy look at her watch. He shrugged and made an apologetic face.

"They have phones in Paris, I'm pretty sure. Durian is starting to—ouch!"

"What happened?"

"—piss me off. Well, fuck you, too. Listen, Kynan, I need to know how to sever a fiend."

"Are you insane?" Kynan said. It occurred to him that she was talking about Carson and severing for a damn good reason. She wasn't asking because she wanted to know but because she wanted Durian to hear and maybe help her find a way around Rasmus. A delay of a second or two could mean the difference between living and dying. Hell. That was damned smart. No mageheld ever lost an opportunity to stick it to his mage. "Are you still there?"

"Yes. Do you have her number or not?" She sounded like a goddamned witch now, and half an inch away from giving him an order.

He gave the number to her and with a reluctant shrug in Maddy's direction said, "I'll be there as soon as I can."

Alexandrine hesitated before she replied, "That might be a good idea."

Kynan disconnected the phone and thought about throwing the thing into the street. "Family emergency," he said.

"Oh?" Maddy leaned forward, resting her forearms on the table. She wasn't bothering to hide what she was. "You're a very interesting man, Kynan Aijan."

He got a view of her cleavage, so he looked, and the

whole time he blocked himself from her for all he was worth. "Honey," he said, "you don't know the half of it."

Maddy, the beautiful witch, smiled and said, "Half is interesting enough, I think."

Kynan grabbed his coffee and her bag and said, "Let's go."

# CHAPTER 26

$X$ia wasn't surprised to feel Alexandrine. He didn't think she was anywhere near him, but hallucinating that she wasn't far took his mind off the pain. The room where Rasmus had him was magically dampened with respect to anything outside of it. Inside? A magical echo chamber. In here, the effect of pulling magic was redoubled. Since none of the kin got past the walls and door, there was no way he could feel any nonmageheld fiend unless he or she was in this room with him. That meant the change in his psychic sense of what was going on had to be an artifact of what Rasmus was doing to him.

Based on Rasmus's behavior and reactions so far, Xia was convinced the mage had no idea he was any different than he had been before he was mageheld. Rasmus didn't know Xia now had access to magic that sourced from a witch. He had to laugh to himself about it, though. Alexandrine's magic made him a fucking mage when she was around, so he could pull her magic. Why, he and Rasmus were practically brothers.

Not that his new talent mattered much right now. His forbidden witch wasn't anywhere near, so instead of blasting her mofo father to hell and back, he lay naked on a metal table under a suffocating magical restraint. Movement was impossible. No matter what Rasmus did to him, and he was doing a lot, Xia was unable to move or touch any magic at all. His autonomic nervous system, however, remained in fine working order.

What Rasmus was doing amounted to a magical vivisection. The sorcerer was determined to have him mageheld again, which was why he wasn't dead yet, and he was going after Xia's bond to Carson and Nikodemus with a scalpel. Sometimes a hacksaw. He switched between assaults on his magic and physical assaults in the hope that near-death would give him an in.

Not so far.

Rasmus kept bringing him back instead of letting his body succumb. Xia would rather die than be mageheld again, but he was afraid he wouldn't get the choice. Rasmus was determined to find a way to take him, and if he succeeded, then Xia was fucked all over again. Then next time he saw Alexandrine, he'd probably have a kill order from her loving father.

He wanted to disassociate from what Rasmus was doing, but he didn't dare take the risk. He needed to be aware so that the minute Rasmus made a mistake—if he made a mistake—he could break free. And then he'd kill the mage with his bare hands. So far, no luck. The best he could do under his present circumstances was separate himself from the pain. Sometimes it worked for a second or two.

The mage sent a sliver of boiling heat into him, and Xia bit back a scream. Not that any sound would have come out. Something in his chest gave way, and for a moment Xia was fully present in his body. His heart felt like it was on fire and withering to ash. A scream bubbled up from his throat, tearing and burning on the way. With his body filled with magically induced fire, he forced himself to concentrate on the chill of Alexandrine's magic. The cold grounded him and gave him a place to hide his sanity.

"Now, now, Xia," Rasmus said. "Enough of that." He pushed his white-blond hair behind his shoulders. The mage was pissed because he'd been trying to break him down for what felt to Xia like hours. His bond to Carson, created when she had severed him from Rasmus, had so far held up to everything the mage had thrown at him. He suspected his possession of Alexandrine's magic played some role in his resistance. Some of what Rasmus had tried so far was brutal even for a mage. Rasmus frowned and muttered to himself as he lay a hand on Xia's bare chest. Fire seeped into him from the contact. "How did she manage this?"

Xia concentrated on the chill of Alexandrine's magic in his belly and let his mind separate once again from Rasmus's probe. Seeing Alexandrine in person, even if only in his desperate imagination, wouldn't be so bad. She was a head trip, that one. Totally hot in the body department and totally into being out there at the edges with him. There was that witch thing she had, too.

From day one, he'd been turned on by her being a

witch, whether she could touch her magic or not. Matter of course for the kin. But he liked that he owned her magic. Alexandrine might not agree, but the truth was, he liked it a lot. He must be the first kin in hundreds of years to have a demon-bound mage of his own. He needed a way to survive this shit with Rasmus so he and Alexandrine could play with what that meant.

Somewhere, far from Xia's present mental space, Rasmus cursed. Xia's air cut off. He was trying *that* again. Fucktard mage. Trying to get his body to give up and die so that he could slip in and take control during the moments before irrevocable death. Hadn't worked the first twenty times he tried it. Well, maybe this time Xia would die.

The air pressure changed. So did the light. Even in his current state, he felt the magical equilibrium balance out. Someone had opened the door and broken the seal. His sense of Alexandrine and her magic rocketed through him. Nice to have her so close while he was dying. Her witch magic felt good, as opposed to Rasmus's, which felt like a sledgehammer to the back of his head. He could feel other individuals, too. Rasmus, in a different way for some reason, and his magehelds, too. Not as kin—that was impossible—but as Alexandrine must feel them.

Concentrating on Alexandrine helped him. She was a fantasy to get him through the moments until Rasmus gave up in rage and just killed him. Rasmus's sledgehammer broke over him, whirling him into an ocean of pain. Which didn't stop until just before the instant of his death.

Xia lay on the table, immobile but alive and holding

on to Alexandrine's magic as hard as he could. He felt one of the kin, too, more strongly than the others, and again, not in the normal way.

"What is the meaning of this?" Rasmus said.

"Fuck you, mage," Xia rasped when he got air into his lungs.

Except, Rasmus wasn't talking to him. His eyes were focused on something across the room.

"Hey, Dad."

Damn. In addition to hallucinating her magic, he was conjuring Alexandrine's voice, too. Hurrah for going insane. Sexual reminiscences were way more entertaining than wondering what Rasmus was going to try next. He thought about what it felt like when Alexandrine went down on him when he was shifted. The woman had talent and enthusiasm, and he was into watching her get him off like that. True statement: His orgasms were better when he was shifted and when she was all small and human and totally turned on by him. His kind of witch. Alexandrine was good in bed and out. Enthusiastic. Fantastic.

"You okay, Xia?"

That was Alexandrine, talking to him through the fog of his agonized body and mind. God love her. Talking to him like she cared about the answer. She must hate him after what he'd done to her and her magic.

"Xia?"

He forced his eyes open, and hell if Alexandrine wasn't standing ten feet from him. Wearing one of his sweatshirts, too. Durian was behind her, the loser mage-held, looking mean and ready to kill like the assassin he was. Nikodemus should have sicced him on Rasmus before it was too late. Pain shivered him down to his marrow.

Nikodemus's former lieutenant reached back and closed the door. The air pressure changed again. But his sense of Alexandrine's magic didn't stop. The double-ply metal surface was made with a layer of crushed rubies in between, which acted as a shield; no magic got through and none got out. With the door closed, they were in a magical echo chamber. His inner ear adjusted to the change in pressure. If he was going to hallucinate about having forbidden sex with Alexandrine, it was odd that he'd hallucinate Durian, too.

"Answer me, Xia." She was close enough for him to see, and her expression was a mix of fear and concern. And irritation, too. Just like a witch.

"You're not really here," he said. But the words didn't come out. They just zoomed around in his head, looking for a way past the freeze Rasmus had on him. God, she was gorgeous. Not model gorgeous. Really, she was only pretty, but she was his pretty now. His. In his insane world here, she cared what happened to him. At least the real Alexandrine was safe from all this.

"Xia?" Alexandrine took a step toward him.

Rasmus threw up a block that diverted energy from the binding that kept Xia motionless and in pain. She stopped moving, but Xia could feel the space around him now, where before he couldn't. Whoa.

Now that he thought about it, this scene was kind of familiar. Not so long ago, it had been Durian on the table getting his rib cage sliced open—he figured it was a matter of time before Rasmus started cutting—and him watching as Carson and Nikodemus came in and blew everything to hell. Now didn't that just suck rotten eggs? He couldn't even have an original hallucination.

He laughed, and damned if the sound didn't emerge from his throat. The magic holding him down eased up a little more, and he discovered he had the use of his extremities. Toes wiggled. Fingers twitched. Oh, what a lucky bastard he was. Come to think of it, he'd seen that happen back when Rasmus and Magellan were sacrificing Durian for the talisman.

The two mages had already killed one fiend that night, but Durian had been the main course. Laid out and ribs cracked open with his body immobilized and his mind completely aware. Xia remembered like it was yesterday, watching Durian's fingers strain toward the talisman and then, at last, tipping the figurine into Carson's hand. Rasmus hadn't told Xia he needed to watch out for the sacrificial victim, so he'd remained conveniently silent while he watched a witch blow Magellan's plans to the clouds.

"Ms. Alexandrine Marit, what a delight to see you again," Rasmus said smoothly. "You will allow me to say how relieved I am that you are unharmed."

The words jerked Xia back into his hallucination about Alexandrine. Only this wasn't right. If he was going to fantasize about the witch, she ought to be naked. Not dressed in leftovers from his closet. And he wasn't inviting Rasmus or Durian to his party.

"Thanks," she said. "I'm lucky I didn't get hurt; that's for sure."

"Ms. Marit." Rasmus had positioned himself at an angle to Alexandrine and Durian. Xia had a perfect view of all three. "While this is a delightful surprise, I assure you, I am engaged at the moment." He lifted his hands. "Durian, you'll take her upstairs to wait for me?"

"I'm sorry to bother you," she said.

Persistent thing, wasn't she? The chill of her magic felt close enough to touch, and so he did, because her magic didn't hurt him, and Rasmus's bindings, as luck would have it, appeared not to extend to sources of magic the mage knew nothing about and that resided outside his physical body.

"But this is important. I had to see you. Life or death, Dad."

Rasmus didn't answer right away, but when he did, he was as cool as ice. "I'm sure it seems so to you. However, as I said, I am quite busy at the moment. Durian will see you get a cup of tea or coffee while you wait."

"No caffeine for me. Stuff gives me the jitters, you know?"

Xia watched her glance over her shoulder at Durian, and when she did, he caught a sense of her fear. She was afraid of Durian, didn't trust him. Smart woman. She was even more afraid of Rasmus. *She was really here.* It occurred to him that if she was here, then he ought to be able to pull from her magic. He tried and got a blast of cold in the back of his head.

"You got herbal?" Her eyes dilated, and if he hadn't been looking at her face, he might never have noticed her reaction when he pulled her magic. "I'll take some of that, if you have it. But in a minute. Not right now." She returned her attention to Rasmus. "I can see you're busy torturing my boyfriend, but I need a minute of your time." She held up her thumb and forefinger, separated by a half inch of air. "Just a minute."

"I am not your boyfriend, witch." Oh, yeah. The words made it past his vocal cords this time. Xia started laughing. He couldn't help it. Jaysus, but she had nerve. He felt her magic come on stronger.

The icy sensation in the back of his head slid down his neck and into his chest. He pulled. Shit, this whole improbable scene was real, wasn't it? At least it was real to him, and in his world, her magic belonged to him, and he could use it. He couldn't touch his magic—hell, he could hardly move his body—but Alexandrine was here. She was facing down Rasmus even though she couldn't do shit against the mage, or his magehelds for that matter, and her magic was on tap for him. He tried to pull more, but he overreached, and all he got was a headache and a sputter of magic that flickered out.

"Boyfriend?" Rasmus said. His voice dripped poison, the hypocrite; his long-time lover was Iskander's twin sister. It was okay for him to take a fiend to bed but not for Alexandrine to do the same?

"Fine." She crossed her arms over her chest. "Boy toy, then. He's my boy toy."

"That's just sick," Xia said. He laughed again. "I'm not your goddamned boy toy, either, Alexandrine."

She rolled her eyes, but he got the impression he'd hurt her feelings. "Fine. How about fuck buddy? Will that work for you, sweetie cakes?" He heard her mutter, "Asshole."

Oh, shit. She was here. Really here.

"Boyfriends get dumped or picked up for fun. No way am I just your boyfriend, baby."

She reached and patted his arm. "Say, Dad," she went on. "Can you answer a question for me?"

"Durian." Rasmus gestured in the mageheld's direction.

Alexandrine pulled Xia's knife from underneath her baggy sweatshirt. *His* sweatshirt. "No giving him orders. And whatever the hell you're doing to Xia, you need to stop it. Right now."

# CHAPTER 27

You're a madwoman," Rasmus said. "Or ignorant. I don't know which is worse." He gestured in Durian's direction.

"Fuck off, mage," Xia told him. Rasmus didn't know Alexandrine couldn't use her magic or that Xia could. If he did, this would be playing out very differently.

"He's a fiend, Ms. Marit. By his nature, he is evil and depraved. Can you truly be ignorant of what a monster like him would do to us if, as you suggest, I let him go?" Rasmus's magic let up enough that Xia's brain stopped burning. "If I were to release him, I assure you neither of us would be safe."

"Gee, I wonder why? Do you think maybe he's pissed off from the torture?"

"Controlling a dangerous animal requires extreme measures."

"This thing is sharp," she said, lifting Xia's knife. "Standing this close to you, I don't think I'm going to miss when I throw it." She grinned and hoped like hell she was convincing. "I've been practicing."

Rasmus took a step back. Xia got a flash of heat in his chest that came from the mage and from Alexandrine's magic. Rasmus was pulling, and he could feel it. "Do you not understand the consequences of allowing such a creature to be free?"

"Uh-huh." She reached over and grabbed Xia's arm, hauling on him. "Can you get up?"

Not really. But he did anyway, sliding off the table with her help. His legs quivered, but he kept his knees locked. He wanted to lean against something, but, like the door, the table had a core of crushed rubies, and the minute he broke contact, he felt one hell of a lot better. His back itched; because Durian was mageheld, Xia shouldn't be feeling him at all. Through Alexandrine's magic, he could, but not as if he were one of the kin. The sensation creeped him out.

"As inconsequential as you are, Alexandrine Marit—"

"Says Kessler on my birth certificate."

"—you are a witch. One of us." Rasmus kept his distance; the mage knew what Xia was capable of, and it was unpleasant and bloody. Magic still constrained Xia from using his own power. He was counting on Rasmus believing he was safer than he really was. "Xia and all his kind are the natural enemies of humankind. It is our special purpose, the purpose of mages, Ms. Marit, to protect those of our race who lack the ability to do so themselves."

"Protect them from what?"

"Monsters." He was talking to Alexandrine as if he couldn't believe she needed any of this to be explained.

"Demons who destroy lives and impose their will on us. Creatures who engage in sexual congress with innocent women for reasons that would sicken you. Rape. Miscegenation. Iniquity you cannot imagine." Like most mages of significant power, Rasmus's voice was a weapon, too. Persuasive and imbued with a magic of its own. "The great Renaissance of Europe and Britain would never have happened if not for the magekind." Rasmus's mouth contorted. "For pity's sake, you poor deluded girl, mages exist to fight the evil you came here to save. If it weren't for us, humans would still be living in the Dark Ages."

She pointed to the ceiling with her free hand. The knife stayed ready to pierce Rasmus's heart. "How many magehelds are up there right now because you've taken over their lives? How many have you killed so you can look thirty-five instead of moldering six feet under?"

"If I didn't control them, they'd be like Xia. A ravening beast who preys on humans."

"That's funny, because the fiends I've met say the same thing about us." She shrugged. "We kill and murder. Torture. Bigotry must be an interspecies thing."

"Until our kind started fighting back, demons murdered and enslaved us. They procreate with our women." He hit his chest with a fist and waved his other hand in the direction of Xia and Durian. "Do you believe either of these creatures had no hand in such atrocities? They're not new on this earth, Alexandrine. Do you think they've never taken a human woman against her will? Have you asked Xia how many he's raped and murdered? Ask him how many times he's taken possession of some innocent and so destroyed a life."

"By whose order?" she softly asked.

"Long before I took him and made him safe."

Xia tried pulling again. The chill started in his head. He didn't figure he'd get more than one chance to take down Rasmus. He had to do this right.

"I'll be honest with you, Dad. That sounds evil to me. If it's not okay for them to control us, then how can it be okay for us to control them?"

"Come a little closer, witch," Xia said. He snarled for effect. "And I'll show you what Rasmus is talking about."

Alexandrine turned from Rasmus to him. Their gazes locked, and, *bam,* their connection went full on. He had everything he needed. She took a step toward him. And more. "This close enough?"

More than close enough. He owned her magic. Flat-out owned it without any of the limitations that so restricted Alexandrine. Going after Rasmus, however, would only bring the assassin down on their asses. Xia probed Durian with Alexandrine's magic and didn't get far. He didn't know how Carson had managed to sever mageholds. If he fucked up, this could go very badly. Durian reached for his chest, pressing a palm to his sternum, where Xia was sure he had a poorly healing wound.

"I don't know what you think you're up to," Rasmus said to Alexandrine. "But do not delude yourself into believing your magic can harm me or Durian."

Xia kept up his search for whatever it was that bound Durian to Rasmus. Rasmus didn't get yet that it wasn't Alexandrine who was pulling.

"If you don't stop, girl, I will release him."

Alexandrine grinned. "Thanks, Dad. Love you, too."

"Get away from Xia." The air overhead crackled. Rasmus gestured, and Xia felt the mage pull. "Durian, make it so."

Xia got a handle on Alexandrine's magic and pulled as hard as he could. She swayed and grabbed Durian's shoulder to keep her balance. Durian flinched, but not because Alexandrine had touched him. Xia had found something in the mageheld that didn't belong. He punched hard, magically speaking.

Rasmus cocked his head, but he still didn't get what was happening. "Your power, my dear child, and please do not mistake that for an endearment of any sort, is insignificant. You're magekind, yes. I don't deny you that birthright. But you can do nothing of interest to me." He hesitated, and Xia watched the flow of his hair as he tipped his head to one side. Rasmus was catching on now that something was happening that he didn't understand. "Perhaps less so now." His voice went low. "Stop that immediately."

"Gee." Alexandrine took a step nearer to Xia and gave him a panicked glance. Her eyes were dilated to the point where there was practically no visible iris. "I have a funny feeling your kind of power isn't everything it's cracked up to be. After all, from what I hear, Carson Philips didn't have any and look at what she managed. Magellan dead. Kynan Aijan on the loose. Xia footloose and fancy-free."

"Carson Philips is bound to the warlord Nikodemus," Rasmus said. "Of course she can now do interesting things." He looked Alexandrine up and down. "Could it be?" He waved a hand. "Durian, if she doesn't leave in the next ten seconds, kill her. I don't care how you do it. If you want her first, by all means. Just see that she's dead when you're done."

"See?" Alexandrine said. "That's what I mean about you guys. That's just not right." She swayed on her feet, and Xia got some of the backlash from her. She was feeling the effects of him pulling through her. "Xia, now would be a good time to take care of things, please."

Xia punched through to the center of Durian's magic. The mageheld stiffened. The result wasn't anything like the kin-to-kin connection Xia was used to. As far as Xia's magic was concerned, Durian remained a nullity. Yet he did feel the other fiend's magic. Durian's power resonated, and right there at the center of everything was magic that didn't belong. Magic that felt more like Alexandrine's than his.

"Time's up," Rasmus said.

Xia touched the pulsing gnarl with the magic of one of the magekind, but he was a southpaw trying to write with his right hand. Everything felt wrong and backward. Durian lay a hand on Alexandrine's shoulder, and through the contact, Xia felt the mageheld's compulsion to act. He also felt Durian's anticipation—a coldhearted and joyful anticipation of killing one of the magekind. He wasn't interested in sex. What he wanted was to kill Alexandrine and pretend he was killing Rasmus. Wasn't that a familiar feeling?

Alexandrine could have tried to save herself. She had his knife. With that, she had a good shot at killing anything within reach of the blade. But she didn't, because she was waiting for Xia to sever Durian or explode something or fry Rasmus where he stood. With no change in expression, Durian slid his hands around Alexandrine's throat.

"Now, fiend," Durian said to Xia. He'd figured it out,

then, what Alexandrine was to him. Their eyes connected. "Do what you must now, or it will be too late." Under Rasmus's compulsion, the defiant delay cost him. Durian's eyes flared copper red as his fingers tightened around Alexandrine's neck. She grabbed the mageheld's hands, but he bent her head back and kept up the pressure.

Xia battered at the knot in the core of Durian's magic. He didn't know how to unravel it. He could see it, could feel it pulsing, but the goddamned mage magic didn't work the same way as his.

At least Rasmus wasn't trying to take him anymore. No, the bastard was watching Durian strangle his daughter. The hell with this cutting-the-knot crap. He sent a shot of her magic into Durian and freaking burst the thing apart. If it killed the mageheld, too damn bad.

Durian's scream echoed off the walls, but his fingers remained frozen around Alexandrine's throat. She got her hands between his arms and broke his hold on her. The mageheld—make that former mageheld, because Xia could feel him normally now, like a ton of bricks on fire—staggered back, palms pressed to his chest. Alexandrine fell to her knees, sucking air.

Rasmus was as good as dead.

The mage took a step forward, then came to a halt. He knew he'd lost Durian; the fear showed in his eyes. Poor little mage. He'd lost control of his killer, and now he was all alone with a fiend—make that two—who'd spent a lot of time dreaming about killing him. With an inchoate cry, the mage rushed Alexandrine. Magic seethed in the air. He grabbed her by her upper arms and yanked her up. "You little fool! What have you done?" He slapped Alexandrine hard enough to whip her head back. She took it with hardly a flinch. "They'll kill us now if I can't get them back."

"No," Alexandrine said slowly. "I think they'll kill you."

"Durian!" Xia shouted. But the former mageheld was on his knees, fighting to stay upright.

Goddamn, his body hurt. Xia lurched toward Rasmus and Alexandrine. He felt Durian, though there was something kind of jacked up about that, and he still had a handle on Alexandrine's magic and a direct connection to her. The talisman's magic fired off in her, too, making her feel like kin to him, to Durian, and probably to Rasmus.

Xia's body turned to ice. Everything happened all at once and overlapped.

Rasmus pulled, and the talisman's magic in Alexandrine boiled over. The mage yelped and leapt back, but he knew one of the kin when he felt one, and he was at last feeling that in Alexandrine. With a smile, he tried to take the part of Alexandrine that was kin. Xia felt the mage's magic at work. "He's in control of you, isn't he?" Rasmus said to her. "All this time, he's been working you."

"No, he's not."

Xia's heart went cold as Alexandrine's upper body bowed back under Rasmus's assault on her kin magic. Xia went after her, but his body wasn't cooperating well enough yet. He wasn't as fast as he needed to be.

Pure fiend-driven chaos ripped through the room. That was him, losing it. She wavered on her feet as Xia lost control, unable to focus the magic burning through her and without a focus for his magic, either. He was going to end up flaming her out if this kept up. He shoved himself into Alexandrine's head without asking permission, and that gave him what he needed—information about how she'd worked her magic when it belonged to her. She dropped to her knees again, wheezing in short, abortive breaths. Rasmus was doing that to her. At the same time he felt the mage taking control of the talisman's magic, Alexandrine screamed. He felt her pain. Shared it and tried to stop what was happening. Xia got air into her lungs despite Rasmus.

They drew a deep breath, but Xia didn't dare ease up. Her demon-bound magic scoured them both, but he knew how to deal with it now. The problem was his choices were limited if he was going to keep Alexandrine alive. He could take over her body and use it to kill Rasmus, or he could make her his demonheld before Rasmus took her first. Neither choice worked. He couldn't use Alexandrine to kill. Not like that. She'd never forgive him. And he sure as hell wouldn't take her mageheld.

Durian slumped against the wall, hands clutching his chest. The fiend looked out of it. Xia knew the feeling. Back when Carson had severed him, he'd passed out. Well, too bad for the assassin. He directed some of the fire raging through him into the other fiend. "Get over it, Durian," he said. "Make yourself useful."

Meanwhile, Rasmus was at least having to work at taking Alexandrine. The mage pulled hard enough that ice formed on the walls. Xia made it to her just as Rasmus released his magic again. A streak of boiling light headed directly for her. The blast hit her shoulder instead of her head, but she still shut down mentally. The mage's second strike was aimed at him. The air above them started popping. Hail hit the floor.

Xia kept his hold on Alexandrine, shielding her from

Rasmus's assault as best he could. Alexandrine staggered to her feet, his knife clenched in her hand. She made a sound, not unlike a sob. She put his knife on the floor and kicked it toward him.

"Alexandrine," he said. "Take Durian with you and get out. Now."

# CHAPTER 28

Alexandrine lunged for the door on legs made of overcooked noodles. After a heart-stopping moment when she thought they were locked in the room, she found the mechanism that disengaged the hardware. Freaking lock! The metal door felt odd when she touched it, as if there were an energy source inside. Her fingers tingled. Freaky. She yanked open the door and whirled, expecting Xia and Durian to be right behind her, ready to get the hell out. They weren't. Durian was barely halfway to the door, and he didn't look so hot, and Xia was still with Rasmus.

She went back for Durian and grabbed his arm. His skin was hot to the touch. "Move it, buster."

All around them, the air alternately sizzled and froze. Rasmus might be down, but he was far from powerless. Xia knelt over her father, his head bowed like he was praying. Her heart collapsed in on itself at the sight. Hadn't that been what Xia wanted all along, more than anything? His moment alone with her father. Ruthlessly, she cut off the emotion; there wasn't time to think about anything but needing to get Xia on his feet and running out the door with her and Durian. Not praying over a body, for crying out loud. Xia clutched the hilt of his knife in both hands and held it over her father's chest.

"Xia!" she shouted.

There wasn't any blood that she could see, not even on the blade. Rasmus's legs twitched in a trying-to-escape kind of kick rather than a waning-seconds-of-life thing. She still wasn't used to not feeling her magic; even worse, the way her father's power came at her through the talisman's magic completely disconcerted her. It was like looking at the world through the back of a mirror. Everything familiar was reversed. Her pulse thumped hard. They weren't out of danger, not by any means. Rasmus was still alive in a house full of magehelds.

Her father's wide-open eyes were fixed on Xia; however, the alarming thing wasn't the rage in his face but his moving lips. He was pulling. Her demon magic vibrated with it. A part of her wanted to be closer to that much power. The sound of running thundered from upstairs.

"Xia!" she yelled again. "He's calling his magehelds." She could feel Xia, kin to kin, the way she felt Durian now. It was trippy, that connection to the two fiends. She had no idea how to interpret what she was getting from either of them. "Whatever you're going to do, Xia, do it now or give it up." Shit, this was going to hell. She gave up on getting any reaction from Durian. She ran to Xia and grabbed him by the arm. "We have to go. Now."

Xia kept muttering, and she didn't know what to do, because the place where her magic used to be was one huge void, and she had no idea how to use the magic she did have. He was using his magic right now, not hers.

Upstairs, something screamed.

"There's no time," she said. Xia turned his head, and for a moment, there she was in his head. She dropped out almost as quickly as she'd dropped in. His irises were white, his pupils huge black discs, his mouth a grimace. "If you're not going to kill him, Xia, disable him. Now."

"Get out," he said. He shoved his knife into her hands.

"Not without you." She went to her knees. Xia was locked in some kind of mental battle with her father, and it had to end. One way or another. She put a hand on Xia's shoulder and practically fried from the heat of their connection. Her body streaked with pain at the amount of magic Xia was holding. Hers and his, and it hurt. She'd never pulled anything like that amount of magic, and she had nothing left to cushion the effect.

Rasmus was wearing his ruby ring on his thumb. Alexandrine reached out and caught his wrist, pinning it to the floor. With shaking hands, she pulled the ring off his thumb. Rasmus's body bowed off the floor, and he shouted what she guessed was an obscenity in his native language, whatever that might be. But the magic flowing between him and Xia didn't stop. Taking his talisman away from him wasn't enough to stop what he was doing.

"Durian!" she shouted.

Durian was leaning against the wall with his knees bent and his hands on his thighs, but at her yell, he looked up.

"Catch." She tossed the ring across the room. He managed to move his hands, but not in any coordinated fashion.

The ruby clinked at Durian's feet. Nothing changed with Rasmus. He was still able to use the talisman. "Shit."

In desperation, she grabbed Xia's knife and dove for the ring at Durian's feet. She slid part of the way there and ended up rolling into Durian's shins. But the ring was in her hand and that's all that mattered. She got her legs underneath her and did the only thing she could think of, which was to grab hold of what little magic she had—the hell with not knowing how it worked. She just opened herself wide and plunged the point of Xia's knife into the stone.

Everything stopped.

Or else she went deaf and dumb and blind to magic.

Rasmus's body went limp, and his head lolled to one side. There wasn't time to figure out what had happened for sure. His chest was still moving, so he wasn't dead. Pity or not? Who knew? She shoved the damaged ring into her pocket and scrambled toward Xia. Behind her, she heard Durian breathing hard.

She grabbed Xia by both arms. Hell, even Xia was loopy. She shook him hard, and his eyes came back from whatever hell he'd been visiting. "Can you walk? Or do I need to carry you? Because I will, if I have to."

She watched him focus on her until his eyes practically crossed. "I love you, Alexandrine," he said.

"You're delirious, sweetie." Right. Wouldn't do for her to forget that Xia hated what she was. They were going to have to deal with that later, when they weren't in immediate danger of death and destruction.

Durian was the next problem. He was on his feet and stable enough, she supposed. He stared at Rasmus with a murderous gleam. With Xia in tow, she went to him and grabbed his arm, too. The former mageheld didn't look so hot. His face was ashen, and beads of sweat formed along his upper lip and dripped down his temples. The smell of blood from him was stronger than before.

"Can you make it out on your own?"

He managed to pull himself away from the wall. One palm stayed pressed to his sternum. The other one was bright with blood. "Yes."

"Great, because it's time to go, boys."

Crap. Whoever was upstairs was heading downstairs now. Something fell hard. She couldn't feel them, but she didn't know if that was because whatever was coming for them was mageheld, or whether she wasn't close enough to feel them, or if she'd flamed out and couldn't feel anything. At this point, she wasn't sure if she could feel anything magical anymore.

"Whatever's coming at us from up there is mageheld," she said. "They should still read me as a witch, so let's hope Rasmus didn't release them. You two, behind me," she said. "Do it now."

They went out like that, with her taking the point. Not so much because she'd taken command as because she was the only one who wasn't completely strung out yet. God knows Xia wasn't himself; Rasmus would be deader than dead if he was. And Durian was worthless right now. She closed the metal door after them, getting that strange deadening in her hands when she touched it. Her back itched the entire time she was exposed to the stairs. Xia turned around and did something to the door that made her head freeze solid.

"Is there another way out?" she asked Durian. "A back door? A window? A secret tunnel?" That last was a joke but nobody laughed. Not even her. Durian and Xia both shook their heads. "Then up we go." She touched Xia's shoulder. He flinched. Great. Now he worse than couldn't stand her. He didn't even want her touching him. Which would piss her off if she had the time for it. She sank onto the riser above Xia and Durian. "Listen up," she said.

Xia's eyes cycled through all the shades of blue again, starting and ending with azure-streaked white. "What?"

"Have I flamed out?" Her heart raced to her throat. The noises from upstairs weren't happy ones. She had a still-loopy Xia, a worthless Durian, no sense of magic herself, and a houseful of mageholds headed their way. Xia's knife was an awesome weapon, but she didn't see herself taking down the dozen or so fiends about to descend on them. "Xia, is there any more of my magic left?"

He swallowed. "Yeah."

"For crying out loud, Xia. Read my mind, would you?" She was too stressed out to care about anybody's feelings. "Yes, there's magic, or yes, I've flamed out?"

"Yes, there's magic left." He touched his fingertip to her forehead, and a connection opened between them. She didn't feel any magic, though. Not his. Not hers. Not Durian's. All she felt was him in her head.

"It'll be all right," he said.

Right. All she had to do was get used to vanilla. "Xia," she said. "It's time to find out if you severing Durian was a fluke or if you can do it again." She figured that was their best shot at getting out—if they severed as many mageholds as they could.

"We just need to be close enough," he replied. He put a hand on her shoulder, the better to pull from her, she supposed, because her stomach filled with ice. Upstairs, something shrieked like a banshee. Xia's irises flashed between neon and midnight blue.

The three of them stood and started climbing the stairs again. With the doorway in sight, Alexandrine came to a halt. For one thing, she was light-headed. For another, the running around upstairs had stopped. Abruptly. The hair on the back of her neck stood up. Her surroundings disappeared. Everything she ever was in her life focused on the stairs and on not falling over in a dead faint.

The first of Rasmus's magehelds appeared at the top of the stairs. Jiminy Cricket, he was a monster. Not in literal form. Just a general observation on the creature she had to face down without a lick of magic to help. *You're a witch, and he's a mageheld.* Repeat as necessary. *You're a witch, and he's a mageheld. He can't hurt you, and he has to do what you tell him.*

He was bigger than Xia and damn near as scary. What hair he had was dark. Three cobalt stripes ran down the left side of his face, starting at the midline of his left eye and moving outward toward his temple. The first stripe actually colored his eyeball. He held a dead fiend by the back of his collar. Oh, yuck. One of his hands was bloody. He was handsome, with a smile to die for that was even creepier than the hand-sized hole where the dead fiend's heart ought to be.

A mageheld couldn't harm a mage, and Alexandrine was pretty sure—though not certain—that she still counted as a mage. Therefore, she had nothing to fear. Right? Right. He might want to rip out her heart, but he couldn't. She hoped.

"Out of my way," she said when he didn't move. She did her best to sound like she expected to be obeyed.

She got her legs moving again, climbing the stairs. Rasmus better not have had time to release his fiends, or they were all going to die a horrible death.

The big mageheld didn't move except to let go of the body he held. Said body hit the floor with a sickening thud. Blood from his hand dripped onto the floor in bright, crimson splashes. She didn't react to the scent of blood. Not anymore. His eyes were pools of cobalt blue, tending to the maniacal, with a hint of insanity thrown in for kicks.

"Coming through," she said, taking another step toward him with her heart in her mouth and expecting any minute he would blast her into a pile of ashes. Or just rip out her heart. Which one was the faster way to go? At the last minute, she realized the mageheld's head wasn't shaved. His hair was slicked back and very long.

"Get out of the way, Iskander," Xia said from behind them. Gee, he sounded just like the old Xia. "That's Harsh's sister, for Christ's sake. No killing her. Got that?"

She turned. "You know each other?"

Xia shrugged. "He's sworn to Nikodemus."

Iskander moved, and the three of them came the rest of the way up the stairs. In the entryway, there were three more dead fiends, all with holes in their chests. And a lot more blood everywhere.

"Looks like you were enjoying yourself," Alexandrine said.

"Where's the mage?" Iskander asked Xia. Apparently, she didn't count. She was light-headed and nauseated. Still deaf, dumb, and blind to magic, too.

"Downstairs," Xia replied. "Restrained for now."

"Kynan said you needed my help," Iskander said. "Doesn't look like it."

Alexandrine picked her way around the dead fiends and tried not to let the sight of all those lifeless bodies get to her. She was feeling even more nauseous. Her stomach wasn't going to put up with this state of affairs much longer. Her head pulsed with the mother of all headaches. "Where are the rest of the magehelds?" she asked.

"Hiding," Iskander said with a dismissive look at the bodies at his feet. "Cowards."

"Xia has to sever them before Rasmus gets out of . . . whatever happened to him."

Xia ran a hand through his hair, but she ignored him. Hell. All three of them were staring at her like she'd grown a second head.

Hands on her hips, she glared at them in turn. She was hollow inside, running on fumes, she realized. "Do you honestly think I'm leaving here without doing whatever is necessary to free anyone held against their will? Tell me you're not that stupid."

# CHAPTER 29

Alexandrine watched Iskander and Durian watch Xia. The two were obviously waiting for the word from Xia. Constitutionally unable to believe Alexandrine could be serious? Yeah, well, they didn't think too highly of witches, now, did they?

Xia shrugged. "She's the boss."

Iskander and Durian got in synch right away. She and Xia, not so much. She couldn't feel much of anything. Maybe a glimmer every now and then, but that was it. All four of them knew they needed to work quickly, since there wasn't any way of knowing when Rasmus would get himself out of whatever bind he was in downstairs.

The first mageheld took a while for Xia to sever, but when it was done, with the fiend on the ground clutching his chest, a layer of frost formed around Alexandrine's bones. Xia recited a phone number she didn't recognize and told the mageheld to call it if he wanted to join up with Nikodemus. By then, Iskander and Durian had two more waiting farther down the hall. She followed Xia and got there in time to see him put a hand to the first one's chest. He pulled, or so she guessed from his expression of concentration. The growing chill in her body was the only way she could tell he was handling magic.

More ice formed in her. The next severance didn't take as long as the first and not as long as the second, either. Proximity to Xia mattered, because whenever she lagged, he'd turn around with an impatient scowl and motion for her to hurry up. The process worked best if she was beside him, with five to six feet away the maximum effective distance. Any farther and he couldn't make it happen.

That became the pattern. Iskander and Durian rousted the magehelds, and Xia severed them, each one faster than the one before. Alexandrine got a little emptier and a little colder every time. Afterward, he gave out that phone number with instructions to call if they wanted. By the tenth, Alexandrine was more or less the South Pole wrapped in a thin outer shell that might or might not be human. By the end, she was shivering and losing her sense of balance. She kept herself upright by staring at the line formed by the right angle of a wall meeting the floor. Following a straight line kept her from flailing about like a dying trout.

She gritted her teeth and made it outside with the others. At least Xia wasn't getting all bent about her lagging anymore. She took her time. Once she was outside, sidewalk lines helped keep her steady. Nobody seemed to care that she was moving slowly, so she took her time. The sidewalk ran out, and she stopped moving.

A car she didn't recognize was in the driveway, its nose about three feet from the sidewalk. A black Lamborghini, unless she was mistaken. Probably Iskander's since the Jag was still there and she knew the Italian car hadn't been there when she arrived.

The tattooed fiend was on a cell phone, talking softly. When he was done, he closed the phone and said, "Nikodemus is back." He looked at Durian. "You coming with us, my friend?"

"Yes."

"You?" Iskander said to Xia.

"Yeah."

Nobody asked what she wanted to do. Why would they? she thought. They wouldn't want to be around a witch any more than they would want to meet Rasmus Kessler for a beer. She stayed at the edge of the driveway, apart from the other three, wishing she'd borrowed six or seven of Xia's hoodies. Awkward moment now. There were four of them and two cars, neither of which seated four, unless you wanted to count the pickup bed.

"Nikodemus know you have his Reventón?" Xia asked. He'd sidled up to the car and put a hand on the hood, stroking the gleaming paint. "You know this is a million-dollar car, right?"

Iskander shrugged. "Kynan told me to get over here ASAP," he said. He grinned, and Alexandrine didn't think she was imagining his tattoos were a brighter blue than just a minute ago. "I hit one-fifty on the Richmond Bridge."

"Sweet," Xia said.

Nobody said who was going with who, but it was more than obvious the four of them weren't going to fit in the Lamborghini. Behind them, Rasmus's house was quiet. Lights were on upstairs, though. One of the newly severed fiends came out with a duffel slung over his shoulder. He paused to face them and to press three fingers to his forehead, first to Xia, then to Iskander and Durian. They responded with a similar motion. And then the fiend did the same in her direction. Go figure. He was probably disoriented like Durian and didn't know what he was doing. When he straightened, he vaulted over the iron fencing along the side of the property and disappeared.

Iskander pressed a fob and the car came to life. "I saw the Chevy at the bottom of the drive," he said.

Alexandrine cleared her throat. "Um." All three looked at her. She fought her stomach and won, enough to speak without feeling like she was going to barf. "Uh. I borrowed it to get here. Hope that's okay. There's a change of clothes in the front for Xia. The keys are in it. And, uh, sorry about the window. It kind of fell down on the way here."

"I've been meaning to tape it shut," Xia said. "It falls down every time I drive it."

"Oh." She wrapped her arms around her midsection, holding on tight to ward off the chill. Her insides still felt like the Antarctic. "Well, then, I guess I feel better about that."

For some reason, the result of her giving up that bit of information was Iskander flipping the Reventón's key fob to Xia. "Meet you at the bottom, then." And he and Durian headed down the drive, leaving her at the edge of the driveway and Xia naked and standing in front of the Lamborghini. Xia pressed the fob, and the doors swung up.

In a way, she was relieved at the way things worked out, because she wasn't sure she could have made it down the driveway on foot. Not without stopping to say good-bye to whatever was in her stomach. She also wouldn't deny she was nervous about being alone with Xia.

"Get in," Xia said.

She took a step, and when she didn't fall over, she took another. Xia walked over and took her elbow. "Come on, baby."

"Don't call me that."

He walked her to the passenger side of the car, and when they got there, she didn't dare look at him; she just kept her head down and got in. Xia went around to the other side and slid into the driver's seat.

"Sweet," he said, running his hands over the dash and along the panel between the front seat and hers. The doors engaged, and then he pressed a button and the motor purred. Alexandrine slumped on her seat and wrapped her arms around her empty body. Xia didn't seem to mind being naked, but she was going to be cold for the rest of her life.

Xia turned the car around and headed down the drive. He engaged the front end lift so they'd make it out of the driveway without scraping the bottom as they headed past the melted iron front gate. Iskander took no prisoners. Must be nice to enjoy your work like that.

On Wildcat Canyon Road, Xia pulled onto the inside shoulder and popped the driver's side door. He stood and caught the bundle of clothes Iskander threw at him. The shoes came next, one then the other. He dropped them on the ground to put on the jeans she'd brought, not bothering with underwear. Then the shirt. Shoes last, no socks. Iskander was already in the Chevy, idling the motor, and swear to God, Alexandrine thought he was caressing the dashboard the same way Xia had caressed the Reventón. Dressed, Xia got back into the car, dropped the driver's side door down, and before long, they were heading to—well, she had no idea.

"Where are we going?" she asked when they'd driven several minutes without a direction she recognized. Shit. Her heart dropped to her toes. He was taking her home. The danger was over, right? The talisman was gone; Rasmus had been given the smack-down of a lifetime.

"Tunnel Road."

"Huh." She waited a bit, then remembered that Tunnel Road led to Highway 13, which led to the Bay Bridge and the City. Xia kept driving. "Be faster to go through Berkeley, wouldn't it?"

He didn't answer right away. She didn't have the benefit of a connection with him, so she had no idea what he was thinking. "Iskander says he got this thing up to one-fifty, but I know it can go two-ten."

She was too empty to care about dying in a car crash, however spectacular, but then he floored it and, hell, she understood his affair with the car. They didn't miss any corners or go crashing down into some cow pasture canyon tucked into the Berkeley hills. In fact, the way the car hugged the road, Alexandrine figured they were stuck to the asphalt. She was hardly scared at all.

Xia got the Reventón down to a mere eighty going back along Wildcat Canyon and then downhill and into North Berkeley. Without the thrill of speed and impending death to keep her awake, Alexandrine bottomed out. Next thing she knew, the car doors were up, there was cold air in her face, and they were parked in front of an enormous house she didn't recognize. "Now where are we?"

He got out but leaned down to answer her. "Tiburon." Tiburon being a Marin County enclave mostly for the extremely wealthy.

"Righty-o." She hauled herself out and thought the front door looked about a hundred miles away. Her balance was improved, though. She didn't need to find a straight line to walk without falling down.

Xia gave the car one last loving stroke before he headed for the house. Ten yards from the front door, he came to a halt.

Alexandrine stopped behind him. "Something wrong?" she asked.

He shook his head. "Carson's here."

"Oh." That would be the Carson Philips everyone worshiped.

"And Nikodemus." He started walking again, and Alexandrine followed. What else was she supposed to do?

The house was gorgeous but in need of someone to clean up. There were moving boxes everywhere, some open but most closed. Empty picture hangers marked the place where something had been on the walls. Were they in the middle of moving in or moving out?

Xia went through a door that led to a downstairs that was as posh as the upstairs part she'd seen. There was somewhat less chaos here, moving-boxes-wise. A glimmer of something tickled in her and then petered out. She heard people talking, and then Xia turned a corner, went through another door, and they were in a living room with a large mahogany table in the middle. Iskander was at the table with Durian, Harsh, and another man she didn't recognize but figured, rightly as it turned out, was Nikodemus. Durian had a plate of cold chicken in front of him, and there were open beers on the table. *Lucifer's Golden Ale*, the bottles read. Good grief. There were little red devil horns on the labels. Durian was chowing down. She and Xia came the rest of the way in. The smell of food made her sick to her stomach. Without a word, Nikodemus picked up a beer and tossed it to Xia. He caught it one-handed.

Harsh got to his feet. "Alexandrine? Are you all right?"

"Hey," she said. She dug her hands deep into the front pocket of her hoodie.

"Where's Carson?" Xia opened his ale but waited to drink any. Of course that's who he cared about.

"Upstairs resting."

"Kynan?"

"Haven't seen him."

Nikodemus lifted his eyebrows and held out a bottle to her. "Lucifer?" he asked. He happened to be sitting close enough that she could have taken it from him.

She lifted a hand, palm out, and shook her head. His sandy-brown hair was shoulder length and a bit shaggy, and he had the most intense blue-gray eyes she'd ever seen. His presence was something. She felt all of them—her brother, Durian, Iskander, and Xia, of course. But of them all, Nikodemus resonated the most. He was a good-looking man. Fiends seemed to have that going for them. "No, thanks."

"Nikodemus, by the way," he said.

She licked her lips. "Nice to meet you." Should she offer him her hand? What was the protocol here? She figured he wouldn't want to touch her, either, what with her witch cooties, and kept her hands in the pocket of her hoodie. "Alexandrine Marit."

"You sure?" Nikodemus said, lifting one of the Lucifers.

"Yeah. Thanks."

"Put the beer away," Xia snarled.

Nikodemus got quiet. "Just being polite," he said.

"I said, put it away."

"Relax, Xia. It's cool." She looked at Nikodemus. "I don't drink, that's all."

"Well, that's a damn shame," Nikodemus said.

She shrugged. "Just the way it is."

"Are you all right, Alexandrine?" Harsh asked again.

She nodded. A big fat lie, but she wasn't going to admit that in front of these men. She didn't know what to do or how to act. Xia wasn't giving her any clues, and she wasn't feeling much like a mind reader. She stood there, a frozen lump.

Nikodemus took a drink from his beer. "Interesting," he said. His eyes followed Alexandrine from her head to her toes, and she didn't think she imagined the way the air felt a little denser around her.

"What?" Xia said.

"She feels like one of the kin."

Xia hadn't touched his beer yet, but he lifted the bottle like he was going to. "So?"

Nikodemus's attention moved to Alexandrine. "And Xia here feels almost like a mage. One of you want to explain that?"

"Well, there was this talisman, see," she said. Her body shook with the cold congealing her insides. If she didn't sit down soon, she might just fall down. Nikodemus reached out and grabbed her arm, and a good thing, too, or she'd have done a face-plant.

"A talisman, huh?" Nikodemus said.

Alexandrine remembered then that she still had Rasmus's ring. She dug it out of her pocket and held it out to the warlord. "This was my father's. He was using it against us." Her arm shook. "Want it?"

Nikodemus studied the ring without touching it. "What happened to it?"

"I stabbed it with Xia's knife."

Xia slipped an arm around her and drew her away from Nikodemus. She let the ring fall to the floor. She heard it hit the ground, but in her head, she saw it falling still, twisting and turning over and over. She was too dizzy to do much but lean against Xia and pray she didn't pass out. Xia held her close to him, but nothing, she thought, that would give away they'd been to bed. Of course, he wouldn't want his buddies to know about that.

"Get your hands off her," Harsh said.

"Fuck off, Harsh." Xia let out a breath. "Alexandrine, I need to talk to you."

She turned her head to look at him. "Yeah?"

"In private."

"Oh."

"Over my dead body, Xia," Harsh said. "I'm not letting you go off on her."

Alexandrine faced her brother. "Would you just butt out?"

At the same time, Xia said, "Fine with me, Harsh. Come on, Alexandrine."

# CHAPTER 30

$X$ia caught Alexandrine before her knees buckled a second time, but she recovered on her own and pushed him away with an elbow jab to his gut. Didn't hurt anything but his pride. Great. She didn't want him touching her. His chest got tight with the fear that she'd tell him to get lost. Would he blame her? Not much. Caring what anyone thought of him was new to him, just like his freedom. But, then, he didn't remember caring all that much about other people's opinions before he ran afoul of Rasmus. Like that mattered. Different life. Different world. The point was that today, right now, he cared what Alexandrine thought. The prospect of her hating him turned his heart to dust.

With a shout, Harsh jumped to his feet when his sister stumbled, and again when Xia caught her. Hell, might as well light a match and watch the fire burn. Nikodemus tipped his head to one side and observed. The warlord was taking everything in. Who the hell knew what

Iskander and Durian had told him while they were alone with Nikodemus. Nikodemus might seem all easygoing and shit, but he didn't tolerate crap or insubordination from anyone. More than any of them, Nikodemus knew they were in a fight for their free existence. He wasn't going to allow anything or anyone to jeopardize that. Like what could happen if one of his fiends was getting it on with a witch. And not just any witch, either.

Durian pushed away his plate of food and leaned against his chair, one hand stroking the center of his chest, right where Magellan had cut him open. The assassin's attention was on Alexandrine, and Xia didn't like it one bit. Durian wasn't popular among the kin, given what he was. Supposedly he hadn't been sanctioned in quite some time, not while he was known to be sworn to Nikodemus. But hell, it was a matter of time before the warlord used his weapon now that he had him back, wasn't it? What better situation than one like this to get it going again. Kill the fiend who got himself tangled up with Rasmus Kessler's little girl.

And Iskander. He was checking her out like he might be interested in some bedroom athletics with her. In addition to the sexual interest in his eyes whenever he looked at Alexandrine, Iskander was giving off all kinds of crazy magic. Nothing much new there. The guy's facial tats still had an interior glow.

Oh, yeah. There was Harsh, too. He wanted to kill Xia just for touching Alexandrine. The fiend was going to dice and sauté Xia's liver if he found out what Xia had done with his precious sister. And for sure Harsh's magic was one-off—only now Xia thought maybe he had a clue about the cause. Not an idea that gave him the let's-sit-

down-and-have-a-chat-about-me-boinking-your-sister-
and-probably-knocking-her-up kind of feeling.

Still holding on to her arm, Xia walked Alexandrine
into the kitchen, the burn of too many eyes following
along. "Look," he said to her when he was sure no one
was eavesdropping. "I don't know what—"

"It's okay, Xia." She smoothed her jeans over her
thighs, sliding her hand to worry at the side seam. "I
won't tell anyone. No worries, all right? Harsh may be my
brother, but my personal life is none of his business. It's
not anybody's business."

He stared at her for about forever, trying to read her
eyes or her expression or her body language, and none of
it helped. She had all these tics going; her eyes weren't
focusing, she was fidgeting with her pants and shifting
her weight, and yet she had her emotions locked down
tight. He had no idea why she was agitated, and he was
afraid to start a connection with her. He'd come so close
to flaming her out tonight; he didn't want to risk finishing
it off for her.

"I don't know what you want," he said. He dragged his
fingers through his hair. Well, fuck this wondering shit.
He wanted to know. Good news or bad. Broken heart or
not. "Is it okay with you if they know about us or what?"

Her eyes narrowed, and she sank onto a chair with her
hands clasped behind her head. Her arms shook. "What
do you want?"

That was an easy one. "To be with you." There. He'd
said it. He'd put himself totally out there for her. Her turn
now.

She looked suspicious, and then understanding dawned.
Sort of, because she got it wrong. "In bed."

"Well, yeah, that, too," Xia said. And anywhere else he could get her. Maybe he hadn't spelled it out quite enough. Without a connection going, he was missing a whole other level of information about her state of mind. Conversation floated in from the kitchen. Somebody raised his voice. He blocked it out. "But that's not what I meant, Alexandrine."

She didn't move. Maybe her eyes did. She wasn't focused on anything that he could tell. Her skin was paler than when they'd arrived. His damn hoodie was way too big on her, and she had her arms tucked into the opposite sleeves. She went white. "I'm going to barf."

"Put your head down." Xia moved to her, cupping the top of her skull in his palm and getting her head down and between her knees. She didn't resist. "Baby," he said, stroking her head, "you have to breathe. Breathe."

"I feel like shit, Xia." Her ribs expanded with a long, slow inhale.

He let go, and she reached up to hold her head. Her fingers tightened over her skull until her fingertips turned white. The whole time, her torso quivered.

He squatted down. "Can I get you anything?"

She lifted a hand and with her head still down, waved a palm at him. He watched her take several deep breaths. After a bit, she lifted her head. "Better," she said. "That's better."

"So we're not going to mention us?" He stayed where he was, less than a foot from her chair. Close enough to smell his shampoo in her hair, the faint lemon trace of his soap on her skin. Jaysus, he felt like a goddamned asshole. An asshole with a train headed straight for his heart.

"It's okay. I don't mind. I mean, why would I?" She

lifted up a bit and crossed her forearms on top of her legs. Her head stayed down, though. Avoiding him, he guessed. "Mum's the word." She mimed zipping up her lips and throwing away a key.

"What if that isn't okay with me?" Looking back on things, he could maybe see where she might not understand that, though his opinion of witches in general hadn't changed, his feelings about her had. She wasn't anything like the witches he'd known or killed. She was Alexandrine, and he had no business thinking she'd want anything to do with him on a permanent basis. Besides what they already had. And from what she'd said, she was used to getting dumped on by guys who couldn't deal with what she was. Which was pretty much what she thought he was—a guy who couldn't deal.

"Xia, I'm still a witch," she said. She met his gaze. "And Rasmus Kessler is my father."

He put a hand on her head and drew his fingers through hair that was the exact same white-blond as her father's. None of his hatred surfaced. Not even a glimmer. From the kitchen came the sound of a chair scraping along the floor.

"What the hell is going on in there?" That was Harsh.

"Yeah," he said. He squatted down again so he could look her in the eye. "You're a witch." He ended up with both hands on her face. "So what?"

Alexandrine bit her lower lip and chewed on it for a while. "Right. Fine. Okay." Her pupils vibrated. Shit, he'd taken her so close to flaming out tonight that she was all crosswise and fucked up, and she never complained even once. She straightened, but that made her eyes go off again, and she held on to the sides of the chair, looking a bit green. "So, are you my boyfriend or my boy toy?" She leaned toward him, wobbly, and he caught her before she fell off the chair.

"Neither." That came out harsher than he meant. That had always been his problem. He had a low-key mood and a pissed-off mood and no moods in between. "Alexandrine, I love you."

"You do not."

"Yes, I do."

"Do not."

He rolled his eyes. Well, he was just going to tell anyone who asked what he'd done with Alexandrine, and she could just deal with it or not. "Look, we'll argue about that later. Right now, we need to go back in there and deal with Nikodemus," he said.

"What for?" She slumped on the chair. She'd been through so much tonight that he hated the thought of asking her to do anything more. Sometimes life just sucked. "He's not going to let you stick around without straightening out a few details. You have some decisions to make." He kept his arms around her, and she didn't do anything to extricate herself. Couldn't, or didn't want to?

" 'Cause I'm a witch?"

"No. Because you're kin now." He pressed a fingertip to her forehead and let her feel him. Just a little. Just enough for her to know. The impulse to take things further burned in him, but he didn't. "He's going to ask you to swear fealty to him. He can't have one of the kin here who hasn't. That means you need to decide if you're going to."

"What if I don't?"

"Then you can't be here."

She fiddled with the too-long sleeves of his hoodie, bringing them down over her hands and clutching the excess in her fists. "Why did you?"

"Because of Carson." She nodded, all guarded and shit, which made him wonder if she was jealous. "But also because I thought if anyone could do something about the mages, it'd be Nikodemus. And I wanted to be a part of that. Killing mages, I mean." He pressed his lips together. "I thought there was a good chance I'd get sent after Rasmus. But now I think Nikodemus has other ideas about what to do."

"Right," she said with halfhearted cheer. "Everybody loves a winner. Go Nikodemus. Down with the mage-kind."

"What Nikodemus is doing isn't about winning or losing, Alexandrine. It's about surviving." He got anxious again about how things were going with them. "But now you have to decide if you're going to be with us."

She tightened her arms across her stomach. "I've always been alone. I think the world means for me to be alone."

"Alexandrine." His chest got all tight, but he got past it. "I won't leave you."

"Sure," she whispered. "That's what they all say, don't they?"

"Do you want to be with me? If you don't—"

"Alexandrine?" Harsh came into the kitchen. All in a rush, Xia felt Harsh in a way he hadn't before. Well, now. Harsh was a piece of work, wasn't he? He turned to look over his shoulder at the man Nikodemus had made his right hand.

"Goddamn it!" Harsh bellowed. He got himself under

control and managed to continue in a more moderate voice. "Get your hands off my sister, Xia."

He leaned into her like Harsh wasn't there. "I don't have any talent for words," he said to her. "You know that about me. I don't care who your father is or whether your brother is Harsh Marit, or whether you're a witch and I'm one of the kin. I want you in my life, Alexandrine."

"What for?" She put her hands on his shoulders and lifted her head to look into his eyes.

"Goddamn it," Harsh said.

"Shut the fuck up," Xia told Harsh.

Nikodemus came out and touched a hand to Harsh's back. "My man," the warlord said. He pushed Harsh's shoulder. "Let them finish here. When they've worked out what they need to work out, they'll let us know. Let's go."

Xia returned his attention to Alexandrine. "You put yourself on the line tonight. For me. You came after me, baby. By yourself." His throat got thick, and he had to wait a bit before he could continue. "Rasmus was only going to do one of two things—take me mageheld again or kill me. If it wasn't for you, I'd be dead. Or worse. So don't go telling me I don't know what you are to me, Alexandrine, or that I don't know how I feel. You're it for me. The only one."

"Says the man who owns my magic." She touched his hair, brushing some behind his ear. "You must hate me for that."

"Hate you?" He snorted. "Don't you get it? Why do you think it's me"—he jabbed a finger to his chest—"instead of Kynan Aijan?"

"Accident?"

"Let's get a few things straight here." He brought Alexandrine off her chair. "There wasn't any accident about your magic. I'm not your boyfriend, and I'm not your boy toy."

Her eyes were calm. Quiet. Very settled. "Then what are you?"

"Yours." Xia brought her into the circle of his arms. "I love you, Alexandrine. I don't even care very much if you don't love me back. I want to be with you. If you don't want to swear fealty to Nikodemus, then I'll find a way to leave here with you."

She stayed close to him, pressing herself against him. He watched the doubt in her eyes slowly fade away. "Wow. That's just really . . . wow." He held his breath while she worked away at that. "Are you sure?"

With his arms tight around Alexandrine, he kissed her. A normal kiss at first and then not so normal because her magic was going all freaky. She had no idea about that, of course, but he sure as hell felt her magical reaction. And the rest of what he felt? Well, people who kissed like that ought to save it for a more private place. He turned his head to one side, exposing his throat to her.

"I'm offering myself to you, Alexandrine Marit, as a permanent thing." Around them the air tingled, and they got a connection going. Not much, but enough that she had a place to anchor herself. "Please, accept me, baby. Because I don't know what I'll do if you say no."

Alexandrine went dead still. He touched a finger to his throat. A line of blood appeared on his skin. "Oh, my God," she whispered. "I feel that. I feel you."

He drew her head to his neck. Her skin was hot. Too hot for a human. Her eyes were dilated, big round black-as-night pupils nearly obliterating her irises. He was feeling the talisman's magic even stronger than before. Her witch magic was going off, too. The way her magic pulsed now, he could incinerate the house with a blink.

Her mouth latched onto his throat, and oh, yes, she tasted. He was able to set aside her magic, leave it untouched while he stayed like this with her. "If you say yes, I'm going to bind us," he said. "The way Nikodemus did with Carson. If that's what you want."

She lifted her mouth from his throat. "Do it."

Before long he'd be wanting to change. Hell, the way he was feeling, he might just take his other form without knowing it. He was twisted higher than he'd been in longer than he could remember. And Alexandrine was just the perfect woman for him.

With his knife, he made a nick in the side of her throat. Blood scent rose between them, and he opened himself to the sensation. Alexandrine pressed herself to him and stared at him. She was kin. He felt her magic, both halves of it. The talisman's power burned in her, and the magic she was born with flowed through him like cool water, alien but almost knowable. Damn. If he ever learned how to pull the two sides together, he'd be invincible.

"Why does that happen?" she asked. She touched the cut on the side of her neck and came away with blood on her fingertip. His insides went taut. She had no idea. No idea at all what this was doing to him. "Why does this make me feel . . . hungry for you?"

"That's how it is for fiends. When one fiend offers to another, there's a connection. Our magic touches deeper." He turned her head to one side. "Come in, Alexandrine," he whispered. He pressed against her, his torso against hers, staying open to her, and it felt good.

In this state, they were open to just about any fiend in the vicinity, which in this case meant Iskander, Durian, Harsh, and Nikodemus, just for starters. They felt good, too. He felt good. And unbearably tight with tension. Better than good. This was right. Alexandrine tilted her head back, and Xia pressed his mouth to her skin; they joined, and just like that, the chaotic power between them swept over them both. He slid a hand around the back of her head, pulled her hard toward him, and bound her to him permanently. Forever. Just like Carson and Nikodemus.

Done. It was done, and Nikodemus could just fuck himself if he didn't like it.

When they came up for air, it was to an audience of Harsh and Nikodemus. Harsh looked like he was going to pop a vein. Nikodemus looked reserved. Thoughtful. The warlord walked over to the counter and leaned against it, arms over his chest.

"You know, don't you, Xia, that she can't be here the way things are now. Probably not you, either, I'm guessing."

"I know." The skin up and down his spine tingled. Nikodemus was pulling, and Xia didn't doubt the warlord could end his life right here and now. His oath of fealty to him was in part responsible for that state of affairs. On the other hand, Nikodemus was one powerful fiend.

"So. How about you explain how you two got this way." Nikodemus lifted a hand to cut off an objection from Harsh. "Not a word. Your sister's a big girl. She can deal on her own. Right now, I need to hear a few things from them."

"Thanks," Alexandrine said.

"One of you better start talking."

They managed it, mostly with Xia doing the telling because Alexandrine was fading out from the effects of severing so many fiends, and he'd not done her a favor by letting magic into them both. She was the color of chalk and shivering off and on like she had the d.t.'s. By the end and with him leaving a lot of stuff out and Alexandrine chiming in every now and then, they got across the highlights of what had happened since Harsh left for Paris.

"You're Rasmus Kessler's daughter?" Nikodemus said when they got to that part. "For real?"

"Yes." Alexandrine hunched over, and Xia put his arm around her.

"That just sucks," the warlord said. He looked at Xia like he'd been too near a pissed-off skunk. "You bound yourself to Kessler's girl?"

"Carson was Magellan's witch."

"Yeah, but that changed, didn't it?" Nikodemus said. He pointed at her. "She can't change who her father is."

"I totally did that on purpose," Alexandrine said. "Picking Rasmus Kessler to be my dad. Look, I'm not the only witch or mage who got tossed out for failing the magical prelims or whatever it is they do when we're three. There's a lot of us who don't feel the love for the people who threw us out." She directed this at Nikodemus. "And don't go thinking I'm the only witch who ended up abandoned on the streets, either."

"No," Nikodemus said. "Matter of fact, I don't think that. Kind of intriguing, don't you agree? Later—if it works out that there's a later—you and I are going to have a nice long talk about some of your buddies."

"Maybe."

He nodded to himself. "Xia explain to you about fealty?" Nikodemus asked.

She nodded, but Xia knew Nikodemus had moved on from the genealogy thing to what mattered more—whether she was going to align herself with the warlord or not.

"You know your boy here is sworn to me." She nodded again. Cautious still. "I could use you both." He grinned. "I'm fine with witches swearing fealty, by the way." His smile got bigger. "So far it's worked out great for me. You want to fight the good fight with us?"

She reached over and grabbed Xia's hand. He squeezed her fingers. "Yeah," she said. "I do."

"Let's get to it."

Xia stayed close during the blood exchange with Nikodemus, and he helped her with the words she needed to say. Nikodemus kept it short and sweet, and when it was over, Harsh was looking gray and Alexandrine was sagging against Xia, who was getting a hard-on. And she, the witch, got her hand between them.

"Get my newest wicked witch upstairs," Nikodemus said. "She needs some rest, I'm guessing. Magic always knocked it out of Carson at first, too."

"Yeah, thanks." Xia brought her closer against him.

"I am not your wicked witch," Alexandrine said.

"Beg to differ there," Nikodemus said. "You sure as hell are."

"I'm your sworn fiend," she returned. Between Xia's body and hers, she moved her hand over Xia's crotch. "But I'm his wicked witch."

"Fuck, yes," Xia said.

# THE DISH

*Where authors give you the inside scoop!*

♥ ♥ ♥ ♥ ♥ ♥ ♥ ♥ ♥ ♥ ♥ ♥ ♥ ♥ ♥ ♥ ♥

*From the desk of Jennifer Haymore*

Dear Reader,

When Sophie, the heroine of A *Hint of Wicked* (on sale now), first came to me describing her problem—that she happened to be married to two men at once, both of whom she loved unconditionally—I rubbed my hands together in glee. What a juicy, wicked dilemma! Yes, of course, I told her, I would be thrilled beyond measure to pen this tale.

"But how on earth will you resolve my problem?" she asked me.

"Easy," said I, proud of my fantabulous solution, and doubly proud of how quickly it had come to me. "You love them both, right?"

"Tremendously!" she declared, nodding vigorously.

"Then you'll live happily ever after with *both* your husbands," I decreed, leaning back in my chair and awaiting her exuberant and everlasting thanks.

Thus ensued a long, uncomfortable silence. Finally, Sophie looked up at me with somber, golden-brown eyes. "Forgive me, but that won't work. Neither of my husbands will accept such a solution."

"Huh. Are you saying they're the possessive cave-man type?"

"Exactly." She leaned forward a bit and lowered her voice so that no one outside my office could hear her. "In fact, I'm certain if either one saw me so much as touch the other, murder might ensue. It's already come close to that. Thank heavens nobody has been shot." She gave me a significant look. "Yet."

"Hmmm," I said. "I could work on them . . ."

Sophie broke me off in mid-thought. "You could 'work on them' for eternity, but you see, there is another problem. One that might negate any possibility of future happiness for all three of us: I am a duchess. In England. In 1823."

"Ah. I see," I said. But alas, I didn't, not really. I figured, okay, if Sophie doesn't want both her husbands, I'll pick one, and we'll go with that. Cocky writer that I am, I thought maybe I could flip a coin. *Ha!*

Soon afterward, Sophie took me on her journey, and . . . *oh my!* It wasn't easy. Given two powerful, honorable, drop-dead gorgeous men, Sophie had to choose the one she wanted to stand beside for the rest of her days. Moreover, in doing so, she had to break the heart of the other man—a man she also still loved.

And I won't even begin to get into the quagmire of 1823 marriage laws! To work everything out without turning Sophie into a criminal, making her child illegitimate, or having her become a pariah or the laughingstock of society? Just about impossible!

Eventually, though, Sophie found her way. By the time I finished writing, I was so glad she let me be the one to share her tale with the world.

I truly hope you enjoy reading Sophie's story. Please feel free to stop by my Web site, www.jennifer haymore.com, where you can share your thoughts about the book, learn some bizarre and fascinating historical facts, and read more about the person who has most recently barged into my office demanding I write his story . . .

Sincerely,

*Jennifer Haymore*

♥ ♥ ♥ ♥ ♥ ♥ ♥ ♥ ♥ ♥ ♥ ♥ ♥ ♥ ♥

*From the desk of Carolyn Jewel*

Dear Reader,

People. Really. I tried to warn you with my first book, *My Wicked Enemy*, but I don't think you were paying attention. I'll try again with *My Forbidden Desire*, my second book (on sale now!). Will you all finally listen up? I certainly hope so. The world is a dangerous

place, and not just in the obvious ways. True statement: Things around you aren't always what they
seem. Same for people, too. Yeah, I know what you're
thinking. How obvious can you get, Carolyn? But really, take a long, hard look at your boss. Is she (or he)
really human? How do you know for sure?

Our capacity to deceive others is far exceeded by
our capacity to deceive ourselves. Keep that in mind
(but not before bed, wouldn't want to keep you up!).

Suppose, for the sake of argument, there really
are monsters among us.

Not the human kind—I think, without further
discussion, we can all agree they exist. I'm talking
about something else. What if there really are creatures like demons or, oh, say, fiends? And "people"
who can do magic. Why the quotes, you ask? Well,
they wouldn't be regular folks like you and me, now
would they?

Who would they be? Mages and witches, of course.
They rose to prominence in the Dark Ages when
they were busy protecting us from demons and the
like. Demons, including fiends, were looking for a
bigger place in the world then. But thanks to the
mages, that didn't work so well. (Thank you, mages!)
Over the years, though, some mages went from being
the good guys to the not-so-good guys, and now the
demons are fighting for their lives. They're sick and
tired of being murdered and enslaved.

That's the backdrop of my books: an all-out
war between demons and fiends and mages and

witches. But what if we take that one step further? What if a demon or a fiend fell in love with a witch or a mage? And now we've got my latest book, *My Forbidden Desire.*

Xia is a fiend. Alexandrine Marit is a witch. He hates witches for some very, very good reasons. Alexandrine isn't sure demons exist and, well, as witches go, she's not much of one . . . until she gets her hands on a talisman. Now Xia has to protect her from some very nasty people. And Alexandrine's view of the world pretty much explodes. What happens after that? You'll have to read it to find out.

Enjoy!

*Carolyn Jewel*

♥ ♥ ♥ ♥ ♥ ♥ ♥ ♥ ♥ ♥ ♥ ♥ ♥ ♥ ♥

*From the desk of Robin Wells*

Dear Reader,

Have you ever been in one of those slumps when everything in your life is going wrong? Well, the heroine of my latest romantic comedy, *How to Score* (on sale now), is in just such a situation, and she decides to hire a telephone life coach to help her straighten things out. Only problem is, the man Sammi is baring her soul to isn't a life coach at all; he's an FBI agent filling in for his brother—and the man Sammi is falling for.

The idea for this book came to me while writing *Between the Sheets*. The heroine of that story, Emma, needed to change her image after being involved in a terrible scandal, and I originally in-tended to have her hire a life coach to help her. Emma had other ideas, however, and the story went in another direction.

The concept of writing a book about a life coach continued to simmer in my subconscious. The topic intrigued me, probably because I'm a sucker for self-improvement plans. I devour magazine articles with titles such as "Organize Your House, Look like Angelina Jolie, Behave like Mother Theresa, Become the Perfect Parent, Stay Serene as a Monk, Clear Up Your Skin, and Scorch Your Sheets in Seven Easy Steps." (The advice never works, but hope springs eternal.)

What kind of woman, I wondered, would go beyond self-help books and actually hire a life coach? Probably a woman with problems on all fronts—problems with her job, problems with her living arrangements, problems with her family, and, most important, problems with her love life. Or lack thereof. The wheels started spinning in my mind. Maybe my heroine's romantic problem could be of her own making. Maybe she had a painful secret that made her inadvertently drive away potential partners. The wheels started spinning faster. Yes! I was onto something!

I then turned my attention to the hero. What kind of man would make the most interesting life coach? Hmmm. He had to be tall, dark, and sexy as sin—that was a given. What if he wasn't a life coach at all? What if he was a highly structured pragmatist who thought everything could and should be solved through logic, careful planning, hard work, and self-discipline—the kind of man who thinks he has all the answers, who believes that if people would just follow his advice, their problems would all be solved? (My husband wants me to point out here that I, personally, have never known, much less married, a man like that.)

What if the hero also had a painful past that made him crave order, organization, and control? (Anyone who has seen my husband's sock drawer will know beyond a doubt that I really, truly did not base this hero on him.)

Once the characters came to life, the story took off. I set the book in Tulsa because I used to live in Oklahoma and know that the city is renowned for its art deco architecture. The museum, neighborhood, and restaurants in my book are fictional, but the issues facing "recent history" preservationists in Tulsa and other cities are all too real.

The secondary romance between the two older characters in the book came as a surprise to me; I originally planned for Sammi's blue-haired artist sister, Chloe, to have a love interest. Instead, Sammi's landlord and boss fell in love as they helped each other deal with past regrets, find self-forgiveness, and learn that it's never too late for new beginnings.

I hope you enjoy reading *How to Score* as much as I enjoyed writing it. I invite you to drop by my Web site, www.robinwells.com, to share your thoughts, read an excerpt from my next novel, or just say hi!

All my best,

*Robin Wells*

*Want to know more about romances at Grand Central Publishing and Forever? Get the scoop online!*

## GRAND CENTRAL PUBLISHING'S ROMANCE HOME PAGE

Visit us at www.hachettebookgroup.com/romance for all the latest news, reviews, and chapter excerpts!

## NEW AND UPCOMING TITLES

Each month we feature our new titles and reader favorites.

## CONTESTS AND GIVEAWAYS

We give away galleys, autographed copies, and all kinds of fun stuff.

## AUTHOR INFO

You'll find bios, articles, and links to personal Web sites for all your favorite authors—and so much more!

## THE BUZZ

Sign up for our monthly romance newsletter, and be the first to read all about it!

# VISIT US ONLINE

@ WWW.HACHETTEBOOKGROUP.COM.

## AT THE HACHETTE BOOK GROUP WEB SITE YOU'LL FIND:

**CHAPTER EXCERPTS FROM SELECTED NEW RELEASES**

•

**ORIGINAL AUTHOR AND EDITOR ARTICLES**

•

**AUDIO EXCERPTS**

•

**BESTSELLER NEWS**

•

**ELECTRONIC NEWSLETTERS**

•

**AUTHOR TOUR INFORMATION**

•

**CONTESTS, QUIZZES, AND POLLS**

•

**FUN, QUIRKY RECOMMENDATION CENTER**

•

**PLUS MUCH MORE!**

Bookmark Hachette Book Group
@ www.HachetteBookGroup.com.